MW01129022

Flashman and the Red Baron

Copyright © Paul Moore 2015

ISBN 978-1519158048


www.paulfmoore.com



This is a work of fiction.
Whilst many of the characters existed, the story
is entirely from the imagination of the author.

In Memoriam


Uncle Jim


Who served with Bomber Command
Lancaster mid gunner

Veteran of 17 raids before, badly damaged,
they crossed the channel one last time
and crash landed on Beachy Head


Per ardua ad astra

## Chapter 1

A thin layer of snow lay on the pavement as I trudged slowly across the square, my pace dictated by the disagreeable nature of the interview to come. I had got used to it over the last few weeks. The summons to another nondescript office, the cold smiles when I appeared, and the downright hostility when I recounted my tale in such a vague fashion. Apparently, every minor official in Whitehall needed to know something about my adventures behind the lines, and when I answered their questions with evasion, they took it as an insult to their intelligence. I was sick of it, but the Colonel insisted I maintain this charade until the interest faded, which he promised it would in time. He didn't say how much time and I was beginning to wonder if it was measured in months or years. At least I hadn't had the pleasure of another summons to the Palace, which was a blessing. Presumably, they had found other fish to fry for the moment and were content that my silence had been guaranteed. They were probably right in that I didn't care in the least about their madcap schemes and the idea of usurping the throne had little immediate appeal. There was plenty of time to decide what to do with my newfound ancestry.

I stopped outside the Portland stone edifice. A brass plaque announced that I was outside the Foreign Office for the umpteenth time. I braced myself for the ordeal and was about to step forward when from the corner of my eye I caught a glimpse of a man approaching me. I hesitated and then looked towards him. He was staring straight at me and for a second or two I had a feeling of doom.

"Major Flashman?" he asked before I had time to turn and run.

"Who wants to know?" I replied, belligerent now it appeared he wasn't about to attack me.

"Buchan, John Buchan.[1]"

---

[1] At this time, Lt Colonel John Buchan had just been promoted and appointed

"The scribbler," I snorted before I could stop myself.

"Well, you could say that I suppose." He sounded offended but I didn't care very much because I was pretty offended myself and in a foul mood with all the traipsing about London for no good reason and a brief assessment suggested no harm would come from being rude to him.

"What are you after then? I have an appointment." I turned to enter the building.

"I know. The appointment is with me," he said to my back.

I turned to stare at him, even more annoyed now it appeared I had been set up.

"With you?" I made it sound like he was wasting my time.

"Yes. With me."

He stared at me and I continued to stare at him.

"Well, out with it then, what are you about?" I asked.

"This way." He turned on his heel and walked quickly away. I considered my options but in the end simply accepted the inevitable and followed a few paces behind him, wondering if I was ever going to have a quiet life again. He turned into Parliament Square and continued away from the Houses, into Great George Street and up to the junction with Horse Guards Road. Here he stopped abruptly and looked all round him. I did the same only I did it in a less conspicuous manner, noticing all sorts of suspicious characters, some in bowler hats, some in uniform, one even in rags and muttering that his sister was a fine plump specimen, not cheap in the old fashioned sense but for a man of my means a bargain and no mistake.

I told him if his sister looked anything like him she was in the wrong business only to find that while my back was turned, Buchan had made a dart for a door just around the corner, leaving me momentarily gaping into space, before I deduced where he had disappeared to. The urchin was pulling faces so I left him to it and followed Buchan through the unmarked door. He closed it behind me and motioned to ascend the staircase. I stopped on reaching the top, allowing Buchan to pass and enter a gloomy and oddly silent

---

to head the Department of Information. He is known to have worked for SIS during the war but little is known of what he actually did. His most famous work, The 39 Steps, was published in 1915.

corridor. We rounded a corner and an open door was allowing some light into the hallway. He stopped and knocked on the frame and a distant voice muttered, "Come in."

I found myself in a large room, occupied at the far end by a large oak desk with a man in uniform sitting behind it, apparently deep in thought. As I approached slowly across the highly polished floor, aware of the possibility of taking a purler, I noted the two stars and crown of a full Colonel. I had absolutely no idea who he was.

"Ah, Major Flashman," he said as I halted gingerly in front of his desk. "Please sit down." He waved airily about while we both searched for a suitable chair. "I think we can safely say that this business with the Emperor is closed, at least for the moment. There will be no further enquiries from the Government, or anyone else for that matter. What do you know about Baron William de Ropp?"[2]

It was so matter of fact, an assumption that I would know something, anything at all about this Baron. I stared at him blankly.

"Not a sausage," I said with some relief.

"Ah." Pause for effect. "Good. That is what I was hoping you would say."

Unwittingly, and entirely out of the blue, I had just been exposed to the sort of comment that is almost always followed by some sort of maniac plan, and maniac plans have an appalling tendency to be dangerous. I will give him this though. He played the game very well as my innards began to dissolve and my brain frantically tried to find an exit.

"We need to know more about him, and you are just the man to find out all there is to know. Well, tea anyone?"

I wanted to scream. I wondered if I would survive the drop from the open window and whether they would pursue me. Of course, they wouldn't need to if I had both legs broken.

"Sugar, Major?"

I grasped the proffered cup, the rattling against the saucer masked by Buchan piling sugar into his and stirring it as a man possessed.

---

[2] Presumably Baron William Sylvester de Ropp, born 1886 in Lithuania. His father came from a family of Prussian noblemen, his mother was a Crimean Cossack. Educated in Dresden, he moved to England in 1910.

"Buchan here will discuss the details, but suffice to say that you will have more or less unlimited powers to find out about this man. You will have to conduct the operation alongside your squadron duties, as otherwise Trenchard will have my guts for garters. So much demand for one so young," he chortled as though I should be proud that they all seemed to want to use me for their sordid schemes. What had I done to deserve this?

I finished my tea, thanked the Colonel profusely for his hospitality and left. Buchan followed me out of the door.

"Who the hell is he then?" I demanded once we were out of earshot.

"Who… you mean you don't know?" I glared at him, daring him to say something even more stupid. "Colonel Stuart is the Count of Albany."[3]

"Never heard of him," I snapped, although my mind instantly wandered back to a conversation in an estaminet some months previously. "And who am I reporting to?"

"Me. And I report to Colonel Stuart."

"And who does he report to?"

"Colonel Sinclair. And that is all I am authorised to tell you."

He looked away and clearly had no intention of saying anything further. I wondered why Sinclair wasn't dealing with me directly and as numerous less than charming reasons presented themselves, I decided not to think about it for the moment. I waited silently, wondering if Buchan was going to continue the conversation, such as it was.

"De Ropp. Odd character. German by origin apparently, came over in 1910, naturalised and loyal to the British Crown possibly, an RFC officer, natural aviator by all accounts, potential traitor. He is with 29 Squadron under Champion de Crespigny[4] near Arras[5] I believe. You will be posted to the same squadron."

---

[3] The 5th Count of Albany, Prince Julius Anthony Henry Stuart claims to be a direct descendant of the Stuarts and therefore of Bonnie Prince Charlie. Taken to its logical but unprovable conclusion, this means that he is the real heir to the British throne and is also descended from Jesus. See 'Flashman and the Knights of the Sky' appendices and appendix below. It is highly unlikely that he held the rank of Colonel in any of the armed forces.

[4] Presumably Major, later Air Vice Marshal, Hugh Vivian Champion de Crespigny. He served from 1915 throughout the war staying in the RAF between

The full import of what he had said took a moment to filter through.

"But I am due a posting to a training squadron as an instructor, staying at home, staying in England, staying away from France, staying away from the bloody Germans, staying, staying...." I tailed off as screaming about staying away from bullets and death and horror was unlikely to help my case. "Can't this bloody Baron be posted here, and then surely I could keep an eye on him properly." It was inspired, if I say so myself. It made sense. Buchan was considering it. "I could also report directly to you in good time if he really is a traitor. You might also find out who his superiors here in London are." Then I overplayed it. "I could live here in London, have an office...." The possibilities swarmed through my mind. Keeping an eye on this de Ropp fellow wouldn't take up much time and I could always embellish my work suitably. It might even last until the damned war finished and I need never go near the front again.

"Impossible. It must be in France. We need something, ah, solid if we are to expose him." The interview was over for the time being. I returned to the cold street.

The real reason for his insistence was obvious of course. My presence in London was becoming a potential embarrassment, and there was nothing more likely to focus the bureaucratic mind than mischief making by subordinates. Perhaps they had dreamed up the entire story to remove me conveniently, although in that case why they couldn't just post me to a squadron..... but then of course I would have made a fuss as I was indeed due an instructors post or a command and I couldn't command in France without commanding in England first[6]. I could have cried. These swine were the ones who had landed me in this mess and my reward was more of the same apparently, whilst they swanned about living the high life, or writing books in Buchan's case.

---

the wars and then serving mainly in Iraq in the second world war. He retired in 1945.

[5] 29 Squadron were based at Izel-les-Hameau at this time.

[6] RFC policy was indeed that new commanders had to lead a reserve squadron in England before being posted back to France. They also required operational experience although at what level was not specified and therefore open to abuse allowing the occasional 'favourite' a somewhat meteoric rise.

There was no way out. France and its jolly life awaited me. Again. I swore under my breath and then thought to hell with it and shouted, "You bastards," at the window. It made no difference.

"There is no need for that sort of language young man," a sharp voice informed me. I ignored the old trout and stalked off, thoroughly out of sorts.

# Chapter 2

I flew to France accompanied by another new flight commander bound for the same squadron. His name was Fred Winterbotham and we hit it off from the start. He was a scoundrel as well and in my mind destined for great things, although no-one would have believed me if I had told them.[7] He readily agreed when I showed him my route to Bapaume via Abbeville, which if you look at any map will highlight my instinct for survival as it went nowhere near the front. Presumably, Fred also did not see the point of throwing his life away uselessly.

My mind was in turmoil again. I had managed to extract a promise from Buchan that once this operation was over, I would be posted to the home establishment and given an instructor's post from which I would hopefully see the end of the war. All I had to do now was to conclude the de Ropp business as fast as possible without appearing to rush it, inform Buchan and that was that. Assuming he kept his promise of course. Knowing what my promises were worth, I had a creeping feeling that it would not be quite that simple and that there was something else going on as well. No doubt, I would find out soon enough.

We landed in the dusk, rolled over to the line of Nieuports and parked ours beside them. Silhouetted in the failing light, they looked quite majestic. One couldn't see the tattered rags that covered them and the bullet-ridden fuselages and wings. Mind you, if I had, it is possible I would have taken off again and never come back. I certainly would have done if I had appreciated the significance of the date. April 1917. Known afterwards as 'Bloody April'[8] when the average life expectancy of a pilot reduced to 17 days.

---

[7] Frederick Winterbotham indeed made his name. He was heavily involved in the operations of MI6 between the wars being made head of the air intelligence section in 1930 and was a somewhat shadowy liaison between the Air General Staff and higher echelons of the Nazi regime before the second war. See Appendix 1.

[8] 'Bloody April' was the worst single month for the RFC during the war. With the battles of Arras and the Aisne as a background, the inferior machines and poor or non-existent training for pilots led to self-perpetuating carnage with new pilots often surviving only a day or two.

But I didn't, so Fred and I wandered into what appeared to be the squadron headquarters and made ourselves at home.

"Ah, expecting you two of course. Bit of a bloody disaster, eh?"

I shivered at the first inkling of what I was about to receive.

"Two Flight Commanders on the same day. Both dead."

The Major grinned at us like the Cheshire Cat, which was appropriate given the lunatic world in which we found ourselves.

"Drink?"

How could we possibly refuse? We made our way to the mess and found the rest of the squadron such as it was. It reminded me of the last time I had been in this situation, albeit in the German equivalent.[9] Tired, terrified, boyish faces gave us the once over and returned to their drinks, games of cards or whatever was occupying their time. Names were mentioned, too many to remember and irrelevant anyway as the vast majority would be gone before the end of the month. Only the senior man in my flight stuck. McIlvenna his name was. He was an Irishman but recently returned from New York.

"What the hell for?" I enquired.

"I got married," he replied. "To the wrong woman." We both laughed.

\*\*\*\*\*\*

The dawn came all too soon, and with it, the attentions of Heskey. I shaved, washed the haze from my eyes and ventured on some breakfast. The machines were buzzing with activity. The clink of metal on metal, mixed with the occasional roar as an engine started, as well as the clatter of guns being test fired filled the air.

"Infantry going over the top shortly. Get out there and give the hun what for."

That appeared to be the extent of the briefing. It was so unlike Hawker's preparation that I was initially baffled and almost asked when the real briefing was to be. But then looking round, I noticed the others getting in their machines. Across the field, the Nieuports of 60 Squadron were moving already. I clambered in and after some initial coughing, managed to start the engine. I rolled out to the edge

---

[9] See 'Flashman and the Knights of the Sky'.

11

of the field and turned into wind. Opening the throttle, the machine began to roll and bump over the grass and in seconds, we were airborne and heading for the front line again. I really couldn't believe I was here.

We climbed steadily up to three thousand feet, the sun as always shining directly into our faces; at least it did once we were above the cloud layer that shrouded everything below two thousand feet. Nice as it was cruising in the sun, it was also pointless as the enemy would be below the cloud looking for easy targets, much as I wanted to stay up high and avoid trouble altogether. Almost immediately, Winterbotham started to glide steadily down toward the ocean of cloud. We skimmed the tops for a few moments and, as always, I couldn't help flinching as we plunged into the white mass, the cloud rush much the same as the ground rush I had experienced in the past, shortly before crashing into it.

The ground appeared again and we flew along just below the cloud layer. The front line drifted below, or at least the old front line did. It was another four miles to the new line after the Canadian victory at Vimy Ridge a few days previously. Today Fritz was going to get more of the same apparently.

I peered at the ground, straining to make out what, if anything, was going on. There was nothing of interest so I returned to scanning the sky for hostile machines. Almost immediately, I spotted them. Winterbotham had seen them already and was signalling an attack. We rolled right, already far enough past them to come out of the sun. As we turned, I knew it was a mistake. I hadn't flown an active show for months, Winterbotham was fresh from England too and the tracer was flying past. Out of the corner of my eye, I saw flames. A Nieuport reared up trailing smoke and fire and was clearly doomed as the formation broke up. In an instant, it was a furious every man for himself melee. I had met Richtofen again.

I couldn't help ducking. I gripped the Vickers, frantically searching the sky for Nemesis. Instead, I found an Albatros coming straight at me from my rear port side. Its nose was winking at me curiously and this held my gaze for the instant it took me to realise this was its two machine guns. A couple of seconds later, bullets shredded my port upper wing. There was an ominous clang somewhere not too far away, as I hauled the machine round to face my assailant. Craning my neck back, I saw him coming into view and gave him a burst from the Vickers. It was ineffective but that and the turn was enough to stop me becoming his latest victim. He rolled towards me and dived underneath, too fast for me to do anything about, and headed towards his next target. I pulled into a steep climb in a frantic attempt to get out of the way. I continued over the top in a sort of Immelmann but stayed upside down, looking down at the battle below. In an instant it was over, dissolved like the morning mist at sunrise. The only problem was the disappearance of all my friends as well as the Germans, and suddenly it felt very lonely.

I climbed higher to get right away from the scene of the action. I levelled off at about sixteen thousand feet, just before the controls became too sluggish and more or less out of effective range of enemy aircraft. I slowed down, peered all around me at the clear skies and then looked down at the front line, visible now I had flown beyond the cloud covering the scene west of the British lines.

It hadn't changed much. The enormous scar defacing the landscape still stretched as far as I could see. At least it did to the north and south. East or west one only had to travel a few miles to return to an odd normality.

It was still hard to make out anything directly below. If there was a battle going on, it wasn't there. My petrol was beginning to run low and I was in home territory again so I began gliding down and heading for the field.

\*\*\*\*\*\*

I walked into the mess and threw my helmet on a table.

"That's one more at least," said a voice behind me.

"Only three then." This was de Ropp.

It was my first encounter with the man himself. It was desperately uninspiring. He seemed to think that three pilots lost wasn't a bad day out. Bearing in mind only ten of us set out in the first place, this was deeply disturbing as it suggested this sort of loss was normal. You may guess what I thought about that.

"Flashman. Harry Flashman." He shook my hand with a grip that was reminiscent of a mangle. I returned it as far as possible and then dragged my hand away before he left me unfit to fly. Typical bloody cabbage eater. No manners. No finesse. Still, bearing that in mind it

13

shouldn't be too difficult to get to the bottom of what he was up to. Assuming I survived that long of course. That would be the most difficult thing of all.

I proceeded to get drunk. My short trip over the lines had reminded me very swiftly how dangerous it was. Even more worrying was that we didn't have a Hawker[10] watching over us. Instead, we had Champion de Crespigny who sounded like a prize dog. At least McIlvenna and his tales of New York enlivened the evening. I finally fell into my bunk past midnight, which probably wasn't a particularly wise idea, as I would be flying tomorrow with a bunch of new pilots to replace those who had failed to return.

---

[10] Flashman is undoubtedly referring to the late Major Lanoe Hawker VC. See 'Flashman and the Knights of the Sky'.

Chapter 3

It wasn't the most pleasant awakening, but neither was it the worst. At least I was in my own bed and I hadn't been privy to the dawn disaster with its attendant haul of casualties. Some poor bastard had received a direct hit from the ground, whereupon his machine had disintegrated. Unfortunately, the blast hadn't killed him outright, or at least that was what his fellows believed from his frantic gesticulating. He then fell three thousand feet to his end. It just didn't bear thinking about.

What I did think about over a leisurely breakfast was the previous day's events. Clearly, our Champion wasn't up to the job, at least not in the same way as the late Major Hawker. I had also arrived in France in the middle of a maelstrom created by the Germans and their superior machines. And as for de Ropp? It was hard to know what to think. He was clearly German by inclination, but my first meeting with him had revealed only that he thought and acted like all the others. If he was working for the other side, it was well hidden. Consequently, I had little idea of how to proceed.

I had to assume that all would become clearer in due course. It was enormously difficult to maintain a false front indefinitely without making some sort of slip. I would just have to wait for that moment and hope I was around to capitalise on it. Easier said than done of course and it didn't exactly encourage me knowing that whilst I was waiting for this moment, I would have to take to the skies regularly to dice with death. A not insignificant part of the problem was how to approach de Ropp himself. I toyed with the idea of making friends with him but that was too obvious. If he WAS playing the game, he would be immediately suspicious and therefore on his guard. If he wasn't, then I would discover nothing anyway. A better idea it seemed to me was to act in an aloof fashion, possibly even vaguely hostile, in the hope of provoking him to some minor indiscretion.

It was all conjecture though and quite possibly a total waste of my time when I could have been occupying a nice comfy billet in England, preferably surrounded by refugee French women from the Moulin Rouge.[11] From here, it was a short step to wondering how

---

[11] This is presumably an oblique reference to the destruction by fire of the

long I would need to stay before announcing that de Ropp wasn't a boche spy and requesting a transfer back home away from Richtofen and friends.

"See the Sea wants you," announced an unmistakable New York drawl.

"Who the hell is…" I started before working it out for myself.

"The Major. No idea why."

Irritated, I stalked down to his office and barged in, just enough this side of insolence not to attract trouble. Nevertheless, he gave me a long hard stare.

"New boys here. Take them up for a spin and show them the ropes."

I looked over my shoulder to see three schoolboys hiding in the corner. I just managed to stop myself rolling my eyes in disbelief.

"Follow me then," I said. They trooped out behind me, saluting the Major who grunted in return. "How many hours in a Nieuport have you all got?"

Silence greeted this complex question. "Well?"

"Two sir," piped up the fair-haired one with the beginnings of a moustache.

"And you two?"

"None sir," came the reply in unison. Jesus. So much for the big idea of training them properly before sending them out over the front. More importantly, they were hardly likely to be a lot of use covering my tail. Still, nothing for it but to go and fly.

As we walked out to the aeroplanes, I gave them a briefing of sorts.

"No point at all in flying round and round landing and taking off again. Either you can do that or you can't, and believe me if you are terrified enough it will be the least of your worries. No, better to try and learn to survive."

They looked marginally happier at this statement. God knows what they had been taught in England, but they certainly knew what the casualty rates were in spite of the attempts at suppression by those in high places[12]. Faced with the same information and lack of training, I would have decamped to somewhere safe, like the Arctic.

---

famous Moulin Rouge cabaret in 1915. It reopened in 1921.

[12] RFC casualty rates varied throughout the war but were generally high for a

I pathetically attempted to explain the art of aerial warfare in five minutes before we clambered aboard and started up. We took off and I led them off towards Paris gesticulating frantically for them to fly closer to me.

It was ridiculous, as expected. None of them had the faintest idea what to do. As for keeping formation, we were like a troupe of clog dancers with two left feet doing the Gay Gordons.[13] How we didn't collide, I'll never know, but having tried to encourage them to come closer, I decided it was actually safer to stay as far as possible from them. God help us, or rather God help me, especially when we went east to where the sky rained lead. I landed again, now thoroughly depressed. The engine stopped and I sat in the cockpit musing on the fate that had brought me back to the front when I should have been instructing from a nice safe office. All thoughts of finding out anything about de Ropp had been chucked in the channel with lead boots on. I had to work out a proper way of staying alive and not being too obvious about it, as clearly I would have no one else to rely on.

---

number of reasons. RFC policy was almost always offensive and so pilots spent a lot of time in enemy territory, something the Germans largely failed to do with a consequent loss in useful intelligence, machines were often obsolete and outgunned and German tactics were markedly superior. It is hard to say whether casualty figures were suppressed but it is unlikely at least on a large scale.

[13] The Gay Gordons is a Scottish country-dance. It was particularly popular in the late 19th and early 20th centuries and consists of couples dancing the same steps, usually in a circle around the dance floor.

# Chapter 4

It was bliss. I was in England, Berkeley Square to be exact. Someone had prepared breakfast which I was about to eat along with my female companion whom I could hear singing merrily as she descended the staircase. As she entered the room, I noticed she was wearing an unusual mixture of army issue boots and a filmy khaki negligee and was carrying a tray with a silver teapot and whisky bottle on it. The delightful singing had been replaced with a much deeper voice getting louder and louder shouting "Major Flashman" and the more I looked the more her face was dissolving into a piratical deaths head. Her big hairy hand grabbed my shoulder and I nearly leapt through the wall as I awoke.

Of all the disappointments, this was becoming all too regular. The daily nightmare of flying and staying alive accompanied by the apparently endless paperwork of a flight commander, all of which was largely pointless as the subjects were rarely around long enough to pay any of their mess bills, culminating in an exhausted collapse into my bunk followed by a rude awakening for more of the same had driven me effectively to the bottle and its night-time effects. As for female company, there was none and no prospect of any in the near future. Not that I could have done anything if the entire cast of the Folies Bergere had danced in in their birthday suits giving me wanton looks.

April was coming to an end. The Americans had officially joined in[14] so all we had to do was wait for them to turn up and win. Then it would be back home with medals for everyone. At least it would for those that survived, and survival at the moment seemed highly unlikely. Life had become an endless grind of dawn excursions over the lines, morning excursions, lunchtime, afternoon trips and evening patrols, all of which were equally likely to prove fatal for the unwary. My instinct for survival at any cost was wearing thin, I suspected I was getting careless and that worried me more than anything as a moments inattention would be enough to see me spiralling earthwards with my machine on fire. As for pursuing the lunatic notion that de Ropp was spying on anyone, I would gladly

---

[14] The United States entered the war on April 6th 1917. Officially it was independent and not one of the allied powers.

have told Buchan to his face that it was nonsense. De Ropp hadn't put a foot wrong and he took part in the same number of patrols as everyone else. He had even shot a couple of boche machines down.

In the few quiet moments, I had begun to wonder what was going on. De Ropp clearly wasn't a problem, so why had Buchan and Albany been so insistent? It didn't make sense. More disconcerting was that if they knew this, why had they sent me to France to find out something they surely knew already?

The real question of course was how was I going to extract myself from the situation without looking foolish and thereby affecting my all-important credit? I couldn't just leave unfortunately. But it had to come to a head soon.

It did.

*****

"Flashman," the Major called out from his office. "Pop over to Dover and pick up a couple of new machines will you. Take someone from your flight, there's a good chap." I could have kissed him.

I set out almost immediately accompanied by a randomly selected Baron de Ropp. It was the usual appalling shambles. It would have been quicker to walk, but I didn't care. I wasn't at the front. We arrived in a haphazard way at Calais and hung around for a ship for Dover but much to my amazement there wasn't one. We took the first available space on a ship bound for London, which suited me anyway as I had resolved from the outset to try to find a way to see Buchan and carry out my threat.

I made a quick tour of the ship, just to check whether its defences against U-boats, aircraft and German battleships were adequate and then retired to the mess for travelling officers where I proceeded to get drunk. De Ropp joined me briefly but the conversation was desultory and boring and he eventually left me to it. Possibly, it had something to do with a little snippet of information I had picked up about the losses of machines in April alone. It was in the hundreds apparently whereas the Germans had only lost one or two[15].

---

[15] In April the RFC lost at least 150 machines with over 300 casualties but the Germans also lost over 100 machines.

Something had to be done about it and in my drunken state, I had probably told de Ropp of my plan for blowing up parliament or something equally foolish. Not that that would have solved anything, as even when sensible chaps like Charlton[16] cancelled postings to France for inexperienced pilots they were overruled, and when Joynson-Hicks questioned Trenchard's methods in the house he was equally ignored. No, I would have to find a less explosive way out of the mess we were all in.

With these happy thoughts flowing through my addled mind I finally gave up my position at the bar and staggered off to find somewhere to sleep. Clearly, it would not be safe to sleep in my quarters so I found a nice safe steel bulkhead somewhere downstairs, took off one boot and collapsed.

I awoke, as I have done a number of times in my life, to face a rather unexpected dilemma. It was not an altogether new one, just unexpected. I had told whoever it was shaking me that I did not require breakfast or tea or even coffee and that they would be better off jumping in the channel now before I threw them in, but they hadn't gone away. Eventually, my eyes had opened slowly to reveal a man standing over me. He was holding a British Service Revolver[17] that was pointing at me.

"For Christ's sake wake up," he snarled.

"What the hell is going on?" I shouted involuntarily. I was rewarded with a hand clamped over my mouth.

"Don't shout again. No-one can hear us down here but I won't be taking any chances."

I stared at him, thoroughly puzzled.

"Now, Major, who exactly are you working for?"

Well that was a facer and no mistake. I wasn't entirely sure myself of course. Bravado, albeit false bravado, seemed in order at this point.

---

[16] Presumably Lionel Charlton DSO, a former flight commander serving in the Directorate of Military Aeronautics who cancelled postings for three pilots who were clearly undertrained only to have Henderson reinstate the posting half an hour later.

[17] Assuming Flashman means British issued, it was probably an American Smith and Wesson .44 Hand Ejector which was the standard officers revolver at the time.

"I have no idea what you are talking about. Now, stop pointing that ridiculous gun at me."

For a moment, I thought it might have worked and my teeth almost stopped chattering in fear.

"Rubbish. No, don't get up. I prefer you on the floor. I will ask one more time, who exactly are you working for?"

I appeared to have very few options. Uppermost in my mind, even above the fear, was the thought that a wrong answer here, assuming I survived, could really put the kibosh on my more or less unblemished career and all would be for naught. Inwardly I cursed the whole crowd of them again. At least I was sure that he wasn't a German spy.

"Buchan, Cumming, Albany, there's a whole bloody crowd of them and I can't wait to be shot of them."

He raised his eyebrows.

"I've heard of Buchan and Cumming, but not Albany. Who is he?"

Acutely aware that anything I said now could be taken down in evidence and used against me, I shuffled about, hummed and hawed and tried to look innocent.

"Come on, come on, we haven't got all day."

My head sank into my hands as I realised I had no option and that yet again I had come across another of those lunatics who are unable to leave harmless chaps like me alone.

"Albany is a Count who works for Cumming. At least I think he does."

It was out. My career was ruined. Maybe my whole life was ruined. I would be disgraced. It made the d'Alprant fiasco[18] look like a game of hide and seek.

The laughter echoed from the steel bulkhead. I glanced up to see de Ropp putting the pistol away.

"But mainly you work for Cumming I suppose?"

I nodded.

"Who watches the watchers eh?"[19] He laughed again. "I suppose I should introduce myself properly. Baron William Sylvester de

---

[18] See 'Flashman and the Knights of the Sky'.

[19] Quis custodiet ipsos custodes? From the Satires of Juvenal. 'Who can watch the watchmen' or more correctly 'Who will guard the guards themselves?' There

Ropp, RFC, etc etc, also employed by Captain Vernon Kell[20] who is the boss of MI5[21]. That's internal security to you and me."

He paused long enough for my expression of puzzlement to turn to a mixture of fear and anger.

"This is a very dangerous game you are involved in here. Have you any idea what they are up to?"

Well there was an easy answer to that. I shook my head.

"Let's find somewhere more suitable and I will explain. The look on your face suggests a large brandy might be in order."

I followed him as he climbed up a couple of decks back to the mess and ordered a couple of brandys. He didn't speak again until we were safe in a quiet corner with the glasses on the table.

"Your court martial[22] caused quite a stir you know. Some very shadowy but influential figures were involved, although Cumming kept out of it. I suspect there was a nasty little power struggle going on behind the scenes and I am somewhat amazed you came out of it intact. It would have been much easier for some had you simply vanished. Still, that's not why I am here. Not directly anyway. What excuse did Buchan give you for watching me then? I guess it is something to do with my boche origin. I can see from your face that it is." My eyebrows had shot up at the mention of the word boche. "And where exactly does friend Winterbotham fit in I wonder."

"You have lost me now. I want no part of any of it. I am going to go and see Buchan and tell him he can keep his meddling and cloak and dagger arrangements and just give me a training command and I will keep my mouth shut." I just about managed to sound calm, like a man who has had enough of being trifled with and just wants to get on with the war in a valiant way from behind the lines.

"Impossible of course."

---

is, as so often, some debate as to whether this was in fact written by Juvenal or inserted into his work at a later date.

[20] It is hard to pin down Kell's rank. Generally referred to as Captain, he was a staff captain before the war, he is referred to as 'Colonel' in the 'Hush Hush' revue performed at MI5 in 1919 and retired as an Honorary Major-General.

[21] The Special Intelligence Bureau was formed at the same time as SIS. Referred to as MO5 it officially became MI5 in January 1916.

[22] See 'Flashman and the Knights of the Sky'.

Had we not been on a ship in the middle of the channel, I think I may have bolted and taken my chances. But, as it was, I was stuck. I could also see him lazily fiddling with his holster.

"I see you will not be persuaded by force," he lied still fiddling with the gun, "so it will have to be by reason alone. I have no doubt that I will convince you to see things my way. So let's make a start by putting all our cards on the table. I will go first."

He paused and stared at the ceiling.

"You and I are both pawns in this game, although I suspect I am a better informed pawn than you. Kell wanted me to watch you because of your link with Buchan. He knew Buchan was up to something, possibly trivial, possibly not, and so I was given the task of finding out what was going on. You see, this war isn't entirely about fighting the Germans." He smiled. "I quickly established that Buchan had his eye on you for some reason so I found out all there was to know about you. You are a difficult man to keep tabs on by the way. You also have someone high up somewhere looking after you because a couple of times I was obstructed by a nameless authority with no apparent reason. I am sure you know best about that but it just meant I had to dig deeper with more subtlety. I eventually found out about the court martial and its result, which puzzled me as well. Why would a court martial return a guilty verdict on what amounted to a murder charge and then let the defendant go free with no punishment and no official record?"[23]

He was staring at me so I stared back, unwilling to enter into the spirit of the thing.

"Obvious really. You have something, or know something that would seriously embarrass those involved. They now have something on you, or at least something that they could hang you with if they so desired, and that they think is enough to keep you quiet. For the moment anyway. I suspect they are really hoping you might end up as another statistic of the western front and save them the bother. So, what is the real story? Well, I don't know either. I suspect that I am being used as well, to keep an eye on you and perhaps find out more about what is underlying all this. I can then tell my masters who will use that information…. wisely? Who knows?"

---

[23] See 'Flashman and the Knights of the Sky'.

Precisely.

My head was spinning. Far from being free of all this nonsense, it appeared I was sinking deeper and deeper in the mire created by my father and his inability to keep his trousers on. Most people just have mad uncles or strange cousins or the mother-in-law from hell. I appeared to have all these plus more. To top it all, I was in a plot where I didn't know the beginning, the middle or the end, although I had a shrewd idea that the end was not something I cared to think about too much.

De Ropp was blowing smoke at the ceiling in a distracted fashion, having presumably said all he was going to say.

"What are you going to do then?" I asked as nonchalantly as possible.

"Me? Do? Nothing. Apart from watch you of course. Kell wouldn't be at all impressed if I didn't do that. What else is there to do? I do not intend to finish up as fertiliser in France at any rate. Assume you feel the same."

"But what about Cumming, and Albany and all the others?"

"What about them? If you mean what are they going to do, I don't know because I don't know what is behind it. If you want a guess, I think Albany, whoever he is, has some plot up his sleeve that he doesn't want anyone to know about. He has dreamed up this scheme to keep you out of his way and keep an eye on me and by extension MI5. Mainly though, he wants you to be his eyes and ears in France, presumably so that if you got wind that we knew what he was up to, you could tell him. As I say, just a guess, but an educated one."

The conversation drifted away from conspiracy onto more mundane things like the fact that we were now steaming down the estuary and I still hadn't decided whether to see Buchan. De Ropp decided it for me.

"Of course you should. Tell him you are here with me and then tell him whatever you like. I don't care what he thinks."

I resolved to go and see him.

"I'll be at the Rag[24] when you're finished."

---

[24] Presumably the Army and Navy club known colloquially as the 'Rag and Famish'.

24

I caught a cab to Trafalgar Square and walked down The Mall and into St James's Park. I wanted to think this over first.

My summary of events was not encouraging. I had no doubt at all that Albany was up to something, presumably something to do with his ancestors and therefore the throne. I thought it was unlikely that he was about to assassinate anyone, least of all good old King George, but the Prince of Wales now? No, it was still too far-fetched. At the very least, any attempt to usurp the throne would mean removing far too many people, so it had to be something more subtle, and maybe that was where I entered the script. Albany clearly had allies, Sinclair perhaps being one of them and he was more than likely a Jacobite at heart otherwise he would not have gone to such lengths to help my Father and I. There were certainly more. Buchan perhaps? Difficult to tell as he could be on anybody's side. Perhaps he considered me an ally although he had a funny way of showing it. Cumming was probably neutral as he had all the instincts of the born survivor.

On the other side then were the Prince of Wales and his sidekick Legh[25], possibly Kell and his band of thugs with de Ropp cheering on from the side-lines. Oh and let's not forget Winterbotham although where he came into it was a mystery as well.

I prayed. Why? Who knows? I prayed for it all to go away. I only wanted a quiet life albeit with certain accoutrements but I could see I wasn't going to get it. I pointlessly rued the day I had let the idiot O'Connell take me flying.

I was getting nowhere. If I was going to see Buchan, I might as well get on with it.

\*\*\*\*\*\*

He wasn't there. I decided to wait despite the decidedly unhelpful attitude of a bespectacled and rather formidable looking woman sitting at a desk at the top of the stairs leading into his offices[26]. An hour passed and clearly, I wasn't going to get past her today, at least not in a conventional fashion. I was beginning to get angry as I

---

[25] This must be Sir Piers Legh. See 'Flashman and the Knights of the Sky'.

[26] MI6 was based in Whitehall Court at this point but Flashman does not say whether this was where he saw Buchan.

had come all this way from France and been threatened with a gun for good measure.

"Tell him I have completed his task," I said and stalked out in fury.

Where to now though? The thought struck me as I started to move involuntarily towards Whitehall. Sinclair. It was his fault I was in this mess. Perhaps I should have it out with him and find out what was going on, as it appeared Buchan couldn't or wouldn't see me. I had developed a sneaking suspicion that he had been in his office and was just avoiding me. My feet took me of their own accord towards Sinclair's lair.[27] As I approached, I reviewed my situation and took a moment to stop and think. Barging right in making demands seemed like the right thing to do but probably wouldn't get me very far. Subtlety was perhaps the order of the day and just for once, I was right. There were enough people around so that I could loiter without causing undue suspicion although an hour hanging around in the lobby wasn't an awful lot of fun but I was rewarded at last by the appearance of the great man himself. I slowly turned away so that he wouldn't see me, let him go past and then followed him out into the street. He didn't look round and immediately headed along Whitehall towards Westminster. For a moment, I thought he was going to turn up Downing Street but he didn't and carried on towards Parliament Square. I was on the other side of the road now and slightly behind him. He suddenly looked round and for an instant, I thought he knew I was there but then he crossed the road and I breathed a sigh of relief. Now in front of me he carried on, turned left onto the square, and headed for the bridge. Halfway across, I tapped him on the shoulder.

"Flashman," he said, sounding unsurprised as he continued walking.

"Finished," I replied.

"Who or what is finished?"

"Your job. Or was it Albany's job. I don't know."

At last he stopped. There was no one around us and just for an inkling I thought he was going to shove me over the rail.

"Albany's. Bloody stupid idea if you ask me."

---

[27] Presumably Whitehall Court.

"Well I'm not asking you, I'm telling you I have done it, de Ropp isn't a traitor, and I have had enough of French food." I think my face was bright red with anger at this point.

"Yes, well, we'll see about that. I presume he is working for Kell's little gang?"

"Christ, if you knew that, why the hell go to all this trouble?"

A passing official of some sort pulled a disgusted face, presumably at all the blasphemy he had heard.

"But I didn't know. I do now though." See what I mean? You couldn't have a sensible conversation with these people. He went on. "What exactly are you after?"

My mood deteriorated from simply angry to livid.

"Mainly I would like to survive this bloody mess, and then never, ever have anything to do with you or Cumming or Albany again."

I turned away and took the two steps to the rail. I briefly considered the ramifications of flinging Sinclair over the rail. I was big enough to do it, but decided I wasn't brave enough, especially in broad daylight in the middle of London.

"Unfortunately, you are stuck with us." His voice had assumed a more placatory tone and I turned to face him again. "And that is not all you are stuck with. Let me get you a drink."

## Chapter 5

"We have a serious problem."

He paused. I stared.

"What do you mean we?" I asked. He now stared as yet again I forced him to consider my true nature.

"I mean, YOU started this and now WE have a problem."

"I started it? Started what for God's sake?"

He threw a worn envelope on the table.

"I believe you gave this to me when you last escaped from Germany. I foolishly let someone else see it[28]."

My mind raced back to my homecoming when I handed over the letter from the Emperor. I hadn't given its contents much thought at all, if any. Now it appeared it was coming back to bite me.

"You see, when I considered what the letter contained, I realised it was beyond my competence. I kept it to myself for a week or two. Then I showed it to Cumming. That was a mistake and is the only time I have seen him so angry."

"Are you going to enlighten me then," I said.

"It is extremely delicate. By telling you, you join the small band that is aware of this letter who have also agreed that should the contents be made public without authorisation, then the full force......"

He paused significantly.

"the full force of the law, as you have witnessed at first hand, be brought to bear on whomever was unwise enough to reveal the said contents. Do I make myself clear?"

"Indeed. Now can we get on with it?"

He gave me a freezing glare and just for a moment, I thought he was going to hit me.

"Read it yourself."


Schonnbrunn Palace

Vienna
1916

---

[28] See 'Flashman and the Knights of the Sky'.

28

Your Majesty,

I write with a degree of fear in my heart, but nevertheless with certainty that I am following the correct course. The war our respective nations are fighting is unwinnable. All nations involved will be destroyed by the cataclysmic battles being fought repeatedly for little real gain. What form our nations will take once the fighting is over is unclear, but I have no doubt it will not be the current one. My greatest fear is the uprising of the masses and thus the end of civilisation as we know it. It would also be the end of our rule as we know it. There must be another way.

We are all cousins. We are a family. We are all, to some greater or lesser degree usurpers. We know the truth. We must come together as a family and bring Europe back from the brink.

I believe the man who conveys this letter may be of use to you. He is resourceful and brave. I believe he would agree with the sentiments expressed within. I believe he could be used to bring us together.

I have expressed the same views to the Kaiser and the Tsar. I have asked the Kaiser to consider withdrawal from Belgium and Alsace Lorraine. I have asked the Tsar to consider a cease-fire and I am willing to sanction an independent Serbia. I implore you to consider the same, to consider negotiation. If we can embrace peace, there may just be a chance for us.

I await your reply.

Charles
Emperor[29]

Sinclair broke the silence. "God knows how he has conceived the idea that you might agree with the sentiments within. Given your ancestry, I should imagine you would be the last person to assist in

---

[29] Emperor Charles I came to the throne in late 1916. He immediately started to seek an end to the war. However, it is not known if he had undertaken any negotiations prior to his accession. Flashman suggests that he had in fact commenced peace overtures whilst still Archduke.

the maintenance of the status quo. Mind you, I probably underestimate your ability to dissimulate. Are you brave?"

"That depends on what you mean by brave," I replied, carefully trying to avoid any answers at all.

"Ha. I suspect you were his only option. Anyway, out with it. What do you think?"

"You send me off on some wild goose chase after de Ropp and then when I get back and tell you it is nonsense, you confront me with this and expect me to tell you what I think?" Well I was angry.

"Yes, that is exactly what I expect you to do. And it wasn't a wild goose chase."

There was a pause while we considered what was to be done. I finished my whisky and ordered another since the Government or someone was paying. Sinclair scratched his head.

"Right, I'll start then and see if we can't salvage something from all this. It wasn't a wild goose chase as I have said. It also wasn't a great idea but Albany has some influence so I had to do something. I knew de Ropp wasn't with us but I didn't know exactly what he was doing or whom he was working for. I also didn't know if the... others were trying to eliminate you for reasons of their own. Oh I know they believe they have you where they want you but however one looks at it, they would be better off if you were dead." My look of horror didn't prevent him telling me the appalling truth although I already knew it really. I gulped another mouthful of the firewater. "God help us all if any of this ever gets into the open."

"You sent me to de Ropp to see if he would try and kill me didn't you?" realisation dawning on me through the slight haze that was descending.

"Yes. But I did send another man to keep an eye on you and I can't help it if you charge off with de Ropp in tow abandoning my watchdog."

"Who.....Winterbotham. Christ." I was holding my head in my hands now. It seemed that whichever way I turned there was one of the buggers looking over my shoulder.

"Anyway, you're still alive as it seems de Ropp didn't want to kill you, only to warn you."

"Lucky me, eh!" His eyes narrowed.

"Luck doesn't come into it. The problem is what we do now. You see, we cannot simply do nothing and hope it all goes away."

I could have cried. I knew you see, that what he said was true. Much as I hoped, it wasn't all going to go away. Worse, I could see already that someone was going to be in the middle of sorting out what we did now, whatever that someone said was going to be ignored and he was going to have to accept being hurled into the soup again. Or he could risk disgrace and abandonment to his fate.

"I am not sure if the King is aware of the letter although there are a few in his circle who are. I suspect the Prince of Wales and Legh. Kell I am not sure about. Possibly not directly but I think he has some knowledge of it. There are so many threads to this, not the least of which is that the Emperor is correct when he suggests that the shape of Europe and this country will not be the same once this war is over. It's changed already of course. The Russians have revolted and the Tsar has abdicated[30]. You probably knew that but what we don't know is where that will go, or where it will end. They are only foreigners but that doesn't mean it won't spread. What you also don't know is parts of the French Army mutinied a few weeks ago. 20,000 men deserted. [31]"

There was a pause while he let that and its implications sink in.

"Well, I am sure it will all end just right, whatever that may be. Good day to you." I got up to leave.

"Not so fast, Major." I stopped. I should have run for it and I knew it, but I couldn't. He knew too much about me. "We haven't finished our discussion yet."

"We both know it isn't a discussion."

"Perhaps not. I need you to go to Germany." He said it like someone says I need you to go to the station. My heart sank into my boots and my liver felt lily like. My face turned its customary red colour, which he probably didn't notice in the smoky gloom, and my feet were like lead as they refused the order to run and run and leave

---

[30] This refers to the February (or March depending on which calendar is being used) revolution which led to the abdication of the Tsar and a period of dual power with a Provisional Government exercising state power whilst the Soviets led the masses.

[31] The French army on the Chemin des Dames had experienced increasing levels of desertion following Nivelle's second Battle of the Aisne. This turned to widespread mutiny towards the end of May 1917 when up to 30,000 soldiers left the front line and many units simply refused to return to the trenches. See appendix.

London and go somewhere safe like the North Pole where no-one had ever been.[32]

"No." I was trembling as I thought I had heard someone say no.

"Fine." Had I heard correctly? "Good day to you Major." He looked away and summoned the bill. I was rooted to the spot. "Still here Major?" It was all wrong. I knew it was all wrong but I was powerless to do anything about it. I turned and left. I hovered in the street for a while looking around me, then instinct took over and I hailed a cab and went to the Rag. Reaction was setting in by this stage so I found a quiet table in a dark corner and set to work on a duck curry and a Talisker.[33] Like my Father, I knew better than to mix my drinks. There was no sign of de Ropp, thank God.

I was halfway through the bottle when a porter came sidling over. I recognised him immediately from my previous exploits[34].

"Evening Jones," I said cheerily with a slight slur.

"Evenin' Sir, you're lookin' well if I might make so bold." I smiled benevolently. "Vere's a rum cully wiv an 'ard 'at in ve porch. 'e asked me to deliver vese telegrams to you. 'e said 'e would wait for a reply." He paused. "I can get rid of 'im if you wanted me to," he said quietly with a knowing leer. Twice in one day, rooted to the spot, frozen with mounting fear, knowing that it wasn't as simple as saying no.

"No," I chuckled, "we'll just see what they say." I resisted the temptation to rip the things open and scream at the contents, nonchalantly tearing the envelope open and picking it all up from the floor.

'Your choice,' the first one said. I opened the second.

'Major Harry Flashman Royal Flying Corps missing from his squadron STOP Last seen in Calais boarding a ship for England STOP Wanted for questioning for murder of French woman STOP Maybe dangerous STOP.

There was a handwritten note saying 'To be sent to all newspaper editors.'

---

[32] It is possible that this statement is incorrect. North Pole exploration was a very controversial subject largely because verification of claims was very difficult. See appendix.

[33] A single malt whisky produced on the Isle of Skye since 1830.

[34] See 'Flashman and the Knights of the Sky'.

The third was addressed to See the Sea and simply stated that I was to be detached from his Squadron for a brief mission on behalf of Trenchard.

"Tell him to tell him that I have reconsidered."

\*\*\*\*\*\*

I woke with an appalling hangover. My head was splitting and I wasn't even sure where I was. I vaguely remembered finishing a bottle and then getting in a cab to go to Piccadilly where I knew a decent brothel. I seemed to recall a voluptuous redhead. What happened next I simply could not remember. Looking around it seemed I had somehow made it back to the Rag but at that moment I was past caring, not a feeling I often succumb to. I lay back again wondering what time it was.

The one thing I did recall was that bastard Sinclair and his threats, my feeble response and how I appeared to be in a right bloody mess again. I considered telling him to send his telegram and try having me arrested for a crime that no-one knew about committed in a foreign country. That was until I realised it had nothing to do with it. Just my name in a paper attached to crime and apparently deserting my squadron would be enough to finish me. I would be dropped by Society without a second thought and there would be no more heroic and rapturous welcomes, just a pelting with rotten tomatoes. I could whine all I liked about the injustice and eventually I would be proved right but 'no smoke without fire' would be the slogan whispered from drawing room to drawing room and my life would end. Of course, my life might well end on Sinclair's mad scheme whatever it was but at least there was a small chance of surviving. I had been across the lines before..... it was all too hellish to think about.

The door opened and my rum cully friend entered uninvited.

"Please to come with me Major."

I dressed quickly once he had left, had a small repast just to keep Sinclair waiting a little longer, and then joined him downstairs. My headache was receding somewhat as we climbed aboard the taxi which took us back to Whitehall and Sinclair's office.

"I am glad you saw fit to reconsider, Flashman. I don't like threatening you but sometimes it is easier just to get to where we need to be. I owe that to your Father."

"If you owe anything to my Father, why the hell do you have to involve me at all?"

"Come come, now. You know as well as I do that fate and your family have left you here. The big thing is how we all come out of it intact and with the right people in the right places. To business." I remained silent while he shuffled some pieces of paper around and looked thoughtful. "This is a casualty return for the recent battles, beginning with the push on the Somme last July." He passed it over the table. "I need not say of course that it is most secret, to be divulged to no-one. I should not really be divulging it to you but I think given what I am going to ask you to do, you should at least have some idea of why."

I couldn't suppress an involuntary gasp. I had just read an account of the first day on the Somme. I had been there of course, watching from above, as apparently 19,000 men died below me. 19,000. It was a staggering figure even to a callous bastard like me who generally worried only about his own survival. No wonder they didn't want the figures to leak out or they might well find a revolution on their hands.[35]

"No doubt you see the problem. We cannot continue to sustain that level of casualties or we won't have anyone left to fight. The Germans are already showing signs of fighting only on the defensive[36], which dramatically reduces the casualty rates. We had worked out that they were going to withdraw and by doing so they have made it much more difficult for us as their defences are now rather good. And apart from anything else, waiting for the Americans could well take a year or so, especially when you consider that the Somme was

---

[35] It is not clear why Flashman thinks the casualty figures were suppressed. It is unlikely but statistics as always could prove anything. Possibly the total figures were not suppressed but equally not promulgated overtly which would explain Flashman's surprise.

[36] The German manpower crisis following the losses in 1916 did in fact precipitate decisions by Hindenburg and Ludendorff to withdraw to the Siegfriedstellung or Hindenburg Line. They planned for defence in depth to defeat the forthcoming Allied offensives whilst certainly realising that they would not win without attacking eventually.

the first battle for many of those recruited in the first weeks of the war[37]. It might well all be over by then, but not in the way we want. So, here we are, not much further forward in terms of overall victory but with a seriously depleted manpower reserve. The question is therefore, what the hell do we do about it?"

"Start a breeding program?"

He gave me a slightly contemptuous stare.

"Let us understand one another. I know you well enough to ignore your facetious remarks, but whether you like it or not, you are still an officer in the RFC and you still work for Cumming and I until such time as we decide you are no longer of use to us. We can make it very difficult for you, as you now appreciate otherwise you would not be here, or, my preferred option, is to make it as easy as possible. It's up to you."

For once in my life, I actually felt slightly humbled. It didn't last long, but I saw his point. What he didn't appreciate was that his idea of making it easy for me meant doing things that risked my life, and you can imagine how I felt about that. Yet again, it appeared that I would have to grin and bear it whilst dissolving inside. I could almost hear my bloody Father laughing. However, I wasn't about to make it easy for him by bursting with enthusiasm for whatever lunatic plan he had in mind. So, I said nothing and waited for him to continue.

The moment passed while Sinclair shuffled some more paper.

"The problem is there is no easy answer. If we simply carry on as we are, feeding more and more men into the grinder, they will eventually revolt. Whether that leads to something more or spreads to England is impossible to say. It might lead to losing the war, more likely it would lead to stalemate. Then what? Stalemate could well lead to revolution as the masses began to wonder what on earth it was all for. There are some developments on the horizon that might help and the Americans will change the balance eventually unless of course the Russians give in[38]. None of which helps right

---

[37] The 'Accrington Pals' (11th Bn East Lancs Regt) being a good example. Formed in September 1914 by the mayor (Captain John Harwood) and corporation of Accrington, they were posted to Egypt in late 1915 to defend the Suez Canal, moving in February 1916 to France where they first saw action on the first day of the Somme battle. Of the 720 men who went into action on the 1st July, 584 became casualties, 235 killed and the rest wounded in half an hour.

now. The machine gun is still king of the battlefield.[39]" He paused to let this sink in. "It would be easy to do nothing and let events take their course, no-one would know and the outcome would be whatever it would be. However, after I gave Cumming the letter and let him calm down, I began to think on it. In theory of course, we don't make deals with the enemy.[40] However, it has been decided that in this case, it is worth a try. Letters have been written. They just need to be sent." He paused again. "I suggest you get de Ropp to brush up your German."

Well if you haven't guessed who was to do the sending, you should have. It was bad enough that he wanted me to go to Germany or Austria or wherever he thought I could do the least damage, but it appeared I was about to join the ranks of the General Post Office. I could have a shrewd guess to whom I was to post these letters as well. How I kept a straight face I will never know.

An hour or so later I left the building. I couldn't go to the Rag, at least not straightaway, as I had to invent some sort of story for de Ropp to swallow. And of course, we would then have to go to Dover to collect the two aeroplanes. One of the worst things that had struck me during our conversations however, was the realisation that the war itself was not going to finish any time soon. If those in authority thought it was likely to end in stalemate, and those same people didn't appear to have any sensible ideas to break said stalemate, then we were all doomed. It would be impossible to survive for years and years flying useless lethal missions over the other side. In short, I was going to die in a flaming ball and there appeared to be nothing to be done about it, although running away would eventually be unavoidable.

"Trying to lose me were you?" said a familiar voice.

"Why would I do that? We've got to get those blasted aeroplanes from Dover and I can't do it by myself."

---

[38] It would probably have been all too clear to the British Authorities that the Russians were on the edge of defeat. The revolution took place in the context of heavy military defeats and much of the Russian army was in a state of mutiny.

[39] In the context of the Somme battles, this was probably true. Overall, it was the artillery that was truly king of the battlefield.

[40] All Governments wish to appear tough when dealing with enemies. Reality of course dictates that negotiations continue and this was as true during the Great War as it is now.

"Of course not. I assume that is where we are going now then?"

"Yes."

It wasn't a long or interesting conversation, but it was correct. After treating myself to some refreshment at the Rag, I left for Dover with de Ropp in tow once again. Quite how he had found me, I didn't know or particularly care to speculate on. I had a nasty feeling he had been following me and that he was somehow privy to all that had gone on between Sinclair, Buchan and co. It was a quiet trip down to Dover.

## Chapter 6

Nowhere was safe. I had awoken again in the middle of the night, sweating and trembling, my mind spinning with Sinclair's last words to me. "We will make contact again once it is time to go." God help me. Blasphemy I know but it seemed like the only place I was going to get it.

I didn't sleep again; at least it felt like I didn't so the appearance of Heskey before dawn was most unwelcome. I abused him as always and he ignored it as always. I couldn't face eating so I struggled into my kit and went outside. The horizon was glowing with the imminent arrival of the sun but I hardly noticed. Apart from anything, I had seen it so many times and it usually heralded the beginning of slaughter of one description or another. Nevertheless, I gazed into the distance until someone reminded me that I was leading the flight and they were all ready.

Airborne again I led them low towards the front, foolishly hoping that any boche would not be able to see us against the brown smear that marked the lines. We crossed into no-mans-land while I decided whether to climb or strafe the trenches just for the hell of it although I guessed it would upset the local footsloggers, or just fly around behind the German lines and look for a target. There was nothing. I had a brief flutter when I realised how close to Douai we were but still nothing. We flew for almost an hour without seeing so much as a sausage. It was eerily quiet. I didn't mind. We landed in time for breakfast and for once, all of us were there. The day passed with another flight patrolling and not losing a single machine and then it was our turn again. The early evening sky had an unnatural glow in the east and there were numerous tall thunderclouds dotted around the sky, leaving large valleys and troughs between them. We flew under one of them and were rewarded with a soaking in the horizontal rain. I spotted Arras in the distance, but it wasn't until we got a little closer I began to see the machines milling around.

I was thinking it looked a bit fraught for my liking when I caught a glint high up behind me and instinctively I knew it wasn't one of ours. Caught between carrying on to join the circus ahead as duty required, or investigating above I banked hard, surprising the others as I hadn't signalled anything, (and myself as I usually wouldn't seek sorrow of any kind but I had the excuse that I hadn't slept and was feeling curiously out of sorts) and at the same time I pushed the throttle forward and pulled on the stick. I pointed upwards and the others followed my arm. For some reason at that point, I took note of who had come with me that evening. De Ropp was there and Winterbotham as well as the two new boys I had tried to teach to fight. Two things struck me. First, I didn't know either of their names, second that there had been three of them. I shivered as I recalled that the third one was dead in a muddy hole somewhere near Bapaume. I dragged my mind back to the task in hand. I was more and more certain it was a hun as we overhauled him. Them, as it turned out.

We climbed hard, only Winterbotham's machine struggling slightly and dropping a little behind although not through want of trying. We got above them and with the setting sun behind occasionally giving us a modicum of cover, we caught them up. A glance over the side told me we were near Arras and heading for the cloud of machines in the distance again, but those nearest had still not seen us. We were just coming into long range of the four Albatros' ahead when there was an enormous roar above me. I hit my head on the coaming as I ducked wondering what the hell had happened and glanced up to see a formation of SE5s, one with a red spinner, passing just above and to my left. Ball.[41]

Typical. Showing off how good he was and now he was about to steal my surprise. Seconds later, I heard his gun open up and one of the Albatros' trailed smoke and rolled over. It carried on rolling and headed for the ground, doomed.[42] It was only then I noticed that the Albatros' were mainly red[43]. My guts dissolved as in my stupid attempt to stay out of it, I had led us into the evening fight with

---

[41] Captain Albert Ball, VC, DSO and two bars, MC. See appendix.

[42] Ball's list of victories shows this one as unconfirmed.

[43] This is probably slightly inaccurate in that only Richtofen generally flew a red painted aircraft, something he began doing when he took command of Jasta 11 in January 1917. The other pilots started to paint parts of their aircraft red to make Richtofen 'less conspicuous', but the colour became an informal squadron identification. It was only in June 1917 when Richtofen assumed command of Jagdgeschwader 1, a 'wing' formation of four Jastas including 11, that the 'Flying Circus' was born. This name came both from the mobility of the unit because they regularly moved by train to new locations and the pilots painting their aircraft in garish multi-coloured patterns.

Richtofen and his gang of chancers. At least the great Manfred himself wasn't there. He was away in Germany apparently being shown off to the fat Hausfrauen as the hero who looked after all their boys. He was even on a postcard.[44]

None of which was particularly comforting as the whole thing was now being led by his brother, the charming Lothar who was steadily catching up his brother in the grim race to see who was best. With that thought lingering, we were in amongst them. There were machines everywhere and I now seriously regretted my rash decision. It struck me that my instincts must be all wrong as they usually led me away from this kind of trouble but tonight the opposite had occurred. In the half a second it took me to think all that I had flown right into the middle of the melee. My guns were firing almost of their own accord as I weaved and climbed trying not to hit anyone. I was just on the point of blasting the tail off of an aeroplane that appeared from nowhere right in front of me when I realised it was one of ours. I rolled frantically and a trail of bullets shot past my cockpit and into the tail of my colleague who woke up and hauled his machine upwards followed by what looked like a yellow aircraft. As I heaved my machine round in a complete 360, I pulled up as well and saw the yellow bastard letting fly again at whoever it was I had nearly shot up. An automatic glance around showed no-one else near enough to cause me any danger so I shoved the throttle forward and tried to climb as fast as I could. The Nieuport was pretty good in a climb and certainly better than the Albatros and I slowly but surely closed the gap[45]. Waiting and waiting with my fingers tense on the trigger as the two machines ahead danced a furious aerial waltz, the SE suddenly turned hard right. I thanked the God of aerial combat, whoever he was, as the Albatros did the same presenting me with a beautiful target I could

---

[44]Richtofen had indeed been recalled to Germany where he was making public appearances, writing his biography and generally being lauded by the German High Command for his fifty victories. He had achieved this milestone during 'Bloody April'. His postcard portrait was everywhere and wherever he went he was mobbed. See appendix.

[45] Relative performance figures for the two aircraft show that the Nieuport 17 had a marginally better climb rate than the Albatros DIII, top speed was broadly similar and both suffered from a weak lower wing that had an alarming tendency to crack or break up in a high-speed dive killing a number of pilots of both types.

not miss. Still no-one else near me I pulled hard and watched the stream of bullets hit friend boche. I hit something important, as the first thing that happened was his propeller was blown off. For a brief moment, I watched it spin away into the void before looking back at what else was going on. There was a whumpf and the engine was on fire, black smoke trailing behind as the aircraft started to head for the ground. I had stopped firing but was following him. In seconds, the whole machine was ablaze and I almost felt sorry for the bastard.

I hauled my nose up again looking for danger and there it was, right above me, the turning, falling, running dogfight.[46] There was an almighty smash caused by a three-way collision. One of ours was being chased by one of theirs, when another one of theirs being chased by one of ours appeared directly in front of our other one and hit him head on. Our chasing machine performed a frantic rolling dive and by some miracle avoided the tangled machines. The other German was much closer and tried but only succeeded in ripping his entire port wing off. I thought I could see the look of horror on his face as his machine began to spin.

An eerie red glow bathed the scene for a few seconds. It was perceptibly darker now but I knew what it was. Someone, probably that bugger Ball, had fired another Very light. Looking round I could see his red spinner in the glow and I watched fascinated as he chased an Albatros into a tall cloud. Feeling lonely, I started to follow. I jumped as another SE5 with a Flight Commander's ribbon appeared as if from nowhere and we both flew into the cloud as well. I still don't really know why I did it. Maybe it was because it was Ball, he of over forty victories. Straining ahead to see where they were we suddenly popped out of the cloud. Ball had gone and so had the German. It was just me and the other SE. I waggled my wings at him and turned round.

It was over. The sky had cleared and silence descended. Alone again I descended to work out where I was and head for home. A crash of thunder nearly had me apoplectic and as I flew over the lines and started to relax a little I realised my hands were shaking

---

[46] The term dogfight has been used for centuries but in relation to air combat can be traced to the latter years of the Great War, being first written down in this context in 1919 by Captain A.E.Illingworth in his book 'Fly Papers' recounting his exploits as an RFC pilot.

uncontrollably. Looking around me, I had a crushing feeling of how insignificant I was compared to the huge clouds towering over me and throwing rain in my face; I was soaked again.

******

Ball was dead. I must have been one of the last to see him as he flew into the cloud. The SE was Billy Crowe from 56 Squadron. The Germans claimed Lothar got him but that seemed like nonsense to me. If anything, Ball was chasing Richtofen and it was unlikely that someone as good as Ball had let himself be turned into the victim. Richtofen had crashed shortly afterwards and described a fight with a naval Triplane. Well I never saw any Triplanes that evening, but then the official report doesn't refer to any Nieuports. A German Lieutenant later described seeing an aeroplane flying over Annouellin upside down with its propeller stopped and crashing. Apparently, there were no bullet wounds on Ball when he was found.

What do I think? He became disorientated in the cloud and lost control of his machine. When he came out of it, he was upside down and not a lot to be done about it. It could have happened to any of us, as we didn't have enough reliable instruments to tell us which way was up when we couldn't see. I resolved not to go flying into clouds without a bloody good reason in future.

Chapter 7

I don't think anyone heard me shout but it woke me up. The vague lingering memory of an appalling dream faded slowly to blackness. The trouble was, too often the dream wasn't far off reality. The continual grind of flying, the associated death and destruction, the forever-changing faces in the squadron all mingled into one long living nightmare. There appeared to be no end. I thought again about what Sinclair had said. The worst nightmare would be when he turned up.

No sooner had I thought it than it became the new reality. I was dreaming again, this time a pleasant little romp involving a legion of voluptuous lovelies when I was shaken out of it. My first thought was Heskey and his infernal early morning cheerfulness so as I awoke I was ready with my usual insults. For one awful moment, I thought I had gone blind. It was as black as pitch, which was odd, as I had got used to waking in the half-light. The hand on my shoulder was a little odd too. Of more concern was the other hand clamped across my mouth. I began to struggle.

"Flashman," hissed a familiar voice, "stop wriggling."

I froze and the hand was slowly removed. I was sorely tempted to shout for assistance and be damned to it, but fear prevented me. Of course, had I known what was in store I would have taken my chance.

"Get up quietly. Collect your things; we will not be coming back."

"What?" I just had the presence of mind to whisper.

"You heard me, now get on with it."

Torn between my natural inclination to disobedience and the commanding tone of Sinclair's voice, I lay perfectly still for a moment while my disordered mind struggled to catch up.

"I'll see you outside in ten minutes." With that, Sinclair left the room.

I stared around me for a while, my eyes slowly becoming accustomed to the gloom. Almost without thinking, I retrieved the few belongings I had, dressed and went outside.

The airfield was quiet as the grave. There was virtually no light and it took me some moments for my eyes to adjust to the gloom. The glow from a cigarette revealed Sinclair, staring into the distance.

"Shall we go?" he announced to no one in particular.

He led me to a waiting staff car and opened the rear door. I stepped in and a gruff voice nearly had me leaping out again.

"How is your German?" said the voice.

Cumming. Come back to haunt me no doubt as promised.

"Passable," I replied wondering what the wrong answer was.

"Not good enough for our purpose." If it hadn't been so dark, he would have been able to see the momentary relief spreading across my face, although if I had stopped to think about it I would have realised that if I didn't go with them I would be up at dawn taking my chance over the lines again. "Have to work on it, I suppose. Can't take too long though, what."

I probably held my head in my hands. I might have cried silently in the dark of the car as we drove at breakneck pace through the French countryside, almost as if we were on a Cook's tour for the damned.

Silence descended over our journey. I hadn't the faintest idea where we were going and after a short period staring through the windows and trying to work it out, I must have dozed off. Perhaps it was the shock.

I woke with a start. The sun was shining straight into my eyes and for a moment, I thought we were heading for the enemy. It was only a moment as I quickly realised I was still in the car and we were still driving, albeit much more slowly. We appeared to be in a port but it wasn't one I knew.

"Dieppe," said my old friend Holmes.[47]

"Well, isn't this jolly. Just like an old school reunion. Where are we going from Dieppe then?"

"Liege. At least you are. Eventually." This was Sinclair.

There have been far too many times in my life when words have failed me. This was yet another of those moments. Far too many of them seemed to involve Sinclair. It is possible my mouth fell open. I know that my mind was completely blank, unable to comprehend what I had just been told.

"I thought you wanted me to go to Germany. Why Liege?" I said after what seemed an eternal silence punctuated only by the noise of the engine.

---

[47] One of Sinclair's men. See 'Flashman and the Knights of the Sky'.

44

"That is where our imperial contact is now," muttered Sinclair.

"How… why… when?" I was virtually blubbing by now. I had been dragged out of my bed in the middle of the night, shanghaied by my own side, and I didn't even know why. Except it had something to do with the Emperor, God help me. Last time I met him, I had nearly been done for several times, albeit not directly by him. Mind you, all his family had a similarly lethal effect on anyone nearby.[48] Which I suppose is why most of them were dead. More worrying however than all of that was the idea that Sinclair had been telling the truth.

\*\*\*\*\*\*

I was back in Blighty. At least I was safe for the moment. I suppose one could say I was lucky really, although I knew it was only a brief respite. It seemed only days ago that I had been in Dieppe boarding a nondescript fishing boat for the apparently unending trip across the channel, a trip I could not remember much of, largely as I had spent most of it heaving my guts over the side. I barely slept in what passed for a cabin and by the time I reached England I would happily have thrown myself over the side. But Sinclair was always around to stop me. I suspect he still had a sneaking suspicion that I might make a run for it. God knows I wish I had.

It was July 1917. The year so far had been one of tremendous upheaval. It had begun with the Germans declaring unrestricted submarine warfare in the belief that they would sink enough ships carrying essential supplies to force Britain to sue for peace. So far, it had mainly forced the Americans to join the fray although Sinclair was correct in that it would be many months before they arrived in Europe. Just before the Americans entered, the Russians had a seizure and threw out the Tsar who had indeed abdicated. They were still fighting but it was anyone's guess how long that would continue. And as for the French, well, Sinclair was right. They had attacked the Germans on the Chemin des Dames where Nivelle[49] had

---

[48] The Flashman family's dealings with the Emperor have indeed been lethal. See 'Flashman and the Knights of the Sky' as well as George MacDonald Fraser's 'Flashman and the Tiger'.

come up with yet another plan for thousands of men to run forward and be mown down by artillery and machine guns in heavily defended positions and finally, after taking more than 100,000 casualties[50], the 2$^{nd}$ Colonial Division amongst others turned up elephant's trunk and refused to fight.[51] The feeling quickly spread and the French army essentially gave up for a period. Nivelle, unsurprisingly, got the sack.

It was different on the British front. There the artillery had been bombarding all month. The gravel crushers had taken Messines Ridge after 19 mines were blown up taking thousands of Germans with them,[52] then hung around for a few weeks, but were now about to attack somewhere else. It didn't matter where of course. I thanked the Lord I was in England.

On a more cheerful note, my German was coming along nicely, but not too nicely. My teacher, who when I asked her name had just stared at me, had warmed to my manly charms enough to consent to calling me Herr Major. She was one of those old dragons we all had in nursery. Indeterminate age, indeterminate personality, cold to the point of freezing. Almost anything would have been better. Anything that is apart from returning to France anytime soon. However, there were the bloody great horns of the dilemma. The more I improved, the nearer came the moment of truth and I dreaded the appearance of Sinclair. I hadn't seen him since we landed in England, but he was near. I could feel it. Mind you, I had had enough of Essex.

After landing from France, we had taken an age to drive through London and out again the other side. I had envisaged a nice hotel, a vision that was rapidly dispelled as the city disappeared behind us. I didn't ask and they didn't tell until we arrived. It was a place called Stow Marys[53] or something. I was tempted to ask 'stow Mary's

---

[49] General Robert Georges Nivelle, French artillery officer, architect of the battle of Verdun and then the 'Nivelle offensive', better known as the 'Second battle of the Aisne' or 'Chemin des Dames'. Following this disaster and the mutiny it precipitated, he was replaced by Petain and sent to command in North Africa.

[50] Casualty figures vary but all sources agree they were more than 100,000.

[51] See appendix.

[52] It is probably impossible to quantify accurately but best estimates suggest the mine explosions caused around 10,000 German casualties.

[53] Stow Maries. Established September 1916 as the home for 37 (Home

what?' but didn't. It was the home of 37 Squadron and appeared to be a new station. I was stashed in the Headquarters at The Grange, Woodham Mortimer. I was instructed to avoid saying much to anybody, to eat alone and pay attention to my teacher, the aforementioned battle-axe. She refused to speak anything other than German to me and it had the desired effect after I had got over my sulk and realised I had no choice but to cooperate. She also instructed me in how to behave; and suddenly I realised they were serious. So serious in fact, that they were teaching me how to be a German. I was stunned by the audacity of it.

******

I was sitting reading a newspaper, a German one I might add, when someone tapped me on the shoulder. My heart nearly leapt out of my mouth as I turned and saw Sinclair.

"Gunther Von Pluschow," he said.

"Who?"

"Famous German aviator, taken prisoner after the ship he was on was forced to dock at Gibraltar, sent to England, escaped and jumped a ship to Holland. He is the only one so far to escape[54]."

"And the relevance of that is?"

"You are going to emulate him, more or less anyway."

I gave him a blank look, as I wasn't sure how going to Gibraltar would help. Fortunately, or not as the case may be, he outlined what the plan was. It was enough to freeze the blood.

I often wonder in my old age how I am still here when so much of my life was attended by lunatics hell bent on shoving me into an early grave. Another of those moments had just arrived. I can still hear Sinclair droning on about his plan; at least I assume it was his plan.

"We brought you here for a reason. You see, a couple of miles away there is a prisoner of war camp. Tomorrow, we are going to deliver you there. You will then spend a short while getting to know the place before attempting to escape. You will succeed of course

---

Defence) Squadron commanded by Lieutenant (later Captain) Claude Ridley.

[54] It is correct that Von Pluschow was the only German prisoner of war to escape from England to Germany.

and make your way to a suitable port. Up to you to choose one and there jump ship for the continent. It would be preferable if you selected someone from the camp to accompany you. It gives your story a better cover and of course once you have gone, the other prisoners will almost certainly report your escape. Once you are ashore, your mission is simple. You will deliver a letter to our contact. After that, I suggest you come home."

He smiled at me whilst I stared back, utterly horrified. As far as I could see, I had just been given a death sentence.

"No need to look so glum about it. Not much here you haven't done before, except perhaps the jumping ship part."

A thought occurred to me, or perhaps it was an inspiration.

"How does all this sit with your mission to protect me given my ancestry?"

"It doesn't really. But then as I am sure you remember, I mentioned there were in fact quite a number of Stuart descendants and whilst we try to keep as many as possible alive and where we can get to them, sometimes there are bigger tasks to complete. This is one of those. Do you listen to anything I tell you?" He paused for effect. "You may recall I pointed out that when all this is over, worrying about the monarchy may be something just for the historians. Let's hope not, eh?"

That was where he left, muttering something about being briefed by someone else who would be along shortly. I stayed in my chair.

\*\*\*\*\*\*

Minutes or maybe hours later, it was hard to tell in the excitement, I had another unwelcome visitor. Buchan. He sidled through the door so quietly I nearly had kittens when he coughed in my ear.

"Ah Flashman," he muttered.

I glared at him. I wish I had shot him there and then although I wasn't armed at the time.

"I think you know something of our plan already. Needless to say, it is of vital, even national importance. It is also top secret. The main difficulty we have is how to get the letter to its destination intact. Oh I know, I know, its carrier will get it there safely." This was in response to my squawk of what I can only describe as hope. "I didn't mean the conveyance, merely how to keep it both in one piece and unseen while you are travelling."

Travelling? You'd think I was setting off on a day trip to Blackpool.

"So, we have a plan to do just that." He smiled as one smiles when one's dog manages to retrieve a stick for the first time. "Two letters. One is real the other fake. The real letter is addressed to the Emperor and contains details of how we could end the war to everyone's satisfaction. The other purports to be from a German agent you have met here in England who wanted to pass on information. It will contain real information of a low but useful level and will help establish your bona fides when necessary. All that remains is to conceal them on your person and we can begin."

I am still not sure how he thought that this hare-brained scheme of his involved a 'we' since as far as I could see it only involved a 'me' and a badly shaken me as well. He had rambled on in the same vein for an hour or so before producing the letters and inviting me to conceal them in the lining of my coat like a true amateur. He held onto them for a moment and with a small tear in his eye, wished me luck knowing that I would probably need it by the shovel. He shook my hand and was gone.

******

The first thing I did was open and read the letters. I had an inkling of what they would say and I was right. One was coded and appeared harmless, the other was dynamite. Being caught by some jumped up officious pipsqueak with either in my possession would ensure me a one-way ticket to the gallows and no mistake. Treason was the least of it.

The next thing I did was to copy them out. I wasn't really sure why but it just felt like the right thing to do. My next decision was what to do with the copies. There was only one answer but it needed immediate action. Fortunately, Buchan and Sinclair had long gone but it was afternoon already. I had been into London twice during my stay. My 'jailers' weren't especially happy about it but I had insisted and they had given in.

I presented myself at the guardhouse as usual, told them what I was doing and breathed a huge sigh of relief when there were no questions. The journey was uneventful and I reached Berkeley Square in good time. I had no illusions about exactly how safe the letters would be in my own house but it was the best I could do. I looked for somewhere obscure to hide them so that at least if the pigs came looking they wouldn't find them easily. Hastily scribbling a covering note which after I'd written it seemed far too much like a will, I searched the staircase for the release switch. I pulled it and behind me, a tiny door swung open in the skirting on the stair wall. Looking around me for the last time and seeing and hearing nothing, I placed the bundle in and shut the door again. No one had seen me arrive and no one saw me leave. As the cab gathered speed from where I had left it across the square, my heart began to slow down again. The journey back was equally uneventful.

My last night of peace was about to begin. I couldn't sleep and didn't fancy drinking myself to sleep. I lay staring at the ceiling, alternately sweating and shivering with fear.

I woke with a start and sat bolt upright. I fumbled for my watch only to find I had been asleep all of ten minutes. Cursing, I flung myself back on the mattress, resigned to a broken night of broken dreams and broken sleep.

Chapter 8

"Get up you jerry bastard, get up."

Rough hands grabbed my shoulders and lifted me bodily out of my pit. My feet hardly touched the floor as I was propelled across the room. Someone opened the door and I was shoved into the corridor banging heavily against the opposite wall. Almost falling, I was held up by a soldier who stank of stale sweat before again being propelled down the corridor and through a door into the cold outside. For reasons only a psychiatrist could explain, I noticed the clear sky and Orion's belt twinkling at me in the dark. Having concluded my astronomical study, I was hurled into the back of a truck conveniently parked nearby. Two soldiers climbed in and we were off. It had all happened so fast it barely registered with my now conscious mind.

I sat up, realising that apart from a couple of new bruises I was unhurt. I peered around me, my mind catching up with events. It was pretty clear what had happened. The original greeting explained that, so there was nothing to be done but grin and bear it. I assumed I was off to prison again.

It seemed to take forever, bouncing and bumbling along rough tracks as the first traces of dawn peeped over the horizon. We got there eventually. A featureless camp appeared in the morning gloom, featureless in that there were nothing but rows of makeshift huts with tents interspersed and the occasional larger hut. The whole was surrounded by a twelve-foot fence with generous helpings of barbed wire to dissuade the escaper.

We stopped at a barrier where a conversation took place between the driver and a guard, the barrier lifted and we drove inside where I was unceremoniously hauled out of the truck and into the nearest building. Clearly, it was a guardhouse and I was shoved into a small cell with a high window and an inspection hatch in the door. There I spent the next few hours wondering yet again if any of this was worth it. Did my standing in society matter in the least? Would it be worth anything anyway when all this was over as if Sinclair was to be believed, we would be lucky to have a royal family and without that, where would your genteel society be? More importantly, where would your less than genteel society be?

My daydream was broken by the cell door opening and an officer and guard entering.

"Guten abend Mein Herr. Ich bin Oberst Schmidt. Ich mochte ihnen einige fragen stellen. Ja?"

It took me a moment to recover from the shock of being addressed in German. It wasn't the German as such, but the dawning realisation that Colonel Smith and his friend believed me to be a German and would treat me as such. Up to now, everything had just been playing games.

"You are a pilot I understand?"

There was a pause. No-one had mentioned interrogation or what I was meant to say when it happened. Consequently I was at something of a loss. So much for their meticulous planning.

"There is no need to be reticent with us, Herr Major Fleischmann. You see we know a lot about you already. Really we only need to confirm a few details to pass on to your authorities."

Standard techniques of course. Pretend you know it all and hopefully he will let something slip.

"Jasta 11 ring any bells? No? Of course not. I suspect Manfred will be wondering where you have got to[55]."

I involuntarily glanced up at the mention of Richtofen, and although the Colonel didn't remark on it he noticed and clearly believed he was onto something.

"I remember watching a scrap in the air, somewhere near Douai I believe. Fascinating. Couldn't take my eyes off it. Every now and then, someone would come dropping out of the sky and crash. Terrible. I don't know how you chaps do it. Still, that will be all for now."

He closed his file and left. The guard glanced at me and closed the door behind him. I was on my own again. They appeared to believe I was one Major Fleischmann. It wasn't very original but then something near the truth was always easier to remember under pressure. I hadn't uttered a word but felt strangely violated as if the Colonel had managed to extract some information, which of course he thought he had.

---

[55] Jasta 11 was commanded by Kurt Wolff for the first few days of July 1917 followed by Wilhelm Reinhard until early August. Richtofen had been moved to command Jagdgeschwader 1 which included Jasta 11.

It occurred to me that I hadn't been searched which was probably just as well as the letters, despite my furious attempts to hide them effectively were inside my boots. They were at least not in the most obvious place having managed to slide them into a small slit cut in the inner upper of the toe area but they wouldn't stand a serious frisk. I sat fretting for some time over whether they would be back to search me and I nearly had kittens when the door opened again but it was just the guard bringing something to eat. I hadn't long finished eating when the light turned off and I realised I was staying in the cell, for the moment at least.

I must have slept, albeit fitfully, as when the door opened again I sat bolt upright blinking in the sunlight. I smelt dreadful and I was hungry again. Unfortunately, there was no more food but at least I was leaving the cell as the guard motioned for me to accompany him. Following him outside, he escorted me to the main prison block and allocated me a bunk. I wasn't sure if this camp was just for officers or all ranks, but whatever it was, I was in an officers only section. I threw my effects on my bunk and looked around. It took all of five seconds to assess the block and facilities, mainly because there weren't many. I then got the shock of my life when an apparition revealed itself in the bunk next to mine, groaned and looked around to see me scrabbling on the floor.

"Juten moyen," I think it said.

"Guten morgen," I replied, my heart in my mouth expecting every second for him to scream 'he's English'. But he didn't.

"Scholtz," he said.

"Fleischmann," I replied.

He sank back into his pit while I stared aimlessly around looking for more Germans and spies and other sinister characters.

"You'll get used to it," the now disembodied voice said.

"I'd rather not if it's all the same."

He laughed, but not in an amused way.

"No choice, brother. Here, another camp, another hut, another tent. All the same. Nothing to do. Food alright though."

We lapsed into silence and I sat on my bunk deep in thought. And so the day passed. There were more introductions, a roll call before lunch, a walk around the camp looking through the fence at the bored guards outside, a desultory game of football, dinner and off to bed. My nerves slowly returned to something near normal after repeating my cover story so many times it almost felt like it was true. Most of them weren't interested in the small village in Bavaria where I had grown up, or that I had gone to England with my late parents when I was quite young and could speak near perfect English. Only one commented that I could almost escape and pass for an Englishman, before laughing at the very idea. All in all, it was better than some of the prisons I had inhabited. It was only when the lights went out that I was forced to confront the reality of the situation again.

I woke with a start. Grey light was seeping through a gap in the window covering, but it wasn't that which woke me. I felt like I was being watched. I lay in my bunk hardly daring to breathe. But nothing happened. Slowly I relaxed and lay staring at the bottom of the bunk above. Day came and with it more of the same. There was a fixed routine which, being German, everyone stuck to. There was only one moment during the day whilst we were having lunch, and pretty poor fare it was too, when I had that feeling again that someone was watching me. Maybe it was just my guilty nature, forever waiting for the tap on the shoulder announcing the latest disaster being prepared for my delectation. By the end of the day, I was wondering how they stood it. The boredom was overwhelming. Every other time I had been incarcerated was as a result of some interfering lunatic and had usually had me quaking with fear at what was about to happen next. This indifference was something else.

Three days I endured before fate intervened. I say fate but of course it wasn't quite like that. It had occurred to me already that I wasn't meant to hang around too long before hightailing it over the hills and faraway, but the idea of selecting one of these Germans to come with me gave me the willies. They would see through me straightaway, at least, I imagined they would. Consequently, I hadn't even begun interviewing for the position of Flashy's assistant.

I was minding my own business, staring into the distance through the fence when I felt rather than heard someone coming up behind me. I froze as it gave me the same feeling I had had of being watched. He, whoever he was, was just behind me. I daren't turn round. It was almost like being a child and covering your eyes so you couldn't be seen.

"Wann gehen wir?"

I spun round.

"You've been watching me."

"I wondered if you had noticed. Anyway, when do we go?"

"What makes you think you are coming with me?"

"Well, it makes sense really doesn't it. Bit tricky trying to convince one of our squarehead friends that we are batting for the Kaiser and then dropping him in the channel half way. Much simpler if we are both on the same team already don't you think?"

"But we're not on the same team."

"I don't mean Cumming and Kell. Ultimately we are conveniently on the same side." If you hadn't guessed already, my friendly shadow, William de Ropp had reappeared in my life. "Of course, I could also be a long lost cousin. Might be useful once we are safely in the Fatherland."

"Why? What do you hope to gain from all this?"

"Nothing. I just do it for the fun." He gave me a sideways look that could have meant anything. "So, back to my original question, when are we going? I assume that is what all this is about. You are going to somewhere on the other side and strangely enough, Kell wants you kept alive. Not suggesting that your friends want anything else of course."

Apparently there were no secrets in SIS anymore.

"When I am ready." I stalked off in a towering rage. I was sure de Ropp was grinning behind me.

******

But when was I going to be ready? I hadn't really got over all the cloak and dagger shenanigans that had led me to this place. I was still reeling from the shock of it all albeit I was bored stiff with prison life. I had even briefly considered staying although I guessed that Sinclair would have something to say about that. I had also considered absconding completely and instead of jumping ship for the continent going somewhere quiet like Scotland. How would anyone ever know if the letters got to their destinations? It wasn't as though anyone would write to the sausage eaters and ask. I began to wonder whether de Ropp really was working for Kell or whether there was more to it.

I slept on it and when I woke I realised I would just have to get on with it. I couldn't stand too much more of this and absconding simply wasn't a realistic option, as of course it never was if I wished to have some sort of life post war. If I survived, which seemed unlikely given the things other people propelled me into. For a moment, I pointlessly cursed my Father again.

The more I thought about it, if I was going to have someone with me it might as well be someone resourceful who appeared to be adept at all things underhand. Someone who also spoke fluent German but who was, to all intents and purposes, actually on the same side. I sought him out.

"Right, got any ideas then?"

"Thought you'd come round to it eventually. As a matter of fact I have. When were you thinking?"

"No point in waiting really. Tonight?"

"Ok. The guards are pretty lax at night. I have been taking a dekko[56] and I think there is a blind spot near one of the corner guard posts. In the dark we can just cut the wire and walk out."

It seemed so simple in daylight. Maybe it was because we weren't actual prisoners, just masquerading, that we didn't really consider the possibility that if we were in fact discovered walking out, the guards might actually shoot us. Mind you, if I had considered that a serious possibility I might never have gone through with it.

---

[56] From the Hindi 'dekho', to look.

# Chapter 9

The day seemed interminable. I walked round and round, occasionally nodding to my new friends, occasionally exchanging the odd word but religiously avoiding de Ropp. Dinner came and went and at long last, darkness descended and the outside lights came on. I made a point of getting into my bunk before the inside lights went out and feigning sleep. I awoke with a start and lay completely still for a minute or two. I could hear someone fiddling about with a latrine bucket, the unmistakeable sounds of a piss and then returning to his bunk. The shadows moving suggested he was at the far end of the room, away from the door I was about to use. I waited what seemed like an age but was probably only a few minutes before gingerly lowering myself to the floor. I picked up my pre prepared roll of clothes and crept towards the door. No-one stirred and I stood before the door, heart pounding, waiting for inevitable discovery. But nothing happened. I unlatched the door, opened it a crack and peeped out. Nothing moved, no sounds, at least none loud enough to make an impression. I slipped out, closing the door gently behind me.

An owl hooted somewhere in the distance. Then again. Then I realised it wasn't a bloody owl it was de Ropp and his call for me to meet him by hut 4. I peered into the gloom, looking for guards snooping about but there were none. I stealthily kicked a stone into the side of the hut with an enormous reverberating crash, freezing like some misplaced gargoyle whilst I waited for the hand on the shoulder, but still nothing happened.

I resumed my slow creep round the hut, flitted across the gap between two huts and suddenly there was de Ropp beside me.

"We're supposed to be escaping without letting anyone know," he muttered, clearly disturbed. I ignored him. "This way."

He beckoned me unnecessarily as he led the way towards the fence. We stopped about fifty yards short and waited.

"Just got to get across that light patch. Only visible from one post and there is only one sentry who is probably asleep. Done it every night so far."

I grudgingly had to admire his planning, as I hadn't really done anything useful in the previous three days, mainly as I had been very busy fretting.

"Go," he whispered in my ear.

I hesitated for a fraction of a second only for him to give me a shove in the right direction. Without thinking, I half stood and half crouched as I half ran towards the fence. I almost ran into it, just stopping myself in time and turned to see de Ropp briefly in the glare of the light before he dropped to the ground beside me.

"Cut a small hole as low down as you can. Don't cut any of it off so that we can try and fold it back into place so it isn't obvious how we got out. They'll discover it eventually but the longer it takes them the better."

I was just starting to frame the phrase "What the hell should I cut it with?" when I felt him shove some cutters into my hands.

"Did you bring your documents?"

I nodded, forgetting it was dark and he could hardly see me but he must have detected the motion, as he didn't ask again. Silence descended for a while as I continued cutting the wire. I finally breathed a sigh of relief as I finished and tentatively pushed the wire out of the way.

"Excellent, now get through, chop chop, there's a good chap."

I scrambled under the sharp edges of the fence and turned to see what was going on. He was almost through. A final pull and the cut fence dropped back into place. With a bit of imagination, one could almost pretend it hadn't happened.

But it had of course and now we had to get moving away from the camp. Even before that though, I had to change out of my regulation issue pyjamas. It only took me a moment. I rolled the pyjamas up intending to get rid of them at the first opportunity and we crept noiselessly away from the fence. I dared a quick glance back. Nothing was happening and it really didn't look like anyone had touched the fence. We faded into the shadows and soon the camp was far behind.

After about an hour, de Ropp suddenly stopped. I stopped beside him, gazing dully into the night sky, vaguely wondering why we had stopped.

"Do you have any idea where we are? Or more to the point where we are going?"

"Of course I do. Rather than gazing at the stars like a love-struck fool, I have been taking us more or less south towards the Thames estuary. When we get there, we will head for Tilbury. Before you ask, we then get a ferry across to Gravesend and then another one to Flushing. In Holland if you didn't know. This isn't a game you know. You seem to think we are safe because we are actually English. Had it occurred to you that if we get caught carrying German papers and dressed as Germans, the local authorities might not see it that way and appealing to a higher authority just might not wash? Unlikely as it may seem, we could end up swinging from a bloody painful rope. Now pay attention and at least look like you are interested in what we are doing."

He had a point really. I hadn't given any of it much thought as it was all too fantastic, but the idea of doing a Tyburn jig in my own country at the behest of some country magistrate was more than I could bear.

"It will be sunrise in a couple of hours and we have got to disappear. We need to change our appearance as well. If they are anything like efficient they will have circulated descriptions. They will be after us not least because we have made them look a bit silly, and whilst the idea of following in the footsteps of Von Pluschow might appeal to us, whatever the reasons behind it the regular authorities will not be in the slightest bit pleased. They will do their best to stop us."

He paused, for effect I assumed.

"You realise of course that Von Pluschow had a sidekick? Trefftz his name was. He got caught somewhere between Donington Hall and London."

He fell silent and I contemplated all that had been said. I wondered what the hell I was doing wandering around England in the dark pretending to be a German.

"Come on."

He led us on into the darkness for what seemed an eternity but was in fact only a couple of hours. The first hint of day appeared in the east. We paused for a rest.

"Over there. Farm buildings. Look quite remote. We can lay up there for the day and take our bearings."

I staggered after him as he strode purposefully towards the what now appeared to be more or less derelict barns. He stopped in the shadow of some trees once we were within a stone's throw and listened. Nothing. Not a squeak. He selected a likely candidate and sneaked up beside it. The main door was ajar. Staying in the shadows, we slipped through the door and stood stock-still. Still nothing. Creeping slowly round the barn in the gloom we found a number of farm tools, an interesting piece of machinery which gave me a nasty kick on the shins, some more or less mouldering hay thinly spread on the floor and a bucket.

It suddenly occurred to me that I was hungry. I very nearly complained about it but thought it would probably only earn me a look of contempt that would do nothing for my current gloominess.

"Here will do," de Ropp announced with an oddly false cheeriness. "You can take first stag."

And with that he went to sleep.

******

The first rays of sun pierced the dark. I could see the dust motes floating in random patterns as they made their way out into the fast spreading daylight. It did nothing for my mood though as the hunger was now joined by thirst and then boredom. I had only been sitting down five minutes. I wondered vaguely where we were and for the thousandth time what had brought me to this. Still, better to be shot while trying to escape than dying in a spinning, burning incinerator. What a choice.

Curiosity got the better of me. I stood up and tiptoed over to the door where we had come in. Staying in the shadow behind the door, I peeped out. The air was still, almost waiting for something to happen. I watched for at least ten minutes, the only noise being a faint snort from the still body behind me. As I stepped out, I knew what I was doing was wrong but a kind of reckless abandon had come over me. Maybe it was the lack of sustenance of all kinds. I had a brief vision of a farm in France where I had spent a jolly couple of days wondering whether I could ever become a Frenchman and deciding I couldn't[57]. I shook my head to clear the memories away.

There didn't appear to be a main house of any kind, just nondescript buildings and barns. I walked along the side of one and stopped at a corner. Slowly I looked round it to see what was there. Nothing. I looked behind me. Still nothing. I carried on looking and

---

[57] See 'Flashman and the Knights of the Sky'.

creeping about from building to building but there was no sign of life. The clearer it became that there was in fact nobody anywhere near, the bolder I became. I wandered in and out of buildings searching now for food as I was virtually at starvation point, having not eaten for what felt like days but of course was in fact only a few hours.

Movement caught my eye. Probably just a bird, although why a bird would be inside the cottage in front of me was a good question. I scurried to the nearest wall and sank down behind it, peering through a small gap towards the window where I thought I had seen whatever it was. All was still again. Perhaps it was just a reflection, maybe even a reflection of me. Maybe I was just being ridiculous.

Nothing moved. I hardly breathed. I stared through the gap but could see nothing. I hesitated, undecided about what to do next. Surely I had just imagined it. I couldn't hear anything unusual. This was England for God's sake. What on earth was I worried about? Carrying German papers maybe?

A face appeared at the gap. I leapt backwards and fell heavily. As I fell, I couldn't help but notice that the face was that of a woman, an attractive woman at that. As I hit the ground, my head snapped backwards and gave a ploughshare behind me a shrewd blow. The light went fuzzy, narrowed and then went out.

\*\*\*\*\*\*

I slowly opened my eyes. There was a strange smell in the air that I couldn't place. The sky was a clear blue above me, except at the periphery where the buildings intruded on the idyllic scene. Suddenly it struck me how I had come to be lying here and panic began to surface. I sat up, looking round me but everything was strangely quiet. Even the birds appeared to be waiting expectantly. There was no sign of the woman. She had apparently vanished into thin air[58]. My mind raced with the possibilities, most pressing of which was that we had been discovered, but by whom? Moreover,

---

[58] 'Vanish into thin air' was possibly coined by Shakespeare with his 'Go; vanish into air; away!' from Othello. The first written adaptation of this phrase as 'vanish into thin air' appears in the Edinburgh Advertiser of April 1822 in an article about the imminent Russo-Turkish conflict.

what did she or they think about my skulking about a deserted farm? Had she discovered us both?

Paralysis gripped me for a moment whilst I seriously considered decamping and letting de Ropp carry the can. Impossible. He had connections and would somehow find me and wreak revenge. I know I would, provided it could be done safely. There was only one solution and that was to find the woman, assuming she hadn't already ratted on us. I slithered back up to the wall and slowly, very slowly peered through the gap again. Nothing to be seen. What would I have done in her position? Gone back into the house? Probably. A true coward would assume that by hiding away and keeping quiet all would be well. But I had no way to tell what she might have done. With my mind racing and my heart doing the same, I realised that my only options were either to go and rouse de Ropp and make ourselves scarce, or go into the house and see if she was there. If she wasn't, then I would have no choice but to take option one.

Steeling myself, I crept along the wall to its end, conveniently out of sight from the window where I had first seen movement. Flat on my face, I slid slowly round the end half expecting any moment to be confronted. Nothing. Inspecting the corner wall of the cottage I realised that by chance I had found the perfect spot to cross the yard without being seen. Before my nerve failed me, I jumped up and half-crouching, half running, sped over to the corner. Now flat against a wall I reassessed my position. As I ran, I had glimpsed a door a few yards away from the corner and without thinking, I moved silently along the wall until I was beside the door. Only when I was beside the door did I notice that it was half-open.

I was sweating profusely now despite the cool morning air and my hands were shaking. It was now or never. I stepped into the doorway, paused for a moment in the gap and then stepped through the door. Whatever I was expecting and on reflection I am still not sure what it was, what it wasn't was silence. I don't know why I thought she would be behind the door. Maybe it was just that childhood fear of the unknown, the monster in the cupboard. Well, there was no monster or anything else for that matter. I stood staring around me for a few seconds wondering what to do next when I saw another half open door on the other side of the room. I was in a kitchen with a table and chairs in the middle and clearly, it had been recently used, as there was a pile of crockery waiting to be washed. I looked out of the window and could see where I had been hiding. I looked away again before I started seeing faces in gaps in walls.

I moved stealthily around the table, taking care not to trip over anything and arrived at the door. Peeping carefully round it I could see there was a passageway leading away into the gloom, itself broken sharply by a distinct ray of light coming from some unseen window at the end. There was just enough light to make out some stairs.

There was a faint thump above me. It was only just audible and then only because my senses were straining to make a nice warm, friendly picture out of this nightmare. My instincts were telling me to run and my legs were getting ready to respond but I couldn't let them take over. I forced myself along the corridor, every nerve screaming to go the other way. I couldn't bear it, but I had to.

I reached the staircase and with infinite care began to climb keeping my feet as close as possible to the edge of the no doubt squeaky wooden stairs. As I reached the top, I made a quick assessment of the scene. Two doors, one closed one open, equidistant from the last step.

I hesitated for a moment too long. From nowhere, a small form shot straight at me hitting me in the midriff, driving all the air from my lungs. Gasping I took an involuntary step backwards realising a second too late that my foot was now over the top of the staircase and my body was already falling. Panic reigned as I scrabbled for a hold on something, anything, but there wasn't one. My scrabbling did however stop me from plunging head first down the stairs and so when I finally stopped falling and realised I was conscious, a little battered but largely alright, I stood up. I was on the point of running for it as that now seemed like the only course available. Normally I have no interest in glancing back at the scene of devastation as that only slows down one's exit from it, but on this occasion my attention was caught by what could only be described as an enormous sob coming from the top of the stairs. I looked away intent on leaving, but stopped. It was the smell that did it.

She was kneeling at the top of the stairs, her head held in her hands sobbing uncontrollably now, oblivious to my predicament and presumably engulfed in her own, whatever that might be. I could only imagine, but as always, it was nothing like what I had imagined.

The smell was the one I had come round to. It got stronger as I climbed the stairs, lifted her up and took her into the room she had come out of. It was obvious that she had been living there for some time. I put her down on the makeshift bed and stood back wondering what to do next.

"Danke schon," she sniffed quietly.

"Bitte schon," I replied automatically.

It took a moment or two to sink in of course. Both of us contemplated for a moment what had just been said before she looked up at me with a quizzical look on her face. She was quicker on the uptake than I was. I gave her my winning smile, for what purpose at that point I really couldn't say. And then it struck me. What she had said and why she was looking at me in that odd way. I would have said it was a look of relief if the bile hadn't been rising in my throat in sudden panic. It wasn't possible was it? How could it be that I had just had an admittedly short conversation in German? In England? Suddenly my feet were made of lead. My winning smile was turning to a strangled stare.

"What IS that smell?" I asked by way of conversation as I could think of nothing else to say. Perhaps I was trying to gloss over the previous transgression. It might have worked except that I had continued to speak in German.

"Cubeb[59]," she replied.

"I…what?" I added helpfully.

She looked down coyly, and just for a fleeting moment, there was a hint of flirtation, the sobs notwithstanding.

"It is something I use in my work. It… relaxes one. Try this."

---

[59] Cubeb is a plant cultivated mainly for its fruit and oil. Mostly grown in Java, it has been known of and used for over 2000 years. It probably arrived in Europe via Indian trade with the Arabs. It was used as a spice as well as medicinally for oral and dental treatments. It was also believed to have aphrodisiac properties when eaten or pasted externally on the genitals of both sexes. It was also used as a treatment for gonorrhoea. In the late 19th and early 20th centuries, it was generally used in cigarette form before its use declined to virtually nothing. It can still be found as an ingredient in Gin.

From a drawer she produced a packet of cigarettes and handed one to me. She lit hers and then mine and I drew in a deep breath. As I smoked, I relaxed. I also began to feel lightheaded.

The more I smoked however, the more flustered I became. I could feel a… a… what? What could I feel? Lascivious probably sums it up. And the more I thought about it, the more I realised that what I needed right now was a decent woman. Well, in fact not a decent woman at all, more an experienced one. Just like the one that was now standing in front of me with a hand on her hip.

It was so sudden I could not now with certainty tell you who started it, but before I could say 'tits' they were out and I was kneading away like a man possessed. Clearly, she had been as deprived as I had. Clothes were flung around the room and having completely forgotten where I was and why, I grappled and groped before finally getting aboard and reaching a sudden but welcome point of no return.

Lying back in the bed, I smoked another of her little cigarettes and again wondered what cubeb was. It certainly made one feel distinctly attracted to the opposite sex and I was even considering a return match until my fast sobering mind remembered where I was and why.

I felt her staring at me and turned my head to look at her. There was obviously some sort of turmoil disturbing her so to prevent any nonsense I asked her who she was.

"Let us say I think we are on the same side but the less you know about me the better." I thought it was highly unlikely that we were on the same side myself but declined to point this out. "I also don't want to know who you are but I admit I am fascinated to know how another German found me in this strange country."

So she admitted it then. She was German and I was now consorting with the enemy in my own back yard.

"Well, I wasn't looking for you if that is what you think." I paused for a moment wondering what to say next knowing that whatever it was carried a huge risk with it and that de Ropp would be having kittens were he around to hear. But he wasn't. He was still sleeping in the barn where I had left him. My watch told me it was barely an hour since we had parted company. "I am a German pilot. I was shot down and captured a few months ago and eventually I was sent to a camp for prisoners at Stow Maries. My friend and I decided to escape as the food was terrible and here we are. Well here I am. He is asleep in the barn."

For a moment, she looked incredulous.

"This cannot be true. It is just like Gunther."

She stopped speaking and there was a long silence. I didn't know what to say and I assumed nor did she. For a moment, I wondered who Gunther was until I recalled a conversation with Sinclair. Apparently, she knew him too. Which led neatly on to how she knew him. And what she did with that knowledge. I decided it was time to break the silence.

"Surely you don't mean Von Pluschow?"

"You have heard of him?"

"Of course. He is our inspiration," which was an inspired response in itself though I say so myself. I could see her thinking.

"So, you wish to follow him? I must help you then. In return you can help me." Tears appeared in her eyes. Now I know I have an effect on the fairer sex but in less than an hour she had nearly killed me, grappled with me like a proper whore, compared me with friend Gunther and then cried because I was about to walk out on her. It is fair to say that women are by far the more complex animal of the species.

"I am sorry. It is so silly and weak of me but I can't help it. You see, those French swine executed her a couple of months ago. You coming here has brought it all back."

"Brought all what back?"

"Margaretha. She was my inspiration. Oh, I know she was only doing it for the money and the excitement, being Dutch and all, but it is for her I keep going. Especially now she is dead[60]." She sobbed a bit more and then pulled herself together. "But we can avenge her. You see, I have a list of them, the French bastards who worked for us who then betrayed her when they thought they were caught and now think they are free again to carry on making money. I had decided to take it back myself. But now...." She smiled at me and I immediately knew what she meant. Yet again, I was firmly wedged between the familiar horns.

---

[60] This can only be Margaretha Geertruida Zelle MacLeod, better known as Mata Hari, executed in France for spying on 15th October 1917. See appendix.

# Chapter 10

I had never seen him so angry. His face was as red as his neck. He could barely speak. He paced around the kitchen that we had taken over to use as a temporary HQ. I had tried explaining the advantages of our newfound ally but it seemed to go in one ear and out of the other.

"I leave you in charge for a few minutes and this is what happens. Good God man. What were you thinking?"

Fortunately, this was all said in German otherwise I suspect our new friend may have smelled a large rat. I didn't reply because the reality was I hadn't actually given it any thought at all, I had just been carried along by events. I was still hungry and I still hadn't eaten anything despite my exertions not so long ago.

"Perhaps we should eat something," I suggested hopefully. Much to my surprise, he agreed and we availed ourselves of the hospitality of our hosts whoever they were. We ate in silence. I occasionally glanced around but de Ropp was staring at his plate and my latest amour was staring at the wall.

"Do you know what? Perhaps you are right. Perhaps fate *has* delivered us here."

He returned to contemplating his breakfast.

"So what do we do now Miss.....?"

She looked at me and I smiled in an encouraging way.

"There is a port not far from here. A boat can take you from there over the river to another port called Gravesend. Here you can find a ship to take you to Holland. Of course, if you allowed me to help, I could perhaps find out some of this for you. And maybe you should stay here until you can take a ship."

Her downcast eyes were hard to read but her glance at me out of the corner of them was full of suggestion, which lifted my spirits.

"Yes, perhaps that is the best course. How long will it take to get this information?"

"A few hours, maybe a day. I have some contacts that will help me. It is the same way Gunther went," she added.

******

We made ourselves at home. I slept for a couple of hours before nervousness woke me wondering if we, or more correctly, I had done the right thing. I then spent a pointless hour alternately inventing stories about why we were there when we were in fact English and panicking over whether she would come back. Eventually calming down due mainly to boredom and de Ropp's apparent insouciance, I began to wonder whether she would be susceptible to my manly charms again. Her glance at me before leaving suggested she was so all it needed was to get rid of de Ropp for a moment or two. Not that I objected particularly to his presence and I doubted he would have any moral qualms, I simply thought he would be a baleful influence and might put me off my stroke.

The next hour I therefore spent cheerily planning our next bout. That done, I took to staring out of the window at the top of the stairs. I didn't feel like eating again. De Ropp joined me in staring and together we contemplated the outside world for some time without speaking.

"You did didn't you, you dirty bastard?"

I gave him my outraged stare and spluttered for a moment or two before admitting that she had been in need of the tender touch of a handsome man and I had felt it more or less my duty to oblige, especially as I thought we now had an ally.

We lapsed into silence again. And there we stayed. The light faded slowly and the stars came out. It was a clear cold night. Sleep overwhelmed me and at some point, I must have moved into one of the bedrooms. It just happened to be the room where I had thrashed the mattress only a few hours previously. For some reason we had not bothered to set a watch. Perhaps we just felt safe or more likely just exhausted from our adventures and maybe because of that I slept the sleep of the dead.

I woke however from a dreamless sleep shivering. Frost covered the windows, the sun shining through projecting the patterns onto the wall beside me. For a moment, I wondered where I was, but remembering was not comforting. There had been no return during the night to warm me up and unbidden my teeth started chattering and not just because of the cold. I sat with the covers, such as they were, pulled around me in a vain attempt to keep warm.

Silence. I wondered what time it was as I had no watch. I assumed de Ropp was still asleep. I began trying to convince myself that all she said was true, that she really was on our side and hadn't just popped down to the local constabulary to bring the rozzers down on us. Of course, that then prompted the question of which side exactly was ours, or at least, which course of action was most in the interests of our real side. Unanswerable, at least until she came back.

The morning dragged on. De Ropp appeared bleary eyed and after a brief muttering about taking risks like that admitted that in fact he had slept very nicely thankyou and was full of the joys of spring. We resolved however to keep a proper watch now until she reappeared. It seemed prudent as well to consider an escape route in the event of other less friendly natives appearing. Having done all this and broken our fast with some tins we found in the kitchen, we settled down to wait.

\*\*\*\*\*\*

The tap on the shoulder had me reaching for the Lewis, at least it did until I remembered where I was. Fortunately, I did it more or less silently. She was back and standing over me with her finger to her lips. I barely moved a muscle wondering what was about to happen that required silence. It was obvious really but it took my mind a moment or two to catch up with my baser instincts. When it did, I noticed the cheeky smile as she clasped my hand and led me silently into the bedroom where, despite my shredded nerves and the fact that she had been up most of the night, I performed a reasonable horizontal quickstep.

Having recovered from my exertions, I began contemplating the immediate future with some trepidation. Not because I thought she had betrayed us now but because whatever she had done I suspected required action from me. I was right.

"We must leave as soon as it starts to get dark. There is a boat this evening to Gravesend and then a ferry leaving for Flushing at first light. You must be on that ferry."

She was very earnest and I wondered what was so important that we must be on the ferry.

"I suppose we should tell de Ropp then."

"Yes. But not everything. I don't trust him completely. Something is not right there."

My heart rate accelerated into dangerous territory and I looked for non-existent escape routes as always. My mouth was suddenly dry and my throat felt like it had a large rock stuck in it. I tried desperately to speak in a normal voice.

"Yes, I thought there was something odd about him as well in the camp. It may just be the er, conditions we find ourselves in of course."

It was hardly normal, more like the last raspings of some Shakespearean actor in one of those interminable death scenes. Et tu Brute. Fortunately, she was somewhat preoccupied as well so didn't appear to notice. I muttered something about getting a drink and went out. I could hear de Ropp in the kitchen downstairs so descended and let him in on my little secret.

"Good," he said when I told him what was going to happen next in our 'Boys Own Adventure'. "About time we made some proper progress. I can't believe there hasn't been more sniffing about for us by the authorities. After all, we are enemy fugitives."

He chuckled to himself for a moment and then began making preparations. For want of something better to do I helped. Madame descended and joined in. Apart from the occasional sideways smirk and an atmosphere one could have cut with a sword so to speak, there was no other sign that I had just had it away with the only female in the room.

When we had packed all there was to pack, which wasn't much to be honest, checked and rechecked our packs, there was still an hour or so to drag by before we could begin, and drag it did. Every noise seemed magnified and I had almost reached breaking point when she finally announced we were leaving. The light was dimming as we left the kitchen. I glanced back wistfully wondering what the hell I was letting myself in for now.

******

I could see lights in the distance at last. It was almost completely dark now and we had just followed her, walking in silence through fields and past the occasional farm, following ancient tracks that appeared to go nowhere in particular. No-one challenged us, mainly because we didn't see anyone until we reached the edge of Tilbury. Even then, no-one said a word to us apart from the occasional good evening. We reached the docks and she pointed out a ticket office of some kind.

"Good evening old girl. Need to get across the other side this evening on the old ferry what? Just the three of us. What? Money? Of course."

I stared stricken at the formidable woman occupying the ticket office. I didn't have any money. Before I could admit this, I felt a small hand at my back and reached round to find a handful of coins. I had to swap the money into my other hand as I was shaking so much now, the old fear back to haunt me at the wrong moment. I handed over a shilling and the bored woman gave me my change and three tickets. The final act in the drama was for her to point to a sign that said 'Gravesend Ferry, this way' with an arrow on it.

"Gertrude[61] tonight. Leaves in ten minutes," she said.

"Thankyou," I said and turned away feeling sick.

"Well, that's the easy part then," said de Ropp managing nicely to find the only way of making me feel worse.

We boarded the ferry and found a secluded place to sit. As far as I could tell, we looked just like fugitives from the authorities but no-one seemed to care and they all ignored us completely. The engine started and we were off, chugging across the river. Gravesend loomed in the distance and slowly filled the view. Before we knew it, we were getting off again. We hung back not wanting to be first off. Somewhere in the middle of the crowd seemed to make sense and we descended from the boat, discreetly following madame as she clearly knew where she was going. We followed her towards the exit before turning abruptly into an alley. She didn't look back and nor did we although I felt a thousand eyes boring into my back, noting what the suspicious characters in coats were doing. She turned again and stopped. We were alone.

"Goedenavond Hilmar," said a voice from the shadows.

As I recoiled into the wall I had the distinct pleasure of seeing de Ropp also similarly undone, a look of utter terror on his face.

---

[61] Presumably the steam packet 'Gertrude', built in 1906 at Canning Town by A.W.Robertson, one of four 'sisters' all used on the Tilbury Gravesend ferry. Sold in 1932 to the New Medway Steam Packet Company and renamed 'Rochester Queen', she was further sold on to M.H.Bland in Gibraltar and renamed 'Caid'. Renamed again in 1949 to 'Djebel Derif', she was finally dismantled in 1962.

"Goedenavond," she replied calmly. "As you can see, they are here."

"You have the money," the voice said quietly in English for some reason.

"Yes."

She handed a bag to the shadow.

"Kommen sie mit," the shadow said with a vaguely seen gesture to us.

I turned to say my farewells, enemy of the state or not. I grabbed her and said, "Goodbye Hilmar."

She immediately stiffened in my grip.

"Do not use that name again until you get to the address I told you. When you do, tell them you are a friend of Hilmar. It is… it is my cover[62]."

There was a short scuffle and wriggle, a tongue briefly between my lips and she was gone into the dark. The shadowy figure turned and started to walk away. We followed, carefully avoiding pools of light from the dock lamps, until we came to a door within a large warehouse door. It was slightly open and the Dutchman slipped through followed by us.

It was gloomy inside, lit only by the moon through a skylight, but at least light enough not to walk into things. We followed our new friend between piles of boxes containing who knows what. We twisted and turned until we were completely lost. Not a word was said. He stopped abruptly and pointed to a door into what looked like a small room.

"Change your clothes in there."

We entered and found a pile of disgustingly smelly seaman's gear along with a ditty bag for our belongings. The clothes were almost solid with salt and more or less stood up by themselves. I selected a charming outfit and changed. I'd like to say that the change in clothes meant we actually looked like seamen but it simply wasn't true. We looked like a pair of dummies dressed up. It would have to do.

Our Dutch friend looked us up and down with a grimace and then beckoned us to follow again. More twists and turns and then a small gap between piles of boxes. We all squeezed through and found

---

[62] Hilmar is a male Nordic name so in this case presumably not her real name.

ourselves in what I can only describe as a hideaway. Two thin mattresses were on the floor and at one end, there was a table with a box on it.

"Eat," he said, "then sleep. You have about four hours before the boat goes. I will come back for you."

The trouble with escaping, as well as all the cloak and dagger arrangements is that it is a thorough bore for a lot of the time. Granted, there are moments of sheer terror and perhaps they are what one remembers, but my God, the boredom. It was the same now. For a moment or two we talked about nothing in particular, not daring to bring up the subject of what the hell was going on, but then we lapsed into silence.

Left with my own thoughts, I considered all that had happened in the last few hours. I tried to sleep but found myself staring at the black space representing the ceiling. Excruciatingly slowly, minutes became hours.

I felt someone shaking me roughly and slowly opened my eyes in the gloom. I must have slept but for how long was anybody's guess. I could hear shuffling and the odd clatter as de Ropp presumably struggled up from his slumber.

"We go," said the Dutchman.

He was smoking and the occasional flare of light from his cigarette was enough for us to follow albeit with the odd suppressed cry of pain from inadvertently colliding with something solid. We emerged after about ten minutes onto a deserted dock. We were in shadow and his raised palm told us to stay exactly where we were. I had a sudden urge to run, not unusual for me as you will no doubt appreciate.

"Walk, follow me."

We did as we were ordered and, attempting not to hurry, we crossed the dockside to where a dim hatch was open on the side of a boat. I couldn't see either end of the boat so it must have been fairly large. I am sure at this point the mariners amongst you would tell me what sort of boat it was and that it was in fact a ship. At the time though, I didn't care what it was as it had all the attraction of an iron maiden. We scrambled through the hatch and followed the Dutchman along a corridor, down a ladder, along another corridor and down another ladder. We didn't see a soul as we descended into the bowels. We stopped at a steel door that the Dutchman opened and gestured for us to enter. Stepping in I realised that my thoughts of an iron maiden were not so far from the truth. We were in some sort of store cupboard with a low ceiling and barely enough room for us to sit down. There was a bucket in the corner but that was the only furniture.

"You stay in here. Do not come out."

He turned and left, closing the door behind him. I now realised just how dark the bowels of a ship are. We sat down as best we could. Conversation was muted to non-existent, not that there was really anything useful to say. We were at the mercy of our Dutch friend and little to be done about it if he turned us in other than pray someone would rescue us.

The din was hellish. At first, I had nearly had another seizure but when no one came to take us away, it became obvious that it was just the working of the ship. I felt it get under way and then it started to rock. An appalling jolt had me remembering a journey across the channel and I began to feel queasy but fortunately, that seemed to be it. The North Sea was obviously in a benevolent frame of mind so my queasiness remained mild. It was a good job because that small room in the dark slopping with vomit would have been next to hell on earth. I dozed fitfully occasionally dreaming and being woken up by harsh reality. I mention this only because one of my awakenings had me tied in knots with my hand wedged in my bag. I was about to take it out when I realised I was clutching at something in what could only be the lining of my coat. It felt like thick paper, or at least folded paper, and surely it wasn't there the last time I had worn my coat. But of course it must have been and I just hadn't noticed it. Hideous thoughts rushed in on me about what it meant and what it was likely to be, none of which filled me with happiness. I would have to look at the first opportunity, provided that wasn't when I was dragged away by the local constabulary.

I didn't sleep again. The hellhole was by now stinking anyway with the accumulated smells of sweat and piss, which hardly made for a restful atmosphere. It was becoming somewhat overwhelming and I wasn't sure I could take it for much longer. De Ropp had hardly said a word for some time, possibly hours. Mind you, he could have been dead for all that I cared at that moment.

Without warning, the door opened. Light flooded in and blinded us temporarily. I staggered to my feet and almost fell down again, the wall conveniently supporting me for a moment or two while the blood returned to its rightful place. The Dutchman waited while we collected our thoughts and belongings and then motioned at us to follow him. We reversed our course through the decks and emerged from the same hatch we had entered. It was dark still; or dark again? I wasn't sure because I couldn't tell how long we had been in the boat and no one seemed interested in enlightening me. He paused on the dock before heading towards some buildings. We followed like sheep. A small door opened as we approached although I couldn't see who opened it. We stepped inside the dark room and the door closed behind us. Clearly, we weren't going via the customs house. Once the door was closed, someone switched a very dim light on. The Dutchman and the other occupant were conversing quietly in one corner, the face of the other man concealed by the Dutchman's back. I heard the rustle of what I took to be money, more muffled grunting and our companion turned and left without a word.

"Guten abend meine Herren, wie gehts?"

De Ropp reacted before I did.

"Tired, sick of travelling. What do we do now?"

I was still reeling from the surprise of meeting another real German. Somewhat ludicrously, I now realised, I had thought that we would arrive in Holland and be left to our own devices but I had reckoned without the German desire to interfere at every opportunity.

"Come with me, I have transport waiting."

We were none the wiser who he was. De Ropp glanced at me and I hid my terror with what I hoped was a noncommittal shrug. I had of course already guessed what was hidden in my coat. It was the list of French agents who were working for... well who exactly? I didn't really know as I only had Hilmar's word for it. I had been vaguely hoping that when we arrived in Holland I would be able to dispose of it somehow and we could vanish into the countryside, pop round to Liege, post our letter, and then get the next train home. Of course, that now looked like the nonsense it was. We were not going to be let go that easily. I quietly thanked the Lord that my German identity was in fact real although quite what I would do if they had dragged the late Major Fleischmann's relatives in to greet the returning hero I hadn't worked out. Just the thought sent a chill down my spine for a moment before I remembered we were a long way from Bavaria. But these were Germans.

We passed through another door into a dingy corridor and followed our new friend down it past numerous closed doors until we reached the end. He opened the door there and we stepped out into an alleyway. There was not a soul to be seen. We didn't stop, turning right and walking silently in single file. The darkness seemed to envelop us as we walked which did nothing for my nerves. As we reached the end, a cab pulled up and the door opened. We were shepherded in and sat down. Still nothing was said. The cab set off through the streets of Flushing. Even in the dark, I could see it was a less than picturesque place. Finally, we stopped at a nondescript house. We clambered out and followed our friend to the front door. He pulled out a key and let us all in.

"Eat and then rest. No-one will disturb you. We have a lot to do tomorrow." With that, he left, leaving me at least lost for words. However in short order, numerous further questions began racing around my head and none of them had appealing answers. I didn't feel like eating but forced down some bread and cheese, which seemed to be all there was. There was no conversation, mainly as there was nothing to say. Neither of us had much idea about what was about to happen as we hadn't really thought this far ahead. Our exploration of the house revealed only an upstairs room with two mattresses in it, so having discovered this we retired for the evening.

For once, there were no nightmares with burning aeroplanes, no artillery to shatter the still of the night, only the light streaming in the window woke me. There was no sign of de Ropp and for one awful moment, I wondered if I had been wrong all along. I heard a clatter below that nearly had me leaping for the window before I stopped and thought about it. Oddly, I could smell coffee and it was this that ultimately led me downstairs having not had a hot drink or even a strong drink for some time.

"Feeling better now are we?"

"Not really."

"Coffee?"

And that was the end of our conversation for the moment. I sipped my coffee staring through the grimy window that only served to confirm my earlier suspicion that this wasn't much of a place.

It felt like hours before anything happened. I had eaten more bread and more cheese until I was thoroughly sick of the whole thing and contemplating whether I would ever eat decent food again when we heard a key in the door. Neither of us moved. Footsteps approached and by the sound of it there was more than one person which was a trifle unnerving. I tried to place de Ropp between myself and the door. Largely futile, but if I had learnt one thing over the years it was that every second counts, especially in a crisis.

Two men entered the room. One instantly recognisable as our friend from the previous evening. The other smiled benevolently. He looked like a teacher peering myopically at us through his cheap spectacles.

"Good morning," he said in English.

A split second discussion took place in my head along the lines of; he spoke in English. It is a test of some kind. Do they know I can speak English, or at least the man I am meant to be speaks English, or did until he met his maker? Do they know who I am? Please God, help me out of this and I promise I will go to church nearly every Sunday.

De Ropp beat me to it. "Why are we speaking in English?" He even looked puzzled. "Don't tell me you think we are English spies? It's true isn't it?" He laughed in what I imagined was his put on ironic laugh. "Of course we both speak English. We both lived there for many years and can almost pass as natives. That's how we got out." This last statement had an edge of contempt in it but the teacher was entirely unmoved.

"How should I know whether you are who you say you are? I have nothing but your word to go on. However, we will know in a couple of hours. Until then, we stay here."

Well that settled it. His masterly understated intimidation meant he was definitely a teacher. We waited.

Nearly six hours passed in silence. Our friend had vanished and left the teacher with us very early on. There was a short period of desultory and boring conversation and then nothing. I wanted to scream but I daren't do anything. It was bad enough that in my low moments I was seconds away from denunciation and being carted off to be tortured. Even the highs had me running for my life down deserted streets and doing something stupid like leaping in the harbour to escape, but worst of all was de Ropp's studied nonchalance, which again had me wondering. Maybe he knew something.

I was almost at the point of irrational behaviour and had considered assaulting the teacher and hoping de Ropp joined in. Once he was dealt with assuming he didn't have a gun in his pocket, which come to think of it was eminently possible, we could abscond and resume my disguise of postmaster general.

The door opened and I nearly had a fit. Too late for escape, this was it, the moment of truth, denunciations and pleading for my life on my knees. The German walked straight towards me and I took a step back unbidden, waiting for the blow. He lifted his hand and grabbed mine, frozen as I now was with terror.

"Heinrich," he said. "Heinrich Flores[63]. I will take you to Hilmar."

\*\*\*\*\*\*

How my heart has stood the regular shock treatment all these years I will never know. My head was properly spinning now. First in the queue was the realisation that they actually thought I was who I said I was. How this had happened, I had no idea. Second, the mention of the name Hilmar. Who on earth was Hilmar? I wasn't supposed to mention this until I got to the Rotterdam address I had been given, assuming I went there of course, but this Heinrich fellow had just blurted it out. Did he know something I didn't? Third, what the hell was I supposed to do now? I had been so busy rogering my Hilmar that I hadn't really given any of this a second thought, but believe me I was now. My life depended on it and one false move would see me tied to a post with bells on.

The journey went by in a blur. Before I knew it, we were in Rotterdam. I tried to discreetly peer at the road signs and see where we were. We stopped and Heinrich motioned for us to get out. 'Binnenweg' the street sign said, which again had my heart pumping, as that was indeed the place Hilmar, my Hilmar, had told me. I knew that 127a was the destination and I was proved correct. It

---

[63]Heinrich Flores was a German language teacher based in Rotterdam. He worked for Hilmar Dierks, one of the better known and long serving Abwehr officers.

looked like a boarding house, which in fact it was. Now that we were here, I was wondering how to drop Hilmar into the conversation, if I should at all as I was also wondering whether I should ever mention her again. Heinrich showed us to our room and 'suggested' we meet later for dinner when we would meet Hilmar. De Ropp seemed utterly relaxed. I lay down. I was exhausted and getting steadily more terrified.

Dinner came all too soon. I was sitting quaking with de Ropp beside me when Heinrich came in accompanied by another man.

"Dierks, Hilmar Dierks[64]," he said, grinning like the Cheshire cat. We both jumped to our feet and shook hands. He looked about my age, blue eyed, tired but alive with energy and dangerous. My innards dissolved again.

"De Ropp. Avoided internment in 1914. Shot down and captured" All eyes turned to me.

"Fleischmann," I stuttered. "Escaped Stow Maries prison camp. Formerly of Jasta 11. Can't wait to get back to it." I grinned in what I hoped was an enthusiastic fashion, immediately regretting it as I remembered these were Germans and I was supposed to be one. They didn't seem to notice.

"I served at the front in 1914," Dierks said almost wistfully, clearly pining for the good old days of instant death by fragmentation. "Just a few months before I got involved with all this." He swept his arm around the room and I took this to mean spying in general rather than decorating.

The conversation lumbered on through the somewhat sparse dinner, but at least they were civilised enough to bring out the brandy and cigars afterwards. I sat alternately puffing and sipping my Napoleon[65], wary of drinking too much but conscious that it had a calming influence on my rather stretched nervous system.

"Hilmar helped us," I said without thinking.

Dierks' eyes lit up and his eyebrows rose unbidden. I could almost see what he was thinking, although perhaps this view was

---

[64]Hilmar Dierks, long serving Abwehr agent. See appendix.

[65] Napoleon cognac should be aged at least six and a half years. Supposedly this is because the Emperor Napoleon insisted his personal barrels of cognac remain untouched while he was away on campaign and when he returned six and a half years later he found he preferred the aged taste compared to the younger variety. Only XO cognac is aged longer.

coloured by my own unsavoury thoughts. However, what I now had to decide on was whether I would proudly hand over the list of French traitors which I had conveniently used to replace Buchan's clumsy coded attempt at useful information. I hesitated, my hand unconsciously fiddling in my pocket before I pulled out the piece of paper.

"She also gave me this." De Ropp's eyebrows shot up which was gratifying. "They are Frenchmen, and they betrayed one of our agents in Paris." De Ropp's eyebrows remained where they were although the look of surprise had changed slightly to something a little more threatening.

"Do you know who?"

"Someone called Margaretha."

He nodded and studied the list intently.

"This is excellent. I think a toast. To Hilmar!"

For a moment, I wasn't sure whether he was toasting himself but finished my brandy anyway. I could see de Ropp was virtually bursting to question my behaviour, but I didn't care. They were only frogs and clearly as trustworthy as me. If they had any sense they would have long gone and if not, well, they weren't as important as saving my own skin, and the best way to do that at this moment was to grovel to this Dierks character as he clearly held all the cards. Plus de Ropp was unlikely to betray me…

As I thought it, my suspicions came rushing back. Was he really who he said he was? Mind you, it was too late now if he wasn't. An icy shiver ran down my spine. The conversation picked up as we discussed the aerial war and I admitted to having flown the Fokker E1. I didn't say when but was pleased to see de Ropp's eyebrows elevated again. There was the odd moment of terror when we probably should have known the answer to Dierks' questions, but both of us managed to deflect him with ignorance due to having been incarcerated. Eventually he yawned and set us off.

"Get some sleep. Tomorrow we travel."

Chapter 11

Our journey took forever and encompassed some of the most boring vistas available from a train window that you will ever encounter. I couldn't believe Belgium was so big. Either that or the train was inordinately slow. We trundled on through, stopping every hour or so to let a troop train or supply train past. Antwerp, Brussels, Waterloo where we got out and inspected the battlefield because Dierks wanted to. Apparently, it was the last time the Germans had fought with the English and he was wondering why we were fighting them now when really we should all be out to fight the French. I couldn't argue with his logic.

We moved on through Mons, the scene of the first reverse for the German Army back in 1914[66], before arriving at somewhere called Avesnes-le-Sec.

The journey had been so dull that up to this point, my senses had been lowered; nothing happening had instilled a false sense of security. Suddenly, this changed as we pulled into a bustling station full of uniforms and hardware.

De Ropp had been somewhat subdued for the entire journey, short of making his feelings known about the list of Frenchmen. For some reason, he thought I should have kept it to myself. I wasn't so sure and said so. Personally, I thought we had been treated well because of it. Now however, he woke up again. Maybe it was the presence of so many Germans or just that we had the feeling of journey's end, at least for the moment.

Dierks shepherded us through the crowd and out of the station where a truck was waiting to take us to an airfield. When we arrived, Dierks led us into an office that announced itself as the administrative headquarters of Jagdgeschwader 1[67], whatever that

---

[66] Presumably referring to the first major encounter between the British and German armies. Although there was an initial repulse for the Germans and they were held up for about two days thus preventing the outflanking of the French Fifth Army, they eventually forced the British to retreat albeit in good order. A German officer (and novelist) Captain Walter Bloem wrote, 'A bad defeat, there can be no gainsaying it. We had been badly beaten, and by the English – by the English we had so laughed at a few hours before.'

[67] Jagdgeschwader 1 was formed in June 1917 with Richtofen as commanding officer. See appendix.

was. He shook hands, muttered something to the office's occupant and left.

"Bodenschatz[68]," he announced. "You are both pilots?"

We nodded.

"Good. We are desperately short of pilots so I think Jasta 11 would be a good place to go."

He smiled at us as if he had just given us the best possible news. My face must have been a picture.

"Surely we are allowed a few days leave before we join," I spluttered in disbelief more than anything. Recovering somewhat, I continued. "I believe my brother died while I was in prison and I would like to visit the people who nursed his wounds in his final hours. I believe they are in Liege."

I looked grave, like a man not to be trifled with who was likely to do something desperate if necessary. Inside, I was wondering what I was going to do if he said no. Or simply dismissed my claim as the nonsense it was.

"Yes, of course you must visit. Just two days, then to your squadron to do your duty," he barked.

We left having both been extended this extraordinary privilege, at least that was the way our office wallah friend made it sound.

"Good," said de Ropp. "I assume we can ditch the pretence that I don't know what you are up to at last?"

"How the hell do you know what I am up to?"

"I pay attention to what is going on around me. You see, Kell and his friends are not unaware of the Count of Albany's little scheme."

"What scheme?" I replied wishing I knew nothing about it.

He paused to savour the moment as a shiver ran down my spine.

"They are all using you, you know. Cumming, Albany, Kell." I didn't say anything. I hadn't imagined I was anything other than a

---

[68] This must be Karl-Heinrich Bodenschatz, a former infantry officer who after recovering from numerous wounds transferred to the Luftstreitkrafte, firstly to Jagd 2 and then Jagd 1 where he was adjutant to Richtofen and eventually Goering. He remained in the Reichswehr after the war and in 1933, having maintained a friendship with Goering, transferred to the Luftwaffe where he served as Goering's adjutant. During the Second World War he was the liaison officer between Goering and Hitler until he was badly injured by the July bomb at the 'Wolf's Lair' in Rastenburg. Briefly imprisoned after Nuremberg, he died in 1979.

pawn in whatever game was going on but this made it sound somewhat more complicated than I expected. I was right. "That letter you are carrying. I presume you made a copy of it and hid it somewhere. That's what I would have done. Except that you are now carrying a slightly different letter to the one that Buchan gave you."

"How.... Why?"

"Well the how is easy. You sleep like a log so it wasn't difficult to search you and I am glad I did or, as you know, we would now be committing treason. Why is a little more difficult. You see, Albany and his backers, whoever they are and I don't know because they are extremely secretive, well, their decision to write to the Emperor supporting his scheme for peace in return for the Emperor naming him as the rightful King caused a few ripples in Whitehall. You are no doubt aware of Albany's reasons for believing he is the rightful king. I have to say they look pretty flimsy to me, but then I am no historian[69]."

I knew very well who was supporting Albany and why. A certain Colonel Sinclair sprang to mind, although it also occurred to me that there had to be more than just Sinclair behind it. I began to wonder who wanted what out of all this, who was involved, who was not involved and whether I would end up stretching my neck for being in the wrong place at the wrong time and having the wrong parents. I could have wept.

"The thing is, we couldn't allow his letter to get too far because not only did it request support from the Emperor, it also portrayed the King as a cowardly usurper who had no heart in the fight. I think he was hoping it would be made public and who knows where that would end."

Indeed.

"So why the hell are we here then?" I said, deeply miffed by this apparent turn of events.

"To carry out your mission. Just with a slightly different text. So we do need to go to Liege."

"What in God's name....? I assume you don't mean our side," I whispered. He tapped his nose. "I assume you have a contact?"

"Of course."

---

[69] See appendix.

And that concluded our conversation for the moment. There followed the usual hours of delay that attended anything military, even the Germans. We were given bunks for the night and told we could leave in the morning.

******

The following morning we had a brief meeting with Bodenschatz who then left us waiting in a cold featureless room. An hour or so dragged by until, without knocking, a man entered the room almost silently. He paused for a moment, clearly weighing us up, before marching over to us and coming to attention with a pronounced click of his heels.

"I am here to... look after you," he announced. "Rudolf Hess at your service, sir."

It meant nothing at the time of course. He was wearing infantry uniform with the rank of Leutnant. De Ropp looked a little crestfallen, as he had clearly thought we were going to be left to our own devices but he soon perked up when it became obvious that Hess meant what he said. So began the next stage of our holiday.

It turned out that Hess was an exceptionally boring companion although this was a virtue as it meant neither of us was particularly required to do any explaining. Of course, he was just a mere Leutnant as well and so probably deemed it prudent to keep quiet. His only foray into conversation was to explain his presence in more detail. Apparently, Dierks had telegraphed our arrival to Douai who had posted us on to this Jagd 1. Jagd 1 had posted us to Jasta 11 who in turn had not been too happy to have our arrival delayed as they were indeed chronically short of pilots but being reasonable chaps they had acquiesced to our demand on the proviso that they could send a 'liaison officer' to accompany us. And, presumably, to make sure we didn't dawdle too much. Hess had been hanging around doing nothing, as he was due to start his pilot training as soon as he had recovered properly from a bullet wound and so Bodenschatz had volunteered him for the job[70].

---

[70]This must be the recently promoted Leutnant der Reserve Rudolf Hess who had served in the German army more or less since the outbreak of the war. He fought at Ypres and Verdun and was injured a number of times. Serving in

We arrived in Liege tired, bored and miserable after another seemingly interminable journey. There had been no sign of a decent drink for hours, no sign of food and more importantly, I hadn't seen hide nor hair of a woman for what felt like years. Our lodgings didn't exactly rectify any of those minor difficulties so I went to bed early.

All too soon, it was morning again and after a miserable breakfast, we set out on our mission. After a couple of false starts with the less than cooperative locals, we found someone who pointed us in the direction of the address de Ropp had shown me. We had explained briefly to Hess what we were going to do but didn't mention why it was in Liege and who exactly we were seeing although it would have been pretty easy to explain away given the number of Germans killed and wounded in the area. He didn't seem that bothered anyway and I guessed he had no reason to assume we were anything other than what we claimed to be.

We knocked on the door of a nondescript house. The door opened and a man stood silently staring at us.

"Sixtus," de Ropp said in a slightly surprised manner.

"Come in," the man said staring at Hess. De Ropp turned round and gave him a nod, which fortunately he took to mean he was surplus to requirements for the moment.

"I will wait in the café we passed, Sir." He turned and left. There was a brief pause while the man Sixtus watched Hess stroll off down the street and then there were introductions all round. I was agog to know who on earth was who.

"This is Major Flashman of the Royal Flying Corps." My legs turned to jelly. "He has a note from your royal cousin, the Prince of Wales to be conveyed to the Emperor."

My face turned its customary red when confronted with apparently innocuous but actually deadly situations from which there is no escape. The mention of Wales had nearly had me choking on my own bile as well. The man Sixtus turned to me and made a slight bow before offering his hand.

---

Romania he received a serious bullet wound and whilst recovering requested a transfer to the Luftstreitkrafte to train as a pilot. He spent most of his convalescence in Bavaria, was with his family at Christmas 1917 and began training in the New Year. Quite why he should be in France at this time is unclear.

"My name is Sixtus and I am a Prince of Bourbon Parma.[71]" I had thought he was a German[72] but this was something else. "My brothers are fighting for the Germans and I am fighting for the Belgians. I have come to believe that this war is futile and so I am prepared to pursue any avenues that may lead to peace and the restoration of the status quo. I believe the Emperor, my brother in law[73], is of the same mind and perhaps the King. I cannot be so sure of the Kaiser but there are always ways and means. I suspect the French may be the stumbling block but I have contacts with the French President. I believe with certain concessions we can finish this to everybody's satisfaction?"

He beamed at me, leaning forward slightly to emphasise that we were all on the same side really and that with a few sensible heads we could sort out the playground squabble and all go home, conkers intact.

There was a moments silence while the smiling continued.

"The letter perhaps?" de Ropp said with a slightly menacing grimace and a raised eyebrow. I shuffled through my pockets before withdrawing an envelope. I glanced at de Ropp and saw the look of horror on his face. Clearly, it hadn't occurred to him that I wasn't a complete fool and that I might have worked out that there was more to his following me around than simple concern for my welfare.

"You....." He tailed off, wondering how he had missed the second copy of the original letter from Albany, unable to say anything now. I gave the letter to Sixtus.

"I believe there are instructions there in how to reply."

He opened the letter and read it through which I was slightly surprised at given that it wasn't addressed to him. I noted the raised eyebrow. He continued staring at the paper long after he had finished reading it, presumably wondering how to deal with this new development.

---

[71] Prince Sixtus of Bourbon-Parma was the half-brother of the last reigning Duke of Parma. It is possible but unlikely that he was related to the Prince of Wales so presumably de Ropp was referring to him as a cousin in royalty rather than family. See appendix.

[72] It would be hard to pin his nationality down as his Mother was Portuguese, his Father Italian and he grew up mainly in Austria and Italy.

[73] Prince Sixtus' sister Zita was married to Archduke Charles in 1911. Charles became Emperor in 1916.

86

****** 

It was always the waking that was the worst and this time was no different. De Ropp was lightning fast. I still wonder now what made me do it, why I didn't just give him the letter from Wales instead of the one Sinclair had given me. After all, it didn't make any difference to me who was King. All I wanted was to go home to a life of unfettered indulgence. Perhaps I just thought it would go away all the quicker. I don't know, but the result was a clout round the head with something solid.

That was the last thing I remembered until I came round on another train. The carriage seemed dark but I could make out two shapes in the gloom. I sat up.

"Back with us at last." This was de Ropp. "You took a funny turn. Lack of food maybe. Still, all alright now. Hess here is taking us to the squadron."

For a moment, I wondered which squadron he meant but I remembered soon enough as it all came flooding back. I looked at de Ropp and his lopsided grin feeling only loathing. We continued travelling more or less in silence until Hess got up to relieve himself. He seemed entirely unaware that there was anything untoward going on. The door closed behind him.

"No hard feelings old boy. Had to be done you know. Couldn't let you have it all your own way, could we now." He smiled. "All part of the game. To be honest, like you, I don't care who is King but Kell pays my wages. Anyway, Sixtus saw your letter as well so he may pass on its contents verbally. Who knows what these people do with all this information. For once, I am with you in thinking we need to get out of here sharpish. Of course not as easy as all that with friend Hess in tow but I am sure once we get to the squadron we can find a way."

Well I agreed with that. I had no desire to hang around, mainly because someone was eventually going to see through us, or I was going to give myself away.

The train trundled on, Hess came back, somehow we ate something and finally we pulled into the station at Douai. We got out and waited while Hess whistled up some transport. It all seemed so normal I had all but forgotten we were going to join a German fighter squadron.

"Back at last," said our old friend Bodenschatz. "Just some formalities and then we'll get you off flying again."

He was as good as his word. Efficient didn't come into it. Papers were presented and signed (I made a pretty good job of my alter ego's signature if I say so myself) and before we could say Fokker we were off again, Hess leading the way. We arrived at the assigned airfield just before dusk where I had the jolt of my life. I had been here before.

# Chapter 12

You have probably already guessed who was waiting for me like the mohel at the brit milah[74]. Richtofen. How I didn't faint clean away from shock I'll never know, and quite why it hadn't occurred to me that this might happen... well it should have done. You know me well enough to know I can usually spot trouble from miles away. It's the avoiding it that I find difficult. But it was odd. The slightly blank look when I was introduced, almost as though he didn't particularly care who I was. And why should he of course. I was just another pilot and would quite possibly be dead shortly. But he should have recognised me. I know I would have done, and although I might not have remembered our meeting straightaway, I would eventually. And in his position, when that occurred, I would then have had me arrested and tied to a post squealing like a pig.

My paralysing horror didn't last long. I couldn't believe he wouldn't work it out and so shaking with terror I asked the next man I met who happened to be Reinhard[75], the second in command, what was up with Richtofen. Of course, I didn't phrase it quite like that but his first words sent a flood of relief coursing through me.

"He shouldn't be flying you know. Got shot down a while back, wounded in the head. Couldn't fly for some time but insisted on coming back." He was shaking his head the whole time he was talking[76].

"What happened to Goering," I blurted out, suddenly remembering that there had been two of the bastards and in fact, the most likely one to remember me was the art fanatic Hermann.

"Who the hell is Goering?" he replied looking puzzled as I nearly collapsed with relief.

"Just someone I crossed swords with some time ago."

"Well, he's not here."

---

[74] The Brit Milah is the circumcision of Jewish boys and performed by the Mohel.

[75] If this is Wilhelm Reinhard, he was at this time commander of Jasta 6 one of the constituent squadrons of Jagd 1. Promoted to Hauptmann in March 1918, he succeeded Richtofen as Jagd 1 commander until his death during a test flight. He was himself succeeded by Hermann Goering.

[76] Richtofen was shot down and wounded in the head on 6th July 1917. See appendix.

Our conversation over, I left Reinhard to his papers and went to my quarters. Needless to say, I didn't sleep very well.

The following morning flew by. Literally. De Ropp and I were assigned an instructor called Lowenhardt[77] who took us to a hangar in which resided a Fokker DR1. It was an unlikely looking flying machine, the designers clearly having decided that in fact they were wrong about needing only one wing, two wings were passé and therefore three were what was required. I was only half listening as my mind was still reeling from the shock of meeting Richtofen again and the need for us to decamp as soon as possible, but I did hear him say something about structural failures that had caused a number of crashes but all was well now. That was something to look forward to then.

Our brief lesson over, we were now expected to get in and fly them. De Ropp looked a little pale but I was relieved to discover that not much had changed since my adventure in the E1. Different speeds, mainly faster, but still just an aeroplane and so it was we took off for a little excursion with Lowenhardt in the lead. I had managed a brief discussion with de Ropp and we had agreed that we couldn't just fly off as they would probably come after us. So it would have to be on our first mission. It wasn't long in coming. They weren't about to give us weeks of training. We were expected to get on with it, as we were experienced pilots. And the April weather was perfect.

Lowenhardt led us southeast away from the main battle area, well behind the German lines where he put us through our paces, first of all in formation, then a bit of stunting which I have to say had me retching, not because the flying made me feel sick, just the thought of the wings coming off if what he had told us about structural failures hadn't been cured. We finished up with a mock dogfight which seemed to finish in a draw all round. Finally, he waggled his wings and we followed him home.

I switched off and realised the sweat was pouring off me in my new German flying gear. I sat in the cockpit for a moment or two

---

[77] This must be Oberleutnant Erich Lowenhardt of Jasta 10 also attached to Jagd 1. Another German 'ace', he claimed 54 victories before dying when his parachute failed to open after bailing out of his stricken aircraft following a mid-air collision with Leutnant Alfred Wenz of Jasta 11 in August 1918.

reflecting on all that had led me to this completely and utterly unreal situation. I saw the commotion out of the corner of my eye. Men running, trucks and vehicles moving in all directions. I heard shouts, even some gunfire and for a moment, I thought we were under attack. I was about to get out of my seat when Lowenhardt appeared beside me and yelled through the din that we were off, there was heavy fighting around Armentieres and that the RFC were out in force. We were fuelled, armed and ready to go and almost without thinking, I was starting the engine. I looked round to see where de Ropp was and the answer was no idea. Someone pulled the chocks away and I trundled over the grass following the mass of garishly painted aircraft that made up the circus. I turned into wind. Another DR1 was beside me and I had a momentary palpitation as I realised it was Richtofen himself.

Terrified beyond description, I shouted 'los gehts'[78] and we were moving, faster, faster, wheels bumped off the ground and then we were airborne climbing away. We formed into a loose gaggle for the transit to the front, climbing all the time keeping the sun behind us. It seemed only seconds before we were there. For one brief moment, I thought we were alone in the sky, no one to be seen, tranquillity itself. And then, like an approaching steam train we were in the thick of it, rolling, diving, upside down, pushed hard down in my seat. There was an almighty explosion, someone had a bomb on-board that was the end of him, lead filled the sky. I waved at a passing Camel and briefly saw the puzzled look on his face before remembering what I was flying, something of a shock because in the heat of the moment it hadn't actually occurred to me that those charming RFC[79] boys would be trying to kill me.

The melee intensified, as did my terror. I hadn't realised how impossible it would be flying for the enemy. I daren't touch my guns in case I inadvertently shot down one of ours but at the same time the ammunition screaming past was mainly coming from them. My worries about the structural integrity of my machine had vanished in the confusion and all I was concerned about now was survival. At

---

[78] Literally 'Here we go', sometimes quoted as an equivalent to the English 'tally ho'.

[79] Officially they were now the RAF having been formed from the RFC and RNAS on the 1st April 1918.

least the Dr.1 was highly manoeuvrable and I explored every aspect of its capability as I hauled it around the sky, rolling frantically, pulling hard to escape a pair of camels that came from nowhere and almost colliding with an RE8. God knows what that was doing there and the look of horror on its crews face told me that they thought their end had come as I flew straight at them before diving below missing them by inches it seemed. I barely had time to draw breath before a Halberstadt, I guessed a CL.II by the look of it, on fire and beginning to break up, plummeted past in front of my nose followed by the camel that had clearly shot him up. My presence sent the camel into a hard turn and I did the same although turning sent me straight back into the fracas. There was an almighty bang and splinters hit my left arm and shoulder, fortunately without penetrating anything important like my skin, but a glance up showed a large hole in the upper wing. I couldn't take much more of this. For reasons I can't begin to fathom I grabbed the guns with one hand, flying with the other. I think in my mind I had decided that the only way out was to shoot my way out regardless of whose side they were on. By way of experiment, I fired a short burst at nothing in particular. I hauled the stick back and came right over the top rolling as I did so and almost instantly the smoke that was filling the sky parted like the Red Sea. And then there were five.

Three German aircraft and two British. What only two of us knew was that there were four British pilots and only one German. One of the Camels was slightly ahead of our ragged flight and one was above and behind and apparently too far away to cause any problems. It had an inevitability about it somehow. Richtofen signalled the chase knowing that as we were heading to the British lines we could turn and take on his colleague once we had dealt with the leader. My heart leapt into my mouth as the reality of what we were doing came home.

My discerning eye for trivia told me that the Camel ahead was from 9 Squadron, RNAS[80]. It dived and rolled getting ever lower in its attempt to escape. Richtofen followed while I flew more or less straight slowly catching them both up. I could feel rather than see de Ropp behind me. How he had found me from the melee God only

---

[80] Flashman would not have known that 9 Squadron RNAS had become 209 Squadron RAF a few days earlier.

knew. Someone started firing, more in desperation than anything, but in looking round I could see we were all a little closer together and everyone was just about in range. Richtofen hadn't fired a shot as far as I could tell, but as we got closer to the ground, clouds of ammunition started to rise past us. Looking round again I realised that the other camel was above but almost parallel with me. For a moment, I wondered what on earth he was doing but it was obvious really. He was trying to save his raggie[81] by scaring Richtofen off although I seriously doubted that that would happen. I saw him open fire but he was too far away. Richtofen was weaving behind the other camel who was so low he was virtually in the trenches. Suddenly, Richtofen turned directly in front of me following the camel. It was instinctive. I pulled the trigger and the dual machine guns opened up. I saw small pieces come off his machine and it trailed a wisp of smoke. I thought I saw him glance round at me and for a second he must have wondered what was going on. The camel pilot beside me certainly did because he stopped firing for a few seconds and then fired everything he had, diving steeply. At this point, I noticed he was aiming at me and just for a second I began to curse him for a fool. Couldn't he see I was friendly? Of course he couldn't, I was just another Dr.1.

Suddenly overwhelmed by panic at the thought of being shot down by my own side, I jammed the throttle open and turned starboard slightly away from my pursuer. The engine screamed as I forced it to do things it probably couldn't do, but glancing behind me I noticed that the camel had had to pull up out of his dive otherwise he would have hit the ground, thereby slowing too much to catch me anytime soon. Looking the other way I saw the other camel also climbing and Richtofen seemingly under control but trailing smoke and with no apparent choice but to land on Morlancourt ridge. De Ropp was a speck in the distance but following me, I thought.

But now what? We were on our own and in seconds, we were behind the British lines. It must have surprised whoever was below

---

[81] Naval slang for close friend. Derived from the idea that friends on board ship would have free run of each other's polishing paste and rags. Also led to the term to 'part brass rags' ie terminate a friendship. First appeared in writing just before the Great War but almost certainly in use in the Navy long before that. Presumably, Flashman's use is because 209 was a naval squadron.

us as no one seemed to react but I knew that wouldn't last long. I considered climbing but that would put us in direct conflict with the RFC, which didn't bear thinking about. The solution was obvious really and no sooner had I thought it than I was preparing to land. I saw a likely field that wasn't completely covered in shellholes and made my approach. It was uneventful, at least up to the point where having landed and slowed the wheels suddenly went down a small hole and I was thrown forward. The last thing I remembered was seeing the gun butts as they hit me in the face.

Chapter 13

I could hear voices with an almost dreamlike quality to them. I lay still, yet again wondering if I was dead or alive and in some hideous dilemma that would not be improved by opening my eyes. Nothing appeared to hurt apart from my forehead, which on closer inspection appeared to have something of a lump on it. There was also some black stuff that I identified as my own dried blood and this convinced me that I was indeed still alive. I would have to do something but for a long moment, I was more or less happy where I was.

The voices came closer, paused and then there was a rattling of a key in the door, which opened. I lay still, eyes still shut, hardly daring to breathe.

"Still aht cold," said an unmistakeably colonial drawl.

The door banged shut and the voices faded away. I opened my eyes and took in my surroundings, such as they were. I was on a bed in what could only be described as a cell. There was a bucket in the corner, and that was it. I pondered the situation, mainly wondering how I came to be here, who they were, who they thought I was and most importantly, what I was going to do about it, all of which needed to be considered before they returned. It might seem obvious to the casual observer; all I needed to do was tell them who I really was and they would hail the conquering hero. On the other hand, if I didn't tell them, presumably they would send me on my meandering way back to England where I could unmask myself before reporting to Albany, or was it Sinclair, or was it Cumming. It seemed so long ago I could barely recall why and how I had arrived in this situation.

Maybe I was still a little dazed and not quite thinking clearly but after getting bored with thinking about it I decided that the best solution was to tell them who I really was. This would, I convinced myself, speed me on my way home.

I stood up, paused for a moment swaying slightly as the blood rushed away from my head, before banging on the door announcing loudly that I was a British officer and what the hell was I doing in this cell.

It took a few minutes before anyone deigned to take notice of my ranting but eventually I heard footsteps in the corridor. I stepped back from the door just as it opened to reveal a large sergeant in what I took to be an Australian uniform.

"Good afternoon," I began. "I realise I may not look the part but I am a British Officer, Major Harry Flashman, late of 29 Squadron and just returned from a mission behind the hun lines. A decent cup of gunfire wouldn't go amiss my good man." I smiled at the sergeant's bemused face. "Chop chop, something to eat would be nice as well."

"Well Sir, we'll 'ave to see about all that." He gave me another puzzled stare, turned round to leave, turned back to say something, thought better of it and shut the door as he left, muttering to himself.

I stared at the closed door for a minute or two before sitting back down on the bed, now feeling extremely hungry and thirsty as well as just a little irritable. It was hours before anything happened but finally there was a scrabbling at the door that opened to reveal as motley a crew as it was possible to find. First up was some oik carrying a tray that appeared to have a gourmet selection of bully beef and biscuits, along with a tin mug containing a brown liquid that was difficult to identify from a distance. Next was my friend the sergeant wearing a relieved look that he didn't have to make any kind of decision about who or what I was. Third, was a pipsqueak of a subaltern who could barely stop himself hopping from foot to foot in his excitement. But it was the final two members of the troupe who held my attention. Major Blake, I discovered later, was the CO of 3 Squadron, Australian Flying Corps based at Bertangles. Colonel Montgomery I knew already.

I stared for a moment and he stared back, as if examining me in detail.

"I was at Sandhurst with a man called Flashman but this is not he."

It was a very short and to the point statement which left me spluttering in disbelief. How could he, the swine, how could he pretend he didn't know me just because I had abandoned him when we set fire to that sniffling little bastard at Sandhurst all those years ago. Words failed me.[82]

---

[82] See 'Flashman and the Knights of the Sky' for the incident Flashman is referring to. Colonel Bernard Montgomery was Chief of Staff of 47 London Division at this time. Quite what coincidence brought him to Flashman's cell is

Before I could recover, they turned and went out, leaving me with my mouth hanging open. I clenched and unclenched my fists, more or less foaming at the mouth, and continued doing this for some minutes before I began raving again. You see, I had also arrived at a possible outcome for this situation that I hadn't previously considered and that was where they thought I was in fact a cabbage eater trying to masquerade as an English officer and therefore a spy, albeit in slightly odd circumstances. There was only one end for someone so discovered and that was the end of a rope. I admit with the benefit of hindsight this was an unlikely outcome but you weren't there and you probably don't have my mile wide yellow streak.

I hollered at the door until I was hoarse and banged on the door 'til my fists hurt, alternately cursing them for the idiots they were and pleading for my life as surely they were officers and gentlemen albeit Australians.

I awoke with something banging hard against my shoulder. I ached all over but didn't have time to feel sorry for myself as there was an insistent voice telling me to get up and out of the way. As I sat up, I realised I had been asleep on the floor and someone had been trying to shove me out of the way with the door. I slithered out of the way and the door opened to allow my friend the sergeant to come in.

"Morning Sir," he said before pausing apparently unsure quite how to proceed. I glanced past him only for the icy grip of fear to assail me unannounced. In the shadows outside the door stood another unidentified man. He was in uniform, but it wasn't a uniform I recognised.

"Major says you's to accompany this 'ere gentleman."

"What for?" I screeched. "Who the hell is he?"

"Don't know Sir."

He stepped to one side and suddenly two more men came in. Before I could do anything, they grabbed my arms, shoved something in my mouth and dragged me out. I screamed, but what came out was more of a choking noise, the gag slipped further into my mouth and I was nearly sick. The cold hit me like a knife as we left the building and I gagged again. I heard the crunch of gravel

unknown.

97

under my feet for a few seconds before I felt hands on my head, pushing me down and shoving me through the door of a vehicle. I sprawled across the seats, felt someone get in beside me and then the unmistakeable feel of a gun barrel against my head.

"Sit still," a voice said.

I sat, not quite still but quivering with fear. I could have screamed and screamed if it hadn't been for the filthy rag in my mouth which I was doing my best not to choke on. My hands were now tingling I assumed because of the rope tied round my wrists, which at least meant I could dispense with the idea of a desperate escape attempt for the moment, that not really being my style anyway. I cursed inwardly, not for the first time. Why me? I did all their dirty work, admittedly unwillingly with a Damocletian sword hanging over me, but I did it, and I still managed to end up with nothing to show for it and deep in the mire.

The vehicle started to move slowly and the fear gripped my bowels ever tighter. Hours it seemed, Flashman hours anyway, I lay on the seat bumping over the appalling roads that meant we were still near the front. We stopped abruptly. I sat up and immediately wished I hadn't. We were outside a cemetery. In that moment, I died yet another coward's death. It was the first but not the last that day.

The door opened and I was unceremoniously hauled out. The two apes who had dragged me out of my cell now shoved me forward towards the brick posts at the entrance to the cemetery. I tried to stop them but together they were far stronger than I was and we made our inexorable way in, each step I imagined taking me closer to my own demise. There was a strange whining noise coming from somewhere. Me, I suddenly realised, and it reached a crescendo as we passed through the gates and glancing to one side, I saw a large pile of earth beside a man sized hole. It was too much. My knees gave way; I died for the second time and started to fall until my chums caught me.

"Jesus," I pleaded, mainly because God had clearly failed in his duty. "Jesus," I said again muffled through my gag but clear in my head. If I had had the wit, I would have cried but I couldn't because it was too unbelievable. These were civilised people who were going to shoot me like a dog and chuck me in a hole. My feet were dragging now as we circled past the hole and the pile of mud and into a straggly group of trees. My loyal appreciation society had now had enough of me and let me go whereupon I measured my length not having any limbs available to stop myself so doing. I lay face down, not having the will to move, waiting for the inevitable. Nothing happened. I lay there for at least twenty minutes and nothing happened.

Every minute of life suddenly seemed precious now it was all going to end. If I could just get the gag out, perhaps I could plead with them. They didn't look wealthy, I could promise them untold riches, at least for the moment, surely there had to be a way. They had their backs to me, almost shielding me from view and then I heard it, and knew it was all over. The tramp of marching feet, the occasional call of the step and the clash of metal. For the third time, my guts dissolved. I closed my eyes tight, waiting for them to drag me upright and tie me to a post. I could hear the orders now as they, whoever they were, halted, grounded their arms and stood easy. Stood easy? Good God, they were going to make me wait for something, or someone more likely to witness the execution of a British officer by his own side and all because they were too stupid to take the gag out and believe me. How I didn't piss myself is a mystery I will never explain.

Seconds stretched into a minute, minutes drifted by and still nothing happened, except the noise increased. It sounded like there was going to be quite a crowd. For some reason, my mind drifted back to a passage in the old bastard's papers when he was a spectator at an execution. I forget who it was but it was quite a spectacle. I had thought those days were over however and I hadn't ever imagined I would be the star turn. For a moment, I even began composing a speech, last words of the condemned and all that, where unlike the roll call of kings and queens who had met their deserved end similarly, I, undeserving of this fate in my humble opinion, would fall to my knees and beg for mercy etcetera. I was assuming that they would give me this opportunity of course. I tried to fight off remembering the other passage I had read where he was tied to the muzzle of a cannon, although oddly it calmed me briefly as he had survived this ordeal. Winking. That was it. That was what he had done. Winked at the nearest soldier. Why in God's name didn't they look at me?

Suddenly there was silence. This was it. The end was nigh.

# Chapter 14

It is possible my mind was temporarily unhinged, but I thought I heard voices. Two voices to be precise. The first appeared to be a vicar, mumbling those well-worn phrases heard at many a funeral; 'I am the resurrection and the life; he that believeth in me, though he were dead, yet shall he live'. Personally, I thought it was unlikely that I would live after my appointment with the firing squad. I also assumed, wrongly as it turned out, that it was in my head. The second voice was much closer, in fact right beside me. It whispered, "You can get up now. Carefully though. We don't want to attract any unwanted attention."

As I say, I think I was a little unhinged because as far as I could tell, the object of a firing squad was to make the unfortunate recipient the centre of attention and no mistake. I lay still, trying to process this information.

"You'll miss it if you don't get up soon," the voice said.

I slowly opened my eyes. How could I possibly miss my own execution? It hit me like the Flying Scotsman. This wasn't my execution. Relief flooded through me, so much so I was nearly sick in my gag. But if it wasn't me, then who? I rolled onto my side. I felt someone behind me fiddling with the rope round my wrists and suddenly my hands were free. I pulled out the gag, spitting the filth out of my mouth and as I recovered, wondered where I should run to and immediately dismissed that thought.

As I stood up straight, I heard the vicar speaking louder now he was closer to me. Some way in front was the crowd I had heard, all facing away from me, and just beyond them, I could see what they were watching. Apparently floating at head height was a coffin with wreaths on it. As I stared, it moved slowly through the cemetery before coming to a halt near the large pile of earth and the man shaped hole in the ground.

"Do you know who it is?" murmured a familiar voice.

"You bastard, this was all your idea wasn't it?"

I had found de Ropp again.

"No actually, at least not this part, but it does rather suit my purpose." I could see him grinning and the temptation to smash my fist into his face was compelling to say the least. If I had been a real man, I might have done it as well. "I don't know what you did to upset that Colonel but he really doesn't like you. Seemed quite happy at the prospect of you rotting in prison for a while. Couldn't have that could we now."

"So who is it then?" I said, more to cover my mixed relief tinged with terror. I was sure now that I would leave the cemetery alive but shaken, though clearly where de Ropp was concerned you could never be certain.

"Your last victim." He paused. "Richtofen.[83]"

My face must have been a picture. "Richtofen? Are you sure?"

"Well he's in that box so unless he makes a miraculous recovery, yes I am sure."

"I meant are you sure I shot him down?"

"I know what you meant. I saw you. You shot him down and flew over the lines leaving me to clear up the mess. Unfortunately for you, you were dressed as a boche at the time and flying a boche aeroplane. So for the sake of good old blighty and the glorious and honourable killing of the worthy foe, your story won't get told. Instead, 'they' have dreamed up a charming controversy for the historians to fight over. Some say it was Brown in that camel, some say it was an anti-aircraft gunner, some say it was a field artillery battery. I say who cares, the bastard's dead."

There was a sudden silence, a couple of muffled orders and then a loud volley of rifle fire which almost had me diving for the trees again until I realised it was just a tribute to the dead enemy. The noise died away and they dropped him into his hole, never to see the light of day again[84].

The crowds started to disperse. We waited until they had all gone.

"What now?"

"Let's get away from here. We're not going back to the squadron if that was what you were thinking."

"Not really. I have had enough of flying thankyou. And Crespigny was a fool. Is he still alive?"

"No idea old boy."

---

[83] Richtofen was buried in Bertangles cemetery on 22nd April 1918.

[84] Not quite true. In fact, Richtofen was reinterred three times, firstly in a military cemetery at Fricourt, then in the Invalidenfriedhof Cemetery in Berlin where the tombstone was regularly hit by bullets fired at escapers trying to cross the Iron Curtain, before finally being moved to the family plot at Sudfriedhof in Wiesbaden.

\*\*\*\*\*\*

"All hands to the pumps, eh Flashman?"

I glared at the only man on earth who could possibly believe that a statement like that was likely to make me jump for joy. Baring. De Ropp had delivered me to Flying Corps Headquarters (although I suspected it had changed its name although no one had thought to enlighten me) and then made himself scarce citing important business in London. I tried this tack as well and was completely ignored for my trouble. I considered simply absconding again but I didn't have the spine for it. Trenchard was gone of course. He had taken up a post as Chief of the Air Staff at the new Air Ministry. His replacement was Jack Salmond.[85]

"You'll take command straightaway of course. Losing the CO is always a blow for a squadron of course. Need a shakeup shouldn't wonder." He grinned benignly at me.

"Of course," I said. What was there to say?

I had been given temporary command of 46 Squadron[86]. I assumed it was because all the more likely candidates were either crippled or dead. Worst of all, it was in France. Someone had conveniently forgotten the stipulation that one must command in England before commanding in France. Apparently, this was because the dire situation demanded it. Of course, I had tried everything I could think of to get out of it. Begging, pleading, threats, all had fallen on Baring's deaf ears and I had known as soon as I met him that it would be a squadron or a court martial, my exploits and destruction of Richtofen all but forgotten in the chaos of the fighting retreat I had only become aware of during my journey with de Ropp. It was touch and go it seemed. Consequently, once I

---

[85] Marshal of the Royal Air Force Sir John Maitland Salmond was commissioned from Sandhurst in 1901. He learnt to fly in 1912 and was seconded to the RFC. He commanded 3 Squadron when they deployed to France in 1914 and spent the rest of his career in the RFC/RAF, rising to become Chief of the Air Staff in 1930.

[86] 46 Squadron suffered a very high casualty rate during the German offensive but there is no evidence that the CO at the time, Major R.H.S.Mealing, was injured or removed from the squadron. It is quite possible he was temporarily relieved for some other reason.

102

had collected my new uniform and kit of course I set off for my new home, fury, anger and terror being my principal emotions at this juncture of my career. In the course of my deliberations and thorough briefing for my new job that I hadn't received, I had heard some of what had been going on on the western front in my absence. With a spectacularly bad sense of timing, I had managed to arrive at the climax of the German offensive.

Apparently, on the 21st March, the Germans had come storming over the hills. Literally, apparently as they had dreamed up some new ways of running forward into overwhelming fire and dying. Although on this occasion, the tactics of these 'stormtroopers[87]' had worked, they had broken through in numerous places and over the succeeding days continued to do so. So began the great fighting retreat of 1918. Of course, jerry had about 50 extra divisions that had moved over from their eastern front after the collapse of the Russians and the signing of the Treaty of Brest Litovsk and the effective surrender of the Russian army[88]. Still, none of it was good news for the allied armies as they staggered backwards under the weight of the German assault. Within a week, Albert fell and the pressure along the whole line continued. The initial part of the offensive ended on the 5th April short of Amiens. They had advanced 40 miles into allied territory in some places and taken 1200 square miles of France. They were welcome to it in my opinion as it consisted mostly of mud.

However, that wasn't the end of it. On the 9th, they started again. Some poor Portuguese division that was about to be taken out of the line got surrounded and annihilated, the British 40th division collapsed although the 55th held on desperately. Next day, Mademoiselle from Armentieres got a pleasant surprise when her clients changed into krauts and Messines ridge changed hands again. On the 11th April, Haig got the wind up, decided that it was all over and issued his backs to the wall order.[89] Apparently, everyone was to

---

[87] In development since 1915, the stormtrooper tactics were initially very successful but tended to run out of steam. They did however herald the blitzkrieg tactics used in the second world war to such devastating effect.

[88] See appendix.

[89] See appendix for transcript of Haig's order.

fight to the last man. It was never made clear whether that included the staff or not. I resolved not to be the last man.

And so it went on. The Germans carried on attacking, losing thousands of men, most of whom were their crack stormtroopers, attacking again, gaining ground, causing huge casualties among the allied forces and slowly but surely running out of steam. By July, it was all over. The allies hadn't collapsed, but had in fact withdrawn mainly in good order allowing the boche to come on and fight against defensive strong points at places of our choosing for once. The Americans were arriving in ever-greater numbers and fought some costly actions, learning lessons they could have avoided if they had only had the sense to ask, but like impetuous children, they didn't. But, as the Duke[90] would have said, it was a close run thing and at one point in June, the front had more or less collapsed and the Germans had reached the Marne river precipitating panic in Paris as citizens began to flee and even the Government drew up plans to evacuate to Bordeaux.

By this time, I wasn't far from being a gibbering wreck. The only reason I hadn't cracked up was that I could smell victory. The arrival of the yanks in their thousands and thousands foretold ultimate success, but I hadn't managed to avoid the action completely and I had a horrible feeling we weren't going to escape whatever was next.

The last few weeks had been one hideous nightmare of ground attacking and despite being the boss, I hadn't been able to shirk anywhere near as much as I had hoped. And still it went on. Every day, over and over again, we took the camels over the lines much too close to the ground for comfort and less and less of us came back.

Here we were again. I was sitting in the cockpit shivering despite the warmth of the early morning. Orders had arrived for us to attack some railway junction or other where there was apparently an entire division of infantry and all its attendant hardware. Fifteen of us were going and I could just about hear the shouts as the engines started. I started my own and waved the chocks away. I trundled slowly down the field trying to keep the sun out of my eyes before turning into wind. The camels were starting to roll and I watched as a pair set off. Then it was my turn, my wingman beside me.

---

[90] Presumably the Duke of Wellington.

104

It seemed only moments before we were airborne and turning to head east, the sun again shining straight in our eyes. The noise of the engines seemed almost to fade into the background as my thoughts drifted unbidden onto the unwritten letters for the five pilots missing in the last week. Of course, it was entirely possible that I would be joining them and then someone else would have to write a letter about me. I suddenly snapped back to reality. For a moment, I had almost given in to despair. But I couldn't. Jesus, I had lasted this long, surely my luck wasn't going to run out now? Surely it couldn't? But of course it could as the regular letters proved. It had even run out for Brigadier General Gordon Shephard, one of the real originals[91]. He was visiting a squadron at Auchel when he spun in from low level. Just a mistake, easy to make, less easy to survive. It made me shiver thinking about it.

Trenches started to pass underneath and in seconds, we were in amongst it. I heard it before I saw it as everything the cabbage eaters had started firing. They were even using artillery. I felt a bloody big shell go by somehow missing everything. The situation rapidly deteriorated as our formation became more and more ragged before dissolving completely into a low-level melee. I watched as a camel ahead of me suddenly pulled up in a climbing turn. Smoke appeared behind him but he did at least look as if he was under control. A line of holes appeared in the port wing as I hurled the aircraft around the sky trying to keep the gunners guessing. We were now only seconds from the target. There was little point in trying to aim at anything in particular so I just aimed in the general direction of the junction where I could see hundreds of troops who had it seemed also noticed us.

---

[91] Captain Gordon Shephard had crossed over with 4 Squadron in 1914 as a flight commander. Sent back home in late 1914 to train new pilots, by July 1916 he was back in France commanding 6 Squadron. 1917 saw him promoted to command a brigade. He was a highly popular brigade commander and took every opportunity to fly reconnaissance missions as well as visiting his squadrons on a daily basis in his Nieuport scout. He made a point of getting to know his pilots and observers personally. On 19th January 1918 as he approached Auchel airfield, he stalled his aircraft in a turn and spun into the ground. He had a reputation as a bold but safe pilot but still made what on the face of it seems a simple error leading to his death. He was 32.

For a fraction of a second, nothing happened. Then hell engulfed me.

The first thing I noticed was a great boot in the essentials. I nearly jumped out of my seat with the shock of it and had it not been for the flattened tin hat that I was sitting on to give the crown jewels a measure of protection, the Flashman bloodline, or at least my branch of it would have ended there and then. As it was, I could feel the swelling and it was not in the least lustful.

The involuntary lurch upwards had pushed the nose of the aircraft down which given my low level was not particularly good news but I instinctively pulled slightly back to level off. My immediate impression was that I was virtually landing in a division of German troops. This led to my decision to pull the trigger, and at a range of what could only have been fifty yards I couldn't miss. I saw bodies flung backwards and a minor explosion that blew a vehicle and those in it to pieces, some of which were blasted above me, so much so that I couldn't avoid them coming back down even if I had wanted to. It must have been gruesome but I didn't particularly care. The throttle was wide open and at thirty feet above the ground, the camel was tearing along and I had no time to concentrate on anything other than flying and firing.

I banked hard to avoid the remains of what must once have been the station, banked again and before I knew it, I was clear of the junction. I pulled up and rolled hard to try to get away from the mess and as I came round, I saw a camel hit the chimney of the station. It must have been the only thing high enough to hit although I guessed afterwards that he had probably been hit already. I continued climbing back towards our own lines.

I was shivering or more likely shaking with the reaction. I hadn't looked behind me once. When I realised this and turned round to look, I nearly had kittens. For a second I thought I was being chased by the boche, not that we had seen any, until I realised they were all camels and they had formed up behind me. A quick count suggested there were two missing.

Suddenly realising I still had full power on I throttled back and slowed down to a more normal cruising speed. Instinctively I headed for the airfield and it was only when I was about to land I realised that there was a camel beside me frantically waggling his wings and gesticulating wildly behind him. Turning to look at what horror was behind me, I saw nothing. It took me a minute for that to register properly and when it did, I nearly gave in. My tailplane was shot to pieces, so much so that it appeared to be a collection of rags waving gently in the breeze. As I looked around, I realized that the entire machine was in much the same state. It looked like bunting from the village fair. The worst thing was that I had been flying it in this state for some time. God knows how it had survived this long without any of the struts collapsing or the wings falling off.

The shaking was getting worse but I had to land it and land it soon otherwise I was pretty sure it was going to break up. There was a field ahead that looked more or less flat and I decided that was the place. I throttled back sinking slowly towards it. There was an almighty groan from somewhere but I daren't look round again. Slowly, slowly I sank towards the ground, hundred feet, don't give up on me now, that would be the height of injustice, fifty feet, thirty, twenty, ten, I pulled gently and floated. The wheels touched and rolled, I cut the throttle completely and waited for it to stop. There was another groan and virtually at walking pace, the port wing subsided onto the ground. The change in weight distribution meant the camel now tipped over onto the starboard wing, which in turn broke off leaving the fuselage upright. I stopped the engine and there was a blissful silence, or at least what passed for silence on the western front. I gripped the sides of the cockpit to stop my hands shaking. I sat still. It was probably the cold but I couldn't feel my legs. After some time I decided that I needed to get out. I put my hands up onto the side of the cockpit again. I was mostly warm as the sun was blazing down but my legs still felt cold for some reason. I tried to haul myself out but I couldn't. Odd. There was no pain anywhere apart from my arse. And then it struck me my legs weren't cold, there was just no feeling at all. I tried again to no avail. Panicky now, I tried rubbing and slapping my legs to get the circulation going but no joy. I sat trapped in the wreckage of the aircraft. It couldn't be true surely. It must be a dream. I slapped my face hard but I didn't wake up. It was going to end here, paralysed, life finished, confined to a bath chair looking at naughty pictures wondering how long I could endure the indignity before I blew my brains out like some I had known.

\*\*\*\*\*\*

I must have passed out. I came round with someone trying to force whisky down my throat.

"He's awake," a voice said.

"Let's get him out then," said another.

There was a rending noise of wood being torn apart and the side of the cockpit was pulled off. Arms seemed to swarm around me and I floated upwards and sideways out of the wrecked aeroplane. I was laid on a stretcher, a face swam into view above me before dissolving into blue sky and then I fainted clean away again.

I woke to a vision of beauty. Looking round I discovered there were several visions, not all of them strictly beautiful. Two nurses, both of whom were in the former category and two men, one of whom appeared to be a doctor and the other, well, hard to tell really. He was not in uniform and was standing in a corner of the ward inspecting his feet.

I was wondering which of them looked the most delicious and which was the most likely to succumb to the Flashman charm quickest when it struck me again why I was there. Fear gripped me as I realised that neither would be succumbing to any charm at all, as I wouldn't be able to get out of bed, let alone sound the charge. I flopped back on my pillow having lifted my head a fraction to inspect the room. This drew the attention of one of the nurses, a buxom redhead I regretted noting.

"Doctor," she trilled cheerily. "The Major is awake."

"Thankyou nurse," the doctor said, glancing over at my inert form then returning to whatever he was doing.

"Here you are Major, a nice drop of water for you."

She winked at me as she passed the glass and I gripped it a little too hard, brushing her hand as I did so and feeling a certain stirring. God it was infuriating. I could have cried. If only my legs were working, if only I hadn't been shot by the blasted boche, if only all these other people hadn't been in the room, if only, if only, if only.

"Thankyou," I said with a sigh but just about managing to return the wink. She giggled quietly and glanced at the others. I took a sip of the water and nearly spat it on the sheets. I just managed to swallow the liquid before looking up again to see my new friend mouthing the word 'gin' at me and putting a dainty finger to her lips. I took another sip and swallowed hard. It was oddly welcome relief.

The nurse stepped back as the doctor stepped over to the bed.

"How are you feeling old boy?" he asked in an uninterested voice. "Bit of colour about you today. Get him something to eat nurse and then I think we might get him up."

I nearly spat my drink out again.

"Up?" I managed to whisper just about audibly. "But I can't walk," I said a little louder.

"What do you mean, can't walk? Who told you that?"

"No-one told me, I just can't. No feeling in my legs." I was on the edge of tears at this point as I felt the imagined disappointment of my new redheaded friend.

"Rubbish, there's nothing wrong with you. Of course, if you hadn't been sitting on that tin hat it might be a different story. Just bruised old boy. Might be a bit painful in the old waterworks for a week or two but other than that, you're as fit as a fiddle."

It took a moment for all this news to sink in. I glanced over at my redhead and winked again, properly this time, with all the lust I could muster in a wink. She glanced coyly back, bent down to pick up the towel she had dropped and said, "I'll get the Major some lunch doctor," before disappearing through the door. She didn't look back which was enough to tell me she was hooked.

"Excellent. Well, once you have had a bite, we'll get you up for a stroll. You'll need to take it easy for a day or two as you have been lying there for nearly a week."

The doctor left the room accompanied by the other nurse who gave me a cold stare clearly meant to convey that she knew what I was thinking and there would be none of that where she was concerned. That left the man in the corner.

He looked up as the others left, waited until the door was closed and sidled over to me looking shifty. Not for the first time I wondered what was about to happen and whether it was truly in the interests of H. Flashman esq as these cloak and dagger people had a tendency to be dangerous and it was obvious that he was in that camp.

"Plantard," he said looking down at me, "Pierre Plantard[92]."

---

[92] This must be Pierre Plantard senior whose son, also called Pierre, was responsible for the 'Dossiers Secrets' which purported to be ancient documents detailing the activities and members of the Priory of Sion and linking them to the

He said it as if I should know the name, which was worrying.

"I 'ave a message for you." He paused looking at the door before continuing. "From Sixtus. You are aware of ze letters zat 'ave been sent between ze monarchs of Europe?" This was said in a barely audible voice. I nodded, my heart in my mouth, wondering if paralysis was a price worth paying to extract myself from whatever was coming next. "Clemenceau is not very 'appy, not very 'appy at all. Nor Poincare[93]. 'e 'as 'ad one letter publish and now what is to be done. Sacre bleu!"

"Which letter?" I whispered trying to look innocent.

"Ze letter from ze Emperor zat Sixtus showed to ze French. Von Czernin[94] said zat Clemenceau was ze biggest obstacle to peace and now 'e is very upset. Very upset indeed."

"Who? Von Czernin?"

"Non, non, Clemenceau, 'e is upset and now it is all finish."

He rambled on in this vein for some time.

I struggled to keep up for a while but slowly it started to become clear. And like the proverbial light being switched on, I suddenly realised I had been part of it. I had forgotten about Sixtus in my desperate attempts simply to stay alive, but he of course was the German Belgian I had given my letter to and who was related to the Austrian Emperor.

Apparently, prior to my sojourn in Belgium as postman, the Austrians had suddenly realised that the war wasn't likely to end well for them and their Emperor who might find himself without an empire to run. Consequently, Charles had decided to try to salvage what he could by attempting to broker peace as long as he could retain his position. By promising that the Kaiser would give up Alsace, that Belgium would be restored and Serbia allowed independence, he had persuaded his brother in law Sixtus to help bring the French on-board. Letters had been written and sent, one of which I had unwittingly carried myself. But then nothing. Nothing

---

Merovingian Kings of France. They were 'officially' condemned as a hoax and Plantard dismissed as a fantasist.

[93] Respectively Prime Minister and President of France.

[94] Presumably Count Ottokar von Czernin. He was appointed as Minister of Foreign Affairs for Emperor Charles I. He was in favour, like the Emperor, of a negotiated peace and strove to achieve that aim throughout his tenure as a Minister.

happened. At least not in Europe anyway. Of course, I had eventually carried a reply of sorts but, well, you have seen what happened. Wales and Albany had both got in on the act. Albany had planned a coup in England to depose the warmongering King who he portrayed as a secret ally of the Kaiser, his relation. In so doing, peace would be negotiated based on the conditions set out by the French and Austrians, and who cared what the Germans and English thought.

With me so far?

Of course, once the Russkis let the Bolsheviks have a go at running their country and having messed it up, pull out of the war with a meaningless treaty that would be dead almost as soon as the ink was dry, the resurgent and newly confident Germans felt they might have a final shot at victory. Peace negotiations were therefore of no interest whatsoever. Unfortunately for them, they had to leave thousands of troops in the newly ceded eastern European territories, which in turn limited the numbers available for transfer to France, but that was mere detail and never going to stop them having another go as I have described. Maybe Von Czernin's outburst was deliberate to provoke the French and scupper any ideas of peace. We'll probably never know. And I'll probably never care. I'd as soon get in the ring with a wild tiger than politicians like these. At least with a tiger, one knew where one stood[95].

It explained a lot, not least about what Albany was up to. I had wondered when I read the letter what it meant. He was clearly hoping that once the dust settled, once he was on the throne, there would be no appetite for more fighting which in turn would give him time to consolidate what would be a monarchy hanging by a thread, especially once his accusations of collaboration became widely known.

Still, it was nice to know they were all looking after me.

---

[95] The Austrian Emperor did indeed attempt to broker peace by contacting the French in early 1917. As with most clandestine negotiations, the details are sketchy at best and filled with claim and counter claim and at this distance impossible to verify. Flashman's details are essentially correct although there is no evidence, other than Flashman's, that an attempt was made to contact the British who would still have been a junior partner and unlikely to have much European influence at the time.

Plantard didn't seem keen on leaving quickly once he had shared all his cheery news. He glanced around the room before going to the door, looking outside and coming back in looking if it were possible more furtive than before.

"I 'ave 'ere ze message from Sixtus for you." He paused while I put it to one side unread. "I 'ave two more sings to say. Sinclair wants you to go to Paris. 'e will meet you outside ze Louvre ze day after tomorrow at six o'clock in ze evening." He paused again while I digested this news, at the same time wondering again how I did it, how, even after surviving all that I had, the bastards came back for more. "And finally, 'e said you may know what 'appened to my cousin?"

For a moment or two, I thought the man must be deranged. How on earth would I know what had happened to his cousin. I had personally known hundreds who had made the ultimate sacrifice for the greater good, so how was I supposed to remember his cousin among the legions of the dead. I was about to disabuse him and tell him the chances of me having known his cousin were slim to nil and the chances of remembering him even less when he spoke again.

"She was, 'ow you say, an 'ostess in St Omer. I sink she 'ad change 'er name. She 'ad rearrange it."

Rearranged it? How could she have rearranged it? And into what for heaven's sake? It struck me like a firebolt from below. D'alprant. Plantard. Well that made it easy of course. I could tell him exactly how I had discovered her spying for the boche, how I had been sent to trap her and how having discovered my knowledge she had tried to use me, threatened me with a gun and finished up lying naked and dead on the steps of her brothel. That would brighten his day up no end[96]. I assumed the hunted look I saved for these occasions at the same time assessing escape routes, limited as I didn't know what floor I was on and I wasn't wearing very much, and violence as a solution. He wasn't a big man, but I had been in bed for a week and hadn't even stood up in that time.

Without warning, Plantard suddenly deflated, sinking onto the bed beside me.

"I knew it. She is dead, non?"

I nodded dumbly. He held his head in his hands.

---

[96] See 'Flashman and the Knights of the Sky'.

"We always knew she would 'ave a bad end. One day you will tell me. Too 'eadstrong," he finished, tapping his head. "I must go."

He stood up, shook my hand and departed, leaving me speechless.

No sooner had the door closed than it opened again. I was about to tell whoever it was that this wasn't King's Cross and to shut the door on their way out when I realised it was my cheeky redheaded nurse.

"Well Major Flashman. I have come to get you up."

She returned my lascivious leer with interest, locked the door and without so much as a by your leave hopped on the bed, partially disrobing as she did so. It must have been months since I had had a woman astride my thighs and there was a loud groan as we got under way, almost immediately muffled by my shirt being stuffed unceremoniously in my mouth. Her head back, back arched, I reached up and popped her charlies out and started kneading away with vigour. She started groaning herself, eyes rolling backwards so I returned the favour and stuffed a pillow in her face. She bit on it, holding it in her mouth like a dog while muffled sighs emanated from within. The climax arrived for her, after which she collapsed onto me while I finished the job. We lay completely still for some time, the pillow both masking our laboured breathing and slowly suffocating us until she suddenly sat up, disengaged, held out her hand and introduced herself.

"The Honourable Lady Victoria Ponsonby, at your service."

"I am not sure Honourable or Lady is the right description," I said, grinning at her. "On the other hand, who cares?"

"I don't. I'm not entitled to use either of them anyway, it just amuses me. Of course, Father might object, but as far as I can tell, all the boys I would have had to choose from to find a suitable husband are dead or crippled and I refuse to spend my life married to a cripple. Apart from that, they were all so boring. You're not boring are you?"

"Not unless you consider tearing round the sky shooting and killing other men in their aeroplanes boring."

"Good. Doc says you are leaving Friday. Until then, I am to look after you and get you up…." she paused for a moment leering at me… "and about. Now come on, out of bed and don't worry about your clothes, I've seen it all before haven't I!"

If I had had any morals at all I would have been shocked at her behaviour, but years of watching men being blown to pieces, burnt to a cinder or riddled with bullets had numbed my already low shock threshold to non-existence. Clearly, she had decided to live life to the full and to hell with the consequences. And she was probably right. Most of the eligible suitors, approved of course by her Father, were buried in the mud of Flanders. As junior officers, they would have been at the sharp end of all the fighting and therefore done a lot of the dying as well. As she helped me swing my legs over the side of the bed, there was another feeling I couldn't place. Puzzled, I dismissed it to continue staring at her while she busied herself with carpet slippers.

******

Having walked around the corridors for a while, the Honourable Lady Ponsonby escorted me back to my room. She then vanished, much to my disgust, to be replaced by the doctor who pronounced me fit although he was happy for me to leave on Friday. After he had gone, I lay on my bed. There was nothing to do but think. The trouble was, despite having a few things to think about, such as Sinclair and his latest lunatic scheme whatever that might be, and the odd letter to read, there was only one thing occupying my mind; and that was the luscious Victoria Ponsonby. Night fell, and I lay staring at the ceiling, seeing nothing, sleep a hopeless fantasy.

If one considers that the day starts at midnight, then the next day was one of the highlights, if not the highlight of my whole war. It began at about two in the morning when the door opened briefly, a curvy figure slipped through, closed the door behind and without further ado, jumped onto the bed and repeated the jolly afternoon performance.

I awoke some hours later. She was still there, lying on her back snoring gently, her warm body close to mine. I almost woke her up and turfed her out as there wasn't strictly room for both of us and I was technically still an invalid. But I realised I couldn't. 'What?' I hear you cry. Flashy not able to push some tart out of bed? It was worrying I grant you, not least because I was beginning to get an inkling of what the strange sensation I had experienced earlier was. I couldn't push her out because, well, I just couldn't. You see, I was in love. I was in lust as well but somehow she was different, not least because she had hopped into bed and got on with it. It wasn't just that, in fact it wasn't that at all, there was just something about her that made the old pump miss a beat.

I daydreamed like this for a minute or two before telling myself to pull myself together. How could I be in love? I had only known her one day. Clearly, my survival and the fact that I wasn't paralysed had affected my mind. Maybe I was going off my rocker. I wouldn't be the first and I had seen plenty and then some of the horrors that finished with the men in white coats taking you away and locking you in a padded room with a battery attached to your testicles[97].

I was just telling myself again to be a man and shove her out when she woke up, snuffled gently, rolled over and set to partners again. How we never woke the entire hospital up I will never know, but on this occasion we finished writhing on the floor with her jaw clamped firmly on my shoulder to at least minimise the racket.

When she came up for air, I was exhausted. My shoulder hurt and there was the beginning of a large bruise. She laughed when she saw it, stood up and admired herself in the window.

"I am not supposed to be here today, but seeing as it's your last day in the madhouse, I thought I would spend it here. Can't think of anything better to do, can you?"

I couldn't. So we spent the day wandering in the grounds of the hospital. Somehow, she conjured some lunch for us to eat in the garden. The weather was splendid, the whisky was Laphroaig but the best part was the romp in the rhododendrons.

The sun was going down as we lay in the shadows, she fiddling with my hair, me dozing fitfully. I was trying not to think of anything, least of all that she had clearly been in the rhododendrons before.

"There's no point," she said suddenly. "This bloody war just seems to go on and on, and what for?"

I was tempted to rebuke her for using such unladylike language but I couldn't. She was right of course.

---

[97] Flashman is presumably referring to electrotherapy, first used as early as the eighteenth century for the treatment of psychiatric conditions.

"I see the way you look at me. You think you are in love don't you? Well that's stupid. You could be dead tomorrow and where would that leave me?"

I didn't say anything but I could tell that despite her protestations, she was drawn to me like a moth to a flame. We were both rogues in our own ways of course and that was probably what made it so delicious.

Somehow, she had commandeered a vehicle for the evening along with a driver. He took us to the nearest town, which with a start I recognised as Le Hameau. I had been here before with 29 Squadron, all that time ago. Whilst I reminisced, she gave him some money to clear off which he happily did and we spent a fine evening in a nondescript restaurant in the town square. The French being French, the waiter happily conspired with us to keep what he imagined was our affair secret, nodding and winking cheerfully with every course. He was about ninety give or take a decade or so which meant dinner took some time but I didn't care.

"You can see me again of course," she said, rather haughtily I felt, late on in the proceedings, "but I won't wait for you."

"I never thought you would."

"Father won't approve, but then he is hardly in a position to throw stones."

"And Father is?"

"Sir Frederick Edward Grey Ponsonby.[98]" No one knows officially that I am his daughter. Ridiculous I know but we have Victoria to thank for all that."

I made a note to find out all I could about this Ponsonby fellow. Clearly, I was smitten; or possibly stricken. Either way there was nothing to be done about it. Well, there was one thing and we did that once we got back to the hospital. When it was over and she was lying beside me again smoking, we fell to conversation again.

---

[98] Sir Frederick Ponsonby served in the Grenadier Guards during the war having previously fought in the Boer war. His Father Henry was Private Secretary to Queen Victoria, his Grandfather General Sir Frederick Ponsonby was wounded at Waterloo. His Aunt was Lady Caroline Lamb, wife to the Prime Minister Lord Melbourne and lover of Lord Byron. They are an interesting family but, although possible, there is no evidence Sir Frederick had any illegitimate children. Sir Frederick was raised to the peerage in 1935 as the 1st Baron Sysonby of Wonersh in Surrey.

"Of course, your Father had something of a reputation at court as I understand. I imagine you are similar. It doesn't matter of course."

She gave me a sidelong glance that told me that it mattered a lot.

"Maybe I am, but that doesn't mean I am incapable of fidelity if required. Who knows...."

I awoke with her shaking my shoulder. The clock said it was past midnight.

"I have to go. Write to me here."

And with that she was gone, leaving me to sleep and ponder all that had happened in such a short time. I also read Sixtus' message. I wished I hadn't.

"The man who brings you this message is a trusted servant. Our plan has failed. They have the list. Do not trust the French. Destroy this message. Sixtus.[99]"

---

[99] Flashman is alluding here to what became known as the 'Sixtus Affair'. Charles I did indeed attempt to broker peace using his brother-in-law Sixtus and wrote a letter to the French President, which was conveyed by Sixtus. When nothing happened, Von Czernin condemned Clemenceau who promptly published the letter in early 1918 causing much angst in Austria. There is no record of Charles having written to King George V but equally there is no record that he did not. Maybe Flashman's revelation may eventually cause further light to be shed on the subject. See appendix.

# Chapter 15

I left early the next morning. I had decided that much as a return bout with the honourable Victoria would be jolly, now was not the time. I had received no orders apart from the instruction from Sinclair, so I decided that I would go to Paris early and make the most of it as no doubt someone somewhere would be waiting in the wings to thrust me back into the cauldron of the western front, and the longer I could put that off the better. It also occurred to me that the safest possible place to be would be with Sinclair.

For once, the train rattled along quite quickly and I arrived at the Gare du Nord before ten. It was very quiet, almost basking in the morning sun. There was no one to meet me, not that I was surprised by that, and I walked out of the station onto the Rue de Maubeuge. I stopped at the first patisserie I found and sat down. I stared along the road at the Basilica of the Sacre Coeur but hardly seeing. My mind was spinning with all that had happened in the last few weeks. I bought myself a coffee and a croissant and sat watching the people go by. Having whiled away an hour or two, I had made up my mind. Hailing a taxi, I set off for Montmartre, where I knew an establishment guaranteed to take my mind off at least some of my woes. I rang the bell and waited. I heard giggling from within and then a statuesque raven-haired woman opened the door.

"Good morning," I began, "I would like to speak with Lucille if I may?"

"Of course, M'sieur. Please come in and 'ave a sit."

I sat in a garish lounge admiring the décor, which seemed to consist mainly of velvet gloves, posters of the Folie Bergere and handcuffs.

"'Arry," a voice said.

"Lucille," I replied getting up to embrace her. Just the feel of the satin dress she was falling out of had my blood pressure rising.

"What can I do for you, my big 'Arry?"

"Everything," I replied.

"Come wiz me," she replied with a wink.

\*\*\*\*\*\*

She did everything. At least, everything I could think of and then some. But it didn't have the desired effect because I was still thinking of the Honourable Lady Victoria as I whipped Lucille round the last bend, she having persuaded me that this was a desirable way to conclude the proceedings. I offered to pay, but she wasn't interested as in her view I had provided her with a significant amount of business in her smaller establishment in Arras thus enabling her to move to Paris.

She told me all about it, how she now only worked for her favourite customers and how she was employing numerous girls and how her reputation for discretion was growing steadily, so much so that she regularly entertained various bigwigs, up to and including Poincare. I suspected there was a little gammon in her claims but I was still interested in finding out who frequented the place despite it being ultimately pointless. I wasn't going to go telling anybody, partly because I didn't care and partly because they had significantly more power than me and I never underestimated the power of the cornered politician.

When I left, it was already mid-afternoon. I ambled down the Champs Elysee doffing my cap to the ladies promenading, basking somewhat in my brief freedom. I climbed the shallow incline up to the Arc de Triomphe[100], paused briefly in the middle to admire the view before continuing on down the hill. In the distance, I could see the Louvre Palace, slowly looming larger as I approached. Passing through the Place de la Concorde, I was acutely aware of two things. First, the Tuileries, the location of the end of the French monarchy and Louis XVI. Second, the Egyptian obelisk and its odd significance in the things I had learnt about the Templars and their descendants. I pondered again all that had brought me to this, whatever 'this' was. Maybe Sinclair would shed some light.

I carried on through the gardens towards the palace, all the time scanning the few people about for signs of trouble. The tap on the shoulder would normally have had me screaming, especially given the cheery note from Sixtus, except that I had half expected it. I stopped and Sinclair stopped with me.

"Shall we take a seat old chum?"

---

[100] In which case strictly speaking Flashman was promenading up the 'Avenue de la Grande Armee'.

"Why not," I replied.

"Your war is over." I could have cried but instead I tried to look disappointed. "Albert was taken yesterday[101], we are moving forward on all fronts. No one will admit it yet but it is all over. Just a case of when the Germans decide to sue for peace." He paused and we sat in silence for a few minutes, mulling over this news. "There will have to be negotiations of course. Europe won't be quite the same as it was. I suspect the Kaiser will abdicate as will the Emperor, which rather puts us all in Queer Street with regard to your little adventures, as neither of them will be in much of a position of influence. Which means that Albany's little plan is dead in the water, not that I ever thought there was much hope for it. Another time."

He looked wistfully into the distance, presumably dreaming of a paradise lost. I didn't interrupt.

"I need someone on the inside."

My heart pounded suddenly. I was alive. I had done my bit and survived. If he was right, and I had no reason to believe otherwise, I could go home a returning hero, back to a life of debauchery and idleness. Briefly, I considered writing to Victoria and decided I would but it could wait a day or two. All I had to do was be someone on the inside.

******

Boredom. Time seemed to be at a standstill, at least compared to the last few years. Paris at least seemed still to be lively and more than a few times the locals spoke of the good old days when Bertie the Bounder had cheered the place up[102]. Admittedly, they weren't your average locals as most were employed in the jollity business and therefore predisposed to showing me a good time, but I still believed them. However, in spite of their educational talents, I still wanted Lady Ponsonby. I had written to her and she had promised to

---

[101] Albert was retaken on the 22nd August 1918.

[102] King Edward VII had been a regular visitor to France all his life and in many ways was a virtual Frenchman. His skills as a diplomat, particularly with the French were unrivalled. On an unauthorised visit to Paris in 1903 he singlehandedly defused the tension over the Fachoda incident in East Africa. For an entertaining and comprehensive biography of 'Berties' relationship with France see 'Dirty Bertie' by Stephen Clarke.

pop over when she next got a few days leave but this seemed almost impossible to get, largely I suspect because there were still heavy casualties at the front. Apparently unwilling just to throw in the towel, the Germans kept fighting and it wasn't until the beginning of September that they were pushed back to the Hindenburg Line[103] from where they had begun their own March offensive. For a couple of weeks I was all but hiding under the furniture as it seemed that the allied armies had run out of steam and I could still hear Baring with his 'all hands to the pumps' speech and Haig with his fighting to the last man nonsense and I still had no intention of being the last man.

Fortunately, Foch and the Americans kicked off the final push at the end of September and by the 5th of October, the allies had broken right through the Hindenburg. Cambrai[104] was the beginning of the end and as the Germans retreated faster and faster, they started abandoning their heavy kit, always a sure sign the end is near. Once the Metz Bruges railway line was crossed, it was essentially all over although there was still a substantial amount of fighting and dying to do by those at the front. Of course the main reason it dragged on longer than necessary was down to the politicians on all sides who could see the cake just out of reach and were scrambling to get at it and eat it before the hated foreigners could get it. And that applied to our own allies as much as the Germans. Nothing would be worse than letting the French get one over on us.

And finally, it was over. Last minute discussions resolved all the details like what sort of cheese should be served with the port at the armistice party, who should sit in what order round the table and whether it was a full dress occasion or would mud stains be acceptable. At 5am in the forest of Compiegne, I was aboard Foch's private train when the boche delegation signed the declaration. The war would conveniently finish at 11 o'clock Paris time. Until then

---

[103] The Hindenburg Line was built in the winter of 1916-17 following the eastern front losses to the austro-hungarian armies requiring German troops to take over more of the line. Combined with losses at Verdun, the Germans needed to reduce the attrition on the western front and so the Hindenburg Line was designed to shorten the front and create strong defensive positions to reduce casualty rates.

[104] Second battle of Cambrai. Fought between the 8th and 10th of October as part of the hundred days offensive. It was an overwhelming success and was probably the high point of the all arms tactics developed since the Somme battles in 1916.

fighting would continue. And continue it did. I discovered long afterwards that nearly three thousand men died on the last day of the war. Some poor Canadian bastard called George Price[105] was shot by a sniper at two minutes to eleven, and a completely mad American called Henry Gunther[106] was killed charging German troops with sixty seconds of war to go. The artillery had a field day firing off all their ammunition so they wouldn't have to carry it anywhere. They dressed this up as putting themselves in the right place in case the war broke out again, which given that the Kaiser had abdicated the previous day seemed unlikely.

But that's to get too far ahead of myself.

When Sinclair told me he needed someone on the inside, in my elated state I just assumed it would be some sort of office wallah thing, writing letters and demanding answers to pointless questions. I should have known better of course but I suspect my outlook was coloured by my not having to go back to the front. Initially it seemed I was right. There wasn't much to do and I loafed around Paris as I have described above. But then as the end neared, it all became deadly serious again. Somehow, Sinclair had pulled some strings and I was told to report to a chateau outside Paris to meet a naval delegation consisting of the First Sea Lord Admiral Rosslyn Wemyss, his deputy Rear-Admiral George Hope and one Captain John Marriott[107], his assistant. Quite why they were all navy was

---

[105] Private George Lawrence Price, 28th Bn Canadian Infantry, is generally recognised as the last British Empire soldier to be killed in the Great War. His patrol was advancing into the village of Havre under machine gun fire and whilst pursuing the German gunner house to house was shot in the chest by a sniper at 10.58. The last British soldier to die was Private George Edwin Ellison. He was killed at 09.30 whilst on patrol outside Mons. He is buried in the St Symphorien military cemetery where his grave coincidentally faces that of Private John Henry Parr, the first soldier to be killed in action during the war.

[106] Private, formerly Sergeant, Henry Nicholas John Gunther was killed at one minute to eleven. Against the orders of his friend and sergeant Ernest Powell, Gunther charged a German roadblock in the village of Chaumont-devant-Damvillers with his bayonet fixed. It is possible he was agonising over his reduction in rank and felt a need to prove himself to his officers and comrades. The German soldiers he approached tried to wave him off but when he fired a shot or two, he was fired on and killed instantly. Appallingly, because of Foch's refusal to countenance the ceasefire requested by the German negotiators even after the signing of the Armistice documents, 11,000 men were killed or wounded on the western front.

never really explained. Of course, I wasn't allowed near the stars of the show and even Captain Marriott was fairly distant in his dealings with me. Not that they amounted to much. I was just told where to be to get on the train that took us into the forest at Compiegne.

I was stuck in a carriage with all the rest of the hangers-on, mainly a group of gabbling Frenchmen who seemed to be constantly arguing about everything from the delights of the train cook who had a very impressive décolletage to whether the battle on the Chemin des Dames had been won because of or in spite of the efforts of the British at Arras. They didn't mention the mutiny that took place afterwards. Maybe they didn't know about it. I wasn't convinced that they really knew the definition of the word 'won' either as describing either battle as a victory was stretching the truth somewhat. I added helpful comments giving the impression that we'd never seen the Armee de l'air and being mainly from the Army they enthusiastically agreed about the uselessness of their air force. It was useful in that it meant they plied me with food and wine. It also loosened their tongues and they started to tell me how they meant to carve up Germany once the hated boche had given in. To listen to them you'd think they had won the war single handed. After a day or two, it was almost possible to forget what we were there for[108].

Then suddenly, I was woken from a deep sleep in a gorgeously comfortable bed by my batman shaking my shoulder. I screamed. As I sat bolt upright I banged my head on his and flopped back down holding it. It took at least a couple of minutes before I was convinced I wasn't about to go over the lines looking for trouble, minutes of sweating and sheer terror I assure you. Once I was coherent, the batman explained that the negotiations were at a critical point, Foch had been roused and they were about to sign the armistice.

I scrambled into my uniform, gulped down the coffee and bread that appeared to be all that was on offer and made my way to the carriage where the ceremony was to take place. There was a solemn

---

[107] Promoted Commander in 1914, he became executive officer of HMS Charybdis, Wemyss' flagship. After a short period attached to the ANZAC staff at Gallipoli, he was appointed Naval Assistant to the First Sea Lord with the rank of Acting Captain.

[108] The German delegation arrived on the 8th November. The negotiations lasted three days.

air about the place. The Germans were looking ashen, as they had apparently only recently heard about the abdication and the fall of the government. Consequently, for a brief period it had looked like they would have to start again but fortunately Hindenburg told them to go ahead and sign the damned thing. He seemed to be past caring.

There's a painting of the carriage scene somewhere. The navy are sitting down of course, the Germans standing, Foch looks as terrifying as a mouse and if the bloody frog who painted it had done it right, you would be able to see me to the left of Vanselow[109]. Everybody signed presumably using their own names and by 5.20am, it was done. All that remained was to tell everybody to stop fighting, which turned out to be easier said than done as I have mentioned. But at 11am on the 11th November, the guns stopped. I missed it as I was fast asleep having gorged myself on the spread made available for those who were working so hard and then returned to my bed. I woke up sometime after lunch. The train was moving and further enquiry told me that we would soon be in Paris again.

******

Sinclair seemed delighted with my little train trip. I hadn't told him anything particularly useful apart from what the Frogs thought they were going to do with Germany. But, I had also 'bumped into' one of the French delegation at Lucille's establishment a couple of days afterwards. He was busily regaling the trollops with tales of derring-do and how he had turned the negotiations singlehandedly. When he saw me, he dragged me into the centre of proceedings.

"My good ami 'Arry was zere also with some uzzer Rosbifs. We decide we share Germany, I sink." He winked at me and continued. "And now, we share you all."

The trollops squealed with excitement, as a proper bacchanalia got under way. Other clients were dragged in, even Lucille herself made an appearance but only to make sure all was in order and that someone was paying. When she left, I took the opportunity to slide

---

[109] Presumably Admiral Ernst Vanselow of the Kaiserliche Marine (Imperial German Navy)

out with her. We retired to her room but for once it was only business I was interested in.

"My boss is interested in information, and our drunken friend downstairs, along with many other of your clients has lots of it. At least, my boss seems to think that. He wondered whether, for a substantial fee, you might be persuaded to pass on any useful information to me."

I smiled my winning smile. I knew she was flattered but I hadn't realised quite how willing she would be.

"I 'ate zem all, zese silly weak men. I will tell you anysing zey tell me or my girls. All I want is you, my 'Arry."

I agreed. I wasn't sure that Victoria would be all that happy with this arrangement if she ever found out about it. However, I wasn't going to tell her so it shouldn't matter. I could foresee difficulties given my character but they were nothing compared to what I had had to put up with at a squadron.

I almost couldn't believe my luck. Sinclair had found me an apartment in Paris into which I had surreptitiously moved the Honourable Lady Ponsonby. I had escaped the Royal Air Force for the moment as he had arranged for me to retain my rank but on detachment to him and my job appeared to be to get information from unsuspecting clients at a brothel where I could pop round for tea at any time. It couldn't last.

Chapter 16

It didn't. I made the most of it while I could though. Between the glorious Lady Victoria with whom I led a most disreputable life and one that would only work in Paris, Lucille and her establishment which I frequented regularly for research and Sinclair, to whom I reported weekly with my little titbits of information, I was getting exhausted again. But it was a different type of exhaustion to that which had nearly done for me so many times over the lines. It was the sort that, returning home after a hard day at the office to find a decent drink awaiting, decent food and a decent bath along with the ministrations of a decent woman, one could find a way to put up with. In my blissful ignorance and my pleasure and relief at finding myself alive and well and living at the expense of the state, I ignored the future completely. Of course, a few months previously, the future could have been measured in seconds, so to have years ahead seemed almost overwhelming. At least it was to a chap like me who had no real intention of working, my current position notwithstanding. Consequently, I had given no thought to any of it.

Like so much of my life, I just drifted headlong with the current. Of course, it was Sinclair that brought me up sharp like a rock in the stream.

"I need you to go to the French Foreign Ministry."

"Why?"

"Because that is where they are negotiating for Europe. I need to find out who wants what."

"How on earth do you expect me to find that out?" I spluttered.

"You really expect me to answer that? I guess your little holiday is over. I will be in England more often than not from now on."

That concluded the conversation. My first reaction once he had gone was annoyance. As he said, it would seem my quiet life was coming to an end. As I reflected though, I realised it wasn't that bad. No one was shooting at me, I wasn't flying round the skies in a lethally flammable wooden crate, I still had all five limbs I had been born with and life was good. But if I had only known where all this would lead…. well maybe we wouldn't have been fighting the same war again twenty years later. But I wasn't to know was I?

\*\*\*\*\*\*

So it was I found myself in the Salle de l'Horloge[110], and fascinating it was too. There was a lot of shouting when I first arrived and it took me at least a day to work out the lie of the land so to speak. The first thing that was obvious to me was that not all the interested parties were there. There were delegations from Italy, France, Great Britain, Japan and the USA. There were no Germans, Austrians or Hungarians, which I suppose given that they had lost, at least according to the allies, made some sort of sense. To hear the Germans, one would be forgiven for thinking it was just an unlucky draw. They seemed to have decided they had been stabbed in the back, at least that was what a Frenchman told me in a quiet moment smoking a cigar. He seemed quite pleased about it, judging by the grin on his face. It was also apparent that all was not well amongst the allies either. The desired outcome was very different depending on who one spoke to. And I did speak to them. At length, very long length. So long in fact that I almost (but not quite!) wanted to go back to the war.

The politicians I am sure found it all very interesting but the reality for us plebs was that it would make no difference whatsoever. The Americans were in a conciliatory mood and had come up with a fourteen-point plan that they considered essential for world peace, whereas everyone else thought it was a basis for negotiation. Wilson,[111] in his speech, had expressed the American desire for a gradual change from autocratic monarchy to republican democracy, which hadn't gone down very well with the British who thought they had a pretty much universally admired system where the monarch was a talking figurehead and not much more. The French obviously believed that any system apart from theirs was nonsense and the Germans, who had no say in it anyway, had just formed a republic and were consequently rooting around for ideas on how to make it

---

[110] The Clock Room in the Quai d'Orsay.

[111] President Woodrow Wilson served from 1913 to 1921. His 'fourteen points' speech made on January 8th 1918 without consultation with his allies was not particularly well received. Clemenceau is said to have commented 'the good Lord only had ten'. Widely known about in Germany before the armistice, the subsequent enormous differences between that and the Treaty of Versailles caused great anger in Germany. See appendix.

work. Of course, the Americans could afford to be conciliatory. They had an ocean between them and the main battlefields.

The French on the other hand wanted Germany to all but vanish and favoured a return to small autonomous states that would cause them no further trouble and could be walked over with ease, preferably resembling the pre Bismarck days. And if the war of 1870[112] could be rewritten or forgotten then that would be useful too. These states would also be effectively bankrupt and unable to afford war again. The British sat somewhere in the middle, realising that both plans were unrealistic and anyway, at some point we would need to start trading again, so really we needed to get them up and running and we would help with all sorts of things that we could sell you for a premium sir.

The Italians mainly wanted food and wine, and the Japanese realised that they were on a hiding to nothing and left. Everyone else who may have wanted a say didn't get one.

Months it took before they reached some sort of agreement. In the meantime, the allied armies had occupied the Rhineland and Alsace Loraine, although the overriding priority for most of the conscripted British was to go home.

June it was before everyone was ready. I hesitate to say happy because they were far from happy. The Germans were summoned to Versailles and in the Hall of Mirrors, the various delegations sat down and signed the treaty[113].

The Germans had almost balked at the reparations demanded of them. In short, they were expected to pay everyone else's bill for the war. The French were delighted as were Lloyd George and Wilson apparently but Keynes from the Treasury remarked that if we went ahead with it and bankrupted Germany they would be back for vengeance eventually[114]. I may have actually dozed off and snored as he was telling me this over lunch at Fouquet's on the Champs Elysees. I claimed it was the effect of all the late nights that I was forced to endure working 'flat out' for His Majesty's government. I

---

[112] Presumably the Franco Prussian war.

[113] Flashman's summary is probably not too far from the truth. See appendix.

[114] Presumably John Maynard Keynes. He was appointed to the Treasury in January 1915 and served as financial representative at Versailles. He resigned his post in disgust at the treaty.

didn't mention what exactly I had been doing at Lucille's of course and why that often meant a late night. Even Victoria seemed impressed although I was careful not to have too many of them when she was around. You see, I really was in love.

Chapter 17

I thought once the treaty was signed, sealed and largely forgotten about, I might be free. Initially I was, but, as it turned out, only for a few months. And it was now, when I should have been most suspicious about everything, I was in fact at my most vulnerable. I was meeting Sinclair again as I had done for months so there was nothing unusual about it. He congratulated me again on all my work to date both during the war and afterwards, hinting that there might eventually be some recognition from on high. I seriously doubted that given my relationship with the palace but one never knew I suppose. However, it meant he had me at a disadvantage when he slipped into the conversation something about my next job.

"Fluent in German, quite an asset I would imagine. Of course, invaluable when you get to Munich."

"Yes," I replied without thinking about it.

"Lots going on there, lots of upheaval. You would still be reporting to Cumming and me of course. Have you heard of the Thule Society[115]?"

"No," I said, suddenly back in the real world.

He must have heard the change in my voice because of what he said next.

"It needn't be a hardship Flashman. You can keep the place here in Paris. And I would caution against returning to England just now."

The word 'Why?' was framed in my mouth but it didn't come out.

"I am sure you haven't told me all that happened when you were behind the lines with de Ropp." He paused at this juncture because I had never told him it was de Ropp that came with me although my look of fear would have confirmed it anyway. "I have my own contacts in Kell's gang which he may or may not know about. Either way, I find things out when I need to and what I found out is that the letter you were carrying for the Emperor, and the one that de Ropp had from Wales, both, or at least the gist of both, found their way from Sixtus into French hands. Initially, I thought that would not be

---

[115] A German occult group noted historically as the organization that sponsored the Deutsche Arbeiterpartei after the war.

a good thing although it was a risk that was always worth taking and denial can be kept up for a long time. Fortunately, the French have their own little secrets that they would rather didn't become common knowledge so for the time being our secret is more or less safe. However, whilst it is safe, it is also complicated. This is where our jumpy friend Plantard comes in. And I imagine you can see why returning to England right now might not be wise. In fact, lying low would be a very good idea."

My mouth opened and closed a couple of times but remained speechless. You see, I hadn't given any of it much thought at all since the end of the war. I had been far too busy pleasuring myself and various women and pretending that I was working. I had seen it all as an amusement, reporting to Sinclair on the goings on at Lucille's house of ill repute that concerned the upper echelons of society. I had even ignored Sixtus' warning. But suddenly, I could see exactly why lying low would be good. Albany's letter had appealed directly to the Emperor and his desire for peace. It had also touched a nerve when it mentioned the likelihood of losing power to usurpers, be they royal or republican and seemed to suggest a never ending land of milk and honey if only the various minor obstacles could be overcome, these being France and the French, Kaiser Bill and King George V. When I had first read it, it seemed pure fantasy but the more I considered it, I realised it was no more nonsensical than the war itself. Of course, de Ropp had brought along a similar letter from the Prince of Wales. I hadn't seen it but from what de Ropp had told me it was a fairly typical example of his correspondence, pretty much insulting everyone and reminding them all that the British Empire was not to be trifled with and if they wouldn't mind ending their petty European squabbles, then that would be fine as long as they all admitted they had lost, especially the French.

The net result though, purely in personal terms was that I had moved a little higher up on His Walesship's nuisance list. What that meant was hard to see, but given their ability to track me down and cause me trouble, it wasn't good news. I suppose if trouble really stirred, it was possible I might vanish. I shivered involuntarily at the thought, remembering Legh's warning at my court martial[116].

---

[116] See 'Flashman and the Knights of the Sky'.

"You won't be going straightaway but I suggest you take a few weeks leave before you do."

I did. And very useful it was too. I spent the first week alternately gnawing my fingers to the bone and threatening to go back to England and expose them all. I told Victoria some of it, naturally leaving out the less reputable parts, and she helped me by laughing uproariously. I got cross and broke some of the furniture, at which point I discovered she had a wild temper as well and I narrowly escaped injury when in blind fury she hurled my revolver at me from close range. It was touch and go for a moment whether I picked it up and shot her or gave her the back of my hand. But I discovered I could do neither of those things and instead stood red-faced and furious squeezing the life out of my number two headdress which I happened to be holding because we were due at the mess for Christmas dinner.

"And," she screeched, "I'm pregnant."

"Who's the Father?" I said out loud before I could stop myself. I admit it wasn't the cleverest thing to say and I silently thanked the Lord that she had already hurled the revolver.

"You are." At which point she fainted.

There was a brief pause in proceedings while she collected herself. I did help her onto a convenient chair and got a vicious stare for my pains. It was difficult to know what to say next as the situation wasn't one I had considered over much. I very nearly asked her how she knew but reconsidered this option and continued staring out of the window.

"Well, it isn't how I imagined it would be either," she said suddenly.

"No," I replied wondering how she imagined it would be.

"You will have to marry me. I am not having a bastard for a child, not least because my Father may well disown me entirely."

I considered this statement for a moment or two, my face turning red again in panic. You see, what I had found out about Lady Victoria's family had convinced me that crossing them was not a path I would be wise to take[117]. There were various male relatives of

---

[117] It is hard to tell who Flashman is referring to here without more information about Victoria's mother and possible siblings. Sir Frederick Ponsonby had one surviving son who would have been aged about 17 at this time and even for

a desperate disposition, some were decorated military men, others the sort of aristocrats who, despite the mounting evidence to the contrary, still believed that they were above the law and putting an upstart in his place for deflowering their admittedly half-sister would be nothing more than a passing sideshow.

"Of course I will marry you. I had been meaning to ask anyway and was just waiting for the right time my darling."

I cringed myself at such cowardly behaviour, but then you weren't there to see her in all her fury. But I was right to say it. In an instant, all her fury had gone, replaced with tears and a heaving bosom that I just managed not to grapple with. Instead, I embraced her, whispering and nibbling her ear, which I knew would eventually lead back to the bedroom, or at least to the most convenient table. Needless to say, we were late for dinner.

******

My leave had long finished. I had heard nothing from Sinclair for weeks. I carried on with my research in a desultory fashion, occasionally taking in more of the cultural wonders of Paris. Victoria was planning our wedding in a hurried fashion for fear that it would soon be obvious to all and sundry why we were getting married. A date was set and a church booked[118]. The vicar seemed largely oblivious to the proceedings, apart from when he delivered what he clearly considered to be an important lecture on the birds and bees which took the form of a largely farm animal related story. He clearly hadn't had any carnal knowledge for some time.

It was the night before my wedding. I hadn't invited my family. Victoria had invited some of hers but was relieved that, on the whole

---

Flashman probably not a serious threat. Given that his Father was Private Secretary to Queen Victoria and his Grandfather was badly wounded at Waterloo, they were probably a typical aristocratic family with all the attendant confidence in themselves.

[118] Flashman doesn't say which church but there has been a Church of England presence in Paris since 1824 when the flood of British residents after the defeat of Napoleon meant that the congregation outgrew the Embassy ballroom. The Hotel Marbeuf was chosen as a suitable location and the Marbeuf Chapel became the first Anglican church in Paris. The 'Old St Georges Church' was built in 1887 on the Rue Auguste Vacquerie.

they couldn't travel because of the short notice. She did receive a somewhat caustic letter from her Father who, given his relationship with her, seemed unduly concerned about my parentage but ultimately slightly relieved to have her off his hands without causing any major scandal. I was staying in the Embassy as Victoria had insisted on maintaining the traditional separation of bride and groom[119]. My companions had also maintained tradition by plying me with alcohol, which I had consumed with abandon. Consequently, when Sinclair appeared at my shoulder, I was roaring drunk. He seemed to want to speak to me alone so after a final slug of whatever I was drinking I stumbled out onto the balcony overlooking the river.

"You must leave the day after tomorrow." He held a hand up to stifle my protest, which was not on account of leaving the arms of my betrothed, more that I had become very accustomed to the comfortable way of life. "I know it is hard on you," (he had got wind of my impending marriage of course) "but duty calls. Your instructions are here." He handed me a large envelope. "Second thoughts, I will have it delivered," he said as he took it away again.

She took it well when I told her by telephone next morning. But then I suspect we were both a little jaded, me from strong drink, her from the sickness that had struck her down more or less every morning for the last few weeks. She was determined not to be incapacitated for the big day and by a supreme effort of will, she survived right through an interminable sermon, the marriage service, the start of the funeral service[120] which was obviously next in the vicar's book, and finally the singing of a hymn, I forget which, after which we processed out of the church, her clinging to my arm in a desperate attempt to stay upright, straight through the guard of honour to the pavement where she heaved her guts into the kerb.

I returned to the slightly bemused crowd and explained that the occasion had overwhelmed my beloved and she would be alright in a moment. I fooled no one of course, least of all the women, but fortunately, none of them cared.

---

[119] Originally, when many marriages were arranged, at least for the ruling classes, this was so the groom couldn't change his mind on seeing the bride. It was also the reason why the bride wore a veil.

[120] Visitation of the sick is after the marriage service in the book of common prayer.

The charades over and done with, we retired to the embassy where there was an uproarious dinner, several largely incomprehensible speeches, more drink and finally an undignified exit into a waiting carriage, which should have swept us off on our honeymoon. Instead, we went home.

I briefly protested about it being my wedding night to no avail and we both fell into an exhausted sleep. The envelope sitting ominously on my desk could wait til the morning.

Dawn came all too soon. It vaguely reminded me of the western front when dawn was a real harbinger of doom albeit on an altogether different scale. Mrs Flashman was still asleep, so I collected the envelope, some coffee, a bottle of whisky and ordered some kippers. I sank into my easy chair, had a slug of firewater to calm my nerves and picked up a knife I used for letter opening. My hands were shaking again, which tells you all you need to know about how I felt. I pulled out various papers and spread them out on a side table. I found what Sinclair liked to call his general synopsis and leaned back to read.

First, there was a summary of the situation in Germany more than a year after the war's end. It was quite depressing. Large parts of the population were hungry and jobless. The Government were struggling to pay the enormous reparations demanded by the French at Versailles, in fact, I got the impression that they were simply trying to avoid paying as they felt it was unfair. I had seen quite a lot of the detail before of course. Law and order were at a very low ebb, particularly as at the armistice, many of the German army had simply vanished, walking back to their homes taking their arms and ammunition with them. Bandits flourished in the remoter areas as people tried to survive in any way possible, theft, murder and armed robbery being especially popular. Central government had all but broken down and many regions had set up their own local authorities, themselves riven with parties of extremists of all colours, not least the communists who had taken over Russia, but also a new kind of right wing paramilitary group that appeared to have surfaced as a reaction to communism. They called themselves Freikorps and seemed hell bent on starting another war if they could find someone to fight. In the meantime, the communists would do. Munich, it seemed, was the hottest of hotbeds for all this strife.

I paused in wonderment.

Continuing, it seemed that the principle adversary for the British Government appeared to be the French who clearly had no qualms about the destruction of Germany. The British however took a more 'enlightened' view, largely I suspect because it would upset the French and because we still had the channel between us and them. It all sounded very jolly and the kind of trouble I would have sold my Grandmother to avoid. But yet again, here I was being coerced into voluntarily kicking over the hornet's nest all for my own good. I had another shot of whisky before continuing.

I was getting closer to the crux of the matter now. It seemed that one Rudolf Hess, whom I had written about in one of my reports and you will recall had bizarrely accompanied us to Liege, had returned to his native Munich after the end of the war[121]. The wicked British had stolen much of his family business in Alexandria and as such, like so many, he was more or less penniless with little chance of changing that situation. Disaffected, he had cast around for other ways to occupy his time and found the Thule society[122] and the Freikorps[123]. He had been a prominent if not a leading figure in many of the street battles that had plagued Bavaria in early 1919 as the communists and Freikorps fought for control of the state and had led an anti-Semitic group distributing leaflets in Munich. Apparently he was now studying at the university of Munich under someone called Haushofer[124], an academic who believed in the superiority of the Aryan races and the concept of 'Lebensraum' whereby Germany would conquer Eastern Europe as additional space to propagate the Aryan race. It all sounded somewhat deluded to me. It also seemed like a storm in a teacup. But it appeared I was to investigate it all.

---

[121] Hess was indeed born in 1894 in Alexandria, Egypt where his Father Fritz was a prosperous merchant. See appendix.

[122] See appendix.

[123] The Freikorps appeared in Germany at the end of the war as returning soldiers banded together to form paramilitary units that largely fought the communists in vicious street battles, often leading to multiple murders and executions. They were given legitimacy by Gustav Noske, the minister of defence who used them to crush the German revolution in 1918-1919 and the Marxist Spartacist League. They also arrested Karl Liebknecht and Rosa Luxemburg, both socialist revolutionaries, before executing them.

[124] Major General Karl Ernst Haushofer retired from the Army after the end of the war. He entered academia specialising in political geography believing German lack of knowledge in this field to be a major cause of their defeat.

Finally, I was to present myself to Sinclair that afternoon for a last chinwag and then I would be off.

I pondered all this for some time until I heard the unmistakeable sounds of life. My wife was awake and the servants were suddenly busy. I greeted her in the dining room where I tucked into another breakfast and she sat looking queasy. Between mouthfuls, I explained that I would be going away for a while although I was sure I would get regular opportunities to return and see how things were progressing. She looked somewhat relieved at this news and I realised that what she really needed were women around her. I was largely surplus to requirements. There were some brief tears, but then she pulled herself together. I almost persuaded her to come back to bed and was halfway there when she suddenly started retching again and put us both off. There was always later. I didn't feel a visit to Lucille was necessary. I would have to write to her and tell her I was going away for a while or she might wonder where I was taking my business and that would never do.

Lunch came and went and there was no sign of my beloved so I set off to walk to Sinclair's apartment. It was some distance away but the weather was glorious and the more I thought about it, the task he had set me didn't seem that onerous in the sunshine. Of course, there could be no comparison to the things I had been forced to do for King and Country and the more I considered, the decent German beer, the hearty food and the buxom women, the more it seemed I might actually enjoy it. There couldn't be much in this society thing, probably just a few old fools and a few young firebrands letting off steam. I doffed my tile to a pair of trollops who happened to saunter by and left them giggling in my wake. The world seemed suddenly benign. Of course, that is usually when one should turn smartly round and run for the hills as fast as possible, preferably disguised and muttering in a foreign language.

******

Sinclair looked very pleased with himself when I arrived.

"I suppose I should congratulate you," he said looking quizzically at me. "However, I suspect given who we are dealing with there is more to it but I won't ask."

137

I was feeling benign myself now so I replied cheerily, "Yes, there is, but it doesn't make any difference."

"Good." He looked slightly suspicious but I ignored it. "To business then."

There wasn't a great deal to discuss. The man Hess was my contact. I was to find him and accidentally a'purpose bump into him. Having done so, I was to let on that I was a former pilot in Jasta 11 and had heard that there was possibly some action to be had against the communists. I could also express amazement that I had met him before and exclaim about the coincidence etc. I would also have to find a way to report to Sinclair about anything I found out. There were a number of agents being sent to Germany, as the government was quite worried. He hinted that my old chum Winterbotham was one of them[125]. I would be allowed to come back to Paris periodically to report. Victoria would understand he thought and she would be busy with the baby anyway. So all was well then.

My optimistic cheeriness didn't last long and suddenly I knew how my wife felt. I wanted to be sick. The more he talked, the more the feeling took me. The bile was rising inexorably, my face was reddening with fear and there was a real risk of evacuating my bowels unexpectedly. Like so often before, I should have run and run and not stopped. Ever. But I didn't, as usual, mainly because at the back of my mind was his throwaway line about lying low along with Sixtus' cheery warning about the French. I knew first-hand what my compatriots were capable of and I was sure that any threat to the throne, real or otherwise, would be crushed. At the same time, I did wonder how Albany had survived so long unscathed. Maybe they just liked having him where they could see him. I sat listening in mounting horror at my inescapable impending doom.

---

[125] Possible but unlikely. Winterbotham spent the immediate post war years farming in Britain, Kenya and Rhodesia.

Chapter 18

I had been in Munich about a month. Nothing whatsoever had happened. I hadn't really sought out any excitement it has to be said, but even so, given the upheaval around me, I probably ought to have seen something. However, it was difficult as I wasn't really sure how to go about my task in a safe yet heroic way. I hadn't even contacted Hess because I honestly wasn't sure how to go about that either. So, I had occupied my time, wandering the streets of Munich, occasionally going out to the airfield and flying the D.VII I had flown down in. Initially I had been very nervous about the whole thing as I had no desire to draw attention to myself. Sinclair had other ideas and had said that that was just the ticket and drawing attention by arriving in an aeroplane was precisely the way to attract Hess as a former pilot. After a month, I wasn't so sure. Fortunately, Germany being that kind of place, the two former Luftstreitkrafte personnel at the airfield who more or less ran the Munich air postal station cheerfully looked after my Fokker and I cheerfully gave them money, although what they really wanted was food and drink. Luckily I also had foreign currency and therefore access to the black market.

So it was that I was at the airfield again having nothing much to do when Klaus the mechanic appeared and muttered about someone wanting to speak to me. He waved in the general direction of the main building. I finished the disgusting coffee that mechanics everywhere seemed to drink and ambled through the bright sun over to the office.

"Leutnant Rudolf Hess[126]," he said saluting and clicking his heels.

It was so unexpected that for a moment I didn't know what to say. I more than half expected him to see straight through me and denounce me. Of course I didn't know to whom he would denounce me the war being over, but then in Germany that wasn't quite true as they had spent most of the last year fighting each other for control of the Government and with millions of trained and demobilised troops available who apparently liked fighting it would be easy enough to recruit an army for any lunatic cause. But he didn't.

---

[126] Strictly speaking he would have had no rank as he was discharged from the armed forces in December 1918.

139

"Major Fleischmann," I eventually replied returning the salute. I assumed a puzzled look for a moment. "I believe we have met before," I said feigning surprise. I scratched my arse in the traditional Flashman method of deep thought. "I have it. Douai. Early 1918." Hess looked pleased in a supplicatory way but was clearly wondering what to say now. "Would you like a spin in the D.VII?"

He nodded and smiled. If he had had a tail, I am pretty sure he would have wagged it. He followed me outside and over to the hangar where it lived. The mechanics were fiddling with something and glanced up as we approached. They just nodded when I explained and dragged it out of the hangar. I gave Hess a rudimentary lesson in the instruments, commented on what a bunch of bastards the communists were, then hopped out of the way to let him get on with it. I didn't look back as I walked away as I knew he was looking at me, but I didn't want him to think I knew. I heard the engine start and increase power as he rolled away. I stopped near the hangar doors and watched with the mechanics as he took off. The D.VII was probably the best fighter that the Germans had produced during the war and towards the end had been more or less unstoppable. I recalled seeing one, although I didn't know what it was at the time, flying almost vertically up underneath a camel who hadn't seen him and as he slowed and was 'hanging on his prop', pour a sudden burst of fire into the underside whereupon the camel caught fire and then disintegrated[127]. It was another of the reasons I had taken to sitting on a tin hat when flying, for all the good it would have done me. But now I watched as Hess did a couple of circuits and then took it up higher and threw it around a bit. He wasn't bad as far as I could tell, especially given that he had only finished training towards the end of the war, had not flown in combat and that since the wars end, flying of any kind by German pilots was thin on the ground. I left him to it and went back into the hangar where Klaus and Manfred were having an in depth political discussion.

---

[127] As Flashman says, the Fokker D.VII was almost certainly the best German fighter produced and its excellent stall characteristics meant it could indeed 'hang on its prop' for a few seconds before stalling allowing it to attack from below. The D.VII accounted for over 500 allied aircraft in the last few months of the war.

"It's no different now. They're still politicians and they're still robbing us and living the high life."

"So you want the communists back? They killed Prince Gustav and the Countess Hella von Westarp[128] and all those others."

"Well, what use were they? Where were they when we were fighting? Anyway, they executed Levine[129]."

"Well, Ebert[130] seems good to me. He says he's not going to pay the shithead French anything and they aren't going to do anything about it are they? They are already in the Rhineland and Alsace and they don't want to be there anyway. And the Freikorps would beat them. If those stupid politicians hadn't stabbed us in the back[131] we would be in Paris now with all those French girls. Their beer is rubbish of course."

I listened a little more than half-heartedly, only because I could write a report about it and send it to Sinclair. They could have been young men anywhere, berating the government and their uselessness. Mind you, much of what they said was true. 1919 had been a fun year all round but especially in Germany. I hadn't taken much notice from Paris but fortunately for me, Sinclair had filled me in at length. Extreme length. I wondered if I now knew more than the politicos themselves.

I won't bore you too much but after the armistice, Germany had fractured alarmingly into communist factions supported by and supporting the Bolsheviks in Russia, and Nationalists directly opposed to them. There had been numerous bloody battles, provisional governments, regional governments, assassinations, murders and general mayhem. It seemed to be worst in Berlin and Munich where for a time a Bavarian Soviet Republic was established. Just before the armistice, someone called Kurt Eisner[132]

---

[128] Presumably Prince Gustav of Thurn and Taxis and the Thule Society Secretary Countess Hella von Westarp.

[129] Eugen Levine was the communist party leader in Bavaria.

[130] Presumably the first President of Germany, Friedrich Ebert in office from 1919 until his death in 1925.

[131] The 'Stab in the Back' myth was propagated in Germany after the end of the war, helped by Ludendorff in particular and his criticisms of the Government and civilian population. Communists, socialists, Jews, Catholics amongst many others were seen as having other loyalties, which contributed to the surrender. It is interesting to note that 12,000 Jewish soldiers died on the two fronts.

141

of the Independent Social Democratic Party had addressed a crowd on the Theresienwiese and demanded amongst other things the abdication of the Bavarian King. Ludwig III duly obliged when the crowd marched to the local army barracks and the soldiers largely joined the crowd. Next day, Eisner declared Bavaria a free state overthrowing the 700-year-old monarchy and declaring himself Minister President of Bavaria. At this stage, he was still distancing himself from the Bolsheviks.

In February, he then contrived to lose the election. Deciding to resign, he was on his way to parliament to announce his decision when a former member of the Thule society called Anton Graf von Arco auf Valley shot him dead.

Next up was Johannes Hoffman, a social democrat who tried in true democrat style to form a coalition government. Within four weeks, this was superseded by the declaration of a soviet republic ruled by Ernst Toller and the anarchists Gustav Landauer and Silvio Gesell. Toller, being particularly foolish described it as the Bavarian revolution of love. Needless to say, six days later it was all over and the communists led by Eugen Levine took over. He immediately started to form a red army, seized the most luxurious houses and gave them to the idle poor and placed factories under the control of the workers. He took hostages because Lenin told him to and that was when Gustav and Hella were executed.

Almost exactly three weeks later, the Freikorps entered Munich in strength and fought the communists to a standstill. The dead numbered in the thousands and the Freikorps arrested hundreds and executed them on the spot. Levine was among the condemned and was shot by a firing squad in Stadelheim Prison. Eventually, everyone got tired of it all and the Deutsches Reich was born, better known as the Weimar Republic. In relative terms, it was a roaring success. As my learned friends had commented, Ebert was in fact a good leader and managed to tread the middle ground with some skill. For doing so, he was criticised and abused by both the communists

---

[132] As a journalist he joined the ISDP in 1917, was convicted of treason in 1918 for inciting a munitions worker strike and spent 9 months in cell 70 of Stadelheim Prison. After his release, he organized the revolution that overthrew the Bavarian monarchy and became the first republican Minister President. Largely due to an inability to organise even basic services, his party was defeated in the 1919 election. Eisner was shot dead on 21st February 1919.

and the nationalists but largely his government performed well, sailing a very tricky path through the Versailles problem. In the end, his loyalties were more to the right than left and his pact with Groener[133] meant he could generally rely on the army to support him, provided he did more or less what they wanted. So, after his formal swearing in on 21st August 1919, a sort of fragile peace descended[134].

"Ausgezeichnet!"

Hess was back. His face was a trifle black and it gave him the bizarre look all pilots were familiar with when he smiled and took his goggles off as his white eyes and teeth shone. I nodded in agreement, as it was a truly excellent fighting aeroplane and I was glad I had not knowingly seen any in combat.

"Shall we have some lunch?"

"Yes, that would be good."

It all seemed bizarrely formal and Hess was more than a little nervous but clearly itching to ask me something. We ate more or less in silence, no more than a few throwaway comments to lighten the mood, until with the arrival of coffee and a move upstairs to an observation room, he started talking.

"I am a member of an organisation called the Thule society. We talk mainly about theories and topics of interest but recently we have become involved in politics. Some of our members have formed the German Workers Party. I don't know how it will develop, but I am going to a meeting tonight. Would you like to accompany me?"

If I hadn't known better I would have wondered whether he was asking me on an assignation but his eyes told a different story.

"Sounds like a great idea," I replied trying to look like it was the best offer I had had all year. At the same time, I wondered again whether I should run for it. Apart from anything, I had no real interest in getting involved with another bunch of deluded non-entities. I yearned to be back in Paris. Perhaps I could go to this meeting and then use it as an excuse to report to Sinclair. Yes, that was it. My face must have shown my enthusiasm at this idea as Hess smiled suddenly and slapped me on the back exclaiming that he

---

[133] General Wilhelm Groener replaced Ludendorff shortly before the armistice.

[134] Flashman's summary of the chaos just after the armistice and the deadly civil strife is accurate.

would meet me at the Hofbrauhaus[135] at seven o'clock. We stood up, shook hands and he left.

******

I arrived early and waited outside the old building. Surprisingly I was quite looking forward to the evening. I hadn't tried the famous beer before and maybe the idea that I would shortly be leaving for Paris had cheered me up. Whatever it was, I was feeling decidedly chirpy. Hess bowled up slightly late and we went in. The meeting was being held on the third floor in the Festsaal. By the time we went in and found some seats, the first speaker was already in full flow and riveting stuff it was too. It sounded much like how I imagined a debate in the House of Lords would be, shockingly dull as a bunch of old men discussed the latest increase in the cost of keeping poor people in the manner to which they were accustomed and what should be done about it if anything. Hess apologised for the speaker and said that he expected the next one to be more interesting. I didn't particularly care because I had a large stein in my hands and there seemed to be plenty of food. More importantly, the waitresses were of the buxom Bavarian type that I had had dreams about and I was idly wondering how to go about the conquest of one of them. Hess interrupted my daydreaming by shaking my shoulder.

"There is someone you should meet," he said before suddenly standing up and manhandling me towards the front of the room. "Dietrich," he called above the clamour.

"Ah, Rudolf," a voice said. A round faced man with a moustache and a dimpled chin who must have been about fifty appeared. "I see you have brought a friend?"

Hess laughed. "This is Major Heinrich Fleischmann," he said glancing at me. I glanced away like an idiot before looking back in horror that they might have noticed my mistake. Fortunately, it was only me that was suspicious and we shook hands.

---

[135] The Hofbrauhaus am Platzl was founded in 1589 by the Duke of Bavaria and is one of Munich's oldest beer halls, originally being the brewery to the old royal residence.

"Dietrich Eckart[136]," he replied. "Ignore this fool," he said gesturing at the man on the stage[137]. "We will soon be rid of him. I understand you don't like communists, Herr Major?"

"Scum," I said without thinking about it.

"Yes," he replied pausing. "Rudolf has told you of our society I think. But, he needs to think bigger. Hence why we are here tonight. Thule has its place but it was no more than talk really. This, however, this is real. There will be an announcement tonight that will influence the course of history in Germany." If he hadn't sounded so serious I would have dismissed him as one of the crackpots that infested speakers corner.

Suddenly, the room went quiet. It was odd really, as there must have been at least a thousand people there. An average size man walked slowly onto the stage and stood perfectly still for a few seconds looking down. I took a gulp of beer and looked around me. Virtually everyone was looking at him and those that weren't, slowly got the message. A voice spoke, almost inaudibly, from the front of the room. I couldn't hear exactly what was said but it was something about Versailles and it triggered murmurs of approval, quickly hushed with vicious glances, not because they disagreed but because they wanted to hear what was next.

"We all know the war was not lost by us, the foot soldiers. We all know it was the November criminals, the socialists, the communists, the Jews that stabbed us in the back, denying us the means to fight with their strikes and betrayal. We had them beaten, we had Russia under our boots, it was only a matter of time before we would win in the west. But no." At this point, there was what I can only describe as a collective groan, an exhalation by hundreds of men who had stopped breathing whilst they listened enthralled by the magnetic appeal of the man on the stage. "Versailles," he whispered. "The ultimate disgrace. However, tonight is the beginning. The beginning of the reversal of that cowardice." Just for a second I wanted to call out, "I was there, I saw them the cowards," but I didn't, not least

---

[136] This must be Johann Dietrich Eckart, born 1868, journalist and politician and with Drexler, Harrer and Feder a founder member of the Deutsche Arbeiterpartei.

[137] This is probably Dr Johannes Dingfelder, an odd homeopathic physician who was known for contributing economic articles to newspapers under a pseudonym, 'Germanus Agricola'.

because I would have had some explaining to do. "We of the Deutsche Arbeiterpartei, no, no longer, we of the Nationalsozialistische Deutsche Arbeiterpartei, we are the saviours, we are the retribution, we will destroy these cowards, we will destroy their treaties, we will march on until we are masters of our own destiny once again."

There was a pause while everyone breathed out again and then there was a roar. It was mayhem. The noise was deafening. Through it all, I could see from our position at the side of the room onto the stage where the speaker looked exhausted and on the point of collapse. He looked up, almost as if he had only just realised the crowd was there, and acknowledged their cheers with a raised hand which only intensified the noise. Quiet descended at last.

"We have a program to rebuild Germany, to rebuild the Reich. First, we demand the unification of all Germans in Greater Germany on the basis of the people's right to self-determination. We demand equality of rights for the German people in respect to the other nations; abrogation of the peace treaties of Versailles and St Germain[138]."

He went on like this for some time. A lot of it sounded entirely rational although a fair amount of it was equally quite mad. He clearly didn't like the Jews very much although across Europe that wasn't an entirely new phenomenon. But, whatever I thought, the crowd lapped it up and by the time he finished, the noise was more deafening than ever[139].

More importantly, while all this was going on it had been nigh on impossible to replenish my stein. The waitresses were all equally taken by the show, but as soon as it finished I managed to catch the eye of one of them. She came over, all Bavarian buxom beauty, and I ordered more food and drink. It was thirsty work I can assure you. Keeping my eye firmly on the developing situation I managed to pay her and pinch her backside at the same time, earning myself a

---

[138] The Treaty of Saint-Germain-en-Laye was signed on 10th September 1919 and dissolved the remains of the Austro-Hungarian empire. It created the Republic of Austria and recognized the independence of Hungary, Czechoslovakia, Poland and the Kingdom of the Serbs, Croats and Slovenes.

[139] This must be one of Hitler's first speeches to a large audience, made on 24th February 1920 when he spelt out the 25 point program that would remain party policy. See appendix.

reproachful look as she walked away. Luckily, I saw her glance back and winked at her at which she smiled. I resolved to make sure I bumped into her later on. It's the small things that turn history of course. I have said it before, but politicians and royalty like to think it is their statesmanship and cleverness that shape the world and the future, whereas you and I know it is the chance meeting, missing the bus, taking the wrong train, tripping over the stairs, pinching a woman's bum that sends fate reeling into the dark spreading fame, glory and woe in equal measure. And had I not pinched her bum... well, we might have averted another war. But I didn't know that. Had I known it of course, I would have done exactly the same thing and hoped for the best because it was glorious...

"We must go," a voice said in my ear.

"No, why, where...." I tailed off.

"We have a meeting which I think.... I think you will enjoy." Hess grinned at me. For a moment, a very short moment I assure you, I thought he had arranged some behind the scenes entertainment and I wondered if I could just take a moment to go and find my big bummed beauty. But no, it wasn't that exciting. Apparently we were going to meet the speaker who had had the audience enthralled. I could think of much better things to do.

Eckart was leading and beckoned us up some stairs. At the top, he knocked on a door, which opened instantly to reveal a large gorilla in what I imagine was a Freikorps uniform. He surveyed us briefly with a lingering stare at me, presumably because I was unknown, and then allowed us into the room. There were a few others there, none that I can recall clearly because there was only one who attracted attention. He was standing surrounded by uniformed men. They all had a sort of hangdog expression and were clearly enthralled by his every word. I listened for a few seconds and realised it was the same stuff he had been spouting to the crowd, but oddly, I was equally transfixed. I suddenly realised, mentally shook myself and looked around at the others. It suddenly occurred to me they all thought it was like the second coming, which was strange given my ancestry. He paused at last and I suddenly found myself being thrust forward beside Hess who was introducing himself.

"This is my friend, Major Fleischmann late of the Luftstreitkrafte like me. He flew with Richtofen in Jagdgeschwader 1 and also escaped from prison in England." I squirmed. "Honoured to meet

147

you," he said looking like he didn't really mean it. "My name is Hitler, Adolf Hitler."

# Chapter 19

Of course, it meant nothing to me then. He wasn't particularly striking, not least because he was about four inches shorter than me[140], in fact he was more odd looking with a curious moustache and slicked back hair. But, there was that magnetism that drew in the unwary and imprisoned them. I shook his hand and he held my gaze for a moment.

"So, what did you make of our plans? Hess here says you are a Thule?" I shivered involuntarily, not because of the question but because I had seen those eyes before, the eyes of the fanatic. He'd get on well with Goering. As for his plans, I hadn't really given them much thought to be honest but I wasn't about to say that.

"Those bastards stabbed us in the back once, how do we know they won't do it again?"

He wasn't expecting that, but equally he wasn't thrown easily.

"They could. But once we have rid society of the Jews and Bolsheviks and their influence, the country will pull together as one."

"What about the French? And the British?"

"The French are weak and contemptible. They will return to their old laziness believing themselves to be safe behind their borders. The British? They will be on our side if we manage it correctly."

I gave in, nodding sagely at the delusions of a man with a thousand supporters in a beer hall before drifting away leaving him to talk to Hess and the others. I watched them all intensely discussing their theories. They wanted someone to blame apart from themselves and there were numerous convenient targets, all a convenient distance away and unlikely to concern themselves with a nationalist party meeting in Bavaria. Once I felt I had enough material to fill out my report to Sinclair, I slid quietly out through the door. There was less noise now but the party, such as it was, was still in full swing. I needed sustenance and sustenance was what I intended to get one way or another. Grabbing a passing stein I circled the room slowly avoiding catching anyone's eye, not that it would have mattered as the majority were past caring having made the most of the refreshments available. I spotted her suddenly at the

---

[140] Adolf Hitler was 5' 8" tall which was the average male height in 1920.

top of the stairs near some curtains. I stared up at her for a moment and almost as if she felt my eyes, she looked down. She winked almost imperceptibly and I mounted the stairs while she waited at the top, one hand on hip. As I reached her, she turned and went through the curtains. I hesitated for a second, just that tiny nagging feeling that something was wrong but decided to hell with it, it was just my ridiculously oversensitive nose for mischief developed from years of trying to avoid it.

It was oddly quiet and oddly dark behind the thick curtains and for a moment, I couldn't see a thing. My eyes were still adjusting when I felt two arms encircle my waist from behind. I was about to turn when I was suddenly lifted off the floor and propelled across the room at some speed. The bile rose instantly as I realised my instincts were right and I was about to scream when I was dumped bodily onto something soft. Winded for a moment I lay face down before someone grabbed me again and turned me over. Before I could move, something soft landed on my face and slowly began to suffocate me. I wanted to scream but in my struggle for breath, I couldn't. I heard a panting noise from above me. I gasped as my assailant moved whatever was on my face and I sucked in air before I was buried again. The panting was getting louder and all of a sudden I realised there was a lot of fumbling going on in my nether regions which in my panic I hadn't noticed. I opened my mouth and found it full of the biggest tits I had ever seen, although technically I still hadn't actually seen them. The realisation of what was going on was a relief I find it hard even now to describe but relief it was and I immediately got to grips with the situation, so to speak. She had somehow, in the few seconds available, completely disrobed and her wandering hands had more or less done the same for me so before I did in fact suffocate I took a more forthright stance and impaled her from below, and in so doing, she reared up freeing me from a slow but ecstatic death. It was only mere seconds before it was all over and she collapsed on me again, pinning me to whatever I was on although this time I had the presence of mind to look to one side.

My breathing slowed as did hers.

"Later," she puffed still slightly out of breath, "we do it again."

With that statement ringing in my ear, she was up and away. I saw the curtains twitch, a brief beam of light and I was alone. I lay still until I started to feel cold. Then I stood up, adjusted my apparel and walked over to where the curtains led back to the real world. There was a small gap and I peeped through. The crowd had thinned somewhat so I had to wait a little while for a suitable opportunity to slip back in unnoticed. Having done so I realised I was thirsty and hungry again. I went back down to the main hall area, found an empty small table with my back to the wall and ordered a schweinshaxe and more beer. There was no sign of my voluptuous lovely, not that I was in a fit state for more bedroom wrestling just yet, but the thought appealed. After all, it made the evening out worthwhile. Plus, as I have mentioned I believe, she had the most gorgeous, enormous breasts, which is probably the best reason for doing anything, just not the most sensible.

I watched the people around me for some time. I could have been anywhere really. I caught snippets of conversation, all of which were trivial and not likely to set the world on fire. It was late now and only the faithful remained. I had seen Hess and promised to join him next day to hand out leaflets to the masses, mainly so he would go away and leave me alone. I had almost given up my wait when she appeared. Without a word, I got up and we left. We walked for ten minutes I guessed before we came to a block of apartments. She unlocked the door, glancing at me with what I can only describe as a lascivious look on her face, led me upstairs and almost before we had got in she was tearing at my clothes.

Well, I had met them before of course but usually one was required to pay and even then, that didn't guarantee enjoyment by both parties. Personally, I preferred the trollops who at least seemed to get some enjoyment from their work. Generally, that meant expensive. Here we clearly had a trollop who just enjoyed it. I was all for it myself.

\*\*\*\*\*\*

I didn't get to sleep much before first light. When I woke, it must have been near midday. She had vanished but I could smell coffee and hear singing from somewhere. I got up to investigate and found her in a small kitchen clad only in a thin robe of some kind. She briefly tried to fight me off but I wasn't having that and we conducted the business on the kitchen table. There was a crash as something slipped off and shattered but she didn't seem to care and nor did I. It was all very jolly.

I discovered her name was Helga Rohm and she was clearly as mad as a hatter. She had a younger brother apparently who had been in the army, not unusual of course, but had then stayed in the Reichswehr[141] before joining Von Epp's Freikorps unit[142]. He had then got himself involved in politics by joining the German Workers Party and had been at last night's meeting to hear the speeches. She enquired whether I had met the star of the show Adolf and I admitted I had in fact been backstage to meet him, which seemed to impress her no end. Luckily for me, being impressed meant she quickly got excited again and dragged me back to the bedroom for another exhausting bout.

When I finally got up again I felt a mere shadow of my former self. I could barely stand but amid protests that she would have to go to work soon, I took my leave. At this point, my rendezvous with Hess seemed slightly more appealing and I set off to meet him in the main square near the Ratskeller[143]. He seemed inordinately pleased to see me and explained excitedly that Adolf was his new best friend and they were going to take over the world, just like Karl had explained.[144] I nodded thinking again how gullible they were but just the right stuff for me to write about at length for Sinclair. There and then I decided to stay another couple of weeks to investigate further and make sure I had everything tip top and Bristol fashion. Of course, I might be able to see Helga again but my work would come first, naturally.

So it was I spent a jolly time peddling propaganda for Hess and his chums, occasionally from the back of a lorry waving a hastily completed flag that was Hitler's idea. It was quite striking really and apparently incorporated the old imperial colours of red white and

---

[141] The Reichswehr was the official name for the German army from 1919 until 1935.

[142] Generalmajor Franz Xaver Ritter von Epp was a career soldier, serving in East Asia during the Boxer rebellion as well as in German Southwest Africa. He commanded a Bavarian Regiment during the Great War and then formed a Freikorps unit which took part in the suppression of the Bavarian Soviet Republic. He was promoted to Generalmajor in the Freikorps in 1922.

[143] Presumably the restaurant in Marienplatz beneath the Neues Rathaus.

[144] Presumably Haushofer.

black with the swastika symbol in the middle. No one was afraid of it then.

Once I had finished my chores, I popped round to the Hofbrauhaus most evenings, sat at the same table until they chucked the drunks out and then waited for Helga. She was a true nymphomaniac, maybe the only one I have ever met. Sometimes, she was so desperate we had to rush upstairs behind the curtains but generally, she managed to contain herself until we got back to her apartment. She never seemed to tire despite the ever more exotic positions we found ourselves in, so much so that I had to invent the occasional excuse not to come round. Luckily, she was so taken with Hess and friends that I only had to mention party business and she virtually shoved me out of the door. Quite how she quelled her appetite on those occasions I didn't like to ask and probably didn't want to know.

It was as I was pondering when exactly to take my leave of all of them and return to visit my beloved in Paris that the Gods gave me a small poke.

Chapter 20

I was mooching about the airfield aimlessly. Klaus and Manfred were trying to fix a problem with my D.VII that was defying all their efforts. I was beginning to get a little impatient for various reasons. I was sick of hearing about plans for 'lebensraum' as Hess called it but I had to endure it, as it was in theory at least my job to listen. Also, Helga was becoming more of a burden than a joy and I needed a break. Paris was the ideal answer but instead I had concocted a story about some family business to deal with in Liege that I hadn't dealt with when we were last there. Hess had nodded and returned to his second favourite subject and I realised he didn't care and apparently nor did anyone else. It was only a matter of getting away but now the blasted aeroplane had decided not to perform.

I was having one of Klaus's appalling coffees again when there was a commotion outside. Vehicle brakes squealed, doors slammed and then there was a loud conversation outside the biggest remaining hangar, which also contained the biggest remaining serviceable aeroplane.

"You must be joking. There aren't any pilots here. You should have brought your own…. hang on though."

Of course, with the benefit of hindsight you wouldn't have seen me for dust, just a fast diminishing shadow disappearing into the woods. Maybe it was the lack of war and danger, maybe boredom, maybe the unconscious desire to get away from Munich for a while and frustration with the D.VII, all combined that had me ambling outside to see what was what. And what it was, was Manfred glancing my way having remembered I was there and pointing to me. The men in front of him turned to me as well. I stopped dead.

"Herr Major," Adolf said, "I, or rather we," gesturing to Eckart who was with him, "need to get to Berlin. Now. Flying is the quickest and best way and I believe there is a serviceable aeroplane in that hangar. I just need someone to fly it."[145]

---

[145] It is generally claimed that the pilot who flew Hitler to Berlin was Generalfeldmarschall Robert Ritter von Greim, a former fighter pilot who briefly succeeded Goering as commander of the Luftwaffe. At this time, he ran the air postal station at Munich. If Flashman is correct, it is possible that Greim, as a committed Nazi in later years, was added to the story later for effect.

Transfixed describes my demeanour perfectly. As far as he was concerned, I was just a minion but at this moment, I was a very useful minion for whatever he had in mind. My personal alarm bells were ringing but they were drowned out by my desire to leave.

"I can fly you. I need to go on to Liege but I will find you a pilot to get you back before I leave. Does that suit? Of course I will need Manfred here to come with me."

Adolf looked at Manfred and he grinned in agreement. I think he thought it would be a bit of an adventure, something that he clearly lacked in his life judging by his yearning for the good old days of the war. Adolf nodded, Manfred shouted for Klaus and the operation got underway. We opened the hangar doors to reveal the great beast. It was a Fokker F II. It hadn't flown very often recently but in Manfred and Klaus it had had two loving guardians who had kept it pretty much in working order. In no time at all, they had hooked up their tractor and towed it out into the open. They were all over it, checking, testing, making sure while I clambered into the cockpit and tried to familiarise myself. It was at that moment that the enormity of what I was about to do started to hit me. I had never flown something this size before although I was pretty sure the principles were the same. If I could find something that gave me an idea of the appropriate speeds for take-off and landing I would be a lot happier. I was beginning to regret my hastiness when I caught my coat on a corner of a side panel and pulled it off. Hidden behind in a large pocket was the bible. At least, it was the bible I needed with all the relevant figures. I breathed an inward sigh of relief. Manfred seeing the look of relief on my face said, "there's nothing to worry about, she's as strong as an ox." Clearly, he had misunderstood my worry.

Klaus appeared. "I have given you all the fuel I can spare but I think you may not have quite enough." He smiled. I looked at the fuel tank gauge and it was no more than half-full at best. It didn't matter. I was leaving Munich for the moment.

The passengers climbed aboard and Klaus closed the door. Keeping a sharp eye on him from the side window he waved that he was ready for me to start the engine. I pushed and pulled and poked at the array of switches in front of me, held my breath, signalled for him to turn the prop thereby priming the engine and waited. It took a few moments but as suddenly as always, the engine burst into life and I was waving Klaus away. As he dragged the chocks out, we started to trundle forward. I made sure we were well clear of the hangar and other buildings and objects before turning towards the end of the field. It took us no more than a couple of minutes before we were in position. I ran the engine up, checked the mags and took a deep breath. I glanced back into the gloom behind me. I could make out the three figures. Manfred and Eckart were deep in conversation, Manfred smiling just for the pleasure of flying again. Adolf seemed to be gripping the seat in fear and staring woodenly out of the tiny window, gulping occasionally at the admittedly rank air inside. I hadn't appreciated that this was the first time he had flown in an aeroplane. Not that I had asked or particularly cared.

I opened the throttle slowly and the noise seemed to increase exponentially. I couldn't hear anything other than the engine but the racket further back must have been appalling. We accelerated slowly across the field. It was very different to a fighter. I tentatively pushed the nose forward to lift the tail and it slowly rose until I was balancing two tons on two tyres[146]. As the speed neared 70kmh I felt it start to lift. There was a bounce, a graze over the grass, another bounce and we were airborne again. Once we were away from the ground it seemed to climb quickly for something so big, astonishingly so although when I thought about it, it made sense as we weren't really carrying the sort of load it had been designed for. Once we were above a thousand feet, I turned slowly to the north and set our course. I hadn't planned on climbing very high as the weather wasn't particularly good and I wasn't particularly familiar with flying across Germany.

Once we had settled into the cruise, Manfred came and joined me in the open cockpit. The first hour or so was uneventful, at least from my point of view. On the other hand, it was torture for one of the passengers. Eckart was gazing down at the country slipping by underneath but Adolf was groaning, or at least he looked like he was groaning because I couldn't hear him, and then every so often he would throw up into a bag. Clearly, flying didn't agree with him although to be fair the weather was awful.[147]

---

[146] The Fokker FII had an empty weight of 1.2 metric tonnes with a gross weight of 1.9.

[147] This was Hitler's first flight and he was airsick although that was not

We had passed east of Frankfurt when I started to wonder about the fuel. I had checked it and Manfred had checked it and we had both come to the same conclusion. We didn't have enough. It was close, but we were going to end up short of our destination.

"Juterbog," he yelled over the racket. "It's an airfield," he shouted in response to my puzzled look, pointing out of the side window. I saw what he meant and immediately started descending towards the field.

"You'd better tell them," I said gesturing towards the passengers. When he came back he was laughing.

"You should see the short one. He says it is a disguise in case there are any communists around."

I turned round to see what he meant. I couldn't believe my eyes. Adolf had transformed himself. Using just a goatee beard, he looked like himself wearing a goatee beard. It wouldn't have deceived a child. I was so incredulous I didn't even laugh and clearly friend Adolf didn't find it funny anyway.

We were approaching the field now and Manfred re-joined me just before we landed. Once we were down, I slowed down and then rolled over to where there were some buildings and some seedy looking characters.

"Leftists," a voice said quietly in my ear as the engine stopped its hellish clattering. I shut everything off that I could recognise and looked out of the window. The 'leftists' looked just like normal people to me. Of course, I had not knowingly seen any before so wasn't entirely sure what they should look like. I noticed that there was the odd red flag dotted about which confirmed who was in charge at least. Maybe I would need a disguise. If it hadn't been so serious it would have been funny in a mad way.

Manfred and I clambered out of the craft and walked towards the office with the biggest flag on. Just behind us came the Marx brothers in their comedy suits. No one gave any of us a second glance, least of all Groucho and Harpo, at least until they started talking loudly about getting to Berlin. They both looked nervous to me, and when another comedy duo confronted us and started asking awkward questions about what we were up to and why we were there, their nerves started to affect me and I began regretting getting

---

unusual.

157

involved just to get away from Helga and her insatiable appetite. I wondered briefly and irrelevantly who was currently filling my boots as I had no doubt at all that she wouldn't be waiting demurely for my return.

"I'm his accountant," I heard Adolf say.

After I had finished my fit of strangled coughing and pulled myself together, I re-joined the conversation. It was so ludicrous they could have been briefed by Buchan.

"Here are my papers," Eckart continued. There was a lot of shuffling and peering.

"What does this company do?"

"We make paper for many purposes. Not money though, that is a specialist trade."

Fatty and Buster[148] conferred for a while.

"We will have to check with our superior." They smirked in our direction as they walked away in much the same way I smirked at the fags as they received a beating that I had caused. Not that that helped my now seriously jangling nerves. I cursed myself for a fool. Why couldn't I see when I was well off? Rogering Helga was exhausting but the only real danger was wearing my pecker off.

"Let's see if we can find some fuel," said Manfred from behind me. He didn't look quite so excited about our adventure now but at least his suggestion gave us something to do and take my mind off some of the less savoury outcomes. We turned and ambled towards the fuel dump. There wasn't much in it, which was a little worrying, and the gate was locked. There was a hut beside it with the door open so Manfred stuck his head in to see if there were any keys. Instead, he found a boy looking ridiculous in a sort of uniform that was far too big for him.

"Can we get some fuel?" The boy looked startled.

"You have to have an order," he stuttered, now looking if anything more terrified.

"Well, where do we get one of those?"

"Sometimes I can do it." I groaned. "Sometimes I have to wait for the Colonel to do it." I groaned again.

"Which is it today?"

---

[148] Presumably Fatty Arbuckle and Buster Keaton who were probably one of the most famous comedy acts of the time.

"It depends."

"On what?" Manfred was beginning to look dangerous as he slowly edged towards the boy.

"On how much you want," the boy replied retreating slowly.

"Well we don't want much. Just enough to get us to Berlin for the moment."

The boy grinned suddenly. "I can do that," he said, grabbing a sheet of paper from a shelf behind him. He started writing on it. "Who is it for?"

Manfred looked blank. Luckily, having a nose for trouble although apparently unable to avoid it, I had taken the precaution of quizzing Eckart about precisely that kind of thing. I don't know why, because I had no knowledge of what he and Hitler were doing going to Berlin, or indeed what was in fact going on in Berlin. It's unlikely that you would have heard of what was going on, especially now, long after the events, but they were important in a small way and played their part in shaping the terrible future of Europe. Of course had I known any of that I would have been on the next flight out to somewhere safe. Like Australia. Or the moon.

Y'see, Germany was still in turmoil. Weimar, as I believe I have mentioned already, was a relatively successful coalition. But like all coalitions, it was damned from the start not least because the Versailles treaty seemed to be extraordinarily harsh to the average man and so the extreme left and right of politics in Germany revived and made a great show of wanting to right the wrongs done by the allies. Of course, what they really wanted was another fight, as long as there was someone else around to do the actual fighting, a bit of power and all that goes with it, wine, women, song, a big flag, grand houses and invites to the most fashionable parties. Being on opposite sides of the spectrum they clashed spectacularly and violently, frequently killing each other in the name of peace but the Weimar Government and Reichs President Friedrich Ebert survived. Until now that is. And Berlin was where the action was and that was precisely where I was heading. Unbeknownst to me, a Korvettenkapitan called Hermann Ehrhardt[149], commander of one of

---

[149] Ehrhardt served throughout the war in the Imperial Navy. He was at Jutland and finished the war as a Torpedo Boat Flotilla commander. He formed the 6000 strong Marine Brigade of the Freikorps at the end of the war.

the most powerful Freikorps units generally known by his name, had refused an order to disband and held a parade instead where the highest-ranking army general, Walther Von Luttwitz[150] had agreed.

Noske[151], the defence minister then removed Ehrhardt's brigade from Luttwitz's command. Luttwitz ignored this and instead agreed to meet Chancellor Ebert where he demanded the dissolution of the government, new elections and of course his appointment as supreme military commander. Ebert and Noske unsurprisingly rejected all this and demanded his resignation instead.

Luttwitz didn't resign. He contacted Ehrhardt and together they decided to take Berlin by force. At this point, he also decided to bring Ludendorff and Kapp[152] into the conspiracy.

At ten o'clock in the evening of the 12th March, Ehrhardt's troops started to march on Berlin. The chancellor called a cabinet meeting. Two decisions were made. One was to call a general strike. The second was to run away and at six in the morning, they did just that, ten minutes ahead of the arrival of the Marine Brigade at the Brandenburg Gate. There they met Luttwitz, Ludendorff and Kapp who then declared himself the new Chancellor and formed a government. Two other important things happened. In Bavaria, the Reichswehr kicked out the social democrat state government and replaced it with a right wing gang led by Gustav Ritter Von Kahr.[153] And across Germany, twelve million people went on strike.

"It's alright," I said. "We are carrying leaflets for the KPD[154], but don't tell anyone."

---

[150] Walther Von Luttwitz served throughout the war in various high-ranking positions. Following the armistice, he was appointed C-in-c of the Berlin area including the Freikorps whom he used to suppress the so called 'spartakus uprising'. In 1919, he was appointed supreme commander of all troops in the Reich.

[151] Gustav Noske, controversial Social Democratic politician elected to the German Parliament in 1906.

[152] Wolfgang Kapp was a Prussian civil servant as well as a nationalist and as such involved with numerous right wing organisations.

[153] Kahr was a lawyer involved with right wing politics although never affiliated to any particular party. He was briefly head of the Upper Bavarian provincial government, was removed during the German revolution in 1918 before succeeding Hoffmann as Bavarian Prime Minister in March 1920.

[154] Communist Party of Germany.

The boy grinned, nodded and winked before hurrying out with a key and opening the gate. Quickly we started loading fuel cans onto a cart. We didn't need a great deal but even that small amount seemed bloody heavy. Convinced we had enough, we started dragging it towards the aeroplane. There was no sign of Eckart and Hitler and for a long moment, I wondered what had happened to them. Not that there was anything I could do about it. Sweating with exertion and an icy lick of fear, we started pouring the fuel into the tank. It didn't take long and was only about a third full when we had finished but it would be enough to get to Berlin. However, only now did it occur to me that it might not be so easy to get out of Berlin if there was something up, and all my senses were telling me that something was indeed up.

Right on cue, Eckart and Hitler appeared. Eckart was smiling. He glanced around as he approached the aeroplane and then muttered, "Fools, all of them. I told them I was a paper manufacturer and was going to Berlin to see the leftists about providing paper for their propaganda. We have appropriate identification of course, but it is false as you know. They swallowed it. If they ever cross my path again, I will have them shot." He laughed aloud at this. Hitler said nothing, mainly because he was looking green at the thought of getting back in the aeroplane.

We took off, Hitler vomiting into a sack and climbed to about two thousand feet. The weather had cleared a little and very quickly we could see the city and then Tempelhof[155]. We landed, turned the engines off and clambered out. It seemed inordinately quiet. We walked into the main building. There was a man at a desk who looked up as we entered. He waited until we approached then got up to greet us. At least he seemed civilised.

"There's no one here. They are all on strike. I am here because I had nothing else to do."

"On strike," Hitler squawked throwing his head back.

"Yes. There are no trains or buses but I can drive you into town if you would like. As I said, I have nothing to do."

Realising that here was a favour he couldn't pass up, Hitler assumed a more conciliatory tone.

---

[155] Tempelhof was officially designated as an airport in October 1923.

161

"Yes, that would be useful. We need to get to the Reich Chancellery[156]."

I thought for a minute I had misheard, but I hadn't. Yet again, I wondered how and why I was selected for these things. What the hell were they doing? It was like arriving in London and asking for the Houses of Parliament.

"Let's go," Eckart said.

Without really making a conscious decision, I got into the car with the others and we set off. The streets were deserted although oddly there was rubbish everywhere. But as we got closer to the centre of the city, we started seeing troops. Eventually, we came up against a roadblock. Eckart and Hitler got out and walked up to the barrier, at which point an armed officer approached them looking menacing. I made myself as small as possible in the back of the car and started looking around for escape routes. There weren't any of course and if the shooting started it would have been pointless anyway.

Suddenly the barrier was moved away, they got back in the car, both grinning, and we drove on. The streets were getting busier and busier now, crammed with soldiers and a few civilians but none of them gave us more than a second glance. Quite what they thought was unfathomable. Equally unfathomable, to me anyway, was how we were able to pass through unmolested. It was also somewhat worrying.

In the distance, I caught my first glimpse of the Brandenburger Tor. As we approached, it was clear it was heavily guarded but again, this wasn't a problem and we passed through the crowds of troops and stopped near the Chancellery. We got out and followed as Eckart and Hitler made their way into the building. We were intercepted and shown into a small room where we waited.

Not for long. The door opened and a round faced moustachioed man entered. He announced himself as Ignaz Trebitsch-Lincoln[157], which was the most unlikely name I had ever heard. He looked terrified.

---

[156] Formerly the palace of Prince Radziwill, the Chancellery building was acquired in 1869 and refurbished opening in 1878 for the Berlin Congress.

[157] This can only be Ignatius Timothy Trebitsch-Lincoln, a Hungarian con-man who led a bizarre yet fascinating life. See appendix.

"You are too late, it is all over, a fiasco. Kapp has resigned. Luttwitz is holding out but he will have to go too."

It dawned on me at last. Somehow, entirely against my will, I was involved in a plot to take over Germany. I wasn't entirely sure who all these people were and what they were doing, but what I was sure of was that they were all a danger to me. And that was not good news. The difficulty was going to be how to extract myself with a whole skin and preferably soon.

"Scheisse," exclaimed Eckart. "What is going on then?"

"They are negotiating. But who knows where that will end?"

"Who the hell are they negotiating with and what for? I thought the idea was to get rid of these Weimar fools."

"Vice Chancellor Schiffer.[158]"

"That useless bastard. A lot of good that will do them."

I heard a door open somewhere and looked around for somewhere to hide. There was nowhere. I wanted to scream and run but I couldn't do either. I remained, frozen to the spot. I heard quick footsteps approaching and my heart climbed into my mouth, accelerating as it did so whilst my largely non-existent lunch prepared to go the other way. The door was flung open and as I recoiled, I barged into Adolf who gave me a vicious stare. Apparently I was the only one who could sense doom approaching. The new arrival was at least known to Ignaz who greeted him with a rictus grin.

"What is the latest news?"

"They are fighting in the Ruhr."

"Who's fighting in the Ruhr?" asked Ignaz with a puzzled look.

"The Communists of course. They have formed an army and taken Dortmund. They have killed hundreds."

"Where…. How….But…. ?"

They were good questions but no one knew the answers to them so consequently, there was a lot of talking, most of which was pointless, and there was a lot of grand gesturing, all of which was pointless. No one knew where this 'army' had come from but over the next couple of hours it became clear there was a crisis developing in the west. Worse, there was a local crisis developing. It

---

[158] Presumably Eugen Schiffer, career lawyer and politician, at this time Minister of Finance and deputy to Philipp Scheidemann.

had become increasingly clear that having provided the means to get to Berlin, I was now considered as part of the staff by Eckart at least. Hitler didn't appear to be so sure. Maybe he recognised a wrong'un when he saw one. Either way, my plan of vanishing at the most opportune moment seemed in serious jeopardy. And in fact, I wasn't now quite so sure that that was the best plan anyway. Whichever way I turned there seemed to be obstacles to absconding successfully. As usual in these cases, I dithered hoping that divine intervention would provide the answer. If you are familiar with my history, you will know that that had never been a useful hope. Still, there was always a first time.

Eckart had disappeared for an hour or so mid-afternoon, leaving me gnawing my fists and trying to look interested. I had at least stopped jumping every time the door opened. I was devouring a dull sandwich and some truly awful coffee when the door opened again shortly after Eckart had returned to my relief.

"Ah, Luttwitz," Eckart said at this new arrival. They shook hands solemnly. Luttwitz looked like he was about to cry.

"I will resign tomorrow. We have failed. The military have not supported us, even though they said they would."

"Is there anything useful?"

"They are going to hold elections. And I retain my full pension rights[159]."

If I hadn't heard it myself I would have assumed they had taken leave of their senses.

"Well that's something."

"Schiffer says Ebert is going to ask Von Seeckt[160] to return to the Reichswehr. Sounds like they are going to need him as well!"

This seemed to conclude the political conversation. No one bothered to introduce me and largely I was ignored to all intents and

---

[159] This is bizarrely true albeit Flashman has the events slightly out of order in that Luttwitz was only offered his full pension when he resigned the next day (18th March – Kapp resigned on the 17th) having briefly attempted to form a military dictatorship.

[160] Johannes Friedrich von Seeckt was a career officer having followed his father into the Army. He served throughout the war notably as Chief of Staff to von Mackensen on the Eastern Front. Following Versailles, he was appointed to organise and head the Reichswehr.

purposes. Afternoon dragged on into evening, Luttwitz finally left, and the question of where we were going to go now surfaced.

"I have many friends and contacts in Berlin," Eckart announced. "They will keep us for the moment. We can be tourists!" He chuckled at this. I wondered again if any of them were quite the ticket and concluding that they weren't, yet again set to wondering how to escape this mess. But for now I had to stay with them as not only did I have nowhere to go, it did in fact seem like the safest option, their deluded ramblings notwithstanding.

We left the Chancellery through some sort of tradesman's entrance. Somehow, Eckart had managed to acquire some transport and we set off into the fast descending gloom. For some reason I was sitting in the front with the driver, which was the only reason I noticed the roundabout route we took. In fact, we passed over the Charlottenburger Chaussee[161] at least twice. At last, we pulled up to a dark gate. The driver got out and disappeared into the shadows. I heard a creaking, and the gates swung back. The driver reappeared, got into the car and we drove through and on up a driveway to a very dark house. We stopped outside the door, which opened almost immediately letting some light onto the scene. The car doors opened and we all got out. A man appeared in the doorway.

"Erich," exclaimed Eckart. There was a grunt from the door. Eckart strode forward followed by Trebitsch-Lincoln. Hitler hung back and so did I until Eckart turned round and beckoned us forward. For a moment, a long moment, I was completely and utterly lost for words. Of all the things that had happened in the last few days, this was up there with the wildest.

"Hitler, Fleischmann, I should like you to meet an old friend of mine. Herr General Erich Ludendorff."

---

[161] Now known as the 'Strasse des 17. Juni'.

165

# Chapter 21

I fought hard to suppress a snort of derision. Here was I, Harry Flashman, late of the Royal Flying Corps and Royal Air Force, cavorting round Germany about to meet the supreme architect of the war itself[162]. If he couldn't protect me, who could? That assumed of course that he wanted to protect a bunch of unannounced visitors who had apparently been conspiring to overthrow the government. On first meeting he didn't seem to care either way which was a little disconcerting but at least he let us stay. Refreshments were found and we retired to a well-furnished room with a fire going. It was all very cosy. It soon became apparent that Eckart, Hitler and Ludendorff were getting deep into a political discussion to which Ignaz and I were not party. I suggested we clear off and leave them to it to which he readily agreed. I announced this to the crazy gang[163] and Ludendorff rang a bell. A servant appeared and escorted us away to an upstairs room where within moments I was dead to the world.

******

Breakfast had long gone when I awoke. The house was quiet but there was a bell on a table so I rang for assistance. An ancient man appeared eventually and announced that there was water in a room along the corridor and that lunch would be available shortly if I wished to descend. Mr Trebitsch-Lincoln was downstairs. I enquired on the whereabouts of the others.

"They have gone sightseeing," the ancient replied.

If the pension revelation was bizarre, this really put the tin hat on it, but I just nodded as though sightseeing was the most normal thing in the world to be doing after an attempted takeover of the country[164].

---

[162] General Erich Friedrich Wilhelm Ludendorff was a career soldier joining the army in 1885. He rose rapidly particular after being appointed to the General Staff. Victories at Liege and Tannenberg led to his appointment in 1916 as First Generalquartiermeister forming the Third Supreme Command with Hindenburg. See appendix.

[163] It is hard to know who or what Flashman is referring to here. The comedy show known as Crazy Week featured the original Crazy Gang but this did not start until 1931 with the name not being used until 1937. Either Flashman is referring to something else or it was not written until after this time.

Having dressed I came down to lunch which consisted of a cold buffet.

"Rather good don't you think?" I nodded rather than indulge in ridiculous pleasantries. "They have gone to have a look around the city."

"You weren't interested then?"

"No, sightseeing is for the dull. Who are you working for, Herr Major?" It took me full aback for a moment and sent a shiver of fear coursing down my spine. "I can tell you have lived in England by your accent."

I stared hard for a moment thinking as quickly and as hard as I could. I had thought already that he was an unusual character.

"I was a prisoner for some time and I did study in England before the war. I was also in India. What about you?" I had realised that it was unlikely that he would spot an English accent if he hadn't heard it before and that therefore it was likely he had spent some time in England as well.

"I was a curate in Kent before I became an MP. But I left in 1910. I did offer my services to the British Government as a spy but they rejected me so I went to the Netherlands and contacted the Germans there."

Another shiver ran down my spine. I think it was the matter of fact way he told me what he had been up to and that it involved conspiring with the enemy, albeit unsuccessfully, that had made my blood run cold.

"Did you ever meet Dierks?"

"No, but I have heard of him. I believe he was after my time. How do you know of him?"

At this point, I decided not to ask anymore smart questions.

"He helped me escape from England."

There was a pause in the conversation while we contemplated each other. I wasn't sure I believed much of what he said and it was clear he had his suspicions about me. How he had arrived at that position was hard to say. Perhaps it was just the recognition of one scoundrel by another. Whatever it was, it was uncomfortable.

---

[164] Flashman's summary of events largely agrees with the historical record of the somewhat bizarre attempted takeover known as the 'Kapp Putsch'. See appendix.

"What are you going to do now?" he asked trying to sound innocent.

"I want to be where the action is." It even sounded false to me. "That means the Ruhr. These communist bastards have got to be stopped." I tried to sound warlike.

"I agree," he replied clearly hoping never to go near the Ruhr. "I could put a word in for you with Eckart? Perhaps you could fly there."

"Perhaps I could."

The conversation petered out but he had set a thought running. If he could get Eckart's blessing and I could get the aeroplane, flying towards the Ruhr would be a good idea. Once I was going, they needn't know where I finished up. Even if someone reported my non-arrival, they would be none the wiser and I doubted they would care anyway. After all, I wasn't an enemy of the state in their eyes, I knew nothing of any great importance and there were plenty of unemployed pilots around, not that Hitler would want another one if it meant he had to fly anywhere. I retired to the grounds of Ludendorff's house to consider my position and avoid Lincoln.

\*\*\*\*\*\*

The tourists arrived home late, presumably having dined elsewhere. Clearly, they had had an enjoyable day as I could hear them laughing uproariously. I stood as they came into the room where a late supper was laid out opposite the roaring fire.

"We have a mission for you, Herr Major," said Ludendorff grinning like an idiot. I adopted the fixed grin that I reserved for these occasions as my face acquired its customary red tinge. As my mind raced, I couldn't help but recall that I had volunteered for this in the first place, and for a moment that gave me a sliver of hope, until I remembered that these were fanatics who believed in their destiny and other such nonsense.

"It shouldn't be too arduous for a man of your talents. You are aware of why we came here of course," Eckart said airily making expansive gestures around the room. "We were to assist the removal of the criminal government and replace it with a more, a more…."

"Nationalist government?" Hitler added.

"Thankyou, however, this has not come about because of those Bolshevik bastards, but it will, it will. For the moment, we must remove the principal from Berlin. Stockholm seems a good option. We have contacts there but getting him out overland would be difficult. In the air…."

He left this sentence hanging. I knew immediately what they were thinking and I am sure you have worked it out too. I'll hand it to them, they played their cards well like the natural publicists they were. It would be hard for me, the pilot with an aeroplane, to slide out of what on the face of it was a simple task and as it happened one I had performed before, albeit unsuccessfully, near Sarajevo a few years previously. Memories of that day gave me the shakes. If you know my history, you'll know how close I came to using an aeroplane to dig my own grave and in fact, it did dig the pilots as I was the only survivor[165]. The silence was weighing on me now and they were all looking at me. Lincoln was giving me a particularly hard stare as if he could see the conflict within. I realised that if I didn't agree smartish, there would be repercussions of an unpleasant nature. I wanted to scream that I was English and didn't care about their plans and governments and even their country but I didn't. Stiffening my upper lip, I assumed what I hoped was a nonchalant air of deep thought and asked a question.

"Does Wilhelm like flying?"

It at least had the virtue of being unexpected and for a moment, they were taken aback.

"He'll have to," said Eckart looking pointedly at Hitler who I am sure was looking green just at the thought of flying again. "That's settled then. As soon as possible I think."

"Kapp will meet you tomorrow then," said Ludendorff with the masterly air of someone who delights in other people taking risks for him. And with that, our little party broke up, Eckart and Hitler to plan tomorrows sightseeing, Ludendorff to his no doubt luxurious rooms, Lincoln to plan our jaunt to the airport and me to sweat and shiver my way through another long night of terror.

******

---

[165] See 'Flashman and the Knights of the Sky'.

The morning came all too quickly. I was woken by Lincoln who had decided that leaving early was the key. He had been out on some sort of scout around and found the city crawling with Freikorps troops. Apparently Von Seeckt, on being reappointed, had immediately summoned the Freikorps, those same troops that the previous day had occupied Berlin on behalf of Kapp, to return to the Government side to suppress the communist uprisings in the Ruhr. Having paraded they set off straightaway, no doubt attracted by the thought of more fighting. At least this meant that by the time we set off, the troops were on their way and not interested in us at all. The journey to the airfield was uneventful and the place was still largely deserted except for our friendly non-striking chap who seemed happy to guide us through. He asked us where we were going and for a long suspicious moment I was looking for the exit but then realised he didn't really care and was just passing the time of day.

"Nuremburg," I replied thinking that would throw anyone who asked off the trail.

The formalities dealt with, we went outside. Manfred had been looking after the F II whilst we had been holidaying in Berlin and fortunately, he had refuelled it, checked it over and made sure all was shipshape so there was virtually nothing to prevent us leaving. The weather was fine and for once, I was actually looking forward to getting airborne, not least because it meant I could leave all the lunatics and fanatics behind. Hopefully, I would never see any of them again. There was one final conversation to have.

"Manfred," I said, and he could tell by the tone in my voice that it was serious. "I am not going back to Munich." I paused to let this sink in. "You are free to leave as you wish."

"I wish to accompany you. I have nothing in Munich anyway." I smiled at this news, mainly as from an entirely selfish point of view, it helped having someone along who knew his business and he was a far more agreeable companion than all my more recent sidekicks.

"Good. Then between you and me, we are bound for Stockholm first. Then, who knows! But don't tell anyone, it is meant to be secret."

We clambered aboard and began our preparations for the flight. I had discovered a planning office in which I found all sorts of useful things like life preservers, some flares, a few rounds of ammunition, various provisions and most importantly some maps, including one

170

of northern Germany and the borders with Scandinavia. The only disturbing thing was the amount of sea there appeared to be between here and Stockholm. At least we would be equipped for all eventualities. I shivered slightly at this thought as in my enthusiasm, I hadn't really considered the events that would lead up to needing a life preserver.

Out of the corner of my eye, I noticed a delegation leaving the building and heading our way. I recognised Kapp from his description. I clambered out of the aircraft to meet them. Lincoln was there as well for some reason. He looked petrified, but not as petrified as Kapp who clearly couldn't wait to get away[166]. Formalities over with, we all mounted up again and the delegation cleared off after what they considered the few minutes necessary for decency. The last I saw of Lincoln was as he led the delegation into the building at speed, intent on self-preservation.

I shivered again involuntarily as what I was about to do hit me. I scanned the airfield for trouble but saw nothing. I could only assume that the restored Government had bigger problems than Kapp. The engine started, we trundled off to the edge of the field, turned round, completed our checks satisfactorily and then turned into wind to begin our take off.

The roar was curiously comforting and for some reason I recalled that first flight with O'Connell all those years ago. I also remembered his demise, which was not quite so reassuring.

The rumbling vibration stopped as we lifted off and climbed away from the field. I circled overhead and set course to the north and safety.

---

[166] Different sources dispute when Kapp left Berlin, however they agree that Kapp did not meet Hitler or Eckart before his departure.

Chapter 22

A land fit for heroes. That's what they had said[167]. It didn't seem like it from where I was standing. I had walked past at least six cripples as I made my way along the royal mile. Most were wearing the remnants of uniforms although I suspected that at least one had never worn it in anger. I hadn't given any of them the money they were demanding from all and sundry. Still, it was good to know that victory hadn't changed the way politicians thought despite the change in the common man and his expectations. Mind you, it would probably take something more significant than a mere war to alter a politician's mind. Once the dust had settled on the war and its aftermath, most of them slunk back to the holes they had come from. And despite the change in outlook of the masses, they didn't really have any power, so consequently, it didn't look like there was going to be revolution in England, at least not yet at any rate. I mention this only because it was all fairly new to me. But I am getting ahead of myself.

I had not really been in England since the end of the war. Paris had its many attractions and Germany had been a royal nuisance until I had managed to escape via Sweden. I liked Sweden. They didn't bother particularly with fighting everyone else. They clearly didn't see the need. The women were extraordinarily attractive, the food was somewhat odd, but the weather had to be seen to be believed. Of course I hadn't actually seen it but I had shared a very comfortable bed with a delicious blonde who regaled me with tales of what they all got up to in winter and why. How they stood it, I'll never know although I supposed voluptuous blondes made the time pass that much quicker.

I had left Sweden by boat and arrived in Paris in time to celebrate the arrival of my firstborn. I confess I had been wondering what my reception would be like having absented myself more or less entirely since Victoria had announced she was in the pudding club. As it turned out, I needn't have worried at all. She embraced me like the prodigal hero I was and promptly gave birth. Thus ensued several months of enforced marital celibacy as I had to promenade around

---

[167] David Lloyd-George in Wolverhampton on 24th November 1918. 'What is our task? To make Britain a fit country for heroes to live in'.

with mother and child showing the fat bundle off to anyone who cared to look. He rejoiced in the name Frederick Harry Victor Flashman after his Grandfather, his Father (whoever he was – I still wasn't completely sure she was telling me the truth) and his Mother or the old Queen depending on how she was feeling. I was getting a trifle bored however as there had been devil a chance of any mischief with the infant getting in the way. Don't get me wrong, I was actually quite impressed with the idea of a son, it was just the reality of a baby that wasn't quite so enchanting. I hadn't even had time to catch up with Lucille although that was something I was determined to put right and that evening if I could help it. But first, I had another meeting to attend. I had contacted Sinclair in London and he had instructed me to meet him as soon as possible but before that he wanted me to meet up with our old friend Plantard. He didn't say why. I couldn't see any harm in it, so I had arranged with my beloved to have a day off from women cooing over my son and heir and I meant to make the fullest possible use of it. Consequently, I had gorged myself at Fouquet's and was now smoking a large cigar waiting for Monsieur Plantard to appear. I was hoping that whatever he had to tell me would be short.

Needless to say really but it wasn't. It was fascinating though, even for me. He had arrived just after lunch, refused to eat anything but ordered a Pernod[168] which he stared at for some time while I contemplated the world outside. We were alone apart from a waiter.

"I know now what 'appened to my cousin." He didn't look up. I shivered as I often do on these occasions. "It is not your fault. She was always too 'eadstrong. Sinclair told me everysing. Pah!" he exclaimed, almost as though that was an end to it. "It is a pity. She could 'ave been a very good agent."

I nodded sagely. Silence descended again.

" 'e is worried. Sinclair. Not about you," he added hurriedly at my look of despair. I couldn't decide whether that was good or bad. "Non. 'e is worried about zis 'Thule society' you have told 'im so much about, and particularly Eckart. You see, Eckart is very wealthy and 'as many influential contacts as you discovered. But, more worryingly, 'e seems to believe some fanciful stuff about a German messiah or redeemer. Your reports indicate zat 'e may have found 'is

---

[168] The Pernod brand is over 200 years old.

messiah and is setting about arranging a second coming. Wezzer 'e believes zat it really is a second coming or just a vehicle to obtain ultimate power is largely irrelevant. Ze fact is, Eckart and 'is friends, once zey start to win significant numbers of followers and zey are well on ze way to achieving zat, become a serious freat to ze stability of Germany and zerefore Europe. France does not 'ave ze appetite for more war and nor does England, so it would be quite easy for someone wiz ze right abilities and resources to take over in Germany. But, what worried 'im most was ze paper referring to ze Spear of Destiny."

For a moment, I wondered what on earth he was talking about, but then I remembered. It was an off the cuff conversation between Hess and Eckart that I happened to overhear. Eckart had been talking in messianic terms again and Hess had been licking his boots when he mentioned this spear.

"If it were only true, the power of the Spear," I had heard Hess say.

"But it is," said Eckart. "When the time is right, we will retrieve it."

"Retrieve it?" exclaimed Hess with a tone of utter disbelief.

"Of course. It is in Vienna."

I had done some research into what they were talking about, purely so I could pad out my latest report, which was looking decidedly thin. I had discovered that the only spear of any note in Vienna was the so-called Spear of Destiny, the lance that some bored roman had supposedly used to hasten the demise of Jesus by stabbing him whilst he was hanging on his cross. The thing about this particular spear was that it supposedly had a crucifixion nail in it as well. I had spent a truly jolly time finding out all about it, writing it all down and sending it off. It had amused me no end to think of Sinclair reading all about a spear in my official report. I could almost hear him cursing me for an idiot and wondering why I was sending him such rubbish. Chillingly, at least from my point of view, he had apparently taken it all very seriously[169].

---

[169] There have been three or four relics claiming to be the 'Holy Lance', supposedly used by the centurion Longinus to pierce Jesus' side and indeed hasten his demise. The Vienna lance came into the possession of the Holy Roman Emperors in the 10th century and was used in the 1273 coronation ceremony.

"You 'ave to go to Edinburgh as soon as possible and meet Sinclair zere. I 'ave somesing to give you zat you must take for 'im. You must guard it wiz your life. I will meet you tonight outside ze Louvre. Shall we say nine o'clock?"

He got up and left without paying. Anyone else would have laughed in his face and told him not to be so melodramatic. I simply sat frozen to the spot, wondering where my foolishness had got me now. Why Edinburgh?

I ordered another slug, and another, just to numb the finer senses that were screaming at me to abscond immediately. I couldn't of course. But the slugs worked a little and at least through the haze I knew exactly what I needed to do next.

******

She had definitely put on some weight around the middle but I wasn't going to tell her. It had to be the fine living of course and it was clear she was living the high life. But it didn't matter to me. She inhabited the real world, one where there were no 'Spears of Destiny' or messiahs. Lucille embraced me as soon as she saw me. It had occurred to me that my idea of finding sanity was somewhat at odds with most people but if you ignored what she did for a living, she was without doubt one of the sanest people I knew. And in a world that seemed to have taken leave of its collective senses, her brothel was an oasis.

I settled down for what was left of the afternoon. I needed to think and this was the only place I could have peace and quiet as well as a little entertainment. Lucille left me with a drink and some food in her own suite while she went back to work, promising me she would come up later. I pondered all that I had done and heard in the last few months. I must have dozed off. Not for the first time I woke to find a near naked woman about to have her way with me and jolly nice it was too. Wide-awake now I got into the spirit of

---

Henry IV reportedly added a silver band inscribed with 'Nail of our Lord' based on the assumption that this was Constantine the Great's lance which supposedly had a nail from the crucifixion embedded in it. In the spring of 1796 when a French army approached Nuremberg, the collection including the lance was removed to Vienna and kept in the Imperial Treasury where it remains.

things and we staggered across to her enormous bed without disengaging, not as easy as it would once have been I can tell you.

In that dreamy aftermath, we talked in a desultory fashion about anything and everything. The war, business, French politicians, Versailles, German politicians, all sorts. She gave me some titbits of news to pass on to Sinclair, none of which was particularly earth shattering.

"America," she said suddenly. "Zat is where I am going when I 'ave enough money. Zat is where fortunes can be made. Anozzer six monfs."

"But, what, what would I do without you?"

"What you 'ave always done."

"But I will miss you." I said it before I thought about it.

"Well come wiz me zen."

I believe she meant it and for at least a couple of minutes I seriously considered it. But it wouldn't do of course. Even I could see that. It would have solved an awful lot of problems but created so many more so I reluctantly declined her offer.

"What about all this?" I asked gesturing around the room.

"Just sings. Ze important stuff I can take wiz me and some of ze girls want to come too. Zey 'ave 'ad enough of French men."

"I have to go," I announced getting off the bed and beginning to get dressed. She watched me for a moment before suddenly getting up and embracing me. When she pulled back there were tears streaming down her face.

"I wish you were coming wiz me."

She kissed me again, then turned and walked to the door grabbing a robe on the way. She didn't look back and I wondered for a moment whether I would ever see her again. It struck me at that moment that in a most odd way, we were in love and I probably had much more in common with her than my truly beloved. I shook my head to clear it and left.

It was nearly 8.30 so I hailed a cab. The journey to the Louvre didn't take above ten minutes so I crouched outside in a dark corner observing the ebb and flow of life.

The hand on my shoulder nearly had my heart exiting via my mouth. I didn't scream but it was close. Fortunately, I recognised Plantard's form in the gloom as I turned. He was muttering something in my ear that I didn't catch but his intent was obvious and I followed him as he dragged me further into the shadow. I felt rather than saw a door open and he pulled me through it and stopped. There was some fumbling and then a match struck and held to a lamp. A warm glow enveloped us. He gestured for me to keep quiet and then turned, beckoning me to follow. We were in a corridor as far as I could tell in the dark. I stumbled along behind him wondering what the hell we were doing, wishing now that I was still wrapped in Lucille's warm embrace. He stopped for a moment and listened, gesturing again for silence. He pulled out a key and to my astonishment inserted it into an all but invisible lock. It turned silently and there was a soft click as a door opened into the wall. If you didn't know it was there, you would have walked past it. Plantard looked around again and then passed through the door pulling me with him. Once in, he gently closed the door, which even from the inside was hard to spot. He walked past me again and I followed into the gloom. Almost immediately, we were at the top of a spiral staircase that we began to descend. I started to count the steps but soon gave up and just carried on down. At the bottom, we passed through a small archway above which I noticed was a symbol. I only noticed because it struck me as unusual to have a Jewish six-pointed star above a museum door, assuming we were still in the museum of course. Beyond the archway was a small circular room with a low ceiling that one could touch with a raised arm. Oddly, there was nothing in it, not a single identifiable thing. I shivered and my throat began to constrict as I wondered if I could outrun him up the stairs.

I jumped when he spoke.

"I can never find it first time." He said it more to himself than me. He backed up against the wall directly opposite the arch and stared over my head at something. I was so confused I hardly dared to turn my head. Suddenly he stepped forward and I lurched back, banging my head against the wall. He looked up and then reached up, touched something with a finger and then pushed. To my further astonishment, a hatch opened in the ceiling, which he pushed hard, and almost with a life of its own it disappeared into the dark. He reached over the lip of the opening and pulled down a rope that had knots in to make climbing it easier. He gestured for me to go up. I hesitated for a second, my heart thumping still and then grasped the first knot. I pulled myself up and almost immediately, my head was through the hatch and in darkness. It was a matter of seconds before I was kneeling on the edge of the hole. I felt the rope move as Plantard prepared to climb.

"Take ze lamp," he said holding it above his head. I reached down behind me to grasp it and lifted it through the hole. Light filled the space around me, for a second almost blindingly so. I squinted for a moment as my eyes adjusted and then as I looked around my mouth actually fell open. Up to that point, I had thought that that was something that only happened in stories.

# Chapter 23

God knows what it was all worth. Tens of thousands, hundreds of thousands? More? Impossible to tell.

"You are surprised?"

Just the look on my face gave him his answer.

"What is it all?"

"It is ze treasure of ze organisation. Ze records, ze 'istory, everysing."

"But what organisation? And why am I here?"

"You know already. It 'as a number of names, some you will know, ozzers not. We are ze descendants of ze knights. Ze knights of Jerusalem."

"The Templars?" I almost shouted it in disbelief.

"Not so loud. No one can 'ear us but we do not take chances in 'ere. Zere is anuzzer sing. We are not sure zat d'Alprant did not betray us. She knew too much in ze end."

Suddenly I knew too what had happened to his cousin. Holmes had told me they had been watching her but it wasn't entirely because she was passing military information to the enemy, it was because she knew about some or all of this. And ultimately, that had led to her demise. I couldn't take it in. I had heard many fanciful and unlikely things in the last few years but this, this beggared belief.

"Sinclair wished me to show zis to you. Of course, 'e is a descendant of Henri de St Clair[170] 'imself, ze original knight of ze Temple in Jerusalem and who brought much of zis back from Outremer after ze Crusades. Of course, 'is heirs took much more to Scotland at ze time of ze great persecution[171] and fought at Bannockburn to prevent ze English from despoiling it all. 'ave a look around. I am sure I 'ave no need to remind you 'ow secret it is."

So I did look around. It was truly fantastic. I am not easily impressed as I have mentioned before but this was another realm entirely. The artwork alone must have been priceless. Some of it was

---

[170] Henri de St Clair was a crusader who fought with Hugues de Payen, the original Templar knight, returning to Scotland in 1100 where he took the title of Baron of Roslin. See appendix.

[171] Presumably the attempted destruction of the Knights by King Philip IV on October 13th, 1307.

more recent work by Botticelli, da Vinci, Raphael and other Renaissance artists. There were paintings, sculptures, metalwork, in fact almost anything you could think of. But the biggest wall was covered in shelves of documents and scrolls. I stopped to look at some of them. They were all labelled and in chronological order and I felt like I was stepping back in time as I worked my way down the wall. Many of the documents related to the royal families of France, England and Scotland. There were family trees galore, many royal, many more relating to long dead knights. But, it was as I got back into ancient history my eyes widened in disbelief. There were plenty of Sinclairs, St Clairs, Stuarts and so on after the crusades. There were a few before but the strands narrowed and narrowed until they arrived at one single point, and it was the same single point Sinclair had told me a few years previously. The messiah himself, Jesus Christ. And it was then I realised that all this, the documents, the art, the secrecy, was related to that one disputed point.

"How long has all this been here?" I asked.

" 'undreds of years. Since ze Louvre was built[172]. Ze masons 'elped design and build it you see and when zey did, zey constructed a number of secret rooms. Ze same was true of many of ze ancient buildings in Paris and London. Persecution 'as always been a problem, especially by ze Casolic church, so secrecy and safety 'ave always been paramount. We simply can't let any of zis fall into ze wrong 'ands."

He reached up and lifted down a file. It was about an inch thick and the size of a large book.

"Zis is an inventory of zis room. It 'as taken me many years to compile in secrecy. I 'ave only just finish it. It also contains 'andwritten copies of ze most important work and zat makes it very dangerous. It needs to be taken to Scotland, to Edinburgh and given to Sinclair. I cannot do it. I am watched a lot of ze time so it would be impossible for me to take it myself. So we need a reliable agent. Sinclair suggested you."

The bastard. He couldn't help himself. If it wasn't bad enough that I had to do his dirty work in Germany, now I was to be his

---

[172] The Louvre Palace was begun as a fortress by Philip II in the 12th century. For those powerful enough it would have been relatively easy to incorporate rooms and passages that either were or became secret.

secret messenger boy, only carrying dynamite into the bargain. For a fleeting moment, it occurred to me that we were in fact the only ones, at least in Paris, who knew of this room and I considered whether anyone would miss Plantard if he accidentally fell through the hatch and broke his neck. I immediately dismissed this as nonsense. He was married and had a son as far as I knew. And anyway, Sinclair would come after me and I would find myself in the Seine with lead boots on. No, yet again I would have to go and make the best of it.

"When do I leave?"

"Right now."

"What!" I spluttered.

"Now. It is 'parfait'. We cannot come back 'ere once we leave. Zey will be annoyed zat zey lost me again so once I let zem find me, I cannot lose zem for some weeks. I 'ave to be very careful. Anyway, it is night time."

That appeared to be the end of the conversation. I took a final look around the room and then lowered myself through the hatch. Plantard followed and then closed it up. Even when I knew where it was, I would have struggled to find the opening again. He gave me the file wrapped in an oilskin cover. Ludicrously, I had nowhere to hide it so I had to shove it in my waistband, which was rather uncomfortable to say the least. Possibly the worst thing however, and one that hadn't really occurred to me until now, was that I didn't really know who I was keeping this secret from. Of course, there were the obvious candidates like the Prince of Wales and his minions, but they wouldn't be tearing round Paris looking for me. It was the unknown pursuers that terrified me. It didn't bear thinking about and a cold shiver rippled down my spine.

We retraced our steps through the arch and back up the spiral stair. When we reached the door we stopped and listened for what seemed an age before he gently turned a handle and opened the door a fraction. There was no light as he had extinguished the lamp and I could almost feel the dark. We listened again, hardly daring to breathe. Nothing. Not a sound. He pulled the door gently open and we slipped silently through. My heart was racing and I barely heard the tiny click of the door closing above the thumping in my chest. We stood and listened again. Still nothing. I felt his hand grasp my arm and pull me along behind him. We walked slowly for some time before he stopped and struck another match to relight the lamp.

"One cannot be too careful," he muttered.

The passage lit up ahead of us and we continued walking, reaching the door to the outside in a couple of minutes. He extinguished the lamp again and listened at the door whilst looking through a tiny Judas hole. After no more than a couple of minutes, he turned to face me.

"You must guard ze manuscript wiz your life." He looked earnestly at me and for a moment, I wondered if he had an inkling about the likelihood of my saving the manuscript instead of my life. God knows what Sinclair had told him. Too much probably. He held out his hand and I shook it. He took a final look through the hole and then opened the door just enough to let me slip out. Up to that point, I had assumed he was coming with me but before I could so much as sniff he closed the door behind me. Instinctively I turned and pushed the door but it didn't move. For no reason other than curiosity, I investigated the door further. There was no handle or visible lock, in fact there was nothing that gave it away as a door. Of course, it occurred to me that Plantard had been on the inside. I turned away from the door and looked around me into the darkness. Seeing nothing, I sidled away out of the recess and along the wall in silence. I came to another dark recess where I stopped again, completely hidden from view. I waited a couple of minutes before moving on to the next recess, and the next until I reached the end of the wall. I could feel my heart racing although when I thought about it, I had no idea why that should be so. I wasn't doing anything particularly dangerous and I was on home territory of a kind and as far as I knew, no one was particularly out to get me. None of which stopped the hairs on my neck standing rigidly to attention.

It was the smell that almost saved me. For reasons I still can't fathom it did save the book. I was frozen to the spot, mainly as I didn't know which way to run. I could see nothing except perhaps a deeper black. Involuntarily, I started sliding very slowly backwards towards the wall, reaching behind me as I did so. My hand touched the sill of a window and as I moved sideways there was an ancient shutter that had clearly not moved in a long time. For a moment, I wondered what I was doing, creeping about in the dark but then the faintest, faintest noise, a whisper of someone breathing instantly stifled. I felt the book and a stab of fear at the same time. Some inner voice told me to get rid of it. I slid it slowly and silently out from behind my back not knowing what to do with it, the solution being instantly formed as I felt the shutter again. Groping into the window recess I felt a gap between the shutter and the wall which would conceal a great deal at least from outside. Slowly, slowly I slid the packet behind the rotten wood until I was sure it could not be seen.

I started to move slowly back along the wall, recess to recess. I was sure I had passed the door and hope was beginning to flare. At which point, I kicked a stone that some inconsiderate had left lying around on the floor. The report was like a gun going off in a confined space. I ran.

I would have made it if it hadn't been for the chain slung between posts that I had forgotten about and didn't see until a second too late. I tried to leap over it but my leading foot caught and I was falling. Even as I hit the ground I was preparing my next move but they, whoever they were, were on me and before I could even scream I felt a rag over my face with the unmistakeable smell of chloroform[173]. I knew I didn't have long and I fought them like a tiger, something I am only compelled to do as a last resort and this seemed very much like it. But it was no good. I could feel my senses failing and my assailants were too many. The light such as it was faded rapidly into blackness.

******

Sunlight streaming through a window woke me. I was in a miserable hovel of a room little better than the cells I had frequented occasionally. It took me some time to recall how I had ended up here and I spent even more wondering why. It did not improve my mood. I jumped as the door was flung open. Three men came in, their faces partially hidden and with hats pulled down low on their foreheads.

For once in my life, I was at a complete loss as to what to say. As I didn't know why I was here, wherever here was, my usual strategy

---

[173] It is highly unlikely that the drug used was chloroform. Despite many references in print, it is difficult to administer in the correct quantity to cause anaesthesia and requires continual application to maintain. It is more likely to be an ether compound which was widely used as an anaesthetic.

of pleading for my life from my knees seemed inappropriate although I was sure that feeling wouldn't last. No one said anything for a minute.

"Do you know Sixtus?" said one of them.

I gaped at them

"Do you know Sixtus?" The menace in his voice was obvious.

"I..... I have met him," I stuttered trying desperately not to commit myself.

"He is the one." This was to his friends. "He is the betrayer."

"No," I squealed, "I can't be. I haven't betrayed anyone."

A hard slap across the face and I stumbled into the wall, feeling my teeth with my tongue and tasting blood. As I stood up again I saw one of them pull out a piece of paper and come towards me. I cowered back against the wall waiting for another blow but he stopped in front of me, straightened out his sheet and turned it round to show me.

"Do you recognise this?"

I felt the colour drain from my face. There, somehow, was the list of Frenchmen that Hilmar had given me and I had given to Sixtus. I couldn't even begin to fathom how it had ended up here and more importantly how they had connected it to me.

"Clearly he does," said another voice. "No further proof is needed."

"Until tomorrow then."

They said this to each other turning their backs on me in dismissal. I could guess what tomorrow had in store and it was enough to send one doolally[174]. Rooted to the spot, I had no idea what to do. Their matter-of-factness had rendered me speechless.

The door slammed closed. I sat down heavily, exhausted. Even terror seemed to have no effect and I sat staring at the wall.

\*\*\*\*\*\*

---

[174] From 'Deolali tap'. Deolali was a British army camp near Mumbai often used as a transit camp for troops moving to or from India. 'Tap' was Persian for malaria or fever.

I awoke shivering and oddly aware that I had been calling out in my sleep. Something about Lenin seemed to be echoing round my head but I couldn't quite place what it was.

There was a scratch at the door and I leapt to my feet, spine tingling as I stepped to the back of the room. The door opened slowly and someone slipped in. Of course, this is where your real hero silently steps behind the intruder, disables him with one blow before making good his escape, taking on hordes of the enemy on the way. If I hadn't been paralysed with fear, I may have briefly considered this course of action.

"Flashman," a voice whispered. "I know you are here. I am here to help you."

Of the many things I had expected to happen in my imaginings, this wasn't one of them.

"Show yourself comrade." There was a hint of irritation. And why had he called me comrade?

"Here," I whispered trying desperately to appear small.

"Good. Do you know what happened to those imperialist bastards? The ones on your list?"

"No."

"They executed them. At least the ones that hadn't disappeared."

There was an odd hint of triumph in his voice. I didn't reply.

"You are one of us. That is why I am helping you get out of here. I will have to give up my cover and run as well but I don't care. I will have struck a blow for Comrade Lenin." He had stopped whispering by this point and in my mounting terror, I grabbed his shoulders. I was about to shake him when he embraced me, continuing with his stream of adoration.

"Shhhhh," I said louder than I meant to.

"Oh, it is alright, they are all drunk, true imperialists. I could fire a cannon beside them and they wouldn't hear. Come, we can go."

I saw his teeth as he smiled and then he turned and left. I followed him out of the door and we walked out, turned into a dimly lit corridor, walked a little further and then through another door into the street.

He turned again to face me, grasped my hand in his, gulped a couple of times and then just nodded.

"Vive la Revolution."

I nodded back, speechless. Then he walked off into the dark. I did the same only a lot quicker. I had to get to the Louvre and then out of France without being caught again, although I suspected my nameless friend was right. By the time my imperialist tormentors had recovered and discovered my absence, I would be far, far away and good luck to them catching a Flashman with a head start and a fast horse.

Chapter 24

It started to rain as I approached the castle. Why Sinclair had chosen the most obvious meeting place in Edinburgh was beginning to disturb me, especially after the effort it had taken to get here. I was sure I wasn't being followed but that didn't seem to matter much. I stopped a hundred yards or so short of the castle gates and looked around again before approaching the sentry.

"Major Flashman for Colonel Sinclair," I told him as instructed.

"One moment sorr," the kilted Seaforth[175] sentry replied turning back into his box. "I'm tae gi' ye this, sorr."

He gave me a thin envelope that instantly started to get wet.

"In here sir," the sentry said pointing to a door. "Nae one will disturb ye."

I entered the small office and the sentry closed the door behind me. Alone, I stared at the envelope for a moment before opening it. I wasn't sure what to expect but it wasn't directions to a church. I knew I was well down on the debit side of the ledger in the eyes of the almighty but surely Sinclair was more of a realist than that. Apparently, I was to go to a village called Roslin about eight miles south of Edinburgh. There was a chapel there and I was to go to the crypt, the entrance to which was to the right of the altar and down some stairs. I was to meet Sinclair there at eight o'clock that evening.

I pondered on the whole thing. Then I gave up. I was sure he had reasons, I just wished they didn't keep involving me. The journey was tedious. I had found the bus station after leaving the castle and discovered there was a bus to Roslin at just before six, which seemed ideal. I spent the next couple of hours alternately eating and gnawing my fingers. I was as jumpy as a cat. I had seen numerous suspicious characters in my circular travels, none of whom had turned out to be anything more than tramps or other loafers. In fact, if anyone looked suspicious it was probably me. Finally, the bus came and I got on. Clearly, it wasn't a popular route as I was the only passenger. Maybe the weather had something to do with it. The bus trundled through

---

[175] An odd coincidence perhaps. The Seaforth Highlanders was created by the amalgamation in 1881 of the 72nd Highlanders (Duke of Albany's Own) and the 78th Highlanders (Ross-shire Buffs).

the outskirts of the city before finally leaving it behind. If anything, the countryside was even more dreary and I must have dozed off. Luckily, I had told the driver where I was getting off and he woke me as he pulled into the village bus stop. There were a couple of other passengers by now but none of them got off and none of them took any interest in me. I stood by the road feeling a little lost.

"Ye're nae frae roond here are ye?" a voice said from behind me.

I spun round instantly to find an elderly man leaning on a gate.

"No," I admitted. "I need to get to the chapel."

"Well, ye've nae far to gae then. Jist follow yon path an' ye'll see it. Odd place. An' it's late. He'll be closed frae the nicht."

"Thankyou for the advice."

I walked away. I had forgotten what it was like out of the cities where everyone saw you coming and knew you were an outsider and wanted to know your business. I daren't look round but I could feel him watching me. I rounded a bend in the path at last and he was gone. A few moments later, I got my first glimpse of the chapel. It was indeed an odd place although I couldn't have said why. I walked through the gates and up to the main entrance. It was very quiet. The main door was half-open. I slipped through and into the aisle and walked towards the altar at the front. I could see an archway to the right. Just above it, carved into the keystone was another six-pointed star. It struck me immediately that I had last seen that in Paris. I briefly stopped at the top of the steps before descending into the crypt.

Relief flowed over me as my eyes accustomed to the gloom and saw Sinclair waiting for me.

"Flashman. Good."

He didn't seem in the least concerned and suddenly I felt foolish for feeling suspicious about it all.

"Do you have it?"

"Yes." I fished the inventory out of my knapsack and passed it to Sinclair.

"You realise how important this is?"

"Not really," I replied suddenly wondering what they hadn't told me.

"Perhaps I should tell you. That manuscript is one of only two copies in existence. Plantard told you it is an inventory of the Louvre temple and it is, but that is not all. What he doesn't know is that hidden within it are original documents dating to the first century. They are from the Gospel of Mary.[176]"

He let this sink in for a moment or two and when he judged I was about to speak shook his head. My mouth closed.

"We must not speak more of it here. Suffice to say it is dynamite for the church. I needed to get it out of France and I had been wondering how to do it for a long time. There are too many watchers keeping an eye on me and my associates, but you are relatively clean."

I didn't like to mention the incident outside the Louvre on the night I had been given the manuscript.

"This however, is my territory. My family have ruled here more or less without mishap since Bannockburn and no one passes the village borders unseen or unreported. By my relations mostly."

He turned and paced around the crypt.

"I am going to show you something. Perhaps against my better judgment but instinct tells me I am right. Very few outside my immediate family know of this and I would like it to stay that way. However, you have earned the right I think to know why all this is important. Follow me."

He passed me and headed up the steps without saying another word. I followed equally wordless. He left the chapel by the side door, closing it carefully behind him. We were in small walled off area with a gate that looked out over scrubby moorland. Stepping quickly to the gate, he opened it, let me pass through and then closed it behind us. He looked around and I saw him nod almost imperceptibly. I knew better than to look but someone was watching us, although in this case I presumed they were on our side, whatever that was.

Night had begun to fall quite suddenly. We walked slowly for no more than a couple of minutes although even then the chapel was more or less out of sight albeit mainly because of the ground falling away in front of us. I saw Sinclair stop again near an odd shaped rock. Clearly, it marked something because he turned abruptly away from it and walked slowly in a completely different direction. I noted

---

[176] The Gospel of Mary was apparently discovered in upper Egypt in the late nineteenth century and taken to Berlin. It contains texts in Greek that date to the second century.

we were descending markedly into what appeared to be a fold in the ground. Very quickly, our heads were below the level of the ground either side of us. We entered a small but deep hollow and stopped. Maybe it was unworthy but it occurred to me that this would be a very suitable place to rid oneself of an irritating appendage. I shook my head to remove that image and looked at Sinclair who had his back to me. He was standing completely still. Then he turned and pointing at the sky said, "Evening Star.[177]"

I looked up at the bright object, which this far north seemed even brighter than normal and stared for a moment. I turned back to say something. He had vanished. It was so unexpected I could barely believe my eyes. I turned around thinking he had somehow got behind me but he wasn't there. There was no way out of the hollow other than to go past me. It was impossible. I moved over to where he had been standing, but there was only a sheer rock wall. I stared at it and then tapped it as if that would help. I was so confused that my natural panic reaction was suppressed. I looked around again, then down at the floor, then back at the wall. There had to be some other way out so I began feeling around the smooth slab. There was nothing and now I was starting to get a little disturbed. I tried the other side and was just considering turning to run when I felt it. There was a gap. As I ran my hand along the edge, I felt something move. There was a tiny puff of cold air and I nearly leapt out of the hollow vertically. As I fell back, Sinclair appeared as if from nowhere out of the gap. I gaped at him from where I was now sitting on the floor.

"How?" was all I managed to say.

He laughed like I had never heard him before, so much so he was almost crying.

"I have longed to do that to someone but I have never had the chance until now," he spluttered through great guffaws.

"Well I hope you enjoyed it," I replied through the beginnings of anger.

"Now don't lose your temper. I really do have something to show you and it really is worth it. Come on, get up."

With this, he helped me to my feet and my anger subsided as quickly as it had come.

---

[177] Otherwise known as Venus.

"Let me show you how it works."

With that, he slipped his hand into the gap I had found and pushed. Something moved away and suddenly, but more importantly silently, there was a gap just large enough for a man to slip through. In a second, he was gone and the gap closed.

"You try it," I heard his disembodied voice say from behind the slab. I found the gap and pushed and as if by magic, the gap appeared again. I stepped through and something I stepped on caused the 'door' to close. It was black as pitch until Sinclair struck a match and lit a lamp hanging on the wall. We were in a narrow corridor that appeared to be cut through the rock although it was hard to tell because the walls were so smooth. I wasn't completely sure but the corridor appeared to head back towards the chapel. Sinclair confirmed that it did as we set off down it. He lit further lamps as we moved but within a minute or so we were at a solid door. There was something odd about it though which I couldn't place until he asked me to open it when I discovered there was no handle. I wasn't surprised given all that had happened so far but I entered into the spirit of the thing and tried to find out how to open it. I knew it was hopeless and so it proved. When I gave up, Sinclair retraced his steps a little and pointed out a tiny recess that was virtually invisible and easily overlooked as the stone was coloured in such a way as to disguise it. He pushed his hand into the hole and there was a slight scraping noise as the door opened towards us.

"Give me a moment to light the lamps," he said so I stood outside the door waiting. A matter of seconds later he called me to come through. The surprise was, in a word, stunning.

Chapter 25

I was at the top of a short flight of steps that led downwards into what I can only describe as a masonic temple, but a temple like nothing I had ever seen. It seemed to shine with the reflected light, the black and white floor polished so that the ceiling was reflected in it. The pillars near the altar were extraordinarily ornate which was unusual but it was only as I descended the steps I noticed that off to one side was another arch leading to another room.

"We are under the ruined wall now." He was referring to the odd wall that seemed to stick out at right angles from the chapel but as far as anyone knew, had never actually been a wall to anything and no one in the village knew of anyone who had ever known anyone who knew any different. At least, that is what Sinclair had told me. I was confused.[178]

"Major Flashman." The formality of it threw me for a moment and I looked directly at where Sinclair was now standing in the annex. "Come in here."

I passed under the arch where I noted there was another six pointed star and stood in the centre of the room wondering what he was going to show me because to all intents and purposes the room was empty.

"We have been keeping a close eye on you for many years as you know. And your father before you although it has been an extraordinarily difficult task given both his and your propensity for vanishing into thin air on a whim. At times, we paid in blood to save his life. His manuscripts don't mention it of course but many of them suggest something of a charmed life, a guardian angel or some such. That was us."

He wasn't making sense and I wondered if he had been at the bottle all afternoon. He was a scot of course. I didn't say anything as I wasn't really sure what to say. Luckily, after a brief pause he continued.

"Your Paget grandmother. That is how the line goes back. From her to her father and his mother. It is all here." He pointed to a cupboard. "Your family tree is in here. It goes back numerous

---

[178] Modern ground scanning apparently shows a large void under Roslin chapel. It has never been excavated or opened in any way.

generations. I will show it to you later. But first, you have to complete the Royal Arch Degree.[179] That is why you are here."

The lights went out and I nearly screamed. There was a sound of rustling nearby and then something was placed over my eyes. I was asked to kneel and a prayer was said. I was then guided forward and told I must descend into a vaulted chamber. Hands lowered me to my knees again and I was told to search in the dark to see if there was anything secreted there. A scroll of some kind was placed in my hands and I was asked what was on it. Of course I could not tell. And so the ceremony went on. And on and on.

What I wasn't sure of at this juncture was whether I actually wanted to be elevated to whatever level this was. I had done no preparation and so had no idea what I had to say or do, if anything. Still, for a change I appeared to have no choice. I went along with it. A deep sonorous voice droned on and on and my eyes must have closed for a second or two and suddenly I felt a gentle push and I was 'lowered' again. There was an odd dreamlike quality to the whole experience and I wondered if they had administered some drug or other. I decided they must have because I didn't actually care very much. I could still hear someone reciting and I had no sooner had the thought than I realised what it was. He, whoever he was, was talking about the excavation of the Jerusalem Temple.

"The glory of this latter house shall be greater than the former, saith the Lord of hosts: and in this place will I give peace, saith the Lord of hosts."

Without warning, the blindfold was removed and suddenly the whole room was lit up almost blinding me. It was as if a starshell had burst in the utter darkness of the western front and it had me reaching for the door. As I staggered back I realised I was against a wall of some kind and in fact, looking round me, I realised I was in a room that had been specially built for this purpose.

"I am and shall be; Lord in Heaven; Father of all."

This apparently was the final act. I felt oddly exhausted with the whole thing.

Another lantern flared and the room was bright enough to see properly. Albany was at the back saying goodbye to two other men whom I didn't recognise. Then he came back to me.

---

[179] See appendix.

"Well Flashman, glad to see you are still alive old boy." He shook my hand imparting as he did so the handshake that apparently marked the descendants of the Stuarts. "One day, we will not need to be so secret." With that, he turned, shook Sinclair's hand and headed for the exit.

"Let me show you what I brought you here for," Sinclair said dispensing with his robe. I followed him back through the arch which I realised was next to the room I had emerged from. I hadn't seen it of course because the door had been closed before. "You realise that this is all our representation of the Temple, don't you," he added.

Standing before a large cupboard, I shivered. Suddenly I felt nervous. He unlocked the door and opened it. For a moment I was so surprised I couldn't speak.

"But there's nothing there."

"There is for those who know where to look." He grinned at me and stepped into the void. Reaching up, he pulled something and a small door in the back opened. I couldn't see what was beyond as for a moment Sinclair filled the space but he slid through and then beckoned me to follow. As I slid into the room he lit another light and this time I was truly shocked. Sitting in the middle of the room was a box. A box like no other on earth, a box that had, if one believed in God, been sent by him to Moses on Mount Sinai and had contained the original ten commandments, a box that had helped the Israelites and Jews in battle but equally slaughtered those that were deemed enemies, a box that rumour had it was fatal to touch. I was truly speechless.

"The Ark of the Covenant." [180]

---

[180] See appendix.

# Chapter 26

The silence was deafening but I didn't know what to say.

"It isn't what you think it is. At least, it isn't what the church says you should think it is. To all intents and purposes it does not exist anymore. We will never reveal its existence and of course no one would believe us if we did, mainly because it isn't deadly and it doesn't perform miracles. It is just a box, albeit one from antiquity. My ancestors found it in Jerusalem during the crusades, walled up in what we think was Solomon's temple. They of course realised the importance of it. They tried to use it for good by denying it to the Pope, but they were doomed to failure from the outset. The Papacy is too strong for all of us, even now although I think it is starting to decline. The war has seen to that. Look around you."

I did and realised that with my attention taken by the Ark, I hadn't noticed the decoration on the wall.

"Start over here."

I went over to where Sinclair was pointing and looked. For a minute I thought I would need resurrecting. It was a family tree, but like none I had ever seen. It started with a man called Solomon and then wound its way through time, passing Joseph, Jesus, Mary and so on. It became so complicated that I rather lost the thread of it until skimming over about a thousand years I reached the restoration and Charles II. And there I found it. Stuarts, Pagets and Flashmans. I was famous. At least, I was famous on a wall that I guessed only a handful of people had ever seen. The next thing that occurred to me was the same as has just occurred to you. How, in the name of all that is holy, had I, Harry Francis Alexander Flashman, ended up on a family tree and thus related to Jesus Christ? Well it was beyond me as well. The Stuarts I could understand as they were a fairly mixed bag of rogues and reprobates but on the whole, Jesus was by all accounts, even the bible, a thoroughly nice chap, the moneychangers and so on notwithstanding.

Interesting though it all was, it wasn't much use to me other than to confirm my status as a target for the Prince of Wales and his friends.

"We should go. You can come back here whenever you like. The guardians will let you in but I would advise not coming too often.

There are very few who even know of the existence of this place and it will stay that way until the restoration."

He said it as though he assumed it was inevitable that someone, presumably Albany, would be restored to the throne. I thought that was unlikely myself but then if you had told me about all of this before the war I would have assumed you were drunk and had you confined.

We retraced our steps out of the chamber and back to the hollow. There we took a slightly different route to a nondescript building that was equipped as an office.

"I need you to go back to Germany," he said quietly before he sat down and pointed me to an armchair. "Your reports were both enlightening and worrying." He paused to let this sink in for a minute. "This Eckart chap concerns me greatly as does his sidekick, particularly as they have powerful friends. We can ignore the coup for now but I think they will try again. I warned them that this would be the problem with making Versailles so punitive but the French want revenge and would really rather Germany fell apart whereas we disagree and would rather they became a peaceful moderating influence in central Europe. What we don't want is aggressive nationalism but that seems to be what we are going to get eventually. But I digress. I am returning to Paris shortly and you should accompany me. You can have a week or two there and then off to Munich again."

My bowels were completely frozen and my face must have been a picture as I considered the implications of all this. I think it was the matter of fact way he told me that I was going back that had my teeth chattering. I had only just escaped for God's sake. But of course, I couldn't do anything about it. The Lord giveth and the Lord giveth again, especially to the undeserving.

"What I am most disturbed about is this Spear of Destiny. I have seen that sort of thing in action and there is no doubt it brings out the fanatic in the most benign people. This Hitler chap seems to have a knack for finding that trait and the Spear will only exacerbate the problem. So I need you to put a stop to it."

I was flabbergasted by now as you can imagine. How on earth was I going to put a stop to anything? More to the point, how was I going to do it and escape with a whole skin? It didn't bear thinking about. But there was more to come.

"Of course, if necessary, it would make all our lives easier if Eckart and friends were to have an unfortunate accident. If needn't be trivial of course."

Well, what can one say? I assumed from the tone of his voice that this statement was meant to cheer me up. A bell rang from the house nearby.

"Ah, supper, good."

We left the office and moved to the drawing room. The conversation, if it could be called that, closed whilst we tucked into admittedly a rather good spread. I didn't eat a great deal as my nerves were jangling furiously and it was with some relief that Sinclair left me alone with a bottle of the local malt. A couple of slugs calmed my immediate fear and I reminded myself that I was for the moment still in the middle of civilisation, Scotland notwithstanding. Half a bottle in I must have fallen asleep and only woke when a servant gently pointed me in the direction of a proper bed. Unusually for me after a fright, I didn't dream anything.

\*\*\*\*\*\*

Nothing happened for a couple of days. In fact, Sinclair vanished on business he said leaving me to make myself free of the facilities. One of the locals introduced me to the delights of playing golf, which to my surprise I both enjoyed and was good at despite the rather pointless nature of the game itself. I almost relaxed and as I wandered the village and the area, it struck me that this would be a good place to live, away from the bustle of the city and more importantly out of reach of my legion of irritants. Except Sinclair of course who was still the major fly in the ointment. I pondered for the millionth time absconding and leaving him to find someone else to retrieve the Spear of Destiny for his collection, which I guessed, was one of the unwritten reasons for my trip to Munich. But as always, I couldn't. I wasn't scared of him anymore and I felt no more obligation to him than I did to the King or the village idiot. I had no desire to return to Munich, not least because it was dangerous and full of fanatics, but I had an odd feeling that if I didn't follow through on all that had happened, I would never be free of them and would live my entire life on the run from someone. There had to be some sort of conclusion to all this. I just prayed it was one that didn't involve me having to fight for my life.

Our departure was abrupt as always and for some reason early in the morning. A car appeared with a driver who said nothing more than 'good morning' and we set off for Edinburgh. Sinclair sat mute looking out of the window, which suited me. By the time we reached the station a grey dawn was approaching. The driver unloaded our valises and hailed a porter who carried them to the First Class section of the train. We boarded and found our compartment, which was reserved just for us. There was a slight delay for reasons unknown and then with the usual whooshes and clouds of steam and smoke, we started to chug forward, slowly picking up speed as we left Waverley station behind us in the gloom.

Breakfast appeared and we ate in silence. Sated I leaned back in my seat and shut my eyes. I must have dozed off, as when I awoke it was broad daylight with the sun streaming into the carriage. I sensed danger immediately but far too late to do anything about it. Sinclair was nowhere to be seen. Instead, there were two huge men poised with what looked like a big sack. I screamed instinctively and held up my arms, simultaneously looking for the door and starting to get up as my legs began to work of their own accord. As I stood, ape number one lunged towards me and I sidestepped him but that only put me between the two of them. I took an almighty swing at number two and caught him square on the jaw. He grunted and took a half step back effectively blocking my exit. I pulled my arm back to hit him again in my now fast rising panic but I was unable to go through with this plan as I was sinking to the floor myself having been hit from behind by something solid. The last thing I heard was a vague 'Sorry Major' as I passed into unconsciousness and hit the floor.

\*\*\*\*\*\*

I came to with a great weight on me as if I was being slowly crushed. I tried to move and found I couldn't. My arms were tied together as were my legs and there was a loose gag in my mouth. I couldn't see much in the dark but I seemed to be surrounded by paper which was distinctly odd. I tried to wriggle but that didn't help at all, so I lay still and listened. Once the hammering heart noises had subsided a little I realised I was still on the train. Or a train. A thousand questions came to mind, none of them useful or answerable. Where the hell was Sinclair? Why hadn't he intervened? Why hadn't he searched the train to find me? Surely he didn't imagine I had just vanished of my own accord? I lay listening to the endless clatter and the seconds stretched to minutes and maybe even to hours, it was hard to tell. I noticed a raging thirst all of a sudden and then I couldn't think of anything else however hard I tried. It felt like I was swallowing my own tongue and more than once I gagged and was almost sick, just stopping myself with the thought that this was a stupid way to die, trussed up like a pig.

I felt the train slow and heard the whistle sound. We stopped with a great sigh and I felt my heart start to hammer again. There was the sound of doors opening and then wherever I was suddenly lit up. Relief flooded through me. Sinclair had had the train stopped to conduct a proper search. I prepared to shout.

Suddenly, the weight on me lifted which threw me slightly and then I was being lifted between two men. Without a by your leave I found myself flying through the air and landing with a thud on something moderately soft, but not soft enough to prevent me being winded and unable to speak. As I strained to regain my breath, there was a scraping and a door slid shut and I was back in the dark. It had taken all of a few seconds. We started to move and I discovered that I was in the back of some kind of vehicle. Whatever it was, it was not comfortable and within moments, my joints were jarring with every bump in the road. We hit a particularly large bump and somehow despite the gag I managed to bite my tongue hard. It was infuriating.

Up to this point, I hadn't really had time to think about what was going on but between jolts I started to consider my position. I had plenty of enemies but most of them were across the channel. As far as I could tell, I was still in England, or possibly Scotland. And that was as far as I got. I simply couldn't fathom what was going on, who was doing it and why. I was also not convinced I wanted to know the answer.

After what seemed another age, the vehicle stopped. I heard doors slamming and then light came in again. I felt movement and then I was lifted again, carried a short distance and dropped onto something hard. Voices, and then a ripping noise and suddenly whatever was covering me was off and I could see. I was lying in a pile of letters and parcels, which instantly explained the paper I had felt but nothing else. Then I saw a face I recognised.

# Chapter 27

De Ropp. If I hadn't still been tied up I think I would have killed him there and then and to hell with the consequences. Instead I shouted 'uh ars ed' at him which translated in my head as 'you bastard'.

"Take the gag off," he said at which someone behind me cut it. "Before you start shouting listen to me. This is all for your own good."

"I doubt that if you are involved," I yelled struggling with my bonds. "Take these off…" As I said it, it occurred to me he wasn't going to unless I promised not to cause a disturbance. "I won't run and I won't kill you," I said.

"I know you won't. Untie him."

The gorilla behind me whom I recognised from the train cut the ropes off and I started to chafe my wrists to get some feeling back. I sat still, mainly because I was in pain.

"I'll say it again, this is all for your own good. In fact, your best friend Sinclair arranged it so before you continue pointing out my parental shortcomings, reflect on that fact."

He could have been lying of course but something told me he wasn't although that threw up more questions than it answered. I sat mute staring at my mutilated wrists wondering again what I was getting into, and more importantly how I was going to get out of it.

"You couldn't go to London."

"Why not? This is England not Germany."

"You just couldn't. Sinclair was being followed. He thought it was something to do with your time in Paris."

Well that was interesting then because clearly Sinclair hadn't told de Ropp everything. Maybe it was something to do with Paris. It was more likely than someone in London, but what bothered me most was the apparent presence of my enemies in both. It seemed I was going to be saddled with all this forever.

"We are in Norfolk. Bircham Newton[181] to be exact. Have you ever flown a Snipe?"

---

[181] RAF Bircham Newton opened in 1918. It was intended as a base for the new Handley Page V/1500 but the armistice intervened before any missions were flown.

I looked sullenly at the floor. I didn't see any reason to be cheerful.

"I'll take that as no then. Not too difficult for a man of your talents I'm sure. We have a day or two here to familiarise yourself, then we leave for Germany and the British Army of the Rhine. Your new uniform is over here. Join me in the mess when you are ready."

At that, he stalked out. I suppose he was used to my tantrums but to hell with it, I had good reasons for them. I couldn't seem to get away from these people and their schemes. I wondered for a moment what would actually happen if I just refused to tolerate it any more. I could just go and live at my house in London and never go abroad again. No one would bother me or shoot at me or send me on lunatic missions, no one would care. But of course it wasn't really like that. There was Victoria and the nipper in Paris, Sinclair himself of course, de Ropp and his employers, His Walesship and his band of thugs, my art lovers from the Louvre, some outraged husbands and no doubt assorted others who would wish me into an early pit. Many of them had already demonstrated how they would make life a misery if I were not to comply with their lunatic schemes. Or maybe I was just judging them by my own standards. It was hard to tell.

I resigned myself again to compliance with whatever this latest madness was, put on my nice blue RAF uniform in which organisation I was apparently a Squadron Leader[182] and set off for the mess. It was conveniently empty apart from de Ropp.

"Most of the squadron are away, which is why we chose this station. We don't need to hide but it would be better if you paid cash and stayed on station until we leave."

I proceeded to try to get drunk. But try as I might, the whisky had no effect apart from giving me a headache. De Ropp had left me to it early on and I had taken residence in a corner until the barman told me he was closing. I slept badly and consequently felt exhausted when they sounded reveille midway through the night. I tried to ignore it as always but to no avail and after an early breakfast, I found myself outside a hangar that contained two stubby looking green aeroplanes. This was the Sopwith Snipe, the last word in

---

[182] The RAF initially used army ranks on formation until August 1919 when an RAF Major became an RAF Squadron Leader.

military aviation apparently. I confess that I, on viewing this wonder, felt slightly underwhelmed by the prospect of flying it.

"They are better than they look," de Ropp said. "I'll show you."

He proceeded to give me a tour of the craft and I could tell he really liked it. To be honest it was impressive. Its speed wasn't much different to anything else I had flown, but that aside, it outperformed its potential adversaries in almost every aspect. I climbed into the cockpit and he talked me through the instrument layout. Nothing particularly unusual there and after a discussion about speeds and handling, we were ready to go. A couple of mechanics appeared and wheeled us out of the hangar. We both started up and rolled away over the field, turned into wind and I opened the throttle. The surge of power was exhilarating, especially compared to the lumbering beast that had been my last foray into the sky. Even compared to the D.VII it was good. We lifted off and it really was as if we had overcome Newton's theory. De Ropp was leading and he climbed out towards the coast. I followed him as he started to throw the aircraft around, rolling right and left, pulling into a steep climb and right over the top into a loop, round again into an Immelmann and then spun down to about a thousand feet. That made me a bit nervous to say the least but I couldn't possibly be seen not to do it. Once we had recovered, we dropped down to wave height and skimmed around the coast. I could almost feel the spray being lifted behind him and for a moment, I felt the joy and freedom of high-speed low-level flight, not a care in the world. We buzzed the beach at Cromer and made a couple strolling on the clifftop jump as we appeared from below them zooming over their heads at no more than fifty feet. Finally, De Ropp waggled his wings and we headed for home.

We reached the station without incident, landed and left the aircraft outside the hangar.

"We leave tomorrow," de Ropp announced to no one in particular. I nodded to myself and went to my quarters to review the situation. Once I had completed that task which took no more than a minute or two I went back to the still deserted mess and ordered some dinner. De Ropp appeared a while later and we sat in silence contemplating this new chapter in our lives.

"Whose side are you on?" I asked suddenly, surprising myself with the question.

"Mine."

"That's not a real answer is it. Not long ago you were busy supporting Kell and his gang and by extension the King and Wales. All of a sudden, you are helping me in a scheme cooked up by Sinclair and his chums. They could not be on more opposite sides."

There was a pause while he considered what I had said and I thought he wasn't going to tell me anything. I started to get up.

"I can tell you some of it," he said quietly.

I sat down again wondering.

"Is it true though, what you are going to tell me?"

"You'll never be sure because you don't trust me. But it is true, yes."

"No, I don't, but you can hardly blame me for that."

Silence descended again and seemed to stretch on endlessly ahead. My eyes felt heavy in the warmth of the sun streaming through the window.

"I have seen too much. I probably know too much and I suspect that there is a fundamental difference between the two sides you talk about. But, Sinclair approached me indirectly. A couple of years ago admittedly. He made it clear that he thought priorities had changed and that in spite of our differences he could see a time where we could, would need to work together and stop fighting each other. I agreed with him at the time and reported back to Kell who ignored me. I took it as just the ignorance of the ruling classes, no different to my native Lithuania. But now, with what you have yourself reported from Germany, I think we have to do something, otherwise we will have another war on our hands. I blame the French."

He fell silent again as I pondered all that had been said. I didn't believe it of course. De Ropp wasn't foolish enough to just change allegiance and decide that working for Cumming was the best thing ever and to hell with MI5. No, there was something else going on but I wasn't going to be told, whatever it was. Well, to hell with them all.

It wasn't a bad assessment.

Chapter 28

The sun was just peeping over the horizon as I walked round to the hangar. I had woken by chance and feeling lively, I got up and had breakfast, strolled around the field and then packed my few belongings ready to leave. I had even cabled Victoria to tell her that her beloved would be spending a few weeks in Paris and to expect my arrival sometime in the late afternoon. She had cabled back with a somewhat lukewarm response that rather left me wondering what to expect. You see, I had simply assumed that I would be greeted as a returning hero regardless but apparently, that wasn't to be the case. Time enough to deal with that when I got there.

We started our engines and rolled away over the rough grass. Turning, I sat staring into the sunlight for a moment, the engine ticking over in front of me, pondering all that had happened and all I had been told. Instinctively I reached into my breast pocket to touch the book. No one knew I had it and nor would they unless I needed it as insurance.

We began accelerating and lifted off together. There was another real moment of exhilaration as I felt the power of the Snipe and without thinking I rolled it right round before turning southwest to head for London and the channel. We flew side by side in a more or less straight line for what seemed like hours before we finally saw the city through the slight haze. The landmarks still stood out however, the majestic dome of St Pauls, the twin spires of the abbey and the clock tower of parliament. We crossed the Thames and continued in a more south-easterly direction until we saw the field at Biggin Hill where we landed to refuel the aeroplanes and ourselves. That done, we took off again and headed for Dover. It was odd really. I hadn't flown across the channel for some years and it seemed awfully quiet in comparison to the last time. But then that was during the war when thousands of ships were plying to and fro all day and night.

The French coast appeared in the haze and we flew over Calais turning southwest again as we did so. The landscape was bleak and dreary but most of all it was empty. We flew on, time dragging somewhat, but eventually the city started to appear in the distance. The sun was sinking towards the horizon by now and suddenly I glimpsed the Eiffel Tower reflecting the light. It all looked so peaceful.

We flew over the top of Le Bourget before gliding gently round until we were into wind and landed side by side. We rolled over to the main buildings and switched off, the silence shocking in its intensity after the racket of the engines. We clambered out and secured the snipes before ambling into the customs hut where we were waved through without any questions. Perhaps it was the uniform that did it. We organised some transport into town and set off to the apartment.

It was much busier as we came into Paris itself. It was almost a relief to hear some noise and the bustle increased exponentially as we trundled up the Champs Elysee. I felt my stomach tighten with what I imagine was a mixture of excitement and an element of fear. I had put Victoria's cable out of my mind until now but as I approached the door it all came rushing back. I rang the bell and there was silence within. I heard de Ropp groan behind me and rang again. At last, I heard footsteps approaching slowly and then the door opened.

"You!" My mouth churned uselessly and nothing further came out.

"Flashman!" He clearly didn't expect to see me either.

There was another of those pregnant pauses with which the lives of the unrighteous are blighted. We all stared at each other. De Ropp said nothing.

"I imagine you were just leaving?"

"First I will take my leave of Victoria."

He turned quickly and headed inside again. De Ropp fortuitously grabbed my arm as I started forward as I had known he would, but I had to be seen to be making after this interloper. My mind had taken several leaps forward in the space of a few seconds and arrived at an ugly but not necessarily correct conclusion. I turned to face de Ropp.

"Think before you act," he said. He was right of course.

"But this is that bastard Wales!"

"Even more reason not to act in haste. Let him go, find out what was going on and then deal with it. If you do anything rash now you may live to regret it. Or not as the case may be."

"Good day to you sir," the Prince of Wales[183] said as he brushed past me accompanied by another man who looked suspiciously like a johndarm[184]. Before I had time to say anything else they were past and on their way down the steps, turning along the pavement and disappearing quickly. For all his bluster it seemed he was a little concerned at what I might do. I passed through the door with de Ropp still in tow. A servant appeared from nowhere and fussed about taking coats and hats and gloves, delaying me I thought uncharitably.

"Where is my wife?" I asked of no one in particular.

"She will be down directly," the servant replied. Well I wasn't having that in my own house. I barged past her and up the stairs. De Ropp had the sense to stay where he was.

"Victoria," I started yelling as temper took over.

She appeared from a doorway and the look on her face stopped me in my tracks. I had been on the point of…. Of what exactly? I didn't really know. I was furious at seeing Wales in my house, but, if I stopped and thought about it, who was I to throw stones? On the other hand, nothing I had done was out in the open, or at least it wasn't as far as I knew, and I didn't make a public show of myself.

"What the hell was he doing here?" I said barely controlling my fury.

"He is a friend of my Father's.[185] Why shouldn't he be here?"

She said it quietly and there was an odd catch in her voice that I couldn't place. At least the cable made sense now. The situation was balanced nicely on a knife-edge. One wrong move and the blade would be searing into my essentials.

"He's a lying bastard who's never had anything but contempt for me and me for him. I never want to see him in this house again."

I thought I had overdone it. It is never easy to tell with females, but on this occasion, more by chance than anything, I had found just the right tone. Suddenly she flung her arms around my neck sobbing.

"He told me such stories. I didn't believe them, any of them, oh I know what it is like being away from home, you must suffer immensely, I missed you terribly."

---

[183] There are no official records but it is possible the Prince was in Paris at this time. He had just returned from a long tour of Australia and New Zealand with a stop in Trinidad on the way home.

[184] Anglicised slang for police from the French 'gendarme'.

[185] Ponsonby held various positions at court. He had been an equerry to Queen Victoria and at this time was Keeper of the Privy Purse for the King.

207

She rattled on like this for some time, so much so that my suspicious mind started to detect a hint of insincerity but before I could do anything about it, she suddenly pushed me on to the couch and without so much as a bye your leave she was aboard and thrashing away like a woman possessed.

Well, you know me. Seize the day and all that. The more I thought about it, the more I wondered but then what? I had suspicions but what would I really do with them? The Prince of Bloody Wales wasn't going to go quietly if he had been up to no good and anything I did would just add reasons for him to have me rubbed out. As for Victoria, well, I was still in love. I had realised it when I saw her sob and even though I couldn't help but think it was at least in part an act, there was nothing that would change that feeling. Well nothing I could think of at the moment.

******

We subsided into married bliss. The baby was performing miracles apparently. I saw him sit surrounded by cushions, which was a marvel. He grinned at me and produced the most noxious gases I had smelt since the western front. Occasionally he joined us for dinner but more often than not, we were out leaving him with a French nanny. I did briefly question the wisdom of this, not because I didn't want to leave him but I didn't want him growing up with too much French influence. I received a sympathetic stare.

I was acutely aware that my time was slipping past again and Sinclair had cabled to tell me he was arriving soon and that would only mean bad news for me. I tried to put it out of my mind and when I couldn't I decided that there was only one way to cure it and that was with Lucille. I hadn't dared to drop in up to now but this was a special occasion that merited special measures. It didn't take too much arranging. Victoria was tired as the baby had been sleeping badly. Teeth she told me, and so when I suggested meeting up with an old friend from the war she hardly batted an eyelid. I kissed her goodbye and left her on the couch virtually asleep.

A cab took me back to the familiar territory of Montmartre and I took an invigorating stroll around the back streets, doffing my tile to the tarts, stopping for a pick-me-up at a little bar I knew whilst I watched the world go by and into the lively brothels. I briefly wondered whether Wales was lurking around somewhere. His grandfather of course had been a frequent visitor in his attempts to upset his mother, but Wales was an altogether different character.

Finishing my drink, I got up, paid and ambled down to my intended rendezvous, thoroughly refreshed and ready for action.

I could only stare at the door with its slightly faded and torn sign announcing that the house was for rent. The lights were off I now realised and it was quieter than the grave. I looked round impotently trying to take it all in and not really believing it but it was clear she had upped and gone, presumably, as she said, to America. I believe I may have sworn loudly, as a couple of passing trollops crossed over to avoid me.

I ranted and raved outside, probably somewhat incoherently, for a few minutes until I realised through my rage that I was beginning to attract attention. It was someone laughing that finally broke the wall of despair and brought me tumbling back to earth. Someone was pointing at me and groping his simpering dolly at the same time and I just caught the look of contempt as they turned away giggling. I looked around and almost instantly, the small crowd of onlookers started to disperse, all except one. I didn't notice him at first as he was in the shadows across the street, but once I was alone again, I saw him move. My normal reaction to someone appearing unannounced in this fashion would have been to run from the scene screaming for the constable, but I was still somewhat bemused by Lucille's failure to inform me of her departure. Consequently, he was on me before I could move.

"I know a good place we can go." He spoke in German, which I thought was odd until I suddenly recalled that I had been raving in German. Why I had done that I could not fathom.

"No thankyou," I replied turning to go.

"But Herr Major, it is very accommodating and the girls...."

He paused while I digested the fact that he somehow knew or had guessed my former rank. It had to be a guess. I stared at him for a moment and he turned his head away.

"Lucille told me all about you." He stopped again to let that little snippet of information sink in. "I was impressed how you managed to get away from those Imperialist bastards, especially without any help from... outside."

It was the way he said it. Imperialist. Suddenly I realised I knew him. He had the most piercing blue eyes and he had been with my little gang of friends from the Louvre although he had remained well and truly in the background. My blood ran cold.

"There is no need to worry. You are on my side. Gregory told me he had let you go as I instructed and they will think it was just him that let them down. Come, let us find somewhere more comfortable where we can talk."

I glanced at his hands, one of which was in his coat pocket and clutching the unmistakeable shape of a gun. He saw me look.

"It was only for my own protection when you recognised me. I didn't want you to do anything foolish before I had explained."

He lowered the weapon and just for a fraction of a second, I explored the option of a fist in the face followed by a knee in the essentials and a lung-bursting sprint, but I knew it wasn't to be. I had seen him in action and I doubted I would survive that avenue.

"Lead on," I said quivering, wanting to believe him and resigning myself once more to whatever fate had in store.

"After you," he replied pointing the way ahead.

We hadn't gone more than two hundred yards when he motioned me towards a nondescript door which opened magically as we reached the steps. It was dimly lit inside in spite of which I could see it was a well-appointed room.

"This way."

I followed him through a door into an office.

"Sit down. We have some business to discuss and then feel free to make use of the facilities here. They are at least comparable to Lucille's establishment. In fact, her girls that didn't want to leave France moved here with her blessing so I am sure you will remember some of them.

I wasn't so sure about that as generally speaking I had only really dealt with Lucille herself. What was a little disturbing was how he knew so much although I suspected I was about to find out.

"I am known as 'Tolstoy[186]'. I work for the republic.... sometimes. Other times I work for sympathetic organisations,

---

[186] An unusual choice of alias for a communist albeit not entirely nonsensical. Presumably, he was calling himself after the author who, particularly in later life, styled himself as something of an anarchist and attempted to divest himself of all

occasionally I have worked for your government. It appears to me that we have a common purpose. This recently attempted coup in Berlin, for example. I know you were involved. Lincoln told me in passing how an unexpected ally of his had helped to prevent the right wing takeover and you had largely succeeded before being forced to help the ringleader escape."

My eyebrows had shot up at the mention of Lincoln and friend Tolstoy had smiled knowingly. Clearly, I had complied with his little plan to test me. Luckily, I wasn't that stupid and had been ready for something like that to happen. It did however confirm my opinion of Lincoln as a chancer who would blow with whatever wind seemed to be of most benefit. Why he thought I was trying to prevent the coup I did not know, although I had probably made enough sarcastic comments in my terror to convince him.

"I am appealing to you as a fellow leftist." Now I was suspicious. Where had he got the idea I was a communist? "I have contacts throughout Germany but very few in Munich or Bavaria. It is very difficult there for people like us, as you may imagine. In fact, there is only one who would be of use and would help you in your quest." He made it sound like a crusade, which, come to think of it, probably wasn't too far off the mark given everything else that was going on. "Between you, and with your contacts, I think you can remove the head of the hydra. Then we will be even."

He was very pleased with himself, particularly his mythological allusion. Of course, I heartily agreed with everything he said having taken note of his lack of resources. I was sure I could avoid his one man. The only jarring note was his comment about being even. The business concluded with a toast to the great Lenin after which, my spirits oddly restored I did as he had bidden and made use of the facilities. And jolly good they were too. Perhaps not quite up to Lucille's standard but a very useful substitute.

---

the trappings of nobility. He died of pneumonia in 1910 having left his wife and travelled south by train, dying in Astapovo train station.

211

Chapter 29

Christmas passed. Sinclair arrived. I tried to ignore it, but he wouldn't go away and it was less than a week before he was badgering me to be gone. De Ropp was no help at all and neither was Victoria. She had recovered her composure pretty quickly I had thought and now despite not having seen me for months on end seemed keen for me to vanish and 'do my duty' as she put it with her tongue firmly in her cheek. I couldn't decide whether there was some ulterior motive although I was fairly sure Wales wasn't due back in the country. So it was I found myself back at the airfield with Sinclair in tow giving me final verbal instructions, which essentially amounted to 'don't get caught with your trousers down or in any other compromising position and most of all don't implicate anyone else, least of all him'. So that was that.

We took off, the snipes still providing an exhilarating boost as we climbed over Paris, the Seine glittering in the winter sun. We flew more or less east, heading generally for Germany again. I think we flew over Luxembourg but it was hard to tell it being just a flyspeck on the map. We flew low over the Rhine and landed at a field near Cologne where the British Army of the Rhine and its attendant Royal Air Force squadrons were based[187]. It brought the St Omer of past times to mind, although the transport all appeared to be the same colour now[188]. We reported to the desk wallah and handed over the reams of paper that apparently accompanied anything military now that the war was over.

"You'll find rooms in the mess sir," he said pointing across a field to a large house in the distance. We toddled off to find somewhere to sleep before we began the next stage of our journey.

Morning came all too soon although for what was probably the first time in military history, no one woke me up with the sparrows and we had what was a very civilised breakfast. Then we left. It felt somewhat strange really. No one cared who we were and what we

---

[187] The British army occupied an area approximately 40 miles by 25 miles centred on Cologne. It was miniscule compared to the area occupied by France and significantly smaller than that occupied by Belgium.

[188] Presumably a reference to the rather haphazard RFC transport arrangements at the start of the war.

were doing. A bored soldier who had taken the bounty[189] and spent it all drove us to the station. I asked him what he had spent it on.

"Women and booze mainly," he replied.

I was impressed. He had taken the fifty-one month payment of fifty pounds, which equated to about a year's pay for a private soldier and spent the lot.

"I hope they were worth it."

"The CO doesn't think so sir. I'm on jankers for the next month. Still this sort of thing is alright."

We reached the station without any further revelations, thanked him and I gave him a tip which I had no doubt would find its way to the nearest brothel.

After the usual German army of officials had checked we were who we said we were, which of course we weren't, we boarded a train for Munich. It departed on time and trundled off into the country for the eight-hour trip. I was bored stiff. I had travelled with de Ropp enough to be comfortable with the prolonged silence but it did go on. And on.

I slept for significant parts of the journey and apparently missed the sights of Koblenz and Wiesbaden among others. Eventually it was over. It was dark and here I was standing in Munich station with my best friend and not much idea of how to proceed.

"Cab sir?" said what was undoubtedly an ex-soldier judging by his greatcoat.

We got in.

---

[189] Re-enlistment bounty offered to NCOs and soldiers. Britain's military commitments at the end of the Great War were considerably larger than at the start. It was reported in 1919 that men were re-enlisting at 700 per day.

Chapter 30

We were back in the apartment that had been rented for me on my previous visit. It was a little cramped with two but it would have to do, especially as on the face of it neither of us had any obvious source of income. Sinclair had provided us with plenty of money for the moment but there would come a time when that ran out if we stayed too long, although as always I was rather hoping it wouldn't be too long.

The big question, for me at least, was what exactly to do next? It was all very well Sinclair pronouncing about what he wanted done and so on, but of course, he didn't have to do the doing. I supposed the first thing to do would be to find Hess again. I didn't give the communists a second thought, mainly because I thought it was unlikely I would encounter them at all in such a staunchly nationalist area. Consequently, having spent a day or two organising ourselves and getting the lie of the land again, I found myself heading for the Hofbrauhaus one evening accompanied by de Ropp. It seemed the obvious choice as a place to start. I don't really know what I imagined was going to happen. My mind was in such turmoil that I was barely thinking straight. So much had happened so fast.

We found an empty corner table and ordered some refreshment. We sat for a couple of hours. The conversation was desultory and boring. Then we went home. The following evening we did the same thing only at a different table. The same thing happened. And so on. For nearly two weeks, nothing happened and I saw nobody that I knew. I was beginning to wonder if they had all given up their cause. Then I saw her. I could hardly miss her really. I watched her across the room and saw that sixth sense that tells you someone is watching. She looked round uncomfortably but I looked away. I had mixed feelings about what I was going to do next but if I am honest, I couldn't see another way. Leaving de Ropp nursing his stein, I wandered off into the throng. It was a Saturday and consequently a lot busier and I was able to lose myself quite effectively in the crowd.

I picked my moment with care. She was walking slowly past me, still, I thought, with an uncomfortable feeling, when she stopped. Like a cobra striking, or so I like to think from my old age, my arm shot out from the curtain, grabbed her round the waist and pulled her into my embrace. What actually happened was my arm shot out from the curtain, struck the stein she was carrying as she turned to see what the movement was and knocked it all over her vast bosom. As she cursed me I dragged her forcibly into the darkness and she was about to scream when I planted my mouth on hers and her baser instincts took over. Recognition sparked a stream of filthy talk in my ear and a change in the balance of power, such that yet again I was bodily heaved onto the same sofa and briefly suffocated before getting to grips properly. I was just recovering from the effort when she ordered me to do it again, using her hands and mouth to full effect. This was one order I wasn't going to slide out of complying with. In fact, quite the opposite.

Temporarily exhausted, we lay entwined chests heaving, hers more spectacularly than mine of course.

"You are back. They told me you were most likely dead or a prisoner but they didn't say why."

I pondered her question for a moment, feeling somewhat betrayed by their assumptions, but then I realised that there was only one possible course of action and that was jolly compliance.

"Well, that probably was the most likely outcome but I managed to get away. It took a lot of effort but....." I tailed off, hopefully implying what a hero I had been. Presumably, she would pass it on to anyone she could and I would be welcomed back as the prodigal, (again – it was becoming a habit!) which would suit my current predicament nicely.

She stared at me, and just for a moment, I thought I had hit the wrong note completely. My face started to burn as the bile rose, but then she grabbed me forcing me back down, her bouncers jiggling nicely and as we set to partners again I could hear her muttering about telling her brother and how he would tell Eckart and Hitler and Hess and a load of others whose names escape me and who became increasingly irrelevant as the seconds passed. They would have been pleased to know that just saying their names out loud seemed to inspire ecstasy in Helga Rohm.

De Ropp looked a trifle piqued when I told him I had made contact although I suspect it was the method rather than the event that irked him. When we left, I bid him goodbye telling him I would see him in the morning. The raised eyebrows said it all but I didn't care. In for a penny and so on, and so I spent an exhausting night in the company of Helga. In the morning, I was a shadow of the man I had once been. I left her gently snoring.

De Ropp was making breakfast when I opened the door. He quickly suppressed his look of fury and offered me some instead. I was grateful and said so, feeling perhaps that I should explain.

"We're in," I said. "She will tell them that I am back and that I have brought another recruit for the organisation."

"Wonderful. A friend of yours called last night. I told him you were out but would be back this morning. He's coming to see you in about, oh, twenty minutes or so." I hated him at that moment. The smug look on his face made it that much worse. "He didn't leave a card in case you were wondering."

I muttered thanks under my breath before finishing my repast and then doing what I could to repair my jaded look although there was in fact very little I could do. A swift wash would help, but that was it.

Mere moments before I finished there was a tap on the door. De Ropp beat me to it although given how much my hands were shaking that probably wasn't a bad thing. Quite why I was so nervous I couldn't decide. Perhaps it was just the unreality of the situation catching up with me bringing back that old pre-flight fear. I held them tightly behind my back to stop them.

The door opened and in walked what for a moment I thought was a boy but with a shock realised was in fact a woman, albeit a severe looking one with a completely flat chest. I glanced at de Ropp but he looked as surprised as I did.

"Comrade Fleischmann?"

"Yes," I said unthinkingly, my mind racing back to a conversation in Paris.

"Comrade Tolstoy ordered me to make contact with you. We are to eliminate the leaders."

It was so matter of fact. I didn't know what to say because there was too much spinning through my head, not the least of which was the fact that she had said this out loud in the middle of the ever so slightly nationalist city of Munich.

"When you say we, who exactly do you mean?"

"You, me and our comrade here."

Well, she didn't mess about.

"Have you a plan then? It's not exactly a simple task to accomplish given where we are."

"I have several plans and we will try them until one of them works. The cause will sustain us in our task until these monsters are dead."

For once in my life, I hadn't for a moment considered an attempt at seduction. Not that it would have worked or made any difference. She was almost asexual, the cause being her prime reason for existing. Well good luck to her. Nothing was worth that. Except that I would have to go along with it all and pretend I felt the same. I suspect that had she been an attractive voluptuous blonde instead of the ugly specimen she was her life may have been different, but who knows.

Without further ado, she cleared the table and produced some paper and pencils from a small sack I noticed she was wearing. She started scribbling silently. Every now and then, she would stop, turn the paper round and look at it before continuing. Eventually pleased with whatever she was doing, she smiled for the first time and turned the paper round to show us. It was labelled 'Hofbrauhaus'.

"This is a plan of their favourite haunt. I have been watching them and listening to them for some time. I was only waiting for the go ahead from Comrade Tolstoy and the news that you had been recruited to begin the operation."

I was surprised on several levels. First, she had been into the lion's den and escaped unharmed, but then I suppose I had witnessed several speeches interrupted by agitators who had got in so it clearly wasn't difficult. Second, her clear enthusiasm for murder and third her desperate need to get on with it. Tolstoy had a lot to answer for.

She rattled on and on drawing ever more detailed parts of the scene of the intended crime and expounding on how we could liquidate Eckart and co. Shooting was a favourite and was top of the list followed by a bomb. She had tried that out apparently somewhere out in the forests and it had worked perfectly, despatching some unsuspecting rabbit to Kingdom come. But shooting it was to be, at least first time. Our job was to work out exactly when with our inside knowledge, acquire some suitable firearms, pop in and bob's your uncle. She made it sound so easy.

It was dusk when I finally managed to get rid of her having spent a joyful evening discussing the finer points of Lenin's master plan. I

217

was exhausted. I hadn't had a proper drink as she had insisted we retain clear heads so no detail was missed but at last I could drown my sorrows and drown them I did. I had persuaded her that I didn't need to see her for a month or more as it would take that long to survey the Hofbrauhaus properly, obtain weapons and deal with the myriad of problems that would arise before any attempt could be made, not the least of which was darling Helga. At least my continual attendance on her wouldn't arouse any suspicion. What I was worried about though was blurting out something incriminating in the throes of passion. I went to bed, thoroughly out of sorts knowing that tomorrow I would be back in the arms of the national socialists, or Nazis[190] as some seemed to be calling them. I couldn't wait.

******

He was at the door like a puppy the next morning. Hess that is. He couldn't believe I was back and safe and he had so much to tell me. But the thing was, we couldn't stay here, there was work to be done so if I and my friend could hurry up.

Before we knew it really, we were outside and in the back of a lorry. Piled on the floor were hundreds if not thousands of leaflets advertising a rally and speech tonight at the Circus Krone near Marsfeld. It was a big venue, much bigger than the Hofbrauhaus.

"Hitler is worried I think although he does not show it." I wondered briefly how he knew then but I didn't ask. "We have to get as many people there as possible."

As he said this I realised we were in the Theresienstrasse and there were lots of people around. Without warning, Hess picked up a handful of the leaflets and hurled them out of the lorry. They fell like leaves and much to my surprise, people picked them up to look at them.

"Come on," he said, "we have a lot to get through."

He could say that again. There were heaps of the bloody things. Still, after a while it was oddly exhilarating, hurling the bundles as

---

[190] Not the National Socialists themselves. More often than not it was used as an insult by others.

far into the streets as possible. It took us at least two hours to empty the truck, but finally it was done[191].

"What now?" I asked.

"Back to Thierschstrasse."

I nodded none the wiser really but swimming with the tide for the moment. De Ropp hadn't said very much but then there wasn't an awful lot to say.

We pulled into Thierschstrasse and stopped outside number forty-one. I was about to ask who lived here but Hess was out before I could say a word. I jumped down, de Ropp followed me and we both followed Hess in a door and up some stairs. Stopping at a dark brown door, he knocked. There was a crash from inside and some muffled cursing before the door opened.

"Ah, Hess. You completed the task?" The voice of Hitler was strained. He was definitely worried.

"Yes, with help from our friends here."

I could tell that Adolf couldn't have cared less about us given the state he was in but with a monumental effort of will he managed to say thankyou for our efforts to publicise his little talk. He even stooped to arranging some coffee and invited us to sit down in his tiny living room that made my place look palatial.

While he was pottering in the kitchen with Hess hovering nearby pretending to help, I had a look around. It really was spartan. I noted Clausewitz amongst others on the shelf[192] and some truly awful paintings. It was only when I looked at them closely I realised they were by the man himself.

Hess came in carrying a tray, which he set down on the table. Hitler stood nervously clasping and unclasping his hands muttering to himself.

"This painting," I said pointing at a sort of grey blue building, "what is it? It is very good."

He looked at me uncertainly for a second or two, blinking quickly before looking away at the painting on the wall.

---

[191] This sounds like a meeting held on the 3rd February 1921.

[192] Presumably 'On War' by Carl von Clausewitz, an influential text still studied today. Clausewitz was a career soldier serving mainly with the Prussian Army. He was present with Blucher during the Waterloo campaign.

"It is the 'Courtyard of the Old Residency' here in Munich.[193] I painted it in 1914."

I half expected him to use that reference to launch into one of his harangues about the stab in the back criminals but he didn't.

"I used to paint a lot then," he said wistfully. "I tried to enter the Vienna Academy, twice in fact, but they wouldn't take me." His face darkened visibly at this admission and he said nothing more.

"Coffee?" said Hess.

We drank our coffee amid a desultory conversation that only livened up a bit when it turned to flying. Hitler had suddenly left the room so clearly Hess felt able to talk. We discussed the various airforces and their strengths and weaknesses. I very nearly set about my own demise by mentioning the E1 and how I had stolen one from under the bloody cabbage eaters noses, fortunately stopping myself before the point of no return and turning it into a somewhat lame story. Luckily, Hess was such a fanatical flyer, largely because he had missed out on most of the action, which was also probably why he was still alive, that the only thing he heard was my description of flying the E1. A lot of it was made up of course because I had to invent on the hoof a believable personal history. It wasn't too difficult because I had seen enough action with E1s, just from the other side of the table. I recounted Hawker's shooting down of the first one and was really getting going with all sorts of tales when I noticed de Ropp glaring at me and realised it was probably unwise to carry on. I found a convenient place to stop and asked if and when we were leaving.

"Yes, soon. I will see what Hitler is doing."

---

[193] It is believed the painting still exists although not on public view. It is stored along with other of Hitler's paintings in the archive of the Army Center of Military History in Washington.

Chapter 31

The atmosphere was electric. I peeped out from the curtains beside the stage. I will never forget the image. On my right, hanging at the back of the stage was an enormous flag. It was blood red with a white circle in the middle and contained within the circle was a black four armed cross, each arm bent to the right at ninety degrees. I had been reliably informed that the black cross was a gammadion cross, a name derived from the similarity to four Greek letter gammas attached to each other. You will know it better as the swastika.[194]

To my left, there was a large crowd. There must have been thousands of them[195]. The noise was incredible. Near me was a group of men in a semblance of uniform. I had heard about them from Helga. They were known as the Saalschutz, or hall protection squad and her brother Ernst was largely responsible for them. They looked very much like thugs to me but I didn't tell her that. Their main talent seemed to be brawling with socialists or if none were available with anyone they took a dislike to. As most of them were former soldiers, they were quite good at this. The chances were they would get to exercise their powers at some point in the proceedings as I doubted that all those present were vigorous supporters and some would definitely be there to cause trouble.

Suddenly the main lights went out. A hush of sorts came over the crowd. There was some scurrying and a loud crash behind me before the curtains moved and out came the man himself. He stared at the crowd for a few moments before bowing his head and looking at the floor. He spoke quietly at first, the crowd straining to hear him. It seemed a bit risky to me because if they got bored with it they would start talking amongst themselves and ignore him but he clearly knew his audience better than I did. As the volume increased, so did the animation, the fist waving and occasional thump of the lectern. He raged about some allied conference or other in Paris that January that

---

[194] The swastika symbol is thousands of years old and there are numerous examples in many ancient civilisations. Hitler claimed he had designed the flag using the old Imperial German colours. It was adopted as the Nazi party symbol in 1920.

[195] There were over 6000 people at the Circus Krone.

had demanded the war repayments be increased[196]. Versailles took a verbal hammering as always which appealed to most of the crowd but their real fury was reserved for the stab in the back cowards who had engineered Germany's downfall, helped by the Jewish plot that had been uncovered in the protocols of the Elders of Zion.[197]

As the speech neared its crescendo, I could see the sweat pouring off him. Something caught my eye and as I turned, I saw a fight break out not five yards away. Clearly, some agitators had managed to get in and had started hurling insults followed by steins. The tinkle of broken glass confirmed this but even before I could react, by looking for the nearest exit I might add, the saalschutz were on their way. I watched in a sort of horrified trance as the brown shirted thugs hauled out their truncheons and waded in. I saw blood fly and bodies go down, I imagined I heard the breaking of bones but I couldn't have done over the noise of the crowd which was cheering and chanting at every utterance from Hitler.

It's easy with hindsight to point out what should have been done or should have happened, but I can say with absolute certainty that that was the night I realised that if Hitler ever held more power, if he managed to take over the Government, and I had seen his cronies try already don't forget, we would have to fight them. Again. Well, someone would have to fight them, as I would be cheering them on from somewhere safe, like America. With Lucille at my side. Well more or less as I assumed that Victoria would come with me of course.

An enormous roar pulled me back into the present. As I listened though I thought I could hear more than just a roar. I could. Slowly, the roar assumed a rhythm as the crowd chanted.

"Sieg heil, sieg heil, sieg heil[198]," over and over and over.

---

[196] Flashman is slightly muddled here. The Paris conference followed the Spa Protocol, which had threatened more occupation if Germany failed to continue the war reparations schedule. The conference formulated a plan for Germany to pay 226,000 million Goldmarks between 1921 and 1963 as well as a fixed percentage of its export values. The German government rejected these proposals as impossible.

[197] The 'Protocols of the Elders of Zion' was first published in Russia in 1903. It purports to be the minutes of a meeting of Jewish leaders that took place in the late 19th century and described their plans for world domination. It was exposed as a fraud in 1921.

There was something else as well. In time with the chanting, the crowd were making some sort of gesture with their arms, their right arms, raising them up and extending them out in front a bit above the horizontal, palm downward. I didn't realise it at the time but this was to be the new greeting for the Nazis[199].

I considered everything I had seen so far. The flag, the messianic speech, the chanting and saluting, the thuggery and the adoration and wondered where it was leading. It had seemed all so trivial when I sent off my reports about the spear of destiny. Now I wasn't so sure.

Hitler stood at the front looking from side to side. It seemed to me that he was almost oblivious of the crowd, drained by the exertion, but he did acknowledge them with a raise of his hand, which just sent them into more ecstasy. I heard glass breaking again above the roar and the saalschutz were there again, this time in bigger numbers as this time there was a proper brawl breaking out. Fists flew and the frenzy seemed to take wings and spread. A stein landed near me and smashed into a thousand pieces that then eerily reflected the half-light. I was on the point of running although I hesitated, not sure which way was safe to go, unusual behaviour for a Flashman I agree, but I hadn't managed to work out a safe exit as the fighting spread around me. As the bile rose in my throat, I suddenly felt a hand on my arm. I turned, fists clenched, face bright red, ready to flee when I realised it was Hess.

"This way," he bawled in my ear.

I followed him without hesitation through the curtains again and into a passage that led to a private room. The noise of the crowd became muffled. Refreshments were on the table including an ample supply of beer. I picked up the nearest stein, half-filled it and then drained it in one gulp. I could have done with something stronger but it at least had the effect of diverting my mind away from the spectacle in the hall.

I heard laughter and the door opened. Hitler came in. I had never seen him so happy. It was almost as if he had taken some drug or other, as if he was a different person, chattering with everyone, waving his arms about, laughing at the smallest joke, clapping

---

[198] 'Hail victory'.

[199] Possible except that the Hitler salute wasn't adopted and made compulsory until 1926.

people on the back. I heard some of what he was saying although it wasn't directed at me particularly. Mainly it was about the speech and its effect on the crowd and how that could be exploited, especially if they could find someone to embrace their ideas who was also capable of leading the German nation. Note that. There was no question at that point of Hitler being the man for the job. It didn't register at the time of course and the previous attempt to take over the government had not involved Hitler at all other than as a spectator.

I wondered if I could slip away. De Ropp had waved as he disappeared into the night some time ago. The thing was, my head was buzzing, there was no chance of sleep and frankly, I didn't want to anyway. There was only one thing I wanted, or rather one person.

At last, the mood seemed to calm and there was talk of leaving. I caught up with Hess and told him I was going. I think I made up some rubbish about it being an inspirational evening out with the lads, couldn't think of a better way to spend my time and so on before grinning inanely, probably somewhat fuelled by alcohol, and trying to find my way out. At last, I opened a door that led to the outside. An enterprising cabbie was waiting for the drunken stragglers whom he could overcharge and overcharge he did. But I didn't care.

He dropped me outside the Hofbrauhaus and having given him far too much money, I stumbled in. Fortunately, I didn't look out of place as it was now after midnight. Rather than sit down, I acquired a glass from a passing waitress and circled the first floor. The band were still going full steam albeit slightly out of tune, not that anyone cared, so I stopped and watched them for a moment or two. I must have been drunker than I thought as the next thing I knew I was being woken by a hand on my shoulder.

"Come with me," a voice I didn't recognise said.

I stood up and swayed a little before obediently following her up the stairs and through my favourite curtains. She was there, not quite naked in all her glory, her mountainous breasts framed by the straps of a black corset, no knickers, stockings and boots. Rather ludicrously, I thanked the girl who had brought me up before she left and then almost fell down as I started to disrobe. Helga joined in and without further ado, we were at it again in the same place as always. The rest of the evening, or morning really, passed in something of a blur. At some point, we left and went to her apartment and continued the jollity before, exhausted from all that had happened, I fell asleep.

It was well after midday before I awoke. I had a headache. I was very hungry and very thirsty. The thought crossed my mind that I couldn't continue with this life for much longer as I would expire. For once, Helga ministered to my every need as opposed to her every need and let me escape without any more bedroom gymnastics. But I had to promise to visit her again as soon as possible.

At last, I got back to my own room. De Ropp was there to cheer things up but I ignored him, had something more to eat and went to bed.

******

And so life continued. Spring dissolved into summer, the speeches and rallies continued and they all led precisely nowhere and I was beginning to get bored, an unusual feeling for me as I had had enough excitement to last a lifetime or two. But bored I was. I felt like I needed to get away from Munich, my supposed mission notwithstanding. I wanted to go to Paris. The difficulty was I would need a proper reason to go and I couldn't find one.

A few more weeks passed uneventfully. I spent too much time in the Café Heck with Hess and Hitler, too much time with Helga, too much time with her vicious brother who whilst intelligent was also a brutal thug, too much time with de Ropp and far too much time with Tolstoy's protégé discussing ever more ludicrous schemes for assassination. I had at least managed to get her to stop her regular loud denunciations of the Nazis, mainly by threatening her, but I was also reaching the point where we would have to try one of her schemes or her impatience would get the better of her. And me.

It was in this atmosphere that the leadership crisis blossomed. It came out of nothing really. Kahr, who had taken over the Bavarian Government in the wake of the Kapp putsch had invited an NSDAP delegation led by Adolf to 'discuss' with him. It didn't say what they would discuss but for the Nazis it was an admission that they were being taken seriously by those in power, many of whom sympathised with the Nazi position. I wasn't there, I was busy organising a trip to Berlin for Hitler and Eckart where they would do some jolly fundraising for the Volkischer Beobachter, the newspaper that the party had bought to spout its propaganda[200], so I didn't see the outcome but apparently they had achieved precisely nothing and consequently Hitler was in a massive sulk afterwards. It seemed he didn't like the idea of joining up with anyone else and sharing power.

It was also about this time that one Dr O.Dickel founded the Deutsch Werkgemeinschaft. This was nothing unusual of course, Bavaria, and Munich in particular were crawling with right wing political groups, most of whom had half a dozen members and met up to talk rot to each other before getting drunk and denouncing everybody who wasn't them. It turned out though that Dickel had something very similar to good old Adolf. Presence and charisma. And he had it in spades. In fact, those who heard him speak and had also heard Hitler generally reckoned that Dickel was the coming man. I even saw him speak. I was at the Hofbrauhaus again, waiting as always for Helga when he made a speech in the Festsaal. If anything, I agreed with those who said he was the future as he made more plausible arguments and didn't rant as much. There was less fighting and it was cheaper in glassware. But it was not to be.

As Dickel's popularity began to climb, the Nazis made approaches to him with a view to combining their operations. Eckart and Drexler were central to this approach and organised a meeting with Dickel. I went along with Hess if only to assuage my boredom. We arrived just after Hitler did and followed him into the meeting. As we entered, we heard shouting.

"You know nothing of the stab in the back cowards, nothing of what it was like to fight in the trenches, nothing of what the people want, nothing about those French bastards and their demands......"

He went on like this barely pausing for breath while Dickel sat calmly watching him. It was only when Eckart and his entourage arrived that he stopped, sat down and looked at the floor. When the introductions were complete, Dickel started making suggestions about how they could join forces. He was clever enough to admit his

---

[200] Eckart and Rohm persuaded General Franz Ritter von Epp, Rohm's commanding officer, to purchase the Volkischer Beobachter from the Thule Society that had owned it since 1918 when it was called the Munchener Beobachter. (Munich Observer)

knowledge of the war was sketchy and nothing compared to an expert like Herr Hitler here, the same Herr Hitler who was now sulking again and hadn't said another word for a couple of hours. It was embarrassing really. Finally, once the various options had been discussed and ignored, Eckart stood, shook Dickel's hand and chivvied Hitler out of the room before everybody went home.

I was busy making dinner having stayed away from the whole lot of them for a week or so when there was a furious banging on the door. For a moment, I considered the back entrance convincing myself in seconds that the stupid Tolstoy woman had given the game away but before I could act on that impulse, de Ropp had opened the door and Hess burst in.

"He's resigned!"

"Who has?" I replied.

"Adolf. But this time he means it."

"Has he done it before then?" I asked.

"Oh, many times, but it is usually just a trick. Not this time."

Hess put on his best grim look as though he had just heard the world was going to end in a day or two and stared into the fireplace shaking his head slowly.

"What will we do?" I wondered.

"I don't know. We can't go on without our inspiration. What would be the point?"

For a long moment, I thought that would be the end of my little mission and thank God for that. I could go back to Paris, Victoria, my son, proper restaurants that had proper wine, proper trollops, in fact, proper everything. Hess turned on his heel and left virtually in tears[201].

It took a couple of days. Eckart and Drexler met for hours on end, sometimes with Hitler present where he apparently demanded that if he were to return, it would only be if he could be dictatorial chairman of the party and that talk of mergers and collaborations would cease immediately.

---

[201] Hitler did in fact regularly have tantrums and resign or threaten to resign but it was more often than not in frustration rather than an orchestrated tactic with an achievable goal. It was a characteristic of his personality – he could not compromise, it was always all or nothing.

Eventually they agreed and instead of going home, I had to resume my double life. Tolstaya[202] was really getting agitated now as we appeared to be no closer to killing anybody, mainly because I had seriously cold feet about the whole thing but was coming to realise that if we didn't do something soon, she might well turn on me.

What I didn't know of course was that fate was just getting nicely wound up and ready for action.

\*\*\*\*\*\*

An extraordinary general meeting was held at the Festsaal where Hitler defended his position, so well in fact that within days he was granted all he wanted. Dickel was persona non grata. Hess wrote a fawning article for the Beobachter dwelling on Hitlers supposed heroism and how he was the only man for the job. The fact that there were no other candidates allowed was apparently irrelevant. Hitler responded to his appointment by wittering on about how he was only the 'drummer and rallier' of the nationalist right and the real leader would be along shortly.[203]

Then on the 26th August, the Reich Finance Minister, one Erzberger, got himself murdered. There was uproar. Ebert[204] declared a state of emergency. Kahr ignored it completely. Food prices started to rise.

Next up, de Ropp and I found ourselves accompanying Rohm on some of his little outings at the behest of Hess. Before we knew it really, we were going to all sorts of meetings looking for trouble and we usually found it, mainly because Rohm seemed to be on a mission to prove himself the toughest gangster in town. You can imagine how I felt about all this but I had no choice. It was highly stressful as well as it was very difficult not to get in the way of assorted fists and weapons and more than once I was clouted with

---

[202] Feminine version of Tolstoy.

[203] It is interesting albeit pointless to speculate what would have happened had Dickel got his way. He was undoubtedly a more moderate and cleverer politician and lacked only the magnetism of Hitler as an orator. If Hitler had not got his way, it is likely the party would have split and the history of the 20th century may well have been very different.

[204] Friedrich Ebert was the first President of Germany from 1919 until his death in 1925.

something and spent an uncomfortable time squirming on the floor amongst the jackboots. The final straw was the 'Bayernbund raid'. Apparently, some worthy called Ballerstedt was speaking, probably about the drains or something equally exciting, but the Nazis had taken a poisonous dislike to him. Not particularly unusual you might say, but on this occasion, they decided to disrupt the meeting. And for some reason, the whole gang was there, Hitler, Hess, Rohm, de Ropp, myself.

There wasn't much of a plan. Someone, I forget who, knew where the power switches were and as we sneaked into the hall, the lights went off. There was immediate shouting and roaring and we surged into the midst of all the politicians, fists and truncheons swinging. What no one had thought about of course was that with the lights out we wouldn't be able to see either. Consequently, Rohm and his gang of roughs just attacked anyone who got in the way. I heard grunting and screams of pain, some of which came from me, as we surged through the hall in the general direction of the speaker. A sudden lull in the noise allowed Ballerstedt to shout for calm. It didn't do him any good, in fact quite the opposite as it attracted Rohm and his best friend who beat him severely. And then the rozzers arrived.

It was quite sudden. A door smashed open and they blew their whistles whilst using the same tactics that Rohm had used, ie, anyone who gets in the way is the enemy and is to be beaten up. Several politicians were injured this way, particularly those that panicked and tried to run. It occurred to me as I was hunting round for an escape route that perhaps a different approach was required. I was against a wall and had been for some time as most of the action was in the centre of the hall and in the dark, I could claim all sorts of heroics after the event whilst staying in one piece to the side. I had felt a door behind me as I slid along the wall keeping out of the way and now I reckoned if I could get back to the door, it might lead somewhere safe.

A body hit the wall beside me and slumped down. Checking it was unlikely to move again and the assailant had vanished for more fun, I stepped over it and continued my search. I felt the handle and turned it. It was unlocked. I opened it a fraction. It was dark inside, not unexpected but I needed to check. Looking round me and seeing nothing and no one, I slipped through the gap, pushing the door not quite closed behind me. I had been hoping for a corridor but it was a store cupboard. I was a little disappointed but it would have to do. I found a corner behind the door and sat down to wait. The noise steadily diminished and suddenly the lights came back on in the hall but not in my hiding place.

I sat still almost not daring to breathe, hoping against hope that the police were as inefficient here as everywhere else. I could hear shouts and general chatter but no one came near me.

Eventually, order was restored and the hall was virtually cleared. Ballerstedt had been carried off along with numerous others from both sides, there had been numerous arrests but now all was quiet. I stayed where I was.

A couple of hours must have passed and I hadn't heard a voice for some time. I stood up and peeped out of the door, which was still ajar from where I had left it. No one had given it a second thought, mainly because being slightly open, it was obvious there was no one in there. An old trick learnt from my father.

It was dark outside and gloomy inside. I let my eyes adjust for a moment and then made my way to the exit. It was open and I stepped outside, looked around and walked home.

De Ropp was there when I arrived.

"Where have you been?" he asked.

"Hiding," I replied.

He raised his eyebrows at this.

"They all got themselves arrested. They will be in court today I think."[205]

---

[205] Ballerstedt pressed charges and Hitler was sentenced to three months in prison for breach of the peace. Two months were suspended but he spent a month in Stadelheim prison in the summer of 1923.

Chapter 32

It was all getting out of hand. I had written a report for Sinclair but when I read it through afterwards it sounded like something from that hysterical woman Austen. I threw it away. I needed a break.

Hess had come round to see us a few weeks after the Bayernbund raid. I told him I was going away for a short period and I think even he could see I was serious. In fact, all he was concerned about was that I would return. I promised I would. He also made me promise I would stay for one more meeting. He said it would be the death of him if I didn't. It was almost the death of me.

It was to be another Hofbrauhaus extravaganza. Hitler would be speaking for most of the evening. All the party faithful would be there. It was going to be a night to remember.

I was sitting alone in my small kitchen, wondering when to leave for the night's entertainment when there was a banging on my door. Without thinking, I got up and opened it. My visitor was most unexpected.

"I have the ideal weapon," she said looking round for once to make sure no one heard her. I dragged her inside unceremoniously before she took it out of the bag she was carrying. "It's a Browning FN1910. It is very accurate and at the range we will need you can't miss." She seemed very pleased with herself. "It was very difficult to get but Tolstoy managed." She went all dewy eyed in admiration whilst I stared hard at the pistol trying to make it go away. "Tonight, we deal a hammer blow to the Nazis."

I was speechless. In my foolish addled mind, I had convinced myself that by prevaricating endlessly she would eventually give up and go away. Instead, here she was armed and dangerous and expecting me to be the performing monkey. I wondered briefly what would happen if I accidentally knocked her under a bus or off a bridge into a river, knowing full well that I would almost certainly be the victim of a similar nondescript accident. She rattled on about her plan and I tried to take it in, if only to try to see some flaw that would mean failure. Apart from the obvious one, me, there was nothing wrong with her plan. If all went as expected, Hitler would start his speech, the crowd would get more and more agitated, the opponents would start heckling, the saalschutz would wade in and a general melee would develop, chaos would be the order of the

231

evening and there would be a perfect opportunity for the selfless assassin, heedless of his own life to put a couple of bullets in the leader. Then we would all stroll home for tea. Apparently, my name would go down in the annals of party history, to be trumpeted from commune to commune, never to be forgotten. Like Martov.[206] I still wonder why men will do the most outrageous things simply for their name to be recorded as the recipient of the 'Order of Most Foolish and Deluded Human Being ever to Live'.

It was in a slightly dazed state that we left for the short journey. I had taken possession of the gun, if only to prevent her from doing something stupid with it. We had agreed that we would enter the building separately and then meet upstairs, coincidentally in the curtained room that I used regularly for my romps with Helga. Well there would be none of that going on tonight, not least because I still could not summon up the least inkling of sexual attraction for my companion. It suddenly occurred to me that Helga would almost certainly be there. And what if she needed refreshment so to speak? There was no answer. It was just a bridge I would have to straddle if the need arose.

The atmosphere in the Hofbrauhaus was electric. The hall was packed, the steins in full flow along with the food, the waitresses looked buxom, there were a few shifty characters of course, one of them being me. I knew she was watching me. I could feel it somehow. I passed the time of day with Hess and Rohm who was there in his official capacity as chief thug. I thought I had managed to avoid Helga completely but without warning, a hand grabbed my arse. I turned to see her winking at me, one hand full of beer glasses, her mouth framing the word 'later' with a nod to the stairs.

I nodded in return. I felt numb. Suddenly a spotlight came on, shining on a door that opened to reveal Adolf. As he entered the room, the chanting began. Automatically I joined in, shivering at the same time. The spotlight followed Hitler as he marched to the side of the room where a large table was against the wall with some boxes as steps up onto it. I still hadn't decided what I was going to do.

---

[206] This must be Julius Martov a contemporary of Lenin who led the Menshevik faction in Russia. Marginalised after the October revolution, he eventually left Russia for Germany in 1920 where he died in 1923. As Flashman implies he is largely forgotten.

Whatever it was, waiting here wasn't the answer so I slowly slid backwards out of the throng. It wasn't difficult in the dark as no one was interested in me. They only had eyes for the leader. By a slightly circuitous route, mainly to avoid Helga who I had spotted listening intently, I reached the staircase. Stopping, I briefly looked around me for trouble but saw none. I climbed the stairs quickly pausing again at the top. It was deserted. I slipped through my favourite curtains quaking in fear. A hand grabbed my arm and I almost fainted.

"This way," she whispered dragging me deep into the gloom. Rounding a corner I didn't know existed I saw a sliver of light ahead of me. I could hear Hitler slowly building the tension in the crowd who were oddly quiet which was of no use to me at all. I needed noise and agitation. Of course, I only needed them if I was actually going to shoot him or indeed anyone. I felt the colour drain from my face with the thought of it.

We reached the light. The opening wasn't very big. It was enough to squeeze the barrel of a pistol through but not much more, which would make aiming quite tricky. Fortunately, it faced directly towards the makeshift stage. I peered through for some time watching the performance.

"Well shoot him then," she said suddenly in my ear. It was so matter of fact.

"Not yet you stupid cow," I replied.

"Why not?"

"They'll know it was us. They'll be on us in seconds."

"That does not matter if we have killed him."

She seemed to believe that our lives were worth expending on this great task. Well, she was welcome to spend hers in that way but quite honestly, if she persisted in this she was going to be the most likely victim. It suddenly occurred to me that she was probably armed with some other weapon. It also occurred to me that I had been in a similar situation not so long ago. I shivered again returning to my vigil.

"I think we will do it my way. There are more great deeds to be done after tonight." It was pathetic but she stopped whispering.

The noise below was starting to build as Hitler got more and more agitated. I could see him in the spotlight, messianic in his oratory, his disciples staring up at him mouths open in admiration. The saalschutz were looking at the crowd, visible in the half-light, ready for action. For some reason at that point Hitler's words made it through the fog of terror and I heard him denouncing some town councillor called Erhard Auer[207] who had had the temerity to survive an assassination attempt. This for some reason had an electric effect on the crowd and I heard raised voices below me.

"Now," she said almost pleading with me to fire.

"Not yet," I replied desperately looking for a way out of this situation.

The crash of glass surprised us and she grabbed my arm again. I flinched away giving her an invisible look of contempt. I briefly wondered if my repulsion at her ugliness would be overcome by violence such as she had planned and quickly decided that it wouldn't.

More glasses were flying, occasionally reflecting the light as they spun through the air. The noise of them shattering was increasing and then I heard the unmistakeable grunting of fighting. One glance told me the saalschutz were on the move and suddenly it seemed everyone was fighting. Hitler carried on speaking although by this time it was more shouting than anything else. There were screams of pain and as I watched I knew the moment of truth had arrived.

---

[207] It seems that following the murder of Eisner in February 1919, there was a virtual riot in parliament. Auer was shot and seriously wounded by Alois Lindner who also killed two others. Such was the politics of the time.

Chapter 33

I aimed the pistol through the gap. Sweat was running down my face. I recoiled as a chair sailed through the air in front of me and then took aim again. Hitler was moving around unusually for him. His arms were waving which was distracting in the gloom and the noise was getting still louder.

I squeezed the trigger. The bang was tremendous and seemed to reverberate round the room. I felt myself more or less shoved to one side as she tried to peer through and see if he was hit.

"Again," she shouted. Clearly, I had missed. I looked through the gap again and took aim. Suddenly I felt dizzy as the blood drained from my head again. I had spotted Hitler and as I aimed, I saw he had drawn his own pistol and was pointing it in the air. He fired at nothing in particular and that set off a barrage of shots. The noise was deafening.

My hand was trembling as I pointed the gun through the gap again. I squeezed the trigger again and just as I fired, there was a crash in front of me and the wall seemed to fall inwards. I felt something heavy hit my arm as I fell backwards, a sharp pain shot through it and I involuntarily fired the blasted gun again, this time taking a chunk out of the ceiling directly above us and causing me to scream in agony at the recoil.

I dropped the pistol and held my arm in that way of the wounded who think that holding their injury might make it better. It didn't and in fact if anything it hurt more. She snatched up the pistol and was about to let fly when a volley of shots hit the wall behind us.

"Time to go," I snarled through the pain and fear.

Crawling, I discovered, is not easy with a broken arm. Every touch seemed like fire but the rising panic at the thought of being discovered drove me on. I reached the curtain and hauled myself upright. I pulled it to one side and peeped out. Not a soul in sight, presumably all attracted by the fight downstairs. I stepped through, not caring if my accomplice was with me or not. The trouble was now that I had to go down as well. I couldn't face it. Instead, I sat down.[208]

---

[208] There were many attempts to assassinate Hitler throughout the period 1920 to 1944, the most well-known being the last serious attempt carried out by Colonel

\*\*\*\*\*\*

That was where Helga found me. I gasped as she fell to her knees beside me and enfolded me in her arms.

"You're hurt," she squealed.

I nodded, suddenly trying to look as though it was just a scratch and that I could shrug it off. The squealing pig sound I made may not have given that impression though.

"What happened to you my love?" she enquired. I was slightly taken aback at the love part but managed to overcome my distress and nod towards the curtains.

"Assassin," I muttered, "in there…"

In my fevered mind, I was hoping for one of two outcomes. The first possibility was that she had escaped behind me and run for the hills. The second more enticing probability was that she was still there and they would find her with the incriminating weapon. This seemed like delicious revenge until I suddenly realised that she would denounce me and whilst they might not believe her, it wouldn't exactly be a reference either. I prayed for her escape.

By this time, reinforcements had appeared in the shape of Hess and a couple of saalschutz men. They pushed through the curtains, itching to find someone or something at least. All they found was the pistol but it was enough. And suddenly, unexpectedly, deliciously I found myself the hero of the hour.

"He tried to stop him but the cheating swine pulled a door down on him and broke his arm." This amongst the slobbers and suffocating attention of Helga who from minimal factual data had reconstructed the entire story, added some embellishments of her own and was now telling anyone who would listen how I had saved Hitler's life. I hardly dared contradict her and frankly, I had neither the energy or inclination to do so anyway. It occurred to me that it might be a useful position to maintain. Until someone asked an awkward question like "How did you know the assassin was up there

---

Stauffenberg at the Wolfschanze using a bomb. Flashman's appears to be the first recorded attempt although details are very thin on the ground and only confirm that it took place in a beer hall and was an attempted shooting in late 1921.

before any shots were fired?" Luckily, no one seemed that bothered about those minor details.

It turned out that in the pandemonium, numerous people had been hurt, some seriously, but no one had been killed despite the amount of ammunition that had been expended. Hitler had continued his harangue, occasionally letting off a round into the mayhem until the police, who had arrived suspiciously late as always, finally cleared the hall into the street and secured the place.

Helga took me to a hospital where my arm was set in plaster and then back to her place where she persuaded me to lie on my back while she had her wicked way with me. It was interesting and painful at the same time. And finally, sleep came, blissful deep sleep long into the morning.

Chapter 34

It hardly seemed real. I was in Paris again. I had escaped the clutches of Munich and all its attendant dangers. I was in a proper bed, with proper food and a semblance of normality had returned. Several months had passed since the incident at the Hofbrauhaus, the baptism of fire as Hitler described it later, months of glorious inaction and idleness. I hadn't seen Sinclair more than twice and he seemed content to leave me alone for the time being. My arm had healed although it had been a long and painful process and I had settled once again into blissful married life with a small child, now two years old and a large bundle of joy for us both. At least that was how any decent novelist would have portrayed it. Reality of course was much more complicated.

After the incident, there had been all sorts of upheaval and recriminations. Naturally, I had described the assassin in detail. I had been hoping they might shoot her on sight, her capture being something I did not need, and I encouraged them in this regard. I believe for a time there was a reward available but I knew it was largely pointless. A thorough search of the upstairs room had not revealed anything useful thank God, but the pistol had exercised their minds more or less continuously. The fact that it was a Browning FN1910 and made in Belgium roused their suspicions enough for me to shiver and when Rohm, during one of his regular discussions with the left, roughed-up a random French communist who under mild torture admitted he had known of a plot that had started in Paris I nearly had a seizure. Unexpectedly though, this turned out to be my salvation, albeit a double-edged salvation, and only temporarily.

We were back in the Café Heck again and the discussion had as always returned to the assassination attempt and Hitler's heroic continuation of his speech whilst firing back that I, in an unguarded moment, admitted to speaking French, still something of a novelty for a German. Further enquiry into this revelation had me desperately trying to dig myself out of a large hole of my own making by telling half-truths and inventions about my past that could only lead to trouble. At one point, I was regaling them with tales of escape and secret agents, Dierks, Hilmar and Mata Hari to name but three, getting myself enmeshed in the murky world of intelligence when the answer to all our problems hit me.

"I could go to Paris and find them," I said.

Silence greeted this statement. They all looked at each other.

"I am not really doing anything here at the moment," I added helpfully.

Suddenly Hitler clapped me on the back.

"Of course that is the answer. You shall go immediately. Report to Hess. And anything else you find out that might be useful...."

Before I knew it, I had become the chief of the Paris bureau of Nazi intelligence. My stories were instantly forgotten and the discussion assumed a life of its own. Delusions of grandeur made their way forward as the network expanded to cover all of France and Europe, especially England, agents in every town, every garrison, every port, rooting out the communists and leftists, sowing the seeds of National Socialism for the greater good of the world. Why I couldn't keep my big mouth shut is a question I have never adequately answered. But it did at least have the desired effect of getting me out of Munich for the time being. Of course, if I didn't find anything there would be an entirely different discussion to have which caused another shiver down my spine. When I left I took de Ropp with me. It amused him of course that I had created yet another mess but he was bored of Munich as well.

"How exactly are you going to explain the wife and child?" de Ropp inconveniently asked as the train took us north. I scowled at him and said nothing. He was right of course. If they took any basic precautions and followed me, they would soon discover my family but to be honest, even I doubted they would, not least because they lacked even basic resources so following me, one of their own, would be pointless. At least this was how I reasoned it out with myself in the dark.

After a month of cringing in the shadows, trying not to be seen with anyone, gnawing my fingernails all night jumping at the slightest noise, a gun at the ready much to Victoria's disgust given that there was a toddler in the house, I realised I had been absolutely right. Apart from a gushing reply to my first report to Hess that I had discovered precisely nothing, I had not heard a peep from Munich and slowly but surely I relaxed as I am wont to do when danger recedes. I am not sure after all this time what exactly I imagined would happen next and how I would extricate myself from the continual intrigue but what I am sure about is that I could not have foreseen any of it.

One of the first things I had done was to tell Sinclair. He was neither pleased or disappointed, just accepting of this new reality. At least he seemed to understand. Slowly he came to realise it wasn't a bad state of affairs and that there were possibilities for my conduit to Germany. I passed on some low level out of date but useful information that went down well and received regular updates on the situation in Munich in return. The situation settled as I have described above.

Married bliss was interesting, we were socially accepted, a nanny imported from England meant that Frederick wouldn't be too French and Sinclair wasn't too much of a bother. Life drifted on and for possibly the first time in my entire life I wasn't being pursued by someone disagreeable.

The news from Munich didn't change much. There was a so-called German day in Coburg in October. The local police banned marching with banners but the Nazis ignored them. For a change there was a pitched battle with the police and the locals who insulted and spat at the marchers. Hess reported that the party now had about 20,000 members, something that made Sinclair sit up in his chair when I told him.

And then suddenly, things started to hot up again. Mussolini swept to power in Italy after the much vaunted (at least later on) march on Rome. It was the first time a fascist party had reached government and whilst it wasn't the Rubicon crossing Mussolini and friends subsequently claimed, it definitely shook the rest of Europe.[209]

A week or so later, Esser[210] pronounced that Hitler was Germany's Mussolini. In December, the VB claimed Hitler was a special leader and the leader that Germany was waiting for. Admittedly, the VB was a little biased but it was the first time Hitler had been associated properly with leadership of a nation. Most of this had reached the ears of the French as well because all of a

---

[209] See appendix.
[210] Hermann Esser was one of the earliest members of the Nazi party. He briefly served in the army at the end of the war becoming a journalist afterwards. He was made editor of the Volkischer Beobachter in 1920.

sudden there was talk of mobilisation. I couldn't believe my ears. Surely they weren't that stupid? But of course they were. Why would they be any less stupid now than eight years before?

Christmas came and went, the weather turned colder and suddenly the French were marching into the Ruhr. It was the telegraph poles that caused it apparently. Sinclair had given me a little warning so that I could pass on the good news to Munich just in time to be useless. A scathing reply came from Hess lambasting the French and their colonial obsession. He seemed to think they wanted to turn Germany into a French colony and Hitler said as much publicly at the Krone. It seemed a trifle odd. Maybe they did. Who knows? The French were always an odd bunch. But whatever they were really thinking, the confrontation, such as it was, petered out with barely a whimper. Hess told me Hitler had ordered a ban on active resistance. Maybe he could see a little further than the end of his nose because the membership was rising steadily[211].

The tension dissipated somewhat as the weeks drifted steadily by and when Hitler lost face at the Mayday socialist rally[212], it seemed it might all be over. A quiet life beckoned. The glorious summer days were spent largely in blissful peace on the banks of the Seine. I had pretty much given up my search for the plot and Hess had largely stopped asking, mainly because I had sent him a continual stream of information at the behest of Sinclair who wanted to maintain the link for the time being. I couldn't see the point myself

---

[211] The French and Belgian Armies marched into the Rhineland on 11th March ostensibly because the Germans had defaulted on their 'wood' payments consisting of 135,000 metres of telegraph poles. The Versailles reparations were self-defeating as they prevented German industry from expanding and producing goods as payment. At this time Hitler made a speech blaming the 'November Criminals', ie claiming the real enemy was within and although popular resistance to the occupation threatened to eclipse the nationalists, Hitler's passive resistance policy did in fact pay off.

[212] The trades unions and communists had planned a large march through Munich on 1st May. It was eventually banned as the politicians began to worry although a demonstration on the Theresienwiese was allowed to go ahead. The right wing organisations had demanded 'their' weapons be returned by the Reichswehr to 'defend' themselves but for once the government stood firm and refused thereby defusing the situation. Hitler was made to look foolish and for a time it was thought his star was on the wane.

and said so but it made no difference and as jobs go it was hardly onerous.

And then September came. And with it, the Deutscher Tag rally at Nuremberg. 100,000 people were present. The march past took two hours. Hitler made an impassioned speech. Ludendorff and Prinz Ludwig Ferdinand of Bavaria were there. The currency started to collapse. From about four marks to the dollar in 1914, there were now 98,000,000. The Central German Reich Government brutally suppressed a communist insurgency with a lot more vigour than they used with the Nazis and then von Knilling[213] declared a state of emergency and appointed Kahr State Commissioner, virtual dictator, in Bavaria along with von Seisser and von Lossow. One of his first acts was to ban numerous NSDAP meetings. The pressure started to mount on someone to do something. People were hungry, unemployed. Industry had nothing to do. Black bread was a 1000 million marks per pound. The only political meetings that were well attended were the Nazis. And then the putsch rumours started.

\*\*\*\*\*\*

"You have to go back." A shudder whipped down my spine at this ridiculous idea. "I need to know what is going on, whether it is serious or not and whether they stand a chance of taking over like Mussolini."

I couldn't fault his logic of course. I had been there and seen it all from the beginning and now because of my own stupidity in making them sound serious, I was going to be hurled back into the fire. My mind raced looking for ways out which didn't exist. I believe I mentioned my family, which received a cold stare.

There was no way out. If I refused, I would be turfed out of Paris with Victoria and Frederick and packed off back to London. I would be persona non grata and my cushy life would end. I might even have to work for a living and that would involve returning to the RAF. Just the thought had me gnawing my nails again, especially as they seemed to be flavour of the month as colonial police and had been in constant action since the end of the war with the attendant

---

[213] Eugen Ritter von Knilling was Prime Minister of Bavaria from 1922 to 1924.

casualties, all of whom were reported heroically in the Times and London Gazette but who were still very much dead in some horrific manner.

And so it was I found myself on the train to Munich. At least that was uneventful. It was dark when I stumbled into the apartment. I was alone this time. De Ropp had vanished on some other business as soon as we had returned to Paris and I hadn't heard from him since. I slumped down in a chair and cried in the dark.

I must have fallen asleep because the next thing I knew I was woken by a persistent banging on the door. I leapt out of the seat like a jack-in-a-box, my senses instantly alight. I had cabled Hess to say I was coming back as I had heard things were getting exciting and I couldn't bear to miss what promised to be a fantastic party and he had agreed that it would be right for me to be there as one of the originals. I wasn't exactly sure what he meant by that but at least I supposed it meant a warm reception. I wasn't wrong.

As I approached the door I had a sudden premonition of who was there. I opened it slowly but as soon as there was space to fit through, it was thrust back and so was I. Resistance was futile. Hands fumbled with my belt and shirt, neither of which were satisfactorily removed amid the grunting and groaning. I thought I heard some mention of 'mein liebchen' and other meaningless pleasantries as I was forced onto the nearest chair. I had been sorely missed and even though she understood that it was important party business she hoped I was back to stay forever in her arms, arms that were now pulling me deep into her if possible even bigger chest. I had no choice of course but to comply and most jolly it was too. At least until afterwards when she was talking somewhat at random about the goings on in my absence.

"Of course they are ready to form a government. Hitler will be the Fuhrer[214], Hess at his right hand. Ernst will be his strong man. I'm not sure about Goering[215] but Hitler likes him."

It is comments like this that have weakened my heart comprehensively over the years. How I am still here I do not know. How I did not collapse instantly I do not know. How this had come

---

[214] The term 'Fuhrer' simply means leader and was common for many political parties at the time.

[215] See appendix.

back to haunt me I did not wish to contemplate. But haunt me it would. The colour had drained from me and I felt faint. I wanted to run and run and never return but I knew I couldn't. And I also knew that in the morning, it would all be over. I would be unmasked and shot.

Needless to say, for possibly the first time in my life I underperformed. Helga seemed a little put out but I couldn't have cared less about that. The few hours left before my impending death dragged by. I didn't sleep a wink. I knew it was hopeless.

******

But of course in the mad world that was Munich in the 20's, nothing turned out quite as I expected. I had watched the sunrise over the city listening to the snoring coming from the other room. I considered breakfast but I wasn't hungry. I considered taking to the bottle, which would at least numb the pain, but in the end, I just sat waiting for the knock on the door. When it came, I was resigned to my fate. I got up, walked to the door, opened it wide and closed my eyes.

"At last!"

Hess barged past me making odd snuffling sounds and waving aimlessly round the room. I watched him for a few seconds wondering if he had a fever of some kind.

"At last," he said again. "It's beginning." Overcome with emotion at this point he stopped and stared out of the window breathing heavily. After a moments silence, I decided I had to say something.

"What exactly is beginning?"

"I can only tell you if you promise to keep it secret. It won't be for long anyway."

He stared at me earnestly, willing me to agree.

"I promise not to tell anyone except Helga who is in the other room."

He nodded which I took to mean that was alright. There was another pause while he controlled himself. For a moment I thought he was going to burst into tears.

"The revolution begins tonight!"

It was impossible to get any more sense out of him for some time. Helga came into the room looking suspiciously at Hess.

"Apparently there is to be a revolution this evening," I said wondering what difference if any it made bearing in mind I had seen at first hand a previous attempt.

"Oh," she said. "Is there any coffee?"

Eventually we persuaded Hess to sit down and eat and at last, we got the full story. He was right. There was going to be a revolution. However, it was only when he told me that I was to be there my hands started shaking. In the brief excitement, I had forgotten all about Goering.

"We will leave here about 7.30 and meet outside the Burgerbraukeller at 8. Kahr will be speaking then. It is so simple, it is brilliant."

The day was agonising, the hours trickling by until at last Hess said, "Let's go… and don't forget your pistols."

Helga waved me goodbye, possibly for the last time and we set off to walk. It was black as pitch. There were few lights on because nobody could afford them. We crossed the Ludwigsbrucke, the Isar glinting at us occasionally with the reflection of the moon and as we came down to the end of Rosenheimer Strasse I became aware that we were not alone. I shivered as I realised that there were lots of groups of men all walking the same way in an eerie silence. It was only then that I actually realised Hess had been serious. How serious only became truly apparent when we got to the Burgerbraukeller.

There were hundreds of men there, most in ex-army greatcoats or similar, but a few had gone a little further and were wearing steel helmets. All of them were armed, most with pistols but some were carrying bigger weapons and some looked like they had a machine gun. My face burned red as the fear surfaced, not that anyone would have noticed. In something of a daze, Hess led us to the front of the group. Here, the tension was palpable. There was little talk although Hitler did greet Hess and I. Then I stepped back straight into the man behind me.

"Watch out," an arrogant voice said.

"Sorry…." I began to say and stopped.

"What's the matter? Seen a communist?"

A couple of them laughed.

"Have we met?" he suddenly said, a puzzled look in his eye.

Inspiration is a funny thing really. It can be lifesaving at times and luckily, for me fear alone has never prevented it for me.

"Jagdgeschwader 1 I think. Fleischmann."

"Of course!" he boomed grabbing my fin and working it like the village pump. "We were heroes then, until these bastards stabbed us in the back."

I vigorously nodded my agreement trying to extricate my hand before he pulled it off.

"We must talk of the old days sometime. But not now. We have a country to take."

He turned away laughing, the sound grating amid the virtual silence whilst I attempted to slide slowly backwards hoping he would forget me, or at least not remember where he had really met me[216]. My heart was pounding and my head was starting to ache. I wondered if this was how all revolutions started.

Without any apparent signal, we all began to move towards the doors. I was much too near the front for my liking but Hess had more or less dragged me to what he described as the place of honour. Someone pushed the doors open and Hitler, flanked by two bodyguards and all brandishing their Brownings, advanced through the thousands strong crowd. He was followed in by the heavy machine gun crew and numerous others. Immediately Kahr stopped speaking as people turned to see what the commotion was. Others climbed on their chairs to see what was going on and the noise was deafening. Suddenly there was a loud bang. I jumped and ducked at the same time thinking all hell was about to break loose but in fact entirely the opposite happened. Near silence descended and as I stood up straight again I realised what had happened. Hitler or his bodyguard, it was hard to tell which, had fired a shot somewhere.

"The national revolution has begun. The hall is surrounded by six hundred armed men. If there is trouble, we will bring a machine gun into the gallery. The Bavarian Government is deposed. A provisional Reich government will be formed. I request your presence next door." This was to Kahr, Lossow and Seisser[217]. "I guarantee your safety."

---

[216] Flashman briefly met both Goering and Richtofen when the latter shot him down. See 'Flashman and the Knights of the Sky'.

[217] Following the declaration of a state of emergency in Bavaria on 26th September 1923, Gustav von Kahr (State Commissioner), Hans Ritter von Seisser (Head of Bavarian State Police) and Reichswehr General Otto von Lossow were appointed as a ruling dictatorial triumvirate. One of their first actions was to ban

Now all hell did break loose. It was like Bedlam and Babel rolled into one. Cheering, shouting, glass breaking, the only thing missing was gunfire but I wasn't entirely sure it was far away. I noticed Hitler and the three wise men heading for a door and took my opportunity to follow, mainly I thought because it would remove me from under Goering's big nose. He was now shouting and trying to establish some order.

"Stay where you are. This is not directed at Kahr or the Army or the police. Stay calm. You've got your beer."

Oddly, that was enough to quieten the crowd as we entered the side room. Hitler for some reason was still waving his pistol about and I guessed from that that it was him that had fired the warning shot. Kahr and friends were looking decidedly uncomfortable.

"I will form a Reich government which I will lead. Ludendorff will head the army, Lossow, you will be Reichswehr minister, Seisser police minister, and you my friend," this to Kahr, "you will be Bavarian head of state. I apologise for having to act this quickly but something had to be done and soon. If it doesn't work out, I have four bullets in my pistol. One each for my collaborators and one for me."

He grinned round at everyone at this last statement. It was hard to tell what they made of it. I thought he had lost his head completely but then I suppose I found it hard to picture Baldwin blowing his brains out if he lost a vote in the commons. Poincare maybe but being French it was more likely he would pop down to the nearest brothel. It seemed a peculiarly German thing this idea of topping oneself after failing to perform adequately.

Hitler headed for the door again and I followed not wanting to be left with Balthazar and co[218]. He clambered back on his chair intent on speaking again. After a brief harangue about the Berlin Jew government and the November criminals, he returned to the present.

"Outside are Kahr, Lossow and Seisser. They are struggling hard to reach a decision. May I say to them that you will stand behind them?"

The crowd roared at this.

---

Hitler's meetings.

[218] Presumably an oblique reference to the three wise men.

"I can say this to you: Either the German revolution begins tonight or we will all be dead by dawn!"

The crowd roared again, minus one who was gaping in disbelief at the idea that this was a death or glory enterprise. Just to confirm a sense of farce worthy of the theatre, Ludendorff chose this moment to appear. He was dressed conservatively in the full uniform of the Imperial Army and shortly after this, the whole gang returned to the stage, Hitler staring around like a child who has raided the sweetshop.

Kahr spoke first.

"I have agreed to serve Bavaria as regent for the monarchy."

I didn't hear what else he said because it was lost in the storm of applause.

Hitler again. "I will direct the policy of the new Reich government." More applause and cheering. Then Ludendorff.

"What a surprise this business is," he exclaimed, clearly planning his exit strategy in case it all went wrong. The applause was a little more muted. He wittered on for a bit before Lossow and Seisser, both looking more than a little agitated also expressed their undying support for the whole operation. Finally, Pohner[219] promised to cooperate with Kahr. Hitler shook hands again with them all, still grinning like the village idiot. And that was it. Success.

Having stood around congratulating each other for a while, someone then asked what was going to happen next.

"We must tell Rohm. And someone should put these placards up."

Even I could see it wasn't much of a plan. The placards announced that Hitler was now the Reich Chancellor, and Rohm was addressing a crowd at the Lowenbraukeller from where he was meant to have secured the Reichswehr headquarters.

There was some more congratulating and some handwringing and then suddenly someone, I forget who, rushed in saying there was trouble at the Engineers barracks. A brief discussion ensued about whether this was important or not and if it was what should be done about it. The general opinion appeared to be that it was important but no one really had any idea what exactly to do about it.

"I must go myself," Hitler announced to no one in particular.

---

[219] This must be Ernst Pohner, Munich Police Chief between 1919 and 1922.

"Good idea," said Hess.

"Excellent. We will leave Ludendorff in charge here."

He left almost immediately, followed by Hess who for some reason was taking a few of the more celebrated members of the audience to a house outside Munich. Ludendorff in his ridiculous comic opera uniform assumed command of the operation and wandered benignly about smiling and shaking hands here and there for all the world like some old buffer at a society wedding. Which of course is exactly what he was.

Kahr appeared from nowhere, his two sidekicks lurking in the background.

"Herr General, we could be more useful if we were allowed to leave don't you think? We would give you our word..."

"Of course, why not. Off you go then."

And so Kahr, Lossow and Seisser departed. It seemed wrong to me as well but I was hardly going to overrule Ludendorff.

And so the evening dragged on, a mixture of farce and fanatics. Hitler arrived back from his little jaunt looking downcast. His feelings weren't improved when he discovered what had happened in his absence. The mood that only a couple of hours ago had been virtually euphoric, was now gloomy and the pall of stale smoke hanging in the air didn't help. The food was gone as was the beer. Groups of men were lounging around as best they could, sleeping on chairs pulled together or lying on the tables. I must have dozed myself, as frankly I was bored stiff. Even I had thought that revolution would be more exciting than this.

In the early hours, a rumour swept the hall that Hitler was going to Berchtesgaden to talk to Prince Rupprecht[220] but it came to nothing. Sometime later there was a cheer when Graf[221] and some other SA men appeared with bundles of 50-billion mark notes to pay everyone with. But they were the highlights. It was now about eight o'clock and I for one was feeling very tired. It slowly became obvious that men were starting to drift off and presumably go home.

---

[220] The last Crown Prince of Bavaria, he commanded Sixth Army at the outbreak of war rising to the rank of Field Marshal commanding Army Group Rupprecht. Widely considered to be the most able of the royal Generals, he realised in late 1917 that the war was lost. He never acceded to the throne as Bavaria was declared a republic but never renounced his right to the throne.

[221] Presumably Ulrich Graf, Hitler's personal bodyguard.

I woke up with Goering shaking me.

"We are going," he said, his face alive with excitement.

"Where are we going?" I replied thinking we would be off to get some breakfast or lunch given the time.

"We are going to march through the city. Hitler and Ludendorff dreamed it up." At least it was something like that. The sound of straws being clutched echoed through the room. But it was true. And before I knew it we were all assembling outside, many of us looking dazed through lack of sleep. I tried to hang back but it was not to be. We formed up with the Nazi standards in front followed by all the bigwigs in a row, Hitler in the centre flanked by Goering and Scheubner-Richter, Rohm, Streicher, Frick and one Fleischmann with the severe wind up.

I looked around and made a quick assessment. There must have been at least a thousand men assembled and the numbers alone gave the marchers confidence. The atmosphere changed again from one of defeat and disillusion to one of confidence that this was the moment when the world would change.

At some prearranged signal, the march set off, Hitler and others again waving their pistols about. Within a couple of minutes, we were on the Ludwigsbrucke again. I noticed with horror that there was a police cordon across the bridge and I glanced at my companions thinking they must stop. But they didn't and I was swept along with the crowd. As we got closer I realised the police were few but armed. I could feel the tension building and my face burning, the bile rising as we marched inexorably over the bridge. And then we were through. The police simply moved out of the way. There were cheers and shouts from the marchers and then as we marched through Isartor I noticed the cheers were from the increasing crowds lining the streets. On we went, up the Tal to Marienplatz in the city centre. I confess that at this moment, I was beginning to believe it might work. More correctly I was beginning to worry it might work.

In the excitement of reaching Marienplatz, it was decided, by whom I don't know, to carry on to the War Ministry and so the whooping and hollering horde, now accompanied by many of the bystanders set off again. Someone started singing the Sturm-Lied[222], which was taken up by all around. The mood was jubilant, and at

---

[222] Storm or storming song written by Eckart.

250

that point, I would say most, if not all, the marchers really did believe this was the beginning.

Even as the leaders came into the top of the Residenzstrasse and saw a much larger police cordon they were not deterred given what had happened on the bridge. Not that they could have stopped anyway as the press behind was considerable.

"Heil Hitler!" someone shouted from the crowd.

"Heil Hitler!" many replied, the shout taken up by the marchers and mingled with the singing.

Then time seemed to stand still. I glanced around me. Hitler was arm in arm with Goering on his right and Scheubner-Richter on his left, both of whom were singing. Rohm and the other front rank leaders were singing as well, arms linked together in defiance. The shouting reached a crescendo, I saw Ludendorff look at Hitler with a smile on his face that suddenly changed to doubt. I looked myself and saw Scheubner-Richter stumble. I saw Hitler's face frown and then with a whoosh like an artillery shell the world sped up and the bullets started flying.

I hadn't heard gunfire in earnest for years but believe me I hadn't forgotten what it was like, especially when one was on the receiving end. A hail of bullets seemed to come from the police cordon while all around me men were drawing weapons and firing back. The noise was horrific, mainly because I was right in the middle of it with nowhere to run. In the seconds that followed Scheubner-Richter falling, I saw Hitler go down as well. Blood splashed on my arm as the man beside me's face disintegrated with a choking, gurgling scream accompanied I might add by my own wail of terror. I lurched away from him only to collide with Goering who shouted something unintelligible before screaming in agony himself and clutching at his leg as he collapsed in front of me. Spinning round desperately looking for a way out, I saw Ludendorff calmly watching from the side of the road. I can only assume the police knew it was him because he stood out like a sore thumb and I realised that was where I needed to be. If only I could make it there.

I crouched down and started to run. Bodies were littering the floor and frankly getting in my way. I nearly ran straight in front of one man who I didn't know but who was firing indiscriminately. I stopped and dropped to the floor more or less in front of him only to see him crumple backwards as a large red stain appeared on his chest. I nearly fainted as I realised another second and that would have been me. On my hands and knees now, I ludicrously crawled towards Ludendorff occasionally taking cover behind the dead.

It stopped. The torrent of lead became a trickle and then stopped. There was no cheering now, just an odd groaning noise. I stayed where I was for a moment to try to get my bearings waiting for the shooting to start again, but it didn't. The marchers and the crowd had scattered in all directions. I lifted my head, why I don't know but I can only assume some instinct told me it was over. I looked behind me to see two men more or less dragging Hitler towards a car. He was clearly badly injured, I hoped terminally, which would be useful if I ever got out of this mess and managed to return to civilisation. Looking towards the police, I saw they were advancing in open order[223], arms at the ready. But it was over. Some men were tending to the wounded, some were standing in surrender, many had disappeared into the side streets or back the way we had come. Ludendorff was still standing to one side looking mightily out of place. I came to a decision. I had to go.

Looking around I could see men still streaming away. Some, like Rohm, were apparently staying, deliberately defying the police who were arresting them as they advanced. Then I saw my way out. About fifty yards back down the Residenzstrasse I saw a group of about five men making themselves scarce. In the centre, limping badly was Goering. That was it. I ran after them trying to look inconspicuous. I caught them up in seconds.

"My God what a battle," I said. "What happened to Adolf? I saw him go down."

"We don't know but we have to get out of here otherwise we will never see Germany rise again."

"Here, let me," as I muscled in beside Goering taking his weight on my shoulders. He looked up at me, his face a mask of pain.

"Thank God it is you Fleischmann and not one of those army cowards. To Austria!"

---

[223] The idea of 'open order' was developed during the American War of Independence. British troops had to adapt to the Americans tactics and in so doing were forced to fight in looser formations, sometimes known as loose files or American scramble. Three 'orders' were used to specify how far apart the troops should be; order, open order and extended order.

Chapter 35

"In this year 1923, the swastika and stormtroopers disappeared, and the name of Adolf Hitler fell back almost into oblivion. Nobody thought of him any longer as a possible in terms of power."

So said Stefan Zweig[224] the author. It seemed he was right. The crisis was over. The mark stabilised, the NSDAP was banned and the various right wing factions splintered into their component parts. Hitler was in prison along with various others and the rest were scattered to the four winds.

After a brief stay in Austria, I had told Goering I had to leave for France. He was happy to see me go for as far as he was concerned I was continuing the struggle from inside enemy territory. Moreover, he was pretty much blotto from morphine injections a lot of the time. He had been shot in the leg and the escape had not helped. And so I had found myself heading for Paris again. It seemed unreal. At long last, I felt my war was over. Even Sinclair seemed to think so when I finally met him. He had taken something of a back seat as well when Cumming died[225] and was succeeded by Hugh Sinclair, a naval officer and former Director of Naval Intelligence who also happened to be a relative of some kind. He also seemed happy for me to stay on in Paris as long as I maintained my links to Germany. Not that that was particularly easy as I had explained in my final report on the subject. The Nazi movement as a whole had to all intents and purposes fractured and vanished after the attempted putsch. There was a trial, which Hitler managed to use for propaganda although no one quite knew why as everyone knew he was finished. The government had re-established order, the economy began to grow, the American banks mortgaged the German railways and other assets, which provided capital for rebuilding. The Rentenmark became the new currency.

Lenin died. Stalin replaced him. MacDonald became the first socialist prime minister of Great Britain. Mallory and Irvine vanished on Everest, Harding and Nelson flew right round the world. The Geneva protocol was adopted by the League of Nations but not ratified. The French withdrew their troops from Germany. Hess was

---

[224] Stefan Zweig was an Austrian author at the height of his fame in the 1920s.
[225] Mansfield Cumming died on 14th June 1923.

sentenced to eighteen months in Landsberg. And Hitler was sentenced to five years.

In December, they were released.

THE END

## Appendix 1.

## Frederick Winterbotham

Group Captain Frederick William Winterbotham was born in Stroud in 1897. He joined the Royal Gloucestershire Hussars Yeomanry at the start of the Great War transferring to the Royal Flying Corps in early 1917. He was shot down on 13th July that year and spent the rest of the war in Holzminden prison camp.

After the war, he took a law degree before becoming a farmer, first in Britain and then in Kenya and Rhodesia before returning in 1929 to join the RAF staff. Initially assigned to the Air Section of SIS he built up the RAF intelligence service, gathering information on military aviation in potentially hostile nations. As part of this, he discovered, through the reports of William de Ropp, that the Germans were training pilots in the Soviet Union in violation of the Versailles treaty. The Nazis, although not yet in power, imagined that Britain, as an imperial nation, would be sympathetic to their aims and quest for power and this led to a visit by Alfred Rosenberg in 1932. Winterbotham used his position in SIS to facilitate Rosenberg's tour and maintained contact with him, regularly visiting Germany over the next seven years. He played the role of Nazi sympathiser so well that he became familiar with many in the highest echelons of the Nazi regime, including Hitler, Goering, Milch and Kesselring.

When war broke out again, Winterbotham was heavily involved with 'Ultra', forming the Special Liaison Units responsible for the delivery of 'Ultra' intelligence to field commanders. It was a very demanding role for all concerned.

Winterbotham left the service in 1946 and concentrated on writing, his book 'The Ultra Secret' being the first to tackle the subject. It was controversial, contained a number of inaccuracies but was nevertheless a vivid first-hand account. Winterbotham concluded that 'we might not have won the war had we not had Ultra'.

Winterbotham died in 1990 aged 92.

# Appendix 2

## French Army Mutiny 1917

By early 1917, nearly one million French men had been killed in action, a truly devastating figure and one that was felt keenly by the French Army, especially the Infantry. Nivelle's 1917 offensive on the Chemin des Dames, billed as a war winner, was nothing of the sort and largely failed with the attendant heavy casualties. He was sacked and replaced by Petain on 15th May. At the end of the month, the increased desertion rate turned to outright mutiny. 30,000 soldiers left the front lines, thousands more refused to return to the trenches. Most were veterans who could see the futility of offensives where the human body was pitted against a storm of artillery and machine gun fire. Most wanted nothing more than the authorities to accept this reality.

At the same time, the Russian revolution was in full swing and news of it was widely published in socialist newspapers.

It was generally reported at the time that mutiny affected more than half of the French Army divisions. In 1983, Guy Pedroncini, biographer of Petain, wrote that of 113 infantry divisions, 49 were affected and of those, 24 were seriously affected and 25 had isolated but repeated instances of mutinous behaviour, ie 43% had been affected.

The infantry of course had borne the brunt of the fighting and therefore of the casualties and this was true in all the main armies. It is hardly surprising that the soldiers who were expected to carry on had had enough and refused to do so. If anything, it is surprising that the soldiers fought on so long.

The aftermath was managed with some care. The authorities, Petain and Poincare in particular, tried hard not to aggravate the situation. In spite of this there were nearly 3500 courts martial of which nearly 2900 men were sentenced to hard labour and just over 600 sentenced to death of which 43 were executed. Petain then offered more regular and longer leave periods and an end to the grand offensives that had so demoralised the infantry. There would be no more attacks 'until the arrival of tanks and Americans on the front'.

The French army remained on the defensive until the last few months of the war when the German offensive and subsequent collapse finished all. The British attempted to restore French morale with Third Ypres, otherwise known as Passchaendaele, but this was largely no more successful than any previous battle.

The first disclosures about the mutiny were not made officially until the release of records in 1967. Many more political papers are due for release in 2017, 100 years after the event.

# Appendix 3

## North Pole Exploration

The North Pole is located more or less in the middle of the Arctic Ocean albeit it is permanently covered with shifting ice. Consequently, unlike the South Pole, no permanent station has ever been constructed there. The nearest land is about 400 miles away on the north coast of Greenland and the nearest habitation is 500 miles away in Canada.

Polar exploration has long fascinated many explorers but has been fraught with difficulty. A Royal Navy expedition commanded by William Parry reached 82 degrees north in 1827. A US expedition in 1871 ended in disaster and another British attempt led by Commander Albert Markham reached 83 degrees north in 1876.

The USS Jeanette tried again in 1879 but the ship was crushed in the pack ice and over half the crew, including its commander George DeLong, died.

April 1895 saw a Norwegian attempt on skis when Fridtjof Nansen and Hjalmar Johansen reached 86 degrees 14' north before turning back and in 1897 a Swedish engineer tried to reach the pole by balloon. This came down about 200 miles north of Kvitoya on the Svalbard archipelago to which the Swedes returned where they died, their remains being found by another Norwegian expedition in 1930.

In 1899, two Italian explorers, Luigi Amedeo and Captain Umberto Cagni tried again, sailing from Norway and set a new record of 86 degrees 34' north but only just made it back to their base camp.

The first man to claim to have reached the Pole was an American, Frederick Cook, in 1908. Unfortunately, he had little proof and this is not generally accepted. Another American, Robert Peary, was for many years credited as the first man to reach the Pole on 6th April 1909, but his claim remains controversial. Research in the last 30 years has been divided with a British explorer, Wally Herbert, finding discrepancies in the navigational records of the journey – Peary was the only trained navigator in the party – as well as contradictions in his companion Matthew Henson's diaries of the trek. However, in 2005, British explorer Tom Avery recreated

Peary's journey using dog sleds and managed to reach the Pole five hours quicker than Peary claimed to have done.

In 1926, US naval officer Richard E Byrd and pilot Floyd Bennett claimed to have overflown the Pole in a Fokker Trimotor. This feat was verified at the time by the National Geographic Society but in 1996 it was revealed that Byrd's solar sextant data that was never checked consistently contradicted his report. It is claimed that the sextant data was impossibly overprecise and was therefore left out of the report circulated at the time.

In 2009, E Myles Standish of the California Institute of Technology, an experienced scientific claims referee stated, 'Anyone who is acquainted with the facts and has any amount of logical reasoning can not avoid the conclusion that neither Cook, nor Peary, nor Byrd reached the North Pole; and they all knew it.'

The first verifiable consistent claim was made by Roald Amundsen on 12th May 1926 when he overflew the Pole in the airship Norge piloted by Italian Umberto Nobile.

An ice station was established by Soviet scientists about 13 miles from the Pole in 1937 and the Pole was overflown again by an RAF Lancaster in 1945.

The first men to set foot on the Pole were Soviet scientists when a 24 strong party flew from Kotelny Island and landed there on April 23rd 1948. They remained for two days before flying back. On May 9th 1949, two more Soviet scientists parachuted onto the Pole and on May 3rd 1952 a US Airforce party landed a Douglas C47 Skytrain at the Pole. This was widely believed to be the first landing until the Soviet arrival was publicised.

In 1968, the first surface conquest of the Pole was completed by four Americans on snowmobiles and then in 1969, four Britons of the British Trans-Arctic Expedition led by Wally Herbert became the first men to reach the Pole on foot albeit aided by dog teams and air dropped supplies. This team also completed the first surface crossing of the Arctic from Barrow in Alaska to Svalbard.

1977 saw the first surface ship reach the Pole, the Russian icebreaker Arktika and in 1982 Ranulph Fiennes and Charles Burton were the first to cross the Arctic in a single season. They went on to complete the first and so far only North South circumnavigation on foot.

Since then many many others have stood at the Pole including Neil Armstrong and Sir Edmund Hillary who arrived in a small ski plane, Hillary becoming the first man to stand at both poles and at the summit of Everest.

Now, it is possible to visit the North Pole as a tourist!

# Appendix 4

## Albert Ball

Born on 14th August 1896 in Lenton, Nottingham, Ball had what might be considered an idyllic childhood. He grew up with his brother and sister attending Grantham Grammar and Nottingham High Schools before moving to Trent College. He learnt to shoot at a young age and had a natural talent for anything mechanical. He served in the Officers' Training Corps and went to work at the Universal Engineering Works when he left school.

On the outbreak of war, Ball enlisted in the Sherwood Foresters and was quickly promoted to Sergeant before being commissioned in October. Itching to see action rather than the training he was conducting, he transferred to the North Midlands Cyclist Company but remained in England. He briefly got engaged and then started taking private flying lessons at Hendon with Ruffy-Baumann.

Not considered anything other than an average pilot, Ball nevertheless gained his Royal Aero Club certificate in October 1915 and immediately applied to transfer to the RFC. Sent to 9 Reserve Squadron at Mousehold Heath, he soloed there before completing his training at the Central Flying School at Upavon. Awarded his wings on 22nd January 1916 he was officially transferred to the RFC.

February 1916 saw him posted to 13 Squadron flying BE2cs on reconnaissance missions and where he was shot down for the first time in March by anti-aircraft fire. Shortly after this he and his observer, Lieutenant S.A.Villiers, began showing the marked aggression that characterise Ball's later career, attacking amongst other things a balloon on 10th April. This led to his being assigned to the squadron's single seat Bristol Scout.

May 1916 saw him posted to 11 Squadron operating a mix of fighters including the Scout, Nieuport 16 and FE2b and this was where his rather unique style came to the fore. Deciding he didn't like the hygiene in his billet he lived in a tent on the flight line before building himself a hut with a small garden.

As a pilot, Ball was always happier as a lone wolf and this was replicated on the ground where he was happiest playing his violin or tending his garden. His engineering interest meant he acted as his own mechanic and often flew without helmet or goggles, his hair longer than regulations permitted.

On 16th May 1916, Ball scored his first victory. Flying a Nieuport he brought down two LVGs on 29th May and a Fokker Eindecker on 1st June. He destroyed a balloon on 25th June plus two more aircraft on 2nd July taking his total to seven.

Temporarily reassigned to reconnaissance with 8 Squadron, he was sent on a mission to drop a French agent behind the German lines although when he landed the agent refused to get out. It was during this period that he was awarded the Military Cross for conspicuous gallantry noting especially the occasion he had attacked six machines in one flight. This was typical of the man. He never heeded the odds and generally attacked on sight although like many, he didn't relish the destruction of his opponents. It was 'either them or me'.

Posted to 60 Squadron, Ball was given almost free rein to indulge his preference for solo missions and it was here he first had his propeller boss painted red, mainly to help his identification for confirmation of his combat claims. By the end of August, he had shot down 17 enemy aircraft.

Leave in England followed and it was now he found his fame had preceded him. Initially, the British Government had suppressed it's aces names but the Somme disaster made publicising some success necessary. Returning from leave he continued his aggressive tactics and by the end of September when he was posted back to England he had amassed 31 victories. He was a national hero.

In November he was invested with his MC and two DSOs by the King and shortly after was the first man to receive the DSO three times. At the end of his leave, he was posted to 34 Squadron as an instructor where he test flew the SE5a. He was not impressed although other pilots did not agree. In February he was made a Freeman of the City of Nottingham and in April he became engaged again to Flora Young.

April 1917 saw Ball posted as Flight Commander to 56 Squadron back on the Western Front. He now had two aircraft, his Nieuport for solo missions and his SE5 for squadron patrols. 23rd April saw his, and the squadron's, first victory when he shot down an Albatros. Numerous others followed and on the 6th May he shot down an Albatros DIII to take his score to 44.

It was becoming obvious however that the Germans were improving their tactics as the heavy battle damage Ball regularly sustained showed. In his last letter to his Father on 6th May, Ball wrote, 'I do get tired of always living to kill, and am really beginning to feel like a murderer. Shall be so pleased when I have finished'.

Like so many of the 'aces' of the Great War, Ball's last flight is shrouded in mystery. Cecil Lewis described it in his excellent memoir 'Sagittarius Rising'. 56 Squadron had run into Jasta 11 near Douai and a running dogfight developed, the aircraft becoming scattered around the sky. Ball was last seen as Flashman describes flying into a dark cloud. The next observation of his aircraft was by Leutnant Hailer, a German pilot who saw him fall out of cloud upside down with the propeller stationery and leaving a cloud of black smoke caused by oil leaking into the cylinders which only happened if the engine was inverted.

When Hailer reached the crash site, Ball was dead. There was no battle damage and no bullet wounds and a doctor subsequently recorded the cause of death as a broken back, crushed chest and multiple fractures.

Oddly, and probably for propaganda reasons, the Germans credited Lothar Richtofen with shooting Ball down but this is highly unlikely as Richtofen claimed a Sopwith Triplane, something Ball never flew. It is most likely that Ball became disorientated in cloud, something that can happen to the most experienced pilot in almost any circumstances, and simply lost control and crashed.

Ball was officially listed as missing on 18th May. At the end of the month, the Germans dropped a message saying he was dead and had been buried with full military honours at Annoeullin. They erected a cross over the grave of the 'English Richtofen' that stated 'Fallen in air combat for his Fatherland English pilot Captain Albert Ball'.

His death was reported worldwide. He was awarded the Croix de Chevalier, Legion d'Honneur by the French and the following day the Victoria Cross. His memorial service in June was attended by large crowds that included his Father and brother Cyril, himself now an RFC pilot.

After the war, Balls grave had a new cross placed on it. When the Imperial War Graves Commission began consolidating British graves into fewer cemeteries, 23 British servicemen buried with Ball were moved to the Cabaret Rouge Cemetery but at the request of Balls father, his was left where it was. He paid for a private memorial to be added. He also bought the field where Ball had crashed and placed a memorial stone there.

There are numerous memorials to Ball, especially in Lenton including two, one inside and one outside, in Holy Trinity Church. In 1967, Trent College established the Albert Ball VC Scholarships and a propeller from one of his aircraft and the original cross from his grave are displayed in the college's library and chapel.

He was without doubt one of my boyhood heroes.

# Appendix 5

## Richtofen

Manfred Albrecht Freiherr von Richtofen was born on 2$^{nd}$ May 1892 into an aristocratic Prussian family in Kleinburg near Breslau, now part of the Polish city of Wroclaw. His early life and education were fairly typical for his class, attending a military school from the age of 11. On leaving school in 1911 he joined an Uhlan Cavalry Unit. After war broke out, his unit saw action on both Eastern and Western Fronts but as cavalry became steadily obsolete, his regiment were dismounted and became dispatch runners and field telephone operators. The final straw for Richtofen was a posting to a supply branch and this prompted him, his interest having been fired by inspecting a military aircraft on the ground, to apply for a transfer to the Imperial German Army Air Service, shortly to be known as the Luftstreitkrafte.

Consequently at the end of May 1915 he joined Flying Squadron 69 on the Eastern Front as an observer. His first 'kill', albeit uncredited, is believed to be a French Farman which he shot down after his transfer to the Champagne front.

After meeting the German ace Oswald Boelcke, he applied to train as a pilot and in March 1916 he joined Kampfgeschwader 2, a bomber squadron, flying the Albatros CIII. He was not rated particularly highly as a pilot and was lucky to survive both a crash in training and flying through a large thunderstorm against more experienced advice.

In August 1916, he met Boelcke again, this time on the Eastern Front where he was searching for candidates for his new fighter unit, Jagdstaffel 2. Within weeks he was back in the west duelling with the allies over France and Belgium.

Richtofen was clearly an unusual character. Following his first confirmed victory, he had a jeweller in Berlin make him a silver cup on which was engraved the date and aircraft type and he continued with this until the dwindling supply of silver made it impossible. He also developed tactics that would generally assure success for himself or his squadron, whereas other aces like Voss or Immelmann tended to be far more aggressive and ignore odds or situations that were not in their favour and attack anyway. This is at least partly why he was so successful and it is difficult to argue with his logic when the overall aim was to win but not at any cost.

November 1916 saw him overcome Lanoe Hawker more or less as I have described in 'Flashman and the Knights of the Sky' and it was shortly after this in January 1917 that Richtofen assumed command of Jasta 11. It was also at this time that he first painted his Albatros red which, given that he was variously described as 'distant, unemotional and humourless' seems somewhat out of character.

His fellow pilots reacted by painting parts of their aircraft red as well, officially to make Richtofen less conspicuous, but red very quickly became Jasta 11's identification. The practice quickly spread throughout the Luftstreitkrafte with different Jastas adopting different schemes and it had tremendous propaganda value and probably contributed indirectly to the demise of many an inexperienced RFC crew. It also led to Richtofen's nicknames; in Germany he was generally known as 'the Red Fighter Pilot', it was only amongst the western allies that the name 'the Red Baron' became common.

By the end of January 1916, Richtofen had 16 victories at which point he was awarded the 'Pour le Merite' more commonly known as 'the Blue Max'. He continued to add to his score before being shot down himself in March, probably by Edwin Benbow in an FE8 of 40 Squadron RFC. He was lucky. Despite a bullet through his fuel tank, he managed to force land without his aircraft catching fire.

April 1917, 'Bloody April', saw him back in his Albatros DIII in which he downed 22 further aircraft making his total now 52, and then in June, a further development in German fighter tactics saw him take command of Jagdgeschwader 1 comprising four Jastas. This was what became known as the 'Flying Circus'.

6th July 1917 was the beginning of the end. During a dogfight with a group of FE2d two seat fighters of 20 Squadron, Richtofen was hit in the head. The wound, though severe was not immediately fatal although it did cause disorientation, partial blindness and a temporary loss of consciousness. When he came round, his aircraft was in a spin from which he recovered in time to make a heavy but survivable landing behind his own lines. Captain Donald Cunnell was credited with the victory although he himself was killed just a few days later by anti-aircraft fire.

Richtofen required numerous operations to repair the damage and unwisely and against orders returned to active service three weeks later. However, by the beginning of September he was on leave and remained so until the end of October. It has been suggested that the long term effects of this wound contributed materially to his death.

By 1918, Richtofen was a legend both in Germany and probably throughout Europe. It was suggested that he should refrain from combat flying as, having deliberately built up his hero status, his loss would be a serious blow to German morale. Richtofen refused.

His final flight took place on 21st April 1918. He was pursuing a Sopwith Camel flown by a novice Canadian pilot, Lt Wilfrid May, when he was attacked by another Camel piloted by another Canadian, Captain Arthur Brown, who had dived steeply at high speed to try and help out but had to climb steeply away to avoid hitting the ground.

At this point, a single .303 bullet hit Richtofen. His heart and lungs were severely damaged but in the last few seconds of life remaining to him, the Red Baron managed to land his Fokker Dr.I in a field north of the village of Vaux-sur-Somme.

Australian soldiers reached the aircraft very quickly, so quickly that Gunner George Ridgway stated that Richtofen was still alive when he arrived and Sergeant Ted Smout reported Richtofen's last word as 'kaputt'.

The aircraft was not particularly badly damaged but was soon virtually dismantled by souvenir hunters. 3 Squadron Australian Flying Corps assumed responsibility for Richtofen.

Controversy has surrounded the Red Baron's demise ever since. At the time, Brown was credited with the kill, but it is now generally believed that this was impossible, partly because his attack was from the wrong side, but more importantly, Richtofen could not have continued his pursuit of May with the wound he died from.

A number of theories have been advanced in support of ground fire, in particular two gunners from the 53rd Battery, 14th Field Artillery Brigade, Royal Australian Artillery. Both fired on the aircraft, but their position at the time does not support the available evidence.

The most likely theory is that an Australian machine gunner, Sergeant Cedric Popkin, fired twice on the aircraft, the second time from the side, and this was when the Baron was hit. Of course, Flashman's evidence suggests that there is another possibility.

Whatever the truth, and like so many similar controversies we will never really know, it is probable that battle stress, the unusual prevailing wind on the day that meant his speed over the ground was higher than normal, his unwise low level crossing of the lines, his one jammed gun and the possible continuing effects of his head wound all contributed to his death.

Richtofen was buried with full military honours in Bertangles cemetery with a guard of honour provided by 3 Squadron AFC. One of the wreaths laid at the time was inscribed, 'To Our Gallant and Worthy Foe'.

This was not however his final resting place. In the 1920s, the French created a military cemetery at Fricourt and Richtofen was moved here. In 1925, his youngest brother Bolko took the Red Baron home intending to bury him near his Father and brother at Schweidnitz. The Government intervened and requested he be buried at the Invalidenfriedhof Cemetery in Berlin and where they held a state funeral.

The Nazis intervened further and set up a huge tombstone simply inscribed 'Richtofen' but during the Cold War this stone was seriously damaged by bullets fired at people trying to escape to the west.

Finally, in 1975, his remains were moved to the family plot at Sudfriedhof in Wiesbaden where he is buried next to his brother Bolko and sister Elisabeth. And here he remains.

He is still the best known fighter pilot of all time and will probably remain so, possibly because he was part of the age when those magnificent men in their flying machines diced with death just getting airborne, and aerial warfare still had a round table like air of chivalry, of knights jousting for the favours of their female audience. To some degree this is true although it does rather gloss over the reality of the appalling deaths suffered by so many. Probably it diverted the masses away from the dreadful reality of attrition warfare, perhaps it over simplified a complex situation, but it did provide real heroes worthy of the title.

# Appendix 6

## Gunther von Pluschow

When war broke out, Leutnant Gunther von Pluschow was based at the German naval station at Tsingtau, China. Towards the end of August, Japan declared war on Germany and a joint Japanese British force attacked the colony. By November, the situation had become critical and Pluschow was ordered to fly out of the colony carrying the Governor's final dispatches. He flew about 150 miles before crash landing in a rice field.

There then followed a hair raising journey on foot and by junk to Nanking where, under surveillance by local officials he bribed a guard at the station and managed to board a train to Shanghai. Finding a friend there, a diplomat's daughter from Berlin, she provided him with documents, money and more importantly a ticket to San Francisco where he arrived in early 1915.

Crossing the United States, he arrived in New York to read in the local press that he was presumed to be in New York. With luck still on his side, a friend managed to acquire more documents that allowed him to sail for Italy, but here his luck ran out. Weather forced the ship to dock at Gibraltar and he was arrested as an enemy alien. They soon discovered his real identity and he was sent to a prisoner of war camp at Donington Hall.

On Juy 4th 1915, he managed to escape again during a storm. This time he headed for London where he disguised himself as a worker, sleeping in the British Museum at night and even managing to take photographs of himself at the docks. He managed to discover that a ferry, the Princess Juliana, was sailing for the Netherlands, via which he arrived home in Germany. Where he was arrested as a spy!

He was quickly positively identified and acclaimed as the 'hero from Tsingtau', decorated, promoted and given command of the naval base of Libau in Latvia. He married, wrote his first book about his adventures and had a son born in 1918.

At the end of the war, Pluschow resigned from the Reichsmarine before eventually sailing for South America where he spent many years exploring, filming and mapping especially in Argentina. In

1931, he was killed in a crash near the Brazo Rico, part of Lake Argentino.

He remains the only man in either world war to have successfully escaped from Britain to Germany.

# Appendix 7

## Mata Hari

Margaretha Geertruida Zelle was born in Leeuwarden in the Netherlands on 7th August 1876. She had an affluent childhood made possible by her Father's oil industry investments. However, a downturn in his fortunes caused his bankruptcy and subsequent divorce followed in 1891 by the death of Margaretha's mother. The collapse of her family saw her move to live with her Godfather.

Margaretha briefly studied in Leiden, hoping to become a teacher but the inappropriate attentions of the Headmaster caused her Godfather to remove her and she eventually went to live in the Hague with her uncle.

Aged 18 and after answering an advert in a Dutch newspaper, Margaretha married a colonial army Captain, Rudolf MacLeod, and the happy couple moved to Java in 1897 where they had two children, Norman John and Louise Jeanne.

The marriage was a disaster. MacLeod was an alcoholic and this almost certainly limited his promotion prospects. He heaped the blame for this on his young wife who briefly left him, and whilst separated studied some of the local traditions, even joining a dance company where she acquired the name 'Mata Hari', a Malay phrase meaning 'Sun'.

The tempestuous marriage continued on and off until in 1899, the two children fell seriously ill, probably with syphilitic complications acquired from their parents despite their denials at the time. Norman died.

After returning to the Netherlands in 1902, the couple separated again finally divorcing in 1907 and although custody of Jeanne was awarded to Margaretha, she lived with her Father who had forced the issue by reneging on maintenance payments. Jeanne also died young aged 21.

In 1903, Margaretha moved to Paris where she began her performing career, initially as a circus rider. She also earned a meagre living as an artist's model. But it was in 1905 that the exotic dancer, Mata Hari, came to the fore. Her first performance at the Musee Guimet was an overnight success and she swiftly became mistress to its owner, Emile Guimet.

Posing as a Javanese Princess, she captivated Paris with what was essentially a strip tease until her many imitators overshadowed her and she performed for the last time in 1915. And that would, probably should, have been that. Except that as a Dutch subject, she had the freedom to travel.

Frequently travelling between Spain, France, Britain and the Netherlands, her movements eventually attracted the attention of Scotland Yard who had her arrested when the ship she was on docked at Falmouth. Under interrogation, she admitted to working for French intelligence and was released. However in 1917, the German military attache in Madrid sent a coded message to Berlin singing the praises of agent H-21, not realising that the code had been broken by the British in 'Room 40', and as a result, Mata Hari was arrested at the Hotel Elysee Palace.

Her trial was by todays standards somewhat farcical. She was accused of causing the deaths of thousands of soldiers through her activities as a spy but neither the British or the French could produce any convincing evidence. It was claimed that some secret ink was found in her room, something she denied saying that it was part of her make-up, but at the time, this was enough to convict her. Her defence was not allowed to directly question any of the witnesses.

Mata Hari was executed by firing squad on 15th October 1917. Her body was not claimed by anyone and so was used for medical research.

In the 1970s, German archive documents were released that confirmed she had been a German agent.

## Appendix 8

## Hilmar Dierks

One of the fascinations for me of writing and particularly about this era is finding snippets of information about truly interesting people of whom very few have ever heard. Hilmar Gustav Johannes Dierks is one of them.

Born in 1889 in Leer, East Friesland, he grew up in a stable conservative family that were devoted to the Kaiser. Hilmar joined the Army and served on the western front in 1914. He was very quickly given an espionage mission. By what means this came about is hard to find but he tried twice to get to England. His career then seems to have largely centred on Rotterdam where he was assisted by a German language teacher, Heinrich Flores. His activities attracted the local police and he was arrested in June 1915 and given a one year prison sentence for jeopardising Dutch neutrality. In 1916 he was known to be in Hamburg.

In the 1920s, Dierks was briefly involved with the Einwohnerwehren and the fight against communism as well as the Kapp putsch. In 1925, he apparently offered his services to SIS although nothing came of it because he would not supply information about Germany. In the early thirties, he was a car dealer and in the late thirties as Nazi Germany expanded its military he was to be found back in Hamburg.

Dierks had numerous agents in the late 30s, quite a few of whom were British or of British origin and each has an interesting story although none quite as interesting as that of Vera Schalburg who may have been Dierks' wife. She was due to accompany him on his last mission to Britain but after a meeting in a Hamburg wine bar, the car they were in crashed and Dierks was killed. The mission was eventually sent to Britain without Dierks but all three agents were arrested within hours, two were eventually executed but Schalburg was apparently released and possibly given a new identity and allowed to remain in Britain. And possibly not, but that is another story.

This is a very brief outline of Dierks story, mainly because there is an excellent essay online written by F.A.C.Kluiters and

E. Verhoeyen which at the time of writing can be found at www.nisa-intelligence.nl, clicking the 'contributions' tab and then scrolling down to 'An International Spymaster and Mystery Man' and clicking on the authors link. There they tell his story far better than I can.

# Appendix 9

## Jagdgeschwader 1

Formed on 24th June 1917 with Manfred von Richtofen as its commander, Jagd 1 was a new departure in the tactics of aerial warfare. It combined four 'Jastas', in this case 4, 6, 10 and 11, into one large fighting unit and came to be known as the 'Flying Circus', possibly because of the brightly painted aircraft and the way the whole unit was moved around the front to where it was needed by train.

The driver for the formation of Jagd 1 was the realisation that the Luftstreitkrafte was outnumbered and always would be. The Jastas, often only six or seven aircraft strong, had already started operating together unofficially, so the Jagdgeschwader merely formalised what was already happening. The biggest change in policy was the mobility, the unit being sent to wherever temporary local air superiority was needed.

One of the biggest drawbacks of forming an elite unit was Richtofen's ability to select his pilots, which meant that Jagd 1 truly was an exceptional force, but many other Jastas were weakened as a result. Conversely, the rising stars often moved on as well to command their own Jastas or Jagdgschwaders.

Operationally Jagd 1 flew from June 1917 until the end of the war. They were first to fly the Fokker Dr.I triplane, Werner Voss scoring ten victories in 21 days in his before they were temporarily grounded. They fought over Cambrai during the autumn offensive and their overall success led to the formation of Jagd 2 and 3.

1918 saw Jagd 1 heavily involved in the German spring offensive and also the death of their commander, Richtofen, who was succeeded by Hauptmann Wilhelm Reinhard. Various moves and heavy fighting saw their combined score increase rapidly passing 500 victories in July by which time they were operating the best fighter of the war, the Fokker D.VII.

Reinhard's death in an accident meant the command passed to Oberleutnant Hermann Goering who remained in post until the armistice, by which time the unit had destroyed 644 allied aircraft losing 52 pilots killed and another 67 wounded.

# Appendix 10

## Count of Albany

The most intriguing thing for me about the Counts of Albany is the vehemence of the debate amongst the historians and conspiracy theorists, the believers and non-believers, most of it conducted behind closed doors or at least at an academic level that most people aren't interested in because it does not affect them in the slightest.

The relevant appendix in 'Flashman and the Knights of the Sky' briefly outlined the claims to the throne and they sound incredible. The 7th Count of Albany, the self-styled HRH Prince Michael James Alexander Stewart claims to be a direct descendant of Bonnie Prince Charlie. A number of historians have dismissed this as pure fantasy as when Henry Benedict Stuart died in 1807 leaving 'only' an illegitimate daughter, the male Stuart line was officially deemed to have died out. The Jacobite claim to the throne today officially rests with Franz, Duke of Bavaria, head of the Wittelsbach dynasty.

It will never be proved definitively who is correct, largely because each side's claims can never be proved. Documents and records can and have been forged, altered, lost or suppressed. The British Government moved heaven and earth to get James II off the throne and replace him with William of Orange, apparently because they were still worried he might turn the country catholic. William and Anne's failure to produce an heir resulted in the Act of Settlement barring Catholics from the throne. This meant that that 'well-known' heir, Sophia, Electress of Hanover and granddaughter of James I would pass over 57 better claimants under the rules of inheritance to sit on the English throne. It makes the recent debate about changing the rules of primogeniture to equalise the rights of male and female, right though that is, seem trivial. As it turned out, it was her son who became George I in 1714.

The point of this, to me at least, is that whether Michael Stewart really is the Count of Albany is irrelevant. When one considers that the succession has been at times farcical, (and I do occasionally wonder why a British Government wanted a minor royal with virtually no connection to England to be King other than to manipulate him) his claim to the throne is probably no more outrageous than some of the people who have in fact sat on said throne.

The idea that anyone could be directly related to and descended from King Solomon sounds ludicrous but is of course entirely possible and there must be many people in the world related to all of ancient history's famous people. The tricky bit of course is proving it, although given that the current royal family (and a few other families in England) can in theory trace their family through multiple generations and back well over a thousand years, there is no reason why someone, somewhere shouldn't be the real Stuart heir to the throne.

We will never know for sure.

# Appendix 11

## Sixtus

Again in my research for this book I came across another of history's interesting but virtually unknown characters and in doing so discovered at least something of the behind the scenes diplomacy that in theory at least could have stopped the Great War in its tracks.

Prince Sixtus of Bourbon Parma was the eldest son of the last Duke of Parma and his wife the Infanta Maria Antonia of Portugal, daughter of King Miguel. Sixtus was the fourteenth of twenty-four children albeit the first twelve were half siblings. As the sixth son, he was named Sixtus.

Italian unification had deposed Sixtus' father from his Duchy but the family were very wealthy and lived a privileged life divided between the Villa Pianore in northern Italy and his castle in Schwarzau, lower Austria. Initially educated at a Catholic boarding school near the Swiss border, Sixtus went on to study law in Paris.

When the old Duke died in 1907, he left a significant fortune mostly to his eldest healthy son, the rest was divided in 1910 following agreement between the two families. In 1911, Sixtus' sister, Princess Zita married Archduke Charles, heir to the Austro-Hungarian Empire.

On the outbreak of war, the brothers enlisted, Sixtus and Prince Xavier into the Belgian Army, Elias (the Duke), Felix and Rene into the Austrian Army.

By 1917, with the war heading towards its fourth year, the Emperor, now of course Charles I, secretly tried to begin negotiating a peace accord using his brother-in-law as his conduit. Zita initiated the contact by writing inviting Sixtus to Vienna. Sixtus contacted the French to find out what their conditions for ceasefire would be; Restoration of Alsace-Lorraine, independence for Belgium and Serbia and the transfer of Constantinople to Russian control. Charles largely agreed, at least enough to be a basis for talks and wrote to Sixtus unofficially telling him to tell the French President that 'he would use all means and influence at his disposal'. There is no record of Charles attempting to contact King George V.

Charles and Sixtus' valiant attempts failed, it appears largely because of a requirement for Italy to cede the Tyrol, but more importantly because the Germans, seeing the imminent collapse of Russia thought they could gain more by continuing the fight on one front and so refused to negotiate Alsace-Lorraine. With 20-20 hindsight, the short-sightedness of this position coupled with the arrogance of the belligerent rulers condemned thousands more men to death.

In April 1918, news of the attempt began to leak into the public domain. Charles denied all knowledge until Clemenceau published the letter signed by him. This heralded a further decline in the empire as Charles' foreign minister, Count Ottokar von Czernin, resigned at the same time feeling he had been let down having not been party to the attempt whilst at the same time successfully negotiating various peace deals in the east. He had also previously made several speeches, presumably with the blessing of Charles, outlining general conditions for peace in Europe along the lines of justice, disarmament, arbitration and freedom of the seas. He had also agreed to the US President Wilson's fourteen point peace plan.

The net result of all this intrigue was Austria becoming even more subservient to its German ally and it would probably be fair to say that the end of the Austro-Hungarian monarchy was sealed at that point.

Shortly after the cessation of hostilities, Sixtus married Hedwige de la Rochefoucauld, daughter of the Duke de Doudeauville. They had one daughter, Princess Isabella Marie Antoinette Louise Hedwig.

Apart from a number of court squabbles over property and inheritance, partly because the French Government had confiscated Chambord castle which was owned by the Bourbons of Parma but under the terms of the Treaty of Saint-Germain had been expropriated because Elias had fought for the Austrians, Sixtus and his family returned to obscurity. They settled in France.

Sixtus occupied himself with expeditions to Africa and writing a number of books. He died in Paris in March 1934. It is interesting to note that in 2004, Pope John Paul II held a Mass of Beatification during which Emperor Charles I was declared blessed for his attempts to broker peace in 1917-18.

# Appendix 12

## Treaty of Brest Litovsk

Stalemate. One of those words which describes so much about the Great War but which is rarely used in the west about the eastern front despite conditions being much the same. Early 1917 saw the near collapse of the Russian economy. The continual strain, large numbers of casualties and food shortages effectively encouraged revolution and in February this critical situation came to a head with the abdication of Tsar Nicholas II. He was replaced by a provisional government, initially headed by Prince Georgy Lvov and then Alexander Kerensky, which continued to support the entente powers and sent a telegram confirming the intention to fight on.

Opposed to this, the leftist parties had started to form 'Soviets' of workers and soldiers deputies as well as an initially paramilitary force, the Red Guards. Given that the Russian Governmental position had not substantially changed, the Germans naturally supported the opposition, in particular the communists or Bolsheviks who were advocating withdrawal. They even allowed Vladimir Lenin to return to Russia from his Swiss exile offering financial help at the same time.

As the Bolshevik influence increased, so chaos reigned. Following the defeat of the Kerensky offensive, soldiers began increasingly to disobey orders, forming committees to control their units and removing the officers. July saw Bolshevik riots in Petrograd and in October by the old calendar, Red Guards stormed the Winter Palace.

On 26th October 1917, Lenin signed a peace decree calling on all the nations to negotiate peace and heralded Russia's withdrawal from the war. The Commissar of Foreign Affairs, Leon Trotsky, appointed Adolph Joffe to negotiate peace.

On December 15th, an armistice was signed and negotiations began in earnest at Brest-Litovsk. The Germans were represented by the Foreign Secretary Richard von Kuhlmann and General Max Hoffmann, the Austrians by Ottokar von Czernin and the Turks by Talat Pasha although the Germans had effective control of the group.

The Russians led by Joffe were all revolutionaries and as such had a very different agenda to the Germans.

The German delegation set out their demands which amongst other things included the annexation of Poland with a buffer state between Germany and Russia, Ukraine established as an independent state and the Baltic states to come under direct German control. The Russian delegation was horrified.

Lenin wanted to sign the agreement believing that peace would allow the Bolsheviks to consolidate their power in Russia. Most of his colleagues disagreed believing that Europe was on the verge of revolution and time was on their side. Numerous other negotiations were taking place outside the main talks. Germany was talking directly to Ukraine, Czernin announced his intention to seek a separate deal if none was forthcoming and Russian frustration led to Trotsky announcing a unilateral end to hostilities.

The German reaction was to resume the war. In two weeks, German troops seized Ukraine, Belarus and the Baltic states. The German fleet steamed into the Gulf of Finland towards Petrograd and there was no revolution in Germany. With no effective choice in the matter, the Soviet Government Central Committee accepted the terms put forward by the Germans which were significantly worse than the original requirements. On 3rd March Georgy Chicherin signed the treaty.

The treaty removed approximately a quarter of the Russian population into German control along with 90% of its coal mines. The Germans appointed new rulers in Lithuania, Latvia and Estonia and occupied their new territories with one million troops, men that ironically could not now be used on the western front. The local populations very quickly became disillusioned with their new masters.

The German Spring offensive in the west benefited from the transfer of hundreds of thousands of troops and possibly for a brief period it looked like the Germans could win the war which would have made twentieth century history very different. It is also possible that had the Russians agreed to the first terms set out by the Germans, or the Germans had not occupied so much territory in the east, the extra troops available may have tipped the balance in their favour. We will never know of course.

The treaty lasted just over eight months with Germany renouncing it just before the final armistice. The German surrender eventually led to their withdrawal leaving a power vacuum which in turn led to a bloody struggle for control of the entire region. Poland and Finland kept their independence but the Baltic states and the Ukraine were absorbed into the Soviet Union. The Second World War led to a further redrawing of the map with the western soviet border moving into Germany until 1991 and the collapse of the communist states.

It is interesting to note Russia's current western border is very similar to the treaty border.

# Appendix 13

## Backs to the Wall

SPECIAL ORDER OF THE DAY
By FIELD-MARSHAL SIR DOUGLAS HAIG
K.T., G.C.B., G.C.V.O., K.C.I.E.
Commander-in-Chief, British Armies in France
To ALL RANKS OF THE BRITISH ARMY IN FRANCE AND FLANDERS
Three weeks ago to-day the enemy began his terrific attacks against us on a fifty-mile front. His objects are to separate us from the French, to take the Channel Ports and destroy the British Army.

In spite of throwing already 106 Divisions into the battle and enduring the most reckless sacrifice of human life, he has as yet made little progress towards his goals.

We owe this to the determined fighting and self-sacrifice of our troops. Words fail me to express the admiration which I feel for the splendid resistance offered by all ranks of our Army under the most trying circumstances.

Many amongst us now are tired. To those I would say that Victory will belong to the side which holds out the longest. The French Army is moving rapidly and in great force to our support.

There is no other course open to us but to fight it out. Every position must be held to the last man: there must be no retirement. With our backs to the wall and believing in the justice of our cause each one of us must fight on to the end. The safety of our homes and the Freedom of mankind alike depend upon the conduct of each one of us at this critical moment.

(Signed) D. Haig F.M.
Commander-in-Chief
British Armies in France

General Headquarters
Tuesday, April 11th, 1918

# Appendix 14

## Wilson's Fourteen Point Plan

On January 8th 1918, President Wilson, without consulting his European allies, made a speech outlining his vision for peace in Europe once the war had ended. At least part of his reasoning was an attempt to disconnect the US from the nationalistic war aims of continental Europe and make a moral case for war, which probably sat better with the views of the American people. Wilson's speech was the only time any of the protagonists stated their war aims, which rather does make one wonder what EXACTLY everyone was fighting for.

I. Open covenants of peace, openly arrived at, after which there shall be no private international understandings of any kind but diplomacy shall proceed always frankly and in the public view.

II. Absolute freedom of navigation upon the seas, outside territorial waters, alike in peace and in war, except as the seas may be closed in whole or in part by international action for the enforcement of international covenants.

III. The removal, so far as possible, of all economic barriers and the establishment of an equality of trade conditions among all the nations consenting to the peace and associating themselves for its maintenance.

IV. Adequate guarantees given and taken that national armaments will be reduced to the lowest point consistent with domestic safety.

V. A free, open-minded, and absolutely impartial adjustment of all colonial claims, based upon a strict observance of the principle that in determining all such questions of sovereignty the interests of the populations concerned must have equal weight with the equitable claims of the government whose title is to be determined.

VI. The evacuation of all Russian territory and such a settlement of all questions affecting Russia as will secure the best and freest cooperation of the other nations of the world in obtaining for her an unhampered and unembarrassed opportunity for the independent determination of her own political development and national policy and assure her of a sincere welcome into the society of free nations under institutions of her own choosing; and, more than a welcome, assistance also of every kind that she may need and may herself desire. The treatment accorded Russia by her sister nations in the months to come will be the acid test of their good will, of their comprehension of her needs as distinguished from their own interests, and of their intelligent and unselfish sympathy.

VII. Belgium, the whole world will agree, must be evacuated and restored, without any attempt to limit the sovereignty which she enjoys in common with all other free nations. No other single act will serve as this will serve to restore confidence among the nations in the laws which they have themselves set and determined for the government of their relations with one another. Without this healing act the whole structure and validity of international law is forever impaired.

VIII. All French territory should be freed and the invaded portions restored, and the wrong done to France by Prussia in 1871 in the matter of Alsace-Lorraine, which has unsettled the peace of the world for nearly fifty years, should be righted, in order that peace may once more be made secure in the interest of all.

IX. A readjustment of the frontiers of Italy should be effected along clearly recognizable lines of nationality.

X. The peoples of Austria-Hungary, whose place among the nations we wish to see safeguarded and assured, should be accorded the freest opportunity to autonomous development.

XI. Romania, Serbia, and Montenegro should be evacuated; occupied territories restored; Serbia accorded free and secure access to the sea; and the relations of the several Balkan states to one another determined by friendly counsel along historically established lines of allegiance and nationality; and international guarantees of the political and economic independence and territorial integrity of the several Balkan states should be entered into.

XII. The Turkish portion of the present Ottoman Empire should be assured a secure sovereignty, but the other nationalities which are now under Turkish rule should be assured an undoubted security of life and an absolutely unmolested opportunity of autonomous development, and the Dardanelles should be permanently opened as a free passage to the ships and commerce of all nations under international guarantees.

XIII. An independent Polish state should be erected which should include the territories inhabited by indisputably Polish populations, which should be assured a free and secure access to the sea, and whose political and economic independence and territorial integrity should be guaranteed by international covenant.

XIV. A general association of nations must be formed under specific covenants for the purpose of affording mutual guarantees of political independence and territorial integrity to great and small states alike.

# Appendix 15

## Treaty of Versailles

Five years after the assassination of Archduke Franz Ferdinand, the Treaty of Versailles was signed in the Hall of Mirrors in the Palace of Versailles. It is a strange work, possibly one of the harshest and most ignored treaties of all time. Much of it is reasonably common knowledge and the terms are easy to find and read should one be interested, so I will confine myself here to an outline plus perhaps some of the lesser known parts.

In essence, the French as the only major western ally with a shared land border, wanted to weaken Germany to the point of impotence. Clemenceau would really have liked to make the Rhine his eastern border but that was an unlikely aim. In the event he achieved demilitarisation, whatever that meant given the increasing mobility of armies, and a rather vague Anglo-American promise to ride to the rescue should the Germans launch another invasion. He also demanded huge financial reparations and an admission of guilt, a slightly odd and even childish demand.

America had outlined its position with Wilson's plan and sought to impose a liberal free trading democratic Europe with the League of Nations as world policeman. It also opposed any harsh treatment of Germany.

Britain as always was probably more concerned with world power and trade, possibly with acquiring as much of the fledgling German empire as it could with little or no idea that within thirty years most of it would be gone. As such, it made no sense to destroy Germany.

By June 1919, the treaty was ready to sign and the Germans were summoned. When they became aware of the terms, Chancellor Philipp Scheidemann and his cabinet resigned in protest. He was replaced by Gustav Bauer who telegraphed his intention to sign provided certain articles were removed. The allied response was to issue an ultimatum saying that if the Germans did not sign, troops would cross the Rhine within 24 hours. Bauer apparently consulted with the military to see if resistance was a realistic option. He was told it was not and so on 23$^{rd}$ June, he sent a telegram to say a delegation was on the way.

Germany was emasculated. It lost 25000 square miles of territory and 7,000,000 people. It lost its colonies and its armed forces were reduced to a size compatible only with defence. Eight battleships, eight cruisers, forty two destroyers and fifty two torpedo boats were decommissioned. The airforce was banned. Germany was required to pay 20 billion gold marks, about $5 billion, in gold or almost any other form. The Rhineland was occupied.

There were two opposing views at the time. John Maynard Keynes predicted that the treaty was too harsh and that it would be counter-productive. On the other hand, American historian Sally Marks said the figure was lenient and it was designed to look harsh but was not.

The French Government signed the treaty but the French people thought Clemenceau had failed and voted him out of office in 1920. He was replaced by Foch, who felt the whole thing was too lenient. "This is not peace. It is an armistice for twenty years," he said.

The British signed the treaty whilst declaring the French to be 'greedy and vindictive'. In 1936 when Hitler reoccupied the Rhineland, Ramsay MacDonald announced that he was pleased that the treaty was vanishing. He hoped that the French had been taught a severe lesson although given the collective myopia prevalent at the time he probably didn't expect that lesson to be as severe and as swift as it turned out to be.

The Americans never signed the treaty. The US Senate required a two thirds vote in favour to pass it. This never happened. But, Wilson claimed, 'at last the world knows America as the savior of the world', which must rate as one of the most arrogant pronouncements ever made.

In Germany, the treaty was widely resented and anyone supporting the treaty viewed as a traitor. Socialists, communists and particularly Jews were treated with suspicion and this atmosphere led to rumours that the Jewish population had not supported the war and had in fact sold Germany out to its enemies. Anyone who had seemed to benefit from the war, including the Weimar politicians, were regarded as having stabbed Germany in the back. Anyone who had instigated unrest before the end of the war, who had instigated strikes in critical armament industries, was seen as having let the soldiers down. It wasn't a large step to believing that, given that German troops occupied French and Belgian territory when they surrendered and that they had won on the Eastern front, they really could have won the war, if only….

Hyper-inflation devastated the German economy. The population blamed the treaty although the real reasons are far more complex. When French and Belgian troops occupied the Ruhr after Germany failed to fulfil its treaty obligations, the government reacted with a policy of passive resistance. Workers ignored any instructions from occupation forces and consequently production and transportation ground to a halt. The public finances collapsed. The policy was reversed in late 1923 and this allowed a currency reform to take place and the negotiation of the Dawes plan which gave Germany breathing space. The economy stabilised as did the country in general.

The stability was as short lived as the resentment was long lived. Worldwide depression beginning in 1929 led the world from crisis to crisis. And in Germany to the resurgence of nationalism and a very different solution to the problems.

# Appendix 16

## Rudolf Hess

Rudolf Walter Richard Hess was born on the 26th April 1894 in Alexandria, Egypt, the eldest of three siblings. His Father Fritz ran an import/export business allowing him, his wife Clara and the family to live in a villa on the Egyptian coast. Rudolf was initially educated in Egypt until 1908 when he was sent to a boarding school in what is now Bonn. He spent three years here before his Father removed him and sent him to a commerce school in Switzerland with a view to him joining the family business. After a year he took up an apprenticeship in Hamburg.

War intervened and like many others, Hess enlisted within weeks initially joining a field artillery regiment. He served on both fronts and was wounded a number of times, the most serious being on the 8th August 1917 when he was hit in the upper chest by a bullet that passed right through him, exiting near his spine leaving a centimetre sized wound. He was lucky. Recovering quickly he was moved to hospital in Hungary and then Germany only two weeks after the injury.

October saw Hess promoted to Leutnant der Reserve and it was during his convalescence period that he applied to train as a pilot. After spending Christmas at home, he passed all the required tests and began training. In October 1918 he was posted to Jagdstaffel 35b based at Givry, Mons. Here he flew the Fokker D.VII although not in action as the war finished before he became operational.

The squadron was disbanded within days of the armistice and Hess was discharged in December 1918. His father's business was taken over by the British.

The vacuum in German society was filled by revolutionaries and political groups of all colours, one of which was the Thule Society. Hess joined both this and the Freikorps, the right wing paramilitary organisation that took part in many of the violent battles for control of Bavaria, and indeed Germany itself, that plagued the country in 1919 and the early twenties.

In late 1919, Hess enrolled on a history and economics course at Munich University. Here he was first introduced to the concept of

'Lebensraum' by Professor Karl Haushofer, the theory being used to justify the armed takeover of territory in Eastern Europe. It was more than likely Hess who passed this concept on to Hitler.

In 1920, Hess met Ilse Prohl, a fellow student whom he married some years later in 1927. They had a son, Wolf, born in 1937. It was this same year, 1920, that Hess first heard Adolf Hitler speak at a NSDAP rally. Inspired by his oratory and realising that they held similar beliefs, particularly with regard to the 'stab in the back' story that Germany had lost the war because of a Jewish Bolshevik conspiracy, Hess joined the party as member number 16.

As the chaos in Germany grew in the early twenties, the NSDAP, now the Nazi party grew as the disaffected joined their ranks. Hyperinflation caused enormous financial problems and when Germany defaulted on their war reparations, French troops marched into the Ruhr. This was the background to Mussolini's march on Rome and then Hitler's attempted coup that became known as the 'Beer Hall Putsch'.

Poorly organised with no real objectives, the coup failed. Hess had two tasks. First he rounded up senior ministers to use as hostages and second he led his own SA unit in an assault on Munich City Hall, mainly to remove the Jewish and Social Democrat councillors to the beer hall. He paused long enough to raise a swastika flag.

When Hess realised the coup had failed, on the advice of Haushofer he took two of the ministers into the mountains intending to take them to Austria. Hess then claims that because of a snowstorm he had to stop at a country house and ask to stay the night. This seems a little unlikely with two hostages, especially as he then claims that when he came out of the house the SA men had driven off with the hostages. It seems more likely, and this is what the SA men claimed, that Hess ordered them to take the men back to Munich.

There is some confusion over what happened next as some claim that Hess called Ilse and explained. She then apparently brought him a bike which he then cycled back to Munich, presumably in the snow. It is much more likely that he continued on to Austria.

Karl Haushofer eventually convinced Hess to return to Germany which he did. He was arrested and given 18 months in prison for his role in the attempted coup. Incarcerated in Landsberg, Hess and

Hitler clearly had some sympathetic guards as they were given adjoining rooms and an extra room to use as a study. It was here that the blueprint for the Third Reich took shape, much of it conceived by Hess. It is also where Hitler wrote 'Mein Kampf', much of which, according to their frequent visitor Karl Haushofer, was also written by Hess.

Released in 1924, the ban on the Nazi party lifted in 1925, Hitler employed Hess as his private secretary and then personal adjutant a few years later as the rise of the party continued until in 1933, when Hitler was appointed Reich Chancellor, Hess was named Deputy Fuhrer and given the cabinet post of Reich Minister without portfolio.

Hess had many roles. He organised the Nuremberg rallies, made numerous speeches, oversaw the activities of overseas members as well as negotiating with major industrialists and financiers. He also issued documents exempting his mentor Haushofer from the anti-Semitic Nuremberg laws.

Unusually, Hess did not seek power or followers. He was utterly loyal to Hitler, popular with the masses and an appalling hypochondriac. He was the real power behind the throne.

He continued flying, taking part in air races near Munich and when war finally broke out again, Hess considered flying on active service again but Hitler refused and in fact banned him from flying at all although he relented to a degree and reduced the ban to one year.

As the war continued, the official story is that Hess became increasingly side-lined as he had no direct role in the war itself and many of his duties had apparently been taken over by Hitler's new favourite, Martin Bormann. With the approach of 'Barbarossa', Hess supposedly became very concerned about Germany fighting on two fronts again and according to the 'victors' unilaterally wrote to the Duke of Hamilton suggesting peace negotiations. Hess believed that Hamilton, a friend of Haushofer, was part of the peace faction present in Britain at the time, something that was largely suppressed and unacknowledged even many years after the war's end. Hamilton didn't reply, as the letter was supposedly intercepted by MI5.

Based on this rather flimsy evidence, on 10th May 1941, Hess took off in his personal Messerschmitt Bfl10E and flew to Britain. Crossing the coast at low level and at night, he evaded three spitfires sent to find him but was unable to escape from a Defiant of 141 Squadron and, low on fuel, Hess bailed out landing on Eaglesham moor near Glasgow. A local ploughman found him and handed him over to the Home Guard who passed him onto the police. He was interviewed and eventually taken to Maryhill Barracks in Glasgow.

The following morning, Hamilton, who was at RAF Turnhouse near Edinburgh, arrived and spoke to Hess alone. Hess admitted who he was at this point having previously stuck to an alias, 'Alfred Horn', and outlined his peace proposals. Transferred to Buchanan Castle, the interrogation continued over the next days and Hamilton met with Churchill and the War Cabinet to discuss the issue.

Hitler was outraged, at least publicly and denounced Hess as mentally deranged, a policy that Goering and others disagreed with on the grounds that it made the entire party look foolish that they had allowed a mentally ill Hess to have so much power.

Over the next few months, Hess appeared to descend further into mental illness and apparently tried to commit suicide. His behaviour became increasingly erratic. He spent three years in Maindiff Court Hospital where he was allowed a degree of freedom before being committed for trial at Nuremberg. Months of deliberation found Hess guilty of crimes against peace and conspiracy to commit crimes but not guilty of war crimes and crimes against humanity. He was sentenced to life imprisonment and sent to Spandau prison in Berlin.

The saga continued. Initially one of seven inmates, Hess was referred to as 'Number 7' throughout his incarceration. He was guarded on a monthly rotation by the four occupying nations, Britain France, United States and the Soviet Union. He had limited access to writing and reading materials, was expected to work and was not allowed to speak to the other inmates. Visitors were allowed but Hess refused all visits until 1969 by which time his wife Ilse was 69 and his son Wolf 32. After this time he had regular family visits.

Unsurprisingly, Hess had a number of bouts of illness and possibly attempted suicide in1977. All six of his fellow prisoners were released, Konstantin von Neurath, Walther Funk and Erich Raeder in the 50s, Karl Donitz in 1956 and Baldur von Schirach and Albert Speer in 1966.

The regime became more and more relaxed as the years passed and Hess' lawyer, Dr Seidl regularly appealed for his release. All these appeals were vetoed by the Soviets, possibly because Spandau was in West Berlin and as such when it was the Soviet month to guard the prison they had access to this area.

On 17<sup>th</sup> August 1987, aged 93, Hess apparently used an extension cord from his lamp to hang himself in the garden summer house. A rather odd note was found thanking his family for all they had done.

Hess was initially buried at a secret location before being moved to a family plot where his wife joined him in 1995. Spandau prison was demolished and every brick pulverised. In 2011, Hess was exhumed and cremated and his ashes scattered at sea. His tombstone bearing the epitaph 'Ich hab's gewagt', 'I have dared', was destroyed.

The conspiracy theories, never far below the surface anyway, appeared again with his death. Seidl felt it was unlikely that a 93 year old man would be capable of killing himself. Wolf Hess claimed his father was murdered by SIS. Hess' medical orderly wrote a book on this theme and was dismissed from his position at his district parliament. The British Government investigated itself, something it is very good at, and the Solicitor General decided there were no grounds for further investigation. Officially that was the end of the story. Except that it refused to go away.

Numerous books have been written on the subject of Hess and in particular his flight to Britain in 1941. The general thrust of the arguments advanced is that Hess had come to meet an influential group in Britain that included members of the Royal Family. This group were supposedly in a high enough position in society that they would be able to negotiate with the Germans for peace. In fact, it is entirely possible that they had already agreed outline terms which would include the removal of Churchill and his supporters.

In their fascinating book, 'Double Standards', Lynn Picknett, Clive Prince and Stephen Prior advance exactly this theory  and suggest that Hess was in fact coming to meet a delegation that included the then Duke of Kent. They further suggest that after the failure of this mission, the Duke of Kent's death in the crash of a Sunderland Flying Boat in Scotland in 1942 was far from being an accident. They also claim that Hess was aboard this aircraft and that the official Hess story is a cover up involving the substitution of another man for Hess. As always, these stories somewhat beggar belief, but their narrative resolves a lot of the anomalies in the Hess story, of which there are many, and in fact is a lot more believable than the official line. It is also interesting to note that when in 1992 the foreign office decided to release its files pertaining to the Hess flight, Foreign Secretary Douglas Hurd kept one file back on the grounds of national security. The book then claims a foreign office source told them that this file contained only a note stating that the files had been transferred on permanent loan to the royal archives at Windsor. They are therefore beyond the reach of anyone except the monarch as the archive is not subject to the freedom of information act!

Further to this claim, another book by Dr Hugh Thomas, a former British Army surgeon also considers the idea of the Hess substitution. He examined Hess in 1973 and noted that he did not have the bullet scars from his First World War wound Therefore, the man held in Spandau was not Hess and it was this man that was murdered in 1987. It would appear this was because the Russians and their new found 'Glasnost' were considering releasing him after years of veto and the British Government simply could not allow this to happen. The other obvious points are why, and more importantly how, would a 93 year old frail man manage a suicide? And equally, why would someone spend a significant part of their life in prison for another man? These are not the only questions that remain officially unanswered.

If there was a 'peace party' in 1941, led by the Duke of Kent with many other important and influential people involved and they were as is claimed ready to meet with Hess as the final part of the negotiation (and not a one off frankly almost impossible mission as officially described), one wonders why Churchill didn't at least attempt to find some common ground. Any settlement would have required Churchill's removal along with Hitler's, but it is interesting that in the biography of Hitler written by Ian Kershaw, there is clear evidence that Hitler did not, at least early on, see himself as the Fuhrer and even expected to stand down at some point.

It is also interesting that Hess spelled out to his captors what he thought would happen if the war continued as opposed to a negotiated peace. War meant the loss of the Empire, virtual bankruptcy and dependency on the Americans as well as Soviet dominance of Europe. Peace meant retaining the Empire, the Americans not involved in Europe and a subdued Russia, assuming that the Germans won the war on the Eastern Front, and German dominance in Europe. Peace with Britain would of course have released large numbers of troops for service in the east so it is not entirely unreasonable to assume the Germans could have won. It is also possible that with Hess around to direct the Fuhrer as he had done up to this point, assuming one accepts the alternative story for Hess, the 'Final Solution' would not have occurred. Hess was a Nazi through and through and as anti-Semitic as all of them but it would appear he was a moderating influence. He objected to the violence of the 'Night of the Long Knives' and largely did not allow it to happen again and whilst the racial policies of Nazi Germany were obscene seen from the 21st century, it has to be remembered that they were not alone in their beliefs, many European countries subscribing to the idea of mass deportation for the Jewish population. It should be noted that later in the war, Churchill was keen for large numbers of concentration camp inmates not to be released in case they made their way to British controlled Palestine!

It is also interesting to note that 70 years after the end of the war, Europe, or at least the European Union, is largely dominated by Germany, Britain has spent decades beholden to the Americans (whose industry in the 1940s was driven by large scale military production and who therefore had a large interest in war rather than peace) and the Russians are now a shadow of their former selves. It is also worth wondering which of the 20th century's dictators was the most murderous. Hitler? Or Stalin?

I personally find the entire story fascinating and time and age has convinced me that Governments of any hue would rather continue crushing their skeletons into the cupboard instead of admitting any wrongdoing whether intentional or not. Of course, if they simply released the files.... But then, even at this distance, there would be uproar at the unnecessary loss of life amongst the many other controversies.

# Appendix 17

## The Thule Society

The Thule Society was originally a study group founded by a Great War veteran, Walter Nauhaus. Also a member of the 'Germanenorden', or 'Order of Teutons', Nauhaus was contacted in 1918 by Rudolf von Sebottendorf, an occultist and head of an offshoot of the Germanenorden, and together they formed the 'Thule Society'.

A major part of the society's beliefs was the idea of the Aryan race and its origins as well as supposed links to 'Ultima Thule' the lost northern landmass sometimes identified with 'Atlantis'. This was the 'home' of the Aryan Race.

The society had less than 2000 members of which about 250 were in Munich. They met in the Four Seasons Hotel and discussed their racial theories and how to combat the supposed menace of the Jews and Communists. Sebottendorf supposedly planned to kidnap Eisner, the socialist prime minister but this failed although the society became involved with the 1919 Bavarian revolution. The short-lived communist government raided the society and later executed seven of their members including Nauhaus, Countess Hella von Westarp and Prince Gustav of Thurn and Taxis.

1918 saw the purchase by the society of the Munchener Beobachter, the ancestor of the Volkischer Beobachter, and in 1919, Anton Drexler who had been working with numerous right wing organisations, and Karl Harrer of the society jointly established the 'Deutsche Arbeiterpartei' (DAP or German Workers Party). In 1919 Adolf Hitler joined the party which by early 1920 had become the 'Nationalsozialistische Deutsche Arbeiterpartei', better known by its short name, the 'Nazi Party'.

This was the peak of the society's fame and its subsequent decline was quick despite many of its members prominent position in the fledgling Nazi party. It was claimed that Hess, Goering, Haushofer, Himmler and even Hitler himself were members although this is highly unlikely. The society folded a few years later.

In 1933, Sebottendorf returned to Germany intending to revive the society and consequently published a book entitled 'Before

Hitler Came', the main thrust of which was that many Nazi ideas were in fact Thulist ideas first. Sebottendorf was imprisoned and eventually exiled to Turkey. He seems to have remained in Turkey for the rest of his life, oddly working for German intelligence (although he may have been a double agent) in Istanbul from 1942-1945 before apparently committing suicide by throwing himself in the Bosphorus on May 8th 1945, the day the war in Europe ended.

# Appendix 18

## The 'Stab in the Back' Myth

The 'Dolchstosslegende' officially derives from a meeting between Erich Ludendorff and General Sir Neill Malcolm. Ludendorff was asked why he thought Germany had lost the war and amongst his reasons suggested that the people at home had failed the army. Malcolm apparently then asked if he meant that 'you were stabbed in the back?' to which Ludendorff reportedly replied, 'Stabbed in the back? Yes that's it exactly, we were stabbed in the back'.

Ludendorff then repeated this tale to the rest of the General Staff and it quickly became known in society. Right wing groups soon began using this as a way to attack the Weimar government.

In 1919, the Weimar government held its own investigation into the war and Germany's defeat and when Hindenburg testified to the committee he quoted from a newspaper article that the German Army had been 'stabbed from behind by the civilian populace'.

Added to these was the fact that the armistice had been signed by a civil authority. Towards the wars end, Germany had been to some degree a military dictatorship with Hindenburg as commander in chief and the Kaiser as head of state. After the early 1918 offensive failed, the German high command arranged for a transfer of power to the civil administration and with the abdication and flight of the Kaiser, it was left to the civilians to agree to a ceasefire and subsequently to the Treaty of Versailles

A book published in 1919 did much to foster the myth. A military census, which showed that the German Jewish population had suffered proportionately in terms of numbers along with the rest of the population, was bastardized and used to claim that Jewish officers had a defeatist mentality and that the Jews in general had taken part only to act as spies and profit from the war.

President Ebert even managed to unwittingly contribute to the myth by greeting returning soldiers with a speech stating that 'they were undefeated on the battlefield'.

As chaos consumed Germany post war, all sorts of groups began fighting for power, particularly in the south where the Bavarian

Soviet Republic, many leaders of which were Jewish, was crushed after only two weeks by the Freikorps, allowing the right wing groups to connect communism and the Jewish population with betrayal and eventually to the 'Dolchstoss'.

Thus the scene was set for the Nazis and Hitler to justify their anti-semitism and use the myth to support their rise to power.

German Jewish veterans published a leaflet in 1920 stating that, '12,000 Jewish soldiers died on the field of honour for the Fatherland'.

Appendix 19

The NSDAP 25 Point Plan


1.We demand the unification of all Germans in the Greater Germany on the basis of the people's right to self-determination.

2.We demand equality of rights for the German people in respect to the other nations; abrogation of the peace treaties of Versailles and St. Germain.

3.We demand land and territory (colonies) for the sustenance of our people, and colonization for our surplus population.

4.Only a member of the race can be a citizen. A member of the race can only be one who is of German blood, without consideration of creed. Consequently no Jew can be a member of the race.

5.Whoever has no citizenship is to be able to live in Germany only as a guest, and must be under the authority of legislation for foreigners.

6.The right to determine matters concerning administration and law belongs only to the citizen. Therefore we demand that every public office, of any sort whatsoever, whether in the Reich, the county or municipality, be filled only by citizens. We combat the corrupting parliamentary economy, office-holding only according to party inclinations without consideration of character or abilities.

7.We demand that the state be charged first with providing the opportunity for a livelihood and way of life for the citizens. If it is impossible to sustain the total population of the State, then the members of foreign nations (non-citizens) are to be expelled from the Reich.

8.Any further immigration of non-citizens is to be prevented. We demand that all non-Germans, who have immigrated to Germany since 2 August 1914, be forced immediately to leave the Reich.

9.All citizens must have equal rights and obligations.

10.The first obligation of every citizen must be to work both spiritually and physically. The activity of individuals is not to counteract the interests of the universality, but must have its result within the framework of the whole for the benefit of all. Consequently we demand:

11.Abolition of unearned (work and labour) incomes. Breaking of debt (interest)-slavery.

12.In consideration of the monstrous sacrifice in property and blood that each war demands of the people, personal enrichment through a war must be designated as a crime against the people. Therefore we demand the total confiscation of all war profits.

13.We demand the nationalisation of all (previous) associated industries (trusts).

14.We demand a division of profits of all heavy industries.

15.We demand an expansion on a large scale of old age welfare.

16.We demand the creation of a healthy middle class and its conservation, immediate communalization of the great warehouses and their being leased at low cost to small firms, the utmost consideration of all small firms in contracts with the State, county or municipality.

17.We demand a land reform suitable to our needs, provision of a law for the free expropriation of land for the purposes of public utility, abolition of taxes on land and prevention of all speculation in land.

18.We demand struggle without consideration against those whose activity is injurious to the general interest. Common national criminals, usurers, profiteers and so forth are to be punished with death, without consideration of confession or race.

19.We demand substitution of a German common law in place of the Roman Law serving a materialistic world-order.

20.The state is to be responsible for a fundamental reconstruction of our whole national education program, to enable every capable and industrious German to obtain higher education and subsequently introduction into leading positions. The plans of instruction of all educational institutions are to conform with the experiences of practical life. The comprehension of the concept of the State must be striven for by the school [Staatsbürgerkunde] as early as the beginning of understanding. We demand the education at the expense of the State of outstanding intellectually gifted children of poor parents without consideration of position or profession.

21.The State is to care for the elevating national health by protecting the mother and child, by outlawing child-labor, by the encouragement of physical fitness, by means of the legal establishment of a gymnastic and sport obligation, by the utmost support of all organizations concerned with the physical instruction of the young.

22.We demand abolition of the mercenary troops and formation of a national army.

23.We demand legal opposition to known lies and their promulgation through the press. In order to enable the provision of a German press, we demand, that: a. All writers and employees of the newspapers appearing in the German language be members of the race; b. Non-German newspapers be required to have the express permission of the State to be published. They may not be printed in the German language; c. Non-Germans are forbidden by law any financial interest in German publications, or any influence on them, and as punishment for violations the closing of such a publication as well as the immediate expulsion from the Reich of the non-German concerned. Publications which are counter to the general good are to be forbidden. We demand legal prosecution of artistic and literary forms which exert a destructive influence on our national life, and the closure of organizations opposing the above made demands.

24.We demand freedom of religion for all religious denominations within the state so long as they do not endanger its existence or oppose the moral senses of the Germanic race. The Party as such advocates the standpoint of a positive Christianity without binding itself confessionally to any one denomination. It combats the Jewish-materialistic spirit within and around us, and is convinced that a lasting recovery of our nation can only succeed from within on the framework: The good of the state before the good of the individual.[9]

25.For the execution of all of this we demand the formation of a strong central power in the Reich. Unlimited authority of the central parliament over the whole Reich and its organizations in general. The forming of state and profession chambers for the execution of the laws made by the Reich within the various states of the confederation. The leaders of the Party promise, if necessary by sacrificing their own lives, to support by the execution of the points set forth above without consideration.

# Appendix 20

## Ludendorff

Erich Freidrich Wilhelm Ludendorff was born on 9th April 1865 in Kruszewnia near Posen in what is now Poland. Descended from minor nobility on his Mother's side, he grew up on a farm. Clearly intelligent, he was sent to a cadet school before being sent to what amounted to a military academy near Berlin in 1882.

In 1885, Ludendorff received his Lieutenants commission with the 57th Infantry Regiment. In 1893 he was selected for the War Academy and this precipitated a rapid rise through the ranks culminating with his joining the Great General Staff under von Schlieffen, responsible for the Mobilization Section. In 1911 he was promoted to Colonel.

As war approached, Ludendorff became heavily involved with testing the Schlieffen plan whilst at the same time he began politically pressing for military funding as he considered war imminent. His scheming resulted however in his dismissal from the General Staff and a posting to command the 39th Fusiliers.

April 1914 saw Ludendorff promoted again to Major-General in command of the 85th Infantry Brigade although when war broke out a few months later he was appointed Deputy Chief of Staff to von Bulow's 2nd Army. It wasn't long before fate intervened again with the death of the General commanding 14th Brigade, Major-General Freidrich von Wussow, which had suffered heavily in the assault on Liege. Ludendorff replaced him and presumably using his extensive knowledge of the area compelled the Belgians and all their forts in the area to surrender by 16th August. The Kaiser presented his 'Pour Le Merite' personally. More importantly, as Ludendorff began the attack on Namur, the Kaiser requested that he be posted east to the 8th Army as chief of staff. With Hindenburg who had been recalled from retirement, they replaced von Prittwitz who was busily advocating withdrawal. Instead, they turned the tables completely at Tannenberg, the Masurian Lakes and the Battle of Lodz, after which Ludendorff was promoted Lieutenant-General.

Ludendorff's power continued growing and in August 1916, after the resignation of von Falkenhayn, he became the real power in Germany albeit as part of a double act with Hindenburg. It is interesting to note that his plans at the time included the formation of what amounted to an Eastern German Empire taking over huge swathes of territory and 'Germanizing' them. His advocacy of unrestricted submarine warfare however eventually led to the American declaration of war.

The last throw of the dice was the western offensive, made possible by the defeat of Russia. The 'stormtrooper' tactics he had developed were on the face of it extremely successful, although it has also been argued that the allied withdrawal was not chaotic but largely carried out in good order anticipating the eventual failure. Exhaustion, lack of supplies and reinforcements led to a complete reversal and the 'hundred days' that led to allied victory.

October 1918 saw Ludendorff appealing directly to the American government in the hopes of better surrender terms, forming a civilian government to which he handed power in the hopes that they would get better terms, deciding to fight on into the winter and then blaming the new government for the humiliating armistice. He considered resigning but changed his mind only to find the Kaiser had dismissed him. He left Germany shortly after eventually arriving in Sweden where he began a writing campaign which, amongst other things proposed the 'stab in the back' theory.

Ludendorff returned to Germany in 1919 where he steadily became involved in right wing politics giving his support to Hitler's fledgling Nazi party. He was involved in the 1923 Beer Hall Putsch and although he was tried for his part in it, he was acquitted. In 1924 he was elected to the Reichstag serving until 1928 at which point he retired.

From obscurity he wrote several books and concluded that the worlds problems were largely caused by Christianity, Judaism and Freemasonry. By the time Hitler came to power he had become an eccentric from which the Nazis distanced themselves although Hitler did attempt to lure him out of retirement in 1935. He furiously refused.

Ludendorff died in 1937 aged 72 and against his wishes was given a state funeral attended by Hitler. He was buried in Tutzing, Bavaria.

# Appendix 21

## Trebitsch-Lincoln

Ignatius Timothy Trebitsch-Lincoln is possibly my favourite of the bizarre characters that populate the history of the early twentieth century. Born in Hungary in1879, he had a Jewish upbringing and after leaving school he attended the Royal Hungarian Academy of Dramatic Art. His restlessness and penchant for theft brought him to the attention of the police from whom he fled in 1897. Apparently arriving in London, he became a Christian missionary and was baptised there in 1899 before setting off for Germany. Sent on to Canada to work, he disagreed with his stipend and after an argument returned to England in 1903.

In 1904 he acquired his anglicised name by deed poll. His gift of the gab somehow brought him into the company of the Archbishop of Canterbury who appointed him as a curate in Appledore, Kent. Shortly after he met the wonderfully named Seebohm Rowntree who employed him as his private secretary and then nominated him as the Liberal candidate for Darlington despite his Hungarian citizenship. This was resolved in May 1909 when he became a naturalised British citizen.

Bizarrely, the January 1910 election saw him wrest the seat from the incumbent Unionist whose family had held the seat for years. His tenure as MP was short-lived. As an unpaid position, Lincoln's financial woes increased and when a second election was called in November, he lost his seat and Darlington reacquired its head.

The following years saw him take a well-trodden route through failed ventures which finished with him offering his meagre services to the British government as a spy. Wisely rejecting this idea, Lincoln then left for Europe and tried the same ploy with the Germans who, clearly not aware of his true nature employed him.

Narrowly escaping arrest on a trip to England, Lincoln went to the United States where he contacted the German military attache, Franz von Papen. Berlin instructed von Papen to have nothing to do with Lincoln who promptly sold his story to the New York World magazine. Later, in 1916, Lincoln managed to get his book, 'Revelations of an International Spy' published in New York.

At this point, the British Government acutely sensitive to the potential embarrassment used the Pinkerton Agency to track him down and have him extradited for fraud. Lincoln was tried and jailed spending three years in Parkhurst Prison. On release in 1919, he was deported.

Returning to Germany, Lincoln slowly wormed his way into extreme right wing circles somehow making the acquaintance of Ludendorff and more importantly Wolfgang Kapp who following the Kapp putsch briefly appointed him his press censor and in this capacity, as Flashman mentions, he met Hitler when he arrived from Munich.

After the putsch failure, Lincoln fled to Budapest, along the way linking up with a reactionary group known as the White International. Naively entrusting him with their archives, Lincoln sold them to various secret services as a result of which he was arrested in Austria and tried for treason. Acquitted he was deported again.

Finding his way to China, he worked for several years for a number of local warlords before converting to Buddhism and becoming a monk. In 1931, having become an Abbot he founded his own monastery. True to form, anybody joining the monastery was required to relinquish all their possessions to Abbot Chao Kung who it would appear also spent a significant amount of time seducing nuns.

By 1937 he had changed allegiance again, this time to Japan although he also wrote anti-Japanese articles for the European press. On the outbreak of war, he offered his services once again to the Germans, the local Gestapo chief Colonel Josef Meisinger suggesting that his offer was serious and backing a scheme to broadcast to the Buddhist community urging them to rise against the British. Himmler and Hess were both interested but following Hess' flight to Britain Hitler put an end to all such schemes.

Following this it appears that Lincoln continued working for the German and Japanese security services in Shanghai until his death in 1943.

# Appendix 22

## The Kapp Putsch

The Weimar Government of 1919 Germany largely consisted of the Social Democratic Party, the German Democratic Party and the Zentrum Catholics. President Ebert, Chancellor Bauer and the Defence Minister Gustav Noske were all Social Democrats. Despite their socialist leanings, the Government had used the generally right wing Freikorps units (which were formed largely from discharged troops) to put down the various communist rebellions. By early 1920, this role was more or less redundant and the politicians had quickly realised that the Freikorps next target may well be them. It seemed wise therefore to disband the Freikorps and a deadline was set for the end of March 1920.

At the end of February, Noske ordered the disbandment of two of the most powerful units, Marinebrigades Loewenfeld and Ehrhardt. Hermann Ehrhardt's unit was formed mainly from Imperial Navy officers and NCOs and had fought throughout the civil strife in 1919. Despite doing the Governments bidding, the brigade was in direct opposition to Ebert.

When Ehrhardt heard that he was to disband, he declared that the unit would refuse the order and instead held a parade. Instead of inviting Noske, General Walther von Luttwitz, commander of all the remaining regular or Reichswehr troops in Berlin, addressed the men saying that he would not allow the unit to be broken up as it was too important.

Noske removed the Ehrhardt brigade from Luttwitz's command, an order he ignored but he did meet Ebert. At this meeting, Luttwitz presented demands from the right wing political parties including the immediate dissolution of the National Assembly, elections, his own appointment as Reichswehr commander and the reinstatement of the Ehrhardt brigade.

Unsurprisingly, Ebert and Noske rejected these proposals and instead demanded Luttwitz's resignation.

At this point, Luttwitz set in train the plan that would see Ehrhardt and his men march on Berlin. It was only now that he contacted a group called Nationale Vereinigung amongst whose members were Wolfgang Kapp and Ludendorff and asked them to be ready to form a new Government.

At about 10pm on the 12<sup>th</sup> March, Ehrhardt gave the orders to march. Noske heard the news about an hour later and began to prepare the military to defend the city. However, the vast majority of regular officers refused the order to fire on the advancing troops leaving Noske deeply disillusioned. At a meeting in the early hours, the politicians made two decisions. The first was to leave the city, the second was to call a general strike, but as neither decision was unanimous talks continued and it was only at 6.15 as Ehrhardt's men approached the Brandenburg Gate that they left.

Luttwitz, Ludendorff and Kapp met Ehrhardt there and moved quickly into the Chancellery with Kapp announcing that he was the new Chancellor and appointing ministers as well as Ignaz Trebitsch-Lincoln as press censor.

It looked very much like the coup had been a success, particularly as most military units supported the putsch or at least did not oppose it. In Bavaria, the Social Democratic state government was removed and replaced by Gustav Ritter von Kahr.

However, with the unions and most socialist parties joining the deposed government in calling for a strike, the people spoke. In Berlin, the strike began on the 14<sup>th</sup> March. Within a day it had spread countrywide. 12 million workers took part and overnight the country was paralysed.

Adolf Hitler who had been in contact with the Nationale Vereinigung flew into Berlin more or less as Flashman described, landing initially outside Berlin to be met by striking workers.

With the machinery of state in meltdown, Kapp and Luttwitz were unable to do anything. Threats of execution were ignored by the workers and within four days the putsch collapsed. The socialists offered elections if Kapp and Luttwitz resigned their newly acquired positions but only Kapp accepted this. Luttwitz held out for another day attempting to establish a dictatorship but the military by this time had begun to desert him.

Luttwitz offered his resignation to ex-Vice-Chancellor Schiffer, now restored, and he accepted at the same time bizarrely granting him full pension rights and suggesting he leave the country.

Ehrhardt's troops marched out of Berlin, but not before they had clashed with civilians heckling them. Opening fire, they killed twelve and wounded many more.

Shortly after this, Kapp left Germany for Sweden, Luttwitz for Hungary and Ehrhardt headed for Bavaria where von Kahr had retained his position.

Despite the short-lived nature of the coup, the chaos continued, especially in the Ruhr where the striking workers had been confronted by the local military and beaten them, leading to an armed uprising and the formation of the Red Ruhr Army. By 22nd March, the entire Ruhr was under the control of the workers army.

Negotiations followed when the unions called off the strike but the Red Ruhr Army refused to disband. Consequently, regular and Freikorps units were ordered into the Ruhr and the workers army was suppressed. Hundreds were killed, many ironically by the marinebrigade Ehrhardt.

Kapp was arrested in Sweden but did not return to Germany until 1922 where he died in prison awaiting trial. Luttwitz returned voluntarily in 1924 under a general amnesty.

Despite the failure of the putsch, the shockwave spread far and wide setting the scene nicely for more resistance, especially in Bavaria, where despite the takeover by Kahr's right wing government, Hitler continued agitating and biding his time.

# Appendix 23

## The St Clairs

The St Clair or Sinclair clan originated in Normandy and are thought to be descendants of the Merovingian Kings. William St Clair came to England as part of the Conqueror's entourage and fought at Hastings before escorting the Saxon Princess Margaret from Hungary to Scotland for King Malcolm. As a result, the family were apparently granted substantial lands near Edinburgh round the village of Roslin by the Scottish King who clearly hoped to benefit militarily from his generosity. William was made the First Baron of Rosslyn in 1070. He was killed fighting the English in one of the frequent border skirmishes.

Knighted by King Malcolm, Sir Henry de St Clair took part in the Crusades, fighting in Palestine alongside Godefroi de Bouillon who formed the Knights Templar Order, its first Grand Master being Hugues de Payens who was married to Catherine de St Clair. Thus the family were intimately linked to the order from its inception. He returned to Scotland after the crusade and lived until about 1153 when he was succeeded by his son, also Henry who was the first of the St Clairs to live at Rosslyn.

The St Clair family remained close to the throne and therefore the power base of Scotland regularly performing military and ambassadorial tasks for the King. The 7th Baron, another Henry, succeeded in 1297 and was present at Bannockburn with his sons in 1314. Of course it is suggested that Bannockburn was turned in the Scots favour by the presence of the Knights Templar who had fled the wrath of the Pope in 1307. He was also present at the Declaration of Arbroath proclaiming Scottish Independence.

After the death of Robert the Bruce, both Henry's sons were chosen to carry his heart to Jerusalem so it could be interred in the Church of the Holy Sepulchre. They never reached their destination as travelling through Spain they fought a battle with the Moors at Teba where both sons were killed. Because of the Scottish Knights bravery, the Moors allowed the survivors to return home carrying the Bruce's heart with them.

Almost a century passed relatively uneventfully until the 11<sup>th</sup> Baron, Sir William, succeeded in 1420. By now an extremely powerful family, they were seen as something of a threat particularly as William's sister Catherine was married to King James II brother, the Duke of Albany.

William was also the founder of the chapel at Rosslyn in 1446 and subsequently divided the Rosslyn lands between his three eldest sons.

Remaining close to royalty, in 1630, the 16<sup>th</sup> Baron was granted the charters from the Masons of Scotland recognising that the Grand Master Mason of Scotland had been a hereditary position in the family since the time of James II in 1441.

The 17<sup>th</sup> Baron, John, was besieged in Rosslyn Castle by Cromwell's troops in 1650, eventually being captured and imprisoned in Tynemouth Castle. Unusually, the castle was not destroyed and this is sometimes attributed to the masonic connections of the St Clairs and their besiegers.

From here on, the St Clairs have maintained their position, the Baronetcy being converted to an Earldom in 1801. They have served in many Governmental positions and fought in various wars. The current 7<sup>th</sup> Earl is Peter St Clair-Erskine.

Appendix 24

## The Royal Arch Degree

If you hadn't already worked it out I confess I am fascinated by the Templars and the more interesting theories about the reasons for their existence. Christopher Knight and Robert Lomas's book, 'The Hiram Key', is for me an absorbing investigation into their activities, especially those that centre on the theory that the Templars discovered something in, or more accurately under, the ruins of the Jerusalem Temple. What that was then infuses the history of Europe in the middle ages and poses so many questions. Why did the French King really attempt to destroy the Templars? Why were there Templar knights at Bannockburn? Why are there Templar relics on the East coast of the USA that predate its supposed finding by Columbus? The list is endless.

One recurring theme I have come across is the idea that much masonic ritual is considerably older than the accepted history of freemasonry and that it also tells a story, a true story. Masonic ritual when studied often sounds like utter nonsense until you apply it to the event or story to which it is related and this is the case with the Royal Arch Degree.

The candidate for this degree, already a Master Mason is questioned before advancing towards a veiled pedestal in a sequence of steps that mimics the actions of a Jewish Priest approaching the Holy of Holies on the First Temple. Shortly after he 'descends' into a vaulted chamber by removing a keystone and there he finds a scroll which he cannot read because of the darkness. The lengthy ritual continues in this vein (most of it is detailed in 'The Hiram Key') and Knight and Lomas propose that it describes in detail the Knights Templar and their discoveries in the ruins of Herod's Temple, ie it tells how Hugues de Payen discovered the scrolls that were the basis of the Templars existence.

In 1894, a group of British Army Officers set out to try and map the vaults below the ruins of Herod's Temple. Led by Lieutenant Charles Wilson, the Royal Engineers confirmed the existence of chambers and passageways often vaulted with keystone arches.

More importantly, they discovered that they were not the first to excavate the temple. Within they found a number of Templar artefacts, all of which are now held in a Templar archive in Scotland.

# Appendix 25

## Ark of the Covenant

The Ark of the Covenant is described in 'Exodus' as containing the tablets on which were inscribed the Ten Commandments and in the New Testament as also containing Aaron's rod, a jar of manna and the first Torah scroll. The Bible relates that a year after the Israelites exodus, the Ark was created in accordance with a pattern given by God to Moses and from that time on, the gold plated acacia chest was carried before the people or the army when on the march.

The Ark accompanied the Israelites on their 40 year desert wanderings being placed in the 'Tabernacle', a sacred tent, whenever they made camp. Legend is central to accounts of the Ark and perhaps the best known from this period are the crossing of the Jordan when the water parted as the priests carrying the Ark entered the river allowing the Israelites to cross and the Battle of Jericho where the collapse of the walls followed the Ark's parade round the city for seven days.

The Ark was not a guarantee of victory however and amongst others the Israelites 'consulted' the Ark after their defeat by Benjamin at Gibeah. After this, the Ark was apparently set up in a more or less permanent Tabernacle at Shiloh and stayed here for some hundreds of years until the Israelites defeat fighting the Philistines. Believing perhaps that the Ark would reverse their fortunes, it was brought to the second battle of Eben-ezer. Here the Israelites were defeated again and worse, the Ark was taken. When this news reached Shiloh, the priest Eli fell dead.

The Philistines apparent experiences with the Ark were not positive. The population of the city of Ashdod were afflicted with haemorrhoids, a plague of mice spread across the lands and when the Ark was removed to Gath and Ekron the people suffered from boils. These events were serious enough for the Philistines to return the Ark to the Israelites who apparently largely ignored it until King David came to the throne.

David decided to take the Ark to Zion, although when one of the drivers of the cart carrying the Ark was struck down dead for touching it, he paused his journey leaving it at the house of Obed-edom, a Gittite. However, when David heard that Obed-edom had been blessed by God, he had the Ark brought to Zion by the Levites. On its arrival, it was placed in the Tabernacle where the Levites looked after it.

The Ark apparently left Jerusalem with the Army and again when David fled the city to get away from his son Absalom's plotting although he subsequently sent it back with Zadok the priest.

When Solomon came to the throne, he constructed the well known temple that bears his name and is so linked with masonic and Templar history. He placed the Ark containing the ten commandments in the Holy of Holies.

In 587 BC, Jerusalem was sacked by the Babylonians at which point the 'known' history of the Ark ends. Ancient Jewish literature, or Rabbinic Literature, contends two opposing theories, first that the Ark was taken to Babylon, second that the Ark must have been hidden somewhere in the Temple. This has of course led to thousands of years of violent dispute about its location, culminating perhaps, at least in Christian society, with the idea that it was the Knights Templar who discovered the Ark in Jerusalem during the Crusades whilst excavating in the ruined Temple of Solomon.

There are other claimants. The book of Maccabees claims that the prophet Jeremiah rescued the Ark and buried it in a cave on Mount Nebo before the Babylonian invasion. Mount Nebo is also possibly where Moses was buried.

The Ethiopian Orthodox Church claims it is kept at the Church of Our Lady of Zion in Axum having been brought to Ethiopia by Menelik I who left a fake in Jerusalem.

The Lemba people of Southern Africa claim their ancestors brought it south.

Other Templar claims are that it was taken to Chartres Cathedral or to Rennes-le-Chateau and thence removed to the United States before the Great War, or even to Warwickshire.

Finally even the Irish got involved digging up large parts of the Hill of Tara looking for it before they were stopped.

We will never know of course. The possibilities are endless if in fact the Ark existed and if it had survived two and a half thousand years since the Babylonian conquest. Perhaps what is most interesting is the fascination it still holds for many.

# Appendix 26

## March on Rome

1919 saw the formation of Mussolini's 'combat leagues' and not long after the 'Blackshirts' or 'Squadristi' appeared on the scene. Violently opposed to the socialists, they were used to crush left wing opposition in the Po valley. As the trade unions lost power, so the new 'fascists' gained winning 36 seats in the 1921 elections forcing Prime Minister Giovanni Giolitti to step down.

Mussolini spent the summer attempting to influence the Government, initially signing a pact with the socialists provoking conflict with the Squadristi and then turning on the socialists in November adopting a Nationalist program and founding the National Fascist Party. By July 1922, the fascists boasted 700,000 members and were instrumental in suppressing socialist opposition. By October, Mussolini was ready to seize power although he reportedly checked with the US ambassador if there would be any objection to a fascist government.

On 22nd October 1922, approximately 30,000 men began to march to Rome. Apart from a few photo opportunities, Mussolini did not accompany his men. On the 24th October, he addressed a crowd of 60,000 at the Fascist Congress in Naples declaring 'Our program is simple; we want to rule Italy'.

On 26th October, former Prime Minister Salandra warned Luigi Facta, the current premier, that Mussolini was demanding he resign. Facta chose not to believe this but as fascist troops gathered outside Rome, he ordered a state of siege for the city. He approached King Victor Emmanuel III to authorise military intervention to restore order but the King refused to sign the appropriate orders instead handing power to Mussolini who had both industrial and military support.

At the time, this seemed a reasonable compromise. Fascism seemed to be on the establishment side although the Kings fear of a civil war given the Squadristi control of much of the country helped him make up his mind. The King asked Mussolini to form a cabinet on 29th October 1922.

Mussolini came to power legally within the constitutional framework, helped by the 25,000 strong blackshirt parade in Rome the same day.

The 'March' later came to be mythologised as the conquest of Italy by the popular majority rather than the surrender to intimidation it undoubtedly was and it soon became apparent to the business and financial leaders that this was not the free market they had thought they were promised. Mussolini's government began to establish state control over many businesses as well as individuals and it was probably no real surprise that he became Dictator in 1924.

# Appendix 27

## Goering

Hermann Wilhelm Goering was born on 12$^{th}$ January 1893 in Rosenhiem, Bavaria, the fourth of five children of Heinrich Goering and his second wife, Franziska. Although born in Germany, his father was serving as consul-general in Haiti having also been the first Governor-General of German South-West Africa. Six weeks after Hermann was born, his mother returned to Haiti and he did not see his parents again until they returned three years later. When they did come home, Heinrich and his family were forced to live on his pension although they were provided with a small castle, Veldenstein, near Nuremberg to live in.

Sent away to boarding school aged 11, the harsh regime and the appalling food convinced him to run away which he did, selling a violin to pay for a train ticket home.

As a boy, Hermann spent much of his time playing at being a soldier and aged 16 he was sent to the military academy at Lichterfelde, Berlin. On graduation in 1912 he joined the Prince Wilhelm Regiment of the Prussian Army. When war broke out, he was stationed in Mulhausen near the French border. Hospitalized with rheumatism as a result of the wetness of the trenches, his friend Bruno Loerzer persuaded him to transfer to the Luftstreitkrafte. His request was refused but he ignored it and started flying with Loerzer as his observer anyway. Unimpressed the Regiment confined him to barracks although this punishment was never carried out as the transfer was finally made official.

Goering and Loerzer flew numerous missions as part of FFA 25, (Feldflieger Abteilung 25) for which they both received the Iron Cross, First Class. Like many observers, Goering went on to complete his training as a pilot and was then posted to Jasta 5. Badly wounded in the hip, he took several months to recover at which point he was sent to Loerzers unit, Jasta 26, in February 1917. His personal tally of victories was beginning to mount up until May 1917 saw him transferred to the command of Jasta 27. Awarded the 'Pour le Merite' in May 1918, he was shortly afterwards appointed to lead Jagdgeschwader 1, Richtofen's Flying Circus, following the death of Richtofen's successor Wilhelm Reinhard. It was not a popular move as Goering's arrogance sat very badly with the highly experienced fighter pilots of the group.

As the war came to an end, Goering was ordered to surrender the squadron, an order he refused, many of his pilots destroying their own aircraft to prevent them falling into enemy hands.

Remaining in aviation, Goering tried barnstorming, was briefly employed by Fokker and then moved to Sweden to work for a Swedish airline. Also working as a pilot for hire he was employed by Count Eric von Rosen to fly him to his castle from Stockholm where he met his future wife, the Counts sister-in-law, Baroness Carin von Kantzow. Goering spent much of 1921 with the Baroness and when Goering returned to Munich to study political science at the University, Carin followed him and they married in February 1922.

Goering joined the NSDAP in 1923 after hearing Hitler speak and he quickly established himself being appointed to lead the SA. His wife often hosted meetings for all the main Nazi leaders. Goering was with Hitler for the Beer Hall Putsch and was in the front rank of the march to the war ministry where they confronted the police. Opening fire the police shot fourteen Nazis dead and wounded many more, including Goering who was hit in the leg. Managing to get away from the debacle, Carin helped him escape initially to Innsbruck where he was operated on and given morphine for the pain. It is generally believed that this is where Goering's drug dependency began.

The Goerings moved to Venice and in 1924 visited Rome where Goering met Mussolini, but their problems became steadily more acute. Carin's health was deteriorating, she was epileptic and her heart was weakening and Goering had to be taken to an asylum as his addiction became more violent. He was eventually released and the Goerings returned to Germany in 1927 when an amnesty was declared. 1928 saw Goering elected as a Nazi representative for Bavaria but their total of 12 seats out of 491 meant their influence was minimal. The Wall Street Crash changed everything and the collapse of the economy was an almost heaven sent opportunity for the Nazis and when another election was held in 1930 they won 107 seats. 1931 saw personal tragedy for Goering when Carin died of heart failure having been seriously ill with tuberculosis and epilepsy.

1932 saw Hitler narrowly beaten by Hindenburg in the presidential elections but enhancing his and the party's status and when a number of influential politicians and businessmen lobbied Hindenburg to appoint Hitler as a leader 'independent from parliamentary parties', Hindenburg reluctantly agreed as two further elections had not allowed a majority government to form.

On 30th January 1933 the cabinet was sworn in with Hitler as Chancellor and Goering as Minister of the Interior for Prussia, Minister without portfolio and Reich Commissioner for Aviation. But this was still not enough.

On the night of February 27th 1933, the Reichstag caught fire. Goering was one of the first to arrive. A communist, Marinus van der Lubbe was arrested and claimed responsibility for the fire. The Nazis called for a crackdown on communists and a decree was passed allowing for detention without trial. 4000 communists were arrested and Goering demanded that they be executed, which was ironic given that General Franz Halder claimed at the Nuremberg trials that Goering admitted to him in 1942 that he had started the fire himself. Goering denied this at the trials.

Through the early 1930s Goering had spent a lot of time with the actress Emmy Sonneman and they married in 1935. The wedding was an enormous event with a reception at the Berlin Opera House and flypasts by Luftwaffe fighters both on the reception night and the following day at the wedding. In 1938, Goering's daughter Edda was born. The family reportedly received well over 600,000 messages of congratulations including one from Lord Halifax.

The next few years saw the Nazis consolidate their position. The so-called 'Night of the Long Knives' occurred in 1934 when the Gestapo and SS removed the perceived threat of the SA, the Treaty of Versailles was increasingly ignored as rearmament continued apace and in 1935 the existence of the Luftwaffe was acknowledged.

War began again in 1939 with the invasion of Poland and Goering's Luftwaffe was initially very successful along with most of the German Armed Forces but as is well known the tide began turning with the 'Battle of Britain'. Goering's radio broadcast announcing that 'If as much as a single enemy aircraft flies over German soil, my name is Meier' came back to haunt him more or less immediately when the RAF bombed Germany on 11th May 1940. The war ran its course and as the Russians approached Berlin,

Goering and many others left Berlin for the last time, Goering to his Obersalzberg estate. As the Reich disintegrated, Hitler expelled Goering from the party after Martin Bormann convinced Hitler he was a traitor, Bormann bizarrely announcing on the radio that Goering had resigned for health reasons. Goering was placed under house arrest.

On 5th May, a Luftwaffe unit freed him and he made his way to the American lines and surrendered.

The Nuremberg trials began in late 1945 and lasted nearly a year, the sentences being passed on 30th September 1946. Goering was sentenced to death by hanging having been found guilty of war crimes and crimes against humanity but he cheated the hangman and committed suicide with a cyanide capsule possibly given to him by an American officer he had bribed.

His body was displayed for the execution witnesses and then cremated and his ashes scattered. His daughter Edda is believed to still be living in Munich.

Made in United States
Orlando, FL
20 May 2023

33315605R00183

And finally, this is the website for Stow Maries aerodrome….

www.stowmaries.org.uk